LILAC NIGHT

Books by the Author

SUMMER SOLSTICE

THE FIELDS OF EDEN

LILAC NIGHT

LILAC NIGHT

A NOVEL OF REVENGE

Michael T. Hinkemeyer

Crown Publishers, Inc.   *New York*

Library of Congress Cataloging in Publication Data

Hinkemeyer, Michael T.
Lilac night.

I. Title.
PS3558.I54L5   1981   813'.54   81-5502
                                      AACR2

ISBN: 0-517-541831

Design by Camilla Filancia

10 9 8 7 6 5 4 3 2 1
First Edition

Lilac Night is a fiction. All characters are creations of my own, and any resemblances to persons living or dead are coincidental. I have taken small liberties with New York's political and educational systems, but since people have been taking liberties with them for some time, I ask the reader's indulgence. Also, I want to thank the young man who handed my wife that sprig of lilacs at Bayville Beach, Long Island, on Mother's Day a few years ago . . .

For WENDY WILDMAN
and JANE LEE HARRIS

PROLOGUE

There is, for each of us, someone.
Someone from the past, perhaps, who writhes
at night in savage rage, awaiting the moment
of vengeance against us for something we have
forgotten, or never knew.
Someone from the present, whose face we see
each day, but whose eyes we have not looked into.
Someone who looms before us through an instant
of awful oblivion.
Or perhaps someone very close.
Someone from yesterday.
Too late, our friends will weep at graveside:
"But all the signs were there! How could they not
have *seen?*"
The answer is simple and deadly:
While we looked hopefully toward the future,
Death stalked us out of the past.
And there is always someone.
Waiting.

Book One

EVIL SEEDS

1

I never felt better in all my eighty-five years," old Miss Blaisdell screeched.

Lean, veined, and indomitable, she stood at a spindly lectern in front of the altar and, with a clattering flash of dentures, blessed "my vessels of the future." That was what she called *her* girls, students at *her* school on the Blackberry River, in Canaan, Connecticut. The campus was bright and cheery, with red bricks, white shutters, and high lilac hedges bordering a long, imperial drive. Only the architecture of the chapel, in which Miss Blaisdell addressed this convocation ending the 1960 academic year, departed from the colonial mode. The chapel was all glass and steel, angles and planes, with gleaming pews of polished oak, cruel to tender haunches.

"When one sinks down into a soft chair," Miss Blaisdell bleated, reiterating a fond maxim, "one inhibits the sinking in of wisdom."

Carol Jean Atwood, who had just completed sixth grade, would usually have endured the bench with patience, smiling inwardly at The Founder's well-meant but windy advisements. But Carol was distracted this evening, and paid little attention to Miss Blaisdell's reedy exhortations. Not to pay attention was unlike Carol; she was a good student and a serious one. She also admired Miss Blaisdell. Education was important, and the old woman had devoted her entire life to others. Carol often saw a similar life of service for herself.

Sitting in chapel on this warm evening in early June, however, Carol was strangely uncertain. She feld odd, unsettled, in the idiom of her peers, "weird." Nothing in her past provided even a hint of explanation for the apprehension settling all about, a peculiar disquiet alien to these familiar surroundings. Not a trace of anything alarming had happened to Carol in her six years at Miss Blaisdell's, nor, really, in the twelve years of her life. Yet now, indecipherably, she experienced a formless premonition of imminence and dread.

Anxiously, her eyes flashed toward the organ beside the altar, a modern masterpiece, with a console as complicated as the control panel in a Concorde, its tiered steel pipes looming over altar and chapel. No sound came from those bleak and glittering pipes, yet Carol was certain she had heard a prelude to terrible chords.

Startled, she glanced around. None of her classmates seemed to have heard anything. Susie Peck had just slashed Robin Auchincloss's paper with her scissored fingers. Marilyn Feibisch was clumsily covering a yawn. Teresa Woolworth and Alicia duPont were communicating in sign language. None of them seemed to have sensed anything unusual. The organist, Almonso Finn, slumped in a pew yards away from the organ itself. Almost as ancient as Miss Blaisdell, Finn endured her speech as if he had heard it fifty-two times before. Which he had.

Carol could not understand her bizarre mood. She ought to be pleased, even happy. School was over, she'd made straight A's again, and summer at Wescott Cove lay ahead like a golden meadow. Tomorrow morning, in fact, Carol's mother would arrive, driven by Rufus, the family's chauffeur, to pick up Carol, clothes, assorted paraphernalia, and motor south to the Cove . . .

Carol stiffened suddenly, certain she had heard again, above the rustle of school uniforms and Miss Blaisdell's babble, a shred of dark music from the monstrous organ. She jerked her head once, twice, clearing her senses. Muffy Wilder, in the next seat, whispered, "Hey. What's with you?"

"Nothing."

But Carol sensed it was not just "nothing." The world, as she had known it, was ending; a curse of foresight was to be hers.

"I have known the greats," Miss Blaisdell proclaimed, pitching her voice even higher, "priests and poets and presidents. Mr. McKinley was my favorite. Now don't snicker," she admonished, in response to a titter from her girls, "it's not so long ago. In your lives, too, the day will come. On which you learn how stealthy time contrives to catch you napping."

She nodded vigorously and clutched the lectern more tightly in long, taloned fingers.

"Well, you are young," Miss Blaisdell admitted, softening her tone, "and you will need to learn many things if you are to be of use to yourself and the world. *If you are to be of use,*" she repeated emphatically.

The students increased their attention slightly—the end was near—and Mr. Finn lifted his head dutifully. "God Bless America" and the "School Hymn" were still to be rendered.

"Three things I leave to you," Miss Blaisdell crowed. "First, never cease trying to improve yourselves . . ."

Yes, there was the sound again, tremulous, evanescent; an organ throb two black octaves below Middle C.

But there *was* no organist at the keyboard!

Outside, the sun dropped, blazing its last. Chapel windows burst into gorgeous fire.

"Second," Miss Blaisdell keened, "remember never to turn your backs on those less fortunate than you."

Carol nodded to herself. She had a natural sympathy for underdogs. But her surge of sentiment was cut off by another organ note, higher on the scale now, but equally disconcerting. It was as if an unseen conductor were chording a symphony of doom. Carol felt gooseflesh erupt on her arms, on her bare legs beneath the uniform skirt. And no one else had heard the chord . . .

"And now let me tell you the last thing," croaked The Founder, apparently as oblivious as all the others to the mysterious music. Miss Blaisdell stopped, rested against the lectern for support; last sunlight scoured each line in her face. Her skin seemed translucent, her eyes tired. But she rallied.

"Don't be preoccupied with the future," she started to say.

Uncharacteristically, her voice faded, trailing off. She stiffened behind the lectern, struck perhaps by a new thought. In the silence, every eye was on her. She did appear to be thinking of something. But Carol Jean knew better. She heard the beginning of a third woeful chord, and she knew that Miss Blaisdell was hearing it too—a shuddering throb of sound, born beyond horizons, clarion call of the end. Dark notes wobbled the spinning earth.

Somehow, Miss Blaisdell mustered the resolve to get hold of herself, although she looked distressed.

"The future . . ." she muttered, trying to find the thread of exhortation.

But now the terrible black chord was deafening. Carol put her hands over her ears. She wanted to scream, to drown out the appalling sound. Muffy Wilder was staring at her.

Then Miss Blaisdell formed words for the third and final thing she wished to tell them. "Death," she called out, her voice high and shrill in the chapel, "is not something that waits for us in the future. No, he is something that stalks us, that comes after us, out of the past. So even when you know he is inevitable, never does he fail to surprise . . ."

Then nothing. For an instant. For a heartbeat. Miss Blaisdell's eyes swept across the chapel ceiling. And discovered, in its farthest reaches, something that caused her to stare with horror upon her vessels of the future, trying wordlessly to communicate to them her ultimate lesson: the knowledge of untellable abyss.

Now Carol heard the doleful chord die out, like thunder rolling on and on to wane in stillness. Carol, and her classmates, saw Miss Blaisdell pirouette around the lectern, as if she were dancing. Gracefully, she twirled. Elegantly, she spun. But then her unseen partner released her. The end of the dance came suddenly, and Miss Blaisdell had time for one last look at the world. Fixing her gaze upon the breathless, awestruck students, she seemed to be seeking one of them.

"You *knew!*" The Founder gasped and crashed down hard upon the marble floor. Her shattered dentures dislodged, skidding across the stone. Veins broke within her, and blood poured from her mouth, running like heavy red cream upon the marble.

Carol was screaming. Miss Blaisdell's eyes, in that last terrible instant, had fallen upon *her.* Carol was screaming, but no one noticed, because everybody else was screaming too.

Almonso Finn lurched to his feet and tottered forward on arthritic legs, bent to observe his employer. Then he straightened up, stiff and woebegone and dignified.

"She's dead," he wheezed in wonder. "She's dead, she's dead . . ."

For Alma Blaisdell, the music had ended. But for young Carol Jean Atwood, it had just begun.

In the cottages later that night, the girls were jittery, and not a few were frankly afraid.

"Dormitories are proper only for prisons," Miss Blaisdell had decreed, before raising her school. And so she had ordered cottages built on her campus, each to shelter twelve students and one prefect, each named after a famous heroine. Carol Jean Atwood, sometimes called CiJi, lived in Carol Kennicott Cottage, sharing an upstairs room with Muffy Wilder, Debra Sterling, and Tiffany Lisch. Muffy and Debra were bright, but lackadaisical. Tiffany loved the whole world. Carol, by common agreement, was the serious one. The four girls were in bed after lights out, attempting through talk to lessen the shock of Miss Blaisdell's demise. To them, The Founder had not been remote, but a vibrant presence. On a schedule never forsaken, she'd visited every cottage once a month for lunch or tea or dinner. It was hard to believe that anyone who wielded a butter knife as if it were a scalpel could ever die.

"I still can't believe it happened." Debra shuddered. "I mean, I just can't. It was *soooo* horrible."

"I know what you mean," Muffy agreed. "I just hope I don't have a nightmare. Or something."

"But just think, I bet Miss Blaisdell is up in heaven right now," Tiffany interjected, looking on the bright side as usual. "You know, seeing God and everything."

"If that's true," wondered Carol. "I mean, I *believe* it is," she added quickly, in response to the reproachful silence of her roommates. "But we don't *really* know, do we?"

The girls shifted in their beds, and thought about it.

"I wonder if—you know . . ." Debra began.

"Wonder if what?"

"Well, like, just at the end? Just before she fell down? It looked like she *saw* something."

"So what?"

"Do you think it's possible to—what I mean is, just before you die, when you're still a little bit alive, do you think you can see over to . . . where you're going to go? 'Cause that's where Miss Blaisdell seemed to be looking."

"No," Muffy disagreed. "I don't think she was looking *at* something. I think she was looking *for* somebody. One of us . . ."

Beneath her blankets, Carol shivered and said nothing. She could not cast off the image of The Founder's final riveting gaze.

"*'You knew!'* That was what she said," Tiffany recapitulated, her sweet voice trembling as she spoke. "So she *was* talking to somebody. But I wonder why."

"I wonder who it was, and what she knew," said Debra.

"I wish *I* knew," Carol said bleakly. Her body felt cold, in spite of the warm spring night. The glow of the moon came softly through the partially open windows. Clouds drifted easily in the night sky, and perfume from the lilac hedges filled the air, a scent evocative and voluptuous. The night lay beautiful beneath stars, but Carol could not enjoy it. She imagined Alma Blaisdell, cold forever, locked in death.

How had she phrased it, in her last words?

"Out of the past," she had said. *"Never does he fail to surprise . . .*

"You knew!"

No, no, Carol pleaded, there in the darkness of Kennicott cottage. *I didn't know anything. How could I?*

"I wonder if Miss Blaisdell is still around here. I mean, do you think she can see us, and everything?" speculated Tiffany Lisch.

The bedroom door opened suddenly, and a rigid figure stood silhouetted in dim corridor light.

"I know we've all suffered a trauma," said Cottage Prefect Georgia Beauchamp, who also taught science and personal hygiene, "but I must insist that you girls get to sleep. Your parents will be here to pick you up tomorrow. And we all want the campus to be as normal as possible. Under the circumstances," she added.

Normal! thought Carol. *Under the circumstances!*

But it was very late, and so after Mrs. Beauchamp closed the door and withdrew, the Kennicott roommates murmured a little while longer, before giving themselves up to sleep.

Except Carol Jean. Enviously, she sensed the others drift away, heard their breathing become deep and regular. Now Carol felt intensely alone, almost abandoned. The darkness around her bed seemed to envelop her like a living shroud, stranding her upon an island of silence.

Think happy thoughts, she encouraged herself. And she tried. But even when she closed her eyes with all her might, Miss Blaisdell's face was there, and within the circle of Carol's world, chords of eerie melody sounded and resounded.

You knew!

Knew what? Lyrics or melody or something else that, in her final breath, Miss Blaisdell had come to understand?

Carol was certain she had never been here before. Inside a spacious building, filled with light. The shimmering windows, high white walls, and starkly modernistic furniture were vaguely troubling. Carol smelled lilacs. Above the ceiling, or beneath the gleaming floor, a smooth oiled click sounded at intervals, evoking the precise function of mechanism. There was, about and within this alarming structure, a quivering of imminence. Carol saw the empty chairs in rows along the walls, as if in readiness for guests. Down along the farthest wall, an electric organ was partially concealed by a gossamer screen. *There is going to be a dance,* she realized, *or there has been a dance, and this is the ballroom of a great house.* Wide corridors led from the ballroom, lost themselves in the distance of the house, trackless in a sheen of wavering light. When she looked again toward the organ, a vase of lilacs stood upon it, some pink and violet, others wintry white.

"Sit down, my dear. Please sit down."

Carol turned toward the voice, but could not tell which of the guests had spoken. The chairs along the ballroom walls were occupied now by elegantly dressed men in white tie and tails and women in long gowns, with diamonds on their fingers, pearls at their throats, sparkling tiaras atop peerless coiffures.

"Miss Blaisdell!" Carol cried, in fearful astonishment, catching sight of The Founder, who waved a butter knife in greeting, and flashed her dentures. But, no, it was not Miss Blaisdell, how could it be, she was dead. This was another woman, a stranger with a smile and a knife.

"*CiJi!*"

Carol glanced around. Who had spoken? She couldn't tell. The guests ignored Carol, not with hostility but merely disinterest. She looked at each of them in turn. All strangers. Yet, like close relations, they seemed alike in peculiar bloodless implacability, watching the empty ballroom with a spiritless anticipation.

"*Child, be seated!*"

The command was followed by other voices, as if the guests had been irritated for a long time, but had restrained their admonishments. "Sit down," some called now, "it is about to begin."

"Sink down into a chair," cried someone else, "sink down, sink down . . ."

"Sit down now!" commanded the woman with the butter knife, curling a tendril of lank hair around the handle of the knife itself. "Here, sit down by me." Her porcelain smile glittered.

"*CiJi!*"

Carol took fearful refuge in the chair. She felt a shrinking where her womb was, or would be. The woman uttered, through motionless blue lips:

"*You knew!*"

Now the gossamer screen was gone. The organ squatted along the far wall, and out of it rose a keening premonitory trill, shivering the lilac petals in the vase.

"*Ooooooohhh,*" sighed the guests, in passionate unison. Carol followed their glittering gaze down one of the corridors, where a dark figure moved, approaching the ballroom. She sensed menace, but the guests seemed not to. They sighed and cooed, lost in sensual delight, and implored the specter to hurry. The organ swelled again, then dipped into the prelude of some quaint tune. The music was beautiful now, subtle, entrancing. Still, Carol perceived a faint dissonance, a flaw so minor it might barely have been noted at all, but which grew irritating, troubling, ultimately horrifying. Until it seemed to be the final anthem of a doomed world, damnation itself.

Then the dark specter swept proudly out onto the ballroom floor, black velvet cape sleek as obsidian lynx, and began to dance. There was something lascivious in the dance, arrogant and assured. Yet it was beautiful too, suggestive of love and desire, forces Carol had sensed in herself, but had barely come to know.

"*CiJi! CiJi!*"

Faster and faster the specter danced, and from the guests rose groans of ecstasy like sounds of pain. Cold fear cupped and fingered Carol's heart.

"What is this?" she cried, turning to the woman beside her. "Please, what *is* this?"

The woman's blue mouth opened in surprise, and her dentures rattled. Carol saw her own terrified face mirrored in the other's eyes.

"But my dear, I thought *you knew*," the woman said, gesturing toward the caped figure, spinning now as the music surged and pounded. "What you are witnessing is *The Waltz of the Dead.*"

Carol sat on the steps of Kennicott Cottage and watched as Rufus, the chauffeur, trundled big trunks over to the car, sweating as he maneuvered between lilac hedges. The violet-pink blossoms were glorious today; their fragrance in the humid air was rich enough to bottle and sell. The day was absolutely splendid. And yet . . .

Carol's mother was inside the cottage, talking to the prefect, surely discussing how Carol Jean Atwood had awakened after midnight, screaming her head off.

Screaming something about death.

Obviously, the All Time Nightmare Prize at Alma Blaisdell's School for Girls. One for the record books, reflected Carol bleakly. Maybe they would award her a silver plaque and hang it in the library.

She had not told her roommates or Mrs. Beauchamp the details of her dream; she was too frightened by the nightmare herself. Moreover, since Carol *never* had nightmares, a private question became difficult to avoid: *Has something gone wrong with me?*

The furtive glances of her roommates at the breakfast table this morning revealed their thoughts on the matter. They had looked at Carol quickly, shyly, over scrambled eggs and raisin toast, not knowing what to say or do. Later, the good-byes had been awkward.

Mrs. Atwood came out of Kennicott Cottage, wearing a smile that was half puzzled, half concerned. She said good-bye to Mrs. Beauchamp, who stood in the doorway and wished mother and daughter a pleasant summer. The long black car waited, and Rufus held open the door.

"How are you, Carol?" he asked cheerfully. But his big grin faded as he looked at her more closely.

"Just fine, Rufus," she answered, embarrassed.

He didn't believe her. "Well, we'll get you down to the beach in no time," was all he said.

Rufus went around to the driver's side, got into the limousine, and settled himself behind the wheel. He turned the key, and the ignition clicked; the engine purred powerfully into life. Glancing into the rearview mirror, Rufus checked to see if everything was clear and pulled away from the cottage. The car floated on fat tires down the long, lilac-lined drive, and Carol watched until the school was out of sight behind trees.

Mrs. Atwood pushed a button, and a glass panel slid upward, separating Rufus from herself and Carol. She wore her most cheerful expression, which, Carol knew, meant that she was concerned. Both her mother and father were warm people, and Carol loved them dearly. But their lives had been steady and unruffled, and so they felt the world to be quite predictable, its apparent anomalies easily explained.

"Want to talk about it, CiJi?" Mrs. Atwood asked, patting Carol's hand.

Carol did, but she didn't quite know how to go about it.

"What did Mrs. Beauchamp tell you?"

Mrs. Atwood pursed her lips. "That you had a nightmare, shortly after midnight."

"That's just what Tiffany said, I bet. She always exaggerates."

"No. Mrs. Beauchamp ran up to your room as soon as she heard the commotion. Now, I think it would be good if you talked about it. Please?"

Carol thought it over. Maybe it *would* be a good idea. Just tell about it, get it off her chest, and go on to enjoy the summer. Even now, as the school fell away behind them, the gripping reality of the dream diminished too.

"It started in chapel," Carol began, "just before Miss Blaisdell . . . fell down."

"In chapel? But Mrs. Beauchamp said—"

"She didn't know about the other things," Carol explained. She told her mother about the mysterious melody, the sense of something disastrous about to happen, and, finally, Miss Blaisdell's cryptic *"you knew."* Carol also detailed her nightmare: modernistic house, lilacs, a counterfeit Miss Blaisdell with a butter knife, last, *The Waltz of the Dead.*

Mrs. Atwood seemed relieved. "Well, thank God there's nothing to worry about," she sighed.

"There isn't?"

"Of course not, dear. I know how much you admired Miss Blaisdell. Her death alarmed you, and your dream transformed the chapel into a house—"

"But what about the organ music?"

"That's just how dreams are. They don't make sense."

"But—but in chapel. I *heard* the organ. I swear I did. And Miss Blaisdell *looked* at me when she said—"

"Come now, CiJi. Dying people do strange things, over which they have no control. The last reflexes, you might say. And, as for the organ, you only think you heard it."

"I do?"

"Of course. If Mr. Finn wasn't playing, you couldn't have heard it. You heard the wind, or some sort of echo in the chapel—the ceiling *is* very high, you know—or you were tired. That's all, dear. When we're tired, or excited, or both, just as you must be with the school year over and summer vacation about to begin, we rather let ourselves go sometimes. Forget about it now and relax. Just be grateful you came to know a person like Miss Blaisdell. You'll never forget her."

That, Carol agreed, was certainly true. Her mother's logical calm was soothing, but she had another misgiving: "What about the waltz? Why a waltz?"

Mrs. Atwood shook her head and smiled. She let a moment go by. Carol's mind wandered. Had she remembered to pack everything? Was her tennis racquet in the trunk?

"What are you thinking about right now?" her mother asked suddenly.

"Why—my tennis racquet," Carol admitted.

"And why not something else? A sweater? A book? One of your friends?"

"I don't know. I just—"

"See?" Mrs. Atwood illustrated. "When one's mind drifts, it can go anywhere. Especially in dreams. Okay?"

"Okay," Carol said, beginning to feel genuinely relieved. She was all right. Nothing was wrong with her; she was perfectly fine. What had been bothering her most deeply—the suspicion that, somehow, she had *known* Miss Blaisdell was going to die—seemed faintly ridiculous now. Thank God for her mother's level-headedness.

"Are we all settled now?" Mrs. Atwood was asking.

Carol nodded and leaned back against the padded leather cushions, no longer so upset. Mrs. Atwood took *Swann's Way* out of her traveling bag.

The big car rolled regally southward, toward Wescott Cove. The Atwoods summered in an eighteen-room "cottage," where white sand separated blue Long Island Sound from a lawn of brilliant green that swept up from the beach to a gleaming white house. It was peaceful and safe and serene. "If money can't buy you respite from the madding crowd," believed Carol's father, Chairman of Atwood Industries, Inc., "then it isn't worth a damn."

Carol was thinking how nice it was to be spending her summer in such a safe, cozy place, when Rufus slowed the limousine to drive through what he always called "this so-called town." It was not really a town, since it possessed neither boundaries nor even a name. It was a grimy collection of teetering houses and ruined stores blighting the highway south of Stamford. Rufus always checked to make sure the car doors were locked when he drove through the place.

Men and boys lounged along the gutters, and gaudily dressed women were with them, drinking from bottles inside crumpled, brown paper bags. Carol's heart quickened with compassion when she saw the hard, lost-looking children squatting aimlessly in sagging doorways. The storms of life, of which she had heard, were the everyday realities of these people. She looked helplessly out the window at the rough men and angry women who glared at the big black car, at the fortunate few behind its tinted glass.

The limo was almost halfway through the town now, and Rufus accelerated slightly, eager to get out. Just ahead, on the right side of the road, a group of about twenty or twenty-five people had gathered around a storefront, yelling, gesticulating, watching something that was going on in their midst. Carol caught sight of the crowd, had just begun to wonder what they were doing, when it happened: a fantastic sequence of perception and event, moving so quickly from one episode to the next that it became a bloody blur of violence and disaster.

First Carol heard the proud, lugubrious blast of an organ.

At the side of the road, the milling figures parted; Carol saw a huge black man beating a boy with a heavy stick. The man held his victim by the neckband of a tattered T-shirt. The boy howled as the blows fell and tried to twist away.

Carol screamed.

She heard a second chord, wavering and dissonant, to *The Waltz of the Dead*.

Mrs. Atwood dropped *Swann's Way*. "Carol," she cried.

Then the boy twisted free, tearing his T-shirt in the process, and, racing blindly to escape the pounding, he dashed into the roadway.

"Oh, God . . ." Rufus groaned and jammed his whole two-hundred-ten pounds down onto the brake pedal. Too late. There was a sickening, hollow *thock*.

Carol and her mother were thrown forward into the glass partition. Carol heard her mother cry out in anguish; the pain in her own body rose and commingled with the third deadly chord of the insane melody.

She scrambled up off the floor of the limousine. Her mother was hunched over, dazed, gasping dryly, and wiping blood from a cut on her left temple.

Rufus lowered the glass partition by pressing a button on the dash. "We got big trouble," he gritted, in a taut, in-charge tone Carol had never heard from him before. "You two reasonably okay?" he demanded, jerking around to have a look.

"Yes," said Carol. She shivered, seeing the boy's black body, limp and limbs askew, in the rude dust of the street.

"I'm cut, but I think I'm all right," Mrs. Atwood managed. "Can we just . . .?"

"Get out of here?" Rufus shook his head. "No such luck. We've been in a big accident, and with all these people around, I couldn't move the car without hurting somebody. Christ, why did that kid have to . . .? I hope the cops get here quick. Just don't unlock the doors."

The outraged crowd gathered first around the ruined body of the boy, then they surrounded the limousine. Several men started to rock it from side to side, trying to turn it over. More men joined them, women and children too. Carol shrank from the car window, driven backward by their angry faces.

Then the big man approached the car. His face was blue with rage and blood. He held the stick in his hand, and rapped on Rufus's window with a massive fist.

"Get outta that car," he yelled, banging on the window. "Get outta that car right now."

"I'm trying, I'm trying," Rufus yelled back, buying time. "But I think I broke my left arm, or my shoulder—"

"Well, you better move or . . ."

The police siren came closer, but to Carol it still seemed a thousand miles away. The car pitched back and forth as the crowd tried to flip it belly up. Carol's forehead throbbed where it had struck the glass partition; her mind could not erase the lingering notes of that phantom organ, a living thing whose song seemed a paean of death. Again, Carol had heard its terrible chords, and again death had appeared to claim a victim.

The car lurched from side to side now, almost all the way over, like a boat on angry water. Carol and her mother clung to each other, thrown back and forth.

"Get outta that car, you hear," yelled the man with the stick, glaring at Rufus.

The police car was very near now, siren shrieking.

"I told you. I got hurt. Can't seem to move my arm," Rufus shouted, gesturing with his right hand.

"You're just working for the bitches in back, I know. It's them I want, not you."

"Look here, Mrs. Atwood," said Rufus, half turning to the rear seat, "if the cops don't show in a minute, I'm putting this car in gear and moving. It's self-defense now."

"You open up!" the big man threatened again. He could hear the police siren too. "Them white bitches killed my boy, driving through here in their big-ass car." He began to pound the stick against the window behind which Carol and her mother pitched and cowered. "A life for a life, you motherfuckers! I got a right to revenge my boy . . ."

With a powerful blow, he succeeded in shattering the glass. A million tiny cracks spread out from the point at which the stick struck, like a sheet of ice smacked by a hammer.

A life for a life," he roared, and drew back the stick to strike again. One more blow, and there would be a hole in the glass. Another, and he could get his arm through, reach the button of the door lock. . . .

But Rufus, knowing something had to be done fast, flung open his door, and leaped out at the man. The two grappled and fell, scuffling on the dusty road. The crowd, amazed for a moment, sprang back from the limo, appraised the fight, and began to close in. The police car screamed up, and the struggle preceding the big man's arrest was nasty, brutal, and short. The man, one Cleophus Watts, had to be forcibly subdued before being hauled away. More police came, an ambulance, and a doctor. A minister arrived, too, wearing black serge and an air of unction. He had authority in the community, and he urged the crowd to disperse, which it did, sullenly. The doctor examined the boy, shook his head. The police radio summoned a hearse to bear away the body of Renfrew Watts, Negro, male, twelve years old.

Summer was pretty much taken up that year by what Mrs.

Atwood forever after called "the incident." Lawyers worked; people remembered and talked; insurance adjusters hovered and haggled; depositions were taken, and reports were filed. Rufus was held inculpable at the inquiry. The accident had not been his fault. He had been driving well within the legal speed limit, and there was no way he could have anticipated Renfrew Watts's dashing into the street, nor could he have stopped in time to avoid hitting the boy.

Cleophus Watts wore suit, sneer, and silence at all the proceedings, but he glared malignantly at everybody, black and white alike. Carol's father, not unsympathetic to Cleophus, expedited the final arrangement, an award of one hundred thousand dollars. Cleophus signed a release stipulating that the matter was closed. "Blood money," he called his award, but Mr. Atwood wasn't splitting hairs. "If money can't buy you freedom from harassment," he said, "then it isn't worth a damn." He'd pay for peace. But one week later, they received a postcard from New Orleans:

> I meant what I said, you rich mothers. A life for a life.
> That's your Christian bible, ain't it?

Two more weeks elapsed, and a mailgram from Las Vegas asserted:

> YOU AIN'T PAID NEARLY ENOUGH YOU KNOW THAT?

And, just before Carol went back to Canaan for seventh grade at Miss Blaisdell's School in early September, there came a telegram from Caracas, Venezuela. Cleophus Watts must have worked on it for quite a while:

> NEVER GOING TO KNOW TIME OR PLACE. YOU WAIT.
> ALL YOU CAN DO. 100 GRAND DONT BUY BACK A LIFE.
> DONT BUY NO SAFETY. DONT EVEN LAST THAT
> LONG.

It was his final message, arriving just when Mr. Atwood was contemplating legal action to end the harassment. But it showed up far too late to bring peace to Carol Jean. She said nothing to anyone, neither parents nor friends, but she was quite certain of one thing. Through a flicker of time, trackless and unintelligible, she had twice sensed the presence of death. In both cases, her premonition had proved correct. So, fearfully, she waited, but the organ sounded no more that summer, nor the next, nor thereafter. *The Waltz of the Dead* became merely a bad dream. Time did its share of healing, distancing Carol from the past, and behind the lilac hedges along the campus by Blackberry River, all was serene. There were no enemies; there was no need for vengeance or the bitter recompense of anguish and blood. The very past curled into itself and fell asleep, and when Carol thought about it, she called it "that strange summer of 1960."

2

In the summer of 1960, when he was twenty, Jack Kenton pumped gas, changed tires, and did lube jobs at a Texaco station in Ridgewood, Queens, where he'd grown up. One unbearably hot day in early July, Buster Pauley dropped in. Jack was using a long wooden stick to measure the quantity of gasoline in an underground storage tank when he spotted Buster crossing the street toward the station. On the football team at Ridgewood's Grover Cleveland High, Jack had been quarterback and Buster a tackle. But that was a couple of years back. Except for these Texaco summers earning money to put himself through City College, Jack didn't spend much time in the old neighborhood. He couldn't remember the last time he'd talked to the guy once voted "The Foulest Mouth in Grover Cleveland."

"Hey there, Kenton," Buster grunted, walking over. "How's your old wazoo?"

Jack withdrew the wooden stick, noted the level at which moisture of fuel marked it, and closed the tank with a heavy steel cap.

"Can't complain," he said. "Yours?"

Buster flashed one of his shit-eating, got-the-world-by-the-balls grins. "Hey, I heard a good one," he said, glancing over his shoulder with counterfeit furtiveness. "Phone rings. Broad answers. Listens. Hangs up. 'Who was that?' husband asks. 'Man who lost a cat,' broad says. 'Cat?' husband says. 'What the fuck's he calling us for?' 'Don't know,' broad says, 'but he was whispering something about finding a little pussy.'"

Buster yelped, appreciating his own wit. "So how you been, hey? Goin' to City College, that's what I hear."

Jack walked across the baking asphalt, past the pumps for Fire Chief and Super Chief, and into the cinder-block station, which was only slightly cooler than outside. Buster followed.

"Yeah, I'm at City," Jack said, writing the gas tank quantity on a clipboard register. "Where'd you hear that?"

"Over at the Harp and Kielbasa Pub, couple of weeks ago, I think it was. Bunch of us was talking about who's going to make it out of Queens, and who's probably still going to be hanging around here when they die."

Jack gave his old classmate an appraising glance. Introspection was not Buster's strong suit, but a couple of aimless years "hanging out" had deepened him, at least to a point where he did some vague wondering about his future.

"Bernice, she always had you figured to be one of the ones to get out," Buster said.

"Bernice?"

"Sure, you remember Bernice. Christ, how could you forget? Social studies class, with that dildo Hartman teaching it? Bernice was second to last in the left-hand row, by the picture of Abe Fucking Lincoln. She wants to get married."

Buster made this last observation with little enthusiasm. Jack could just about imagine Bernice, dimly recollected now as a calculating gumcracker, telling Buster about work, wages, responsibility and ambition.

"What the hell," Jack said, to cheer Buster a little. He shrugged. So many of his old classmates at Grover Cleveland were having trouble making plans, getting started, breaking away. Those things would not simply happen, either. If you wanted to break away, to get out, first you had to *decide* to do it, and then you had to be willing to *do* it. Jack had decided to give it a hell of a try, and he was already pretty sure he would do all right. A well-built six-footer— swimming, baseball, football—he knew he was an attractive quantity. Moreover, he figured he had at least a decent supply of brainpower, and he enjoyed work. He was pretty sure he would do all right. But he didn't want to do just "all right." He wanted to do a lot more, and go a lot farther, although he was as yet uncertain exactly what or where. *What can happen?* he figured. *Either I make it or I don't.*

Buster tried, in succession, the peanut machine, the candy machine, the soda machine, and the telephone, hunting for stray coins. "You remember Bernie Lipschitz?" he asked, not looking at Jack.

So this was the purpose of Buster's visit. "Damn right I do," Jack said, "painfully. All-Conference guard from Canarsie High, over in Brooklyn. Sacked me at least half-a-dozen times during that game, senior year. Very dirty with elbows and knees. He even *bit* me once. What about him?"

"He's after my ass, that's what . . ."

A battered old Studebaker bounced into the lot then on ruined shock absorbers, rolled over the rubber hose, and dinged the bell. Jack had to leave Buster in the station while he put a dollar and seventy cents worth of Fire Chief in the Studebaker, driven by a harried mother, who screamed at four preschoolers in the backseat while she counted out coins to pay for the gas. Jack took the money, feeling sorry for the woman. The Studebaker lurched away, belching oily exhaust. Buster watched Jack ring up the sale and put the coins in the cash register.

"Couldn't you just pocket that?" he asked. "Your boss ain't here, and who's to know?"

"The gas gets measured and the money gets counted. A discrepancy would show up sooner or later. It's a system."

Buster looked gloomy. "There's always some fucking system," he grunted, "and I ain't in on any of them."

"You were talking about Bernie Lipschitz," Jack reminded him, deflecting ruminations on felony.

"Yeah," Buster said, as if he had been trying to forget it. Jack thought the big guy actually looked scared. "Yeah, he's after my ass. That's what I'm here about."

Jack tilted his head slightly to the side, an unconscious mannerism he had when confronted with surprising information. "That's what you're *here* about?" he asked.

Buster looked sheepish. "We always got along pretty well, you and me," he said quickly, giving information true enough but somewhat outdated, "and you know how to handle yourself and use your fists."

"If I handle myself, I don't have to use my fists," Jack replied. "Why don't you just go ahead and tell me what this is all about?"

Buster kicked the concrete floor a couple of times with the toe of a combat boot. "Well, I ran into Lipschitz at the Harp and Kielbasa, couple days ago, and he wants to fight."

"Just like that?"

"Well, I dumped a pitcher of beer on him."

"I see."

"Because he was messing with Bernice. He was feeling her up, is what it was. In a back booth. I woulda killed him there, except the bartender called the fucking cops. So we're supposed to have it out tonight in that little park behind the high school. Tha. monkey-jumping Lipschitz is big, man."

"Why don't you just not show up?"

"What? *What?* Then Lipschitz will go all around saying I'm gutless. *And* Bernice will find out."

"Maybe Lipschitz won't show."

"Oh, he'll show," said Buster dolefully. Then he screwed up his resolve. "I can take him, though. The bigger they are, you know."

"What do you need me for?"

"I thought you might come along and, sort of, act as my second. Like in a duel, sort of. You can handle yourself, and I don't want things getting out of hand. Like, I might lose control, or something."

Jack thought it over. He had a tentative date tonight to take Jane, an old high school friend now home on vacation from the University of Buffalo, to see Doris Day in *Please Don't Eat the Daisies* at the RKO in Flushing. Maybe he could even talk Lipschitz and Buster out of killing each other. He could go to the movie after that.

"What time is the bout set for?"

"Soon as it gets dark. You'll come?"

"Yeah. What can happen? Besides, you blocked well enough to get me through football without scrambling my brains."

"Great," said Buster, relieved. "All you have to do is make sure he don't kick me when I'm down."

"I thought you said you could take him?"

"Sure I can take him. But you never know, I might go down. Hey, I'll stop by and pick you up. We can walk over to the park together. You gonna be home?"

"Yes. No, wait. I get paid tonight. I'll go home, clean up, and come back here to pick up my money. See you here around eight-thirty."

"Okay. I got to go now. Bernice wants me to go with her and take a look at this ring she found in a jewelry store. She said she wants to make sure I don't have to spend too much on her, so she found one that's only a carat-and-a-half."

"Thoughtful girl," said Jack and shook his head as Buster walked off across the street and disappeared into Mel and Irma's Tavern. Buster did his serious drinking and thinking at Mel and Irma's. The Harp and Kielbasa Pub was strictly social stuff.

The rest of the afternoon passed uneventfully; Ridgewood lay near death in the heat. By late afternoon, traffic was almost nonexistent, and waves of vapor shimmered over the asphalt in the Texaco lot. Jack oiled and lubed three cars, changed two tires, and had two Cokes. His boss, a thick-necked, phlegmatic named Kohler, dropped in, checked the cash register, and went back home to drink beer and watch soap operas on television. Jack leaned back in a chair, propped his feet up on the grimy desk, and read the *New York Times*. Khrushchev was blustering; Kennedy inveighed with alarm, and Nixon pointed with pride. Out there, in the real world, all kinds of things were happening, but Jack Kenton still had two years of college to go. He also had to decide what to do about the draft. He could take his chances that it might miss him, or enlist and get it over with, or perhaps try for an officer's commission. He was thinking about this last possibility when Jane drove her old Rambler into the station lot. A cute but sad-looking girl was in the car with her. Jack walked over to them. "Hi," he said.

"I don't feel like the movie tonight," Jane said. "Let's drive out to Babylon Beach instead."

"Fine with me," said Jack. "Pick me up over at the park behind the high school, okay? About nine-thirty, or so."

"Anybody you know for Sheila? She just broke up with her steady."

"Somebody *honest*," said Sheila petulantly, requesting a virtue obviously not possessed by her ex-steady. Sheila was dark, lithe, and intense.

This would not be a match made in heaven. "You remember Buster Pauley from high school?" Jack suggested.

"Yuk!" said Sheila, and Jane groaned.

"It's all I can do on short notice."

"I thought I heard Buster was getting married to Bernice," Jane said.

"No, I'm sure that's just a rumor."

"No, I heard it from Bernice."

"Is that the same Bernice who used to sit by the picture of Abe F. Lincoln in social studies?"

"What?" asked Jane, puzzled.

"Nothing. Look, Sheila, I'll see what I can do. But it might have to be Buster."

"Ohhhh . . ."

"Well, look at it this way. At least he's honest."

"You've got a grin you're going to have to grow into, Jack," observed Sheila. "You look like a pirate."

"Why are you going to be over at the park?" Jane wanted to know.

"High level diplomacy. I'll explain later. Here comes Kohler, the manager. Buy fifty cents worth of regular, or something. I need this job to pay tuition for my accounting courses."

Buster Pauley was waiting at the station when Jack showed up, and he shadowboxed around a bit to the bafflement of night manager Clyde Wotsen, who counted out Jack's pay.

"I had four shots of cherry vodka," Buster confided, as he and Jack set out for the park.

"That was a good idea?"

"John L. Sullivan used to do it. In the old days of barefisted boxing. John L. Sullivan used to drink a quart or more during every match. If you get hit, you don't feel it as much." Buster danced a little as he walked, and punched the air vigorously. "I'm going to kill that fucking Lipschitz. Did I tell you I was going to try to get in the New York City Police Academy?"

"Hey, good. You'd be a natural."

"Think so? Either that or electrical engineering. If I marry Bernice, I got to have a job, and I got to marry her if I want to keep getting it from her. That's what she told me. And I'm good at electrical stuff. I know that. But there's more money in being a cop."

Jack himself was interested in money, but he hadn't considered law enforcement an especially promising avenue to wealth. "In being a cop?" he asked.

"Sure. Come on. You know how it goes. Was you born yesterday, or something? Them cops are into everything. Everything," he repeated, with emphasis. "They say if you can't double your salary in five years by, you know, off-the-books stuff, you got no place in the uniform."

"Yeah, and if you get caught, the highlight of your social life will be shuffleboard in the prison yard."

"The trouble with you, Kenton, is you don't think positive. Bernice, she keeps telling me you're going to go places and everything, and maybe so, but you just watch me, too."

They walked down the clean, treelined streets of Ridgewood and cut over toward Grover Cleveland High School, a squat bulky monstrosity hunching against the twilight.

"I hate that fucking place," Buster said. "What are you studying over in Manhattan there?"

"Economics. Banking. Model theory."

Buster thought that over. "I had a model airplane once. Took it over to Flushing Meadow Park and sent it up. Fucker crashed into a fucking tree."

"Too bad," Jack said.

"Hear the one about the madam?" Buster wanted to know.

"I don't think so."

"Madam sends in her income tax form, puts down for her occupation 'Whorehouse Proprietor.' Internal Revenue sends form back, saying can't be whorehouse owner, it's against the law. So madam sends form in again, says 'Chicken Raiser.' Phone call comes from IRS: 'Madam, you're lying about your occupation.' 'Am not,' she tells the guy; 'raised at least a thousand cocks this year, so what the hell would you call it?'"

Buster roared at his own joke.

"Not bad," said Jack, laughing too.

"I didn't get my high school rep for nothing."

They cut across the street, skirted the candy store by the high school—Buster's hangout prior to Mel and Irma's—and went down the block toward the park. Streetlights came on as they walked.

"You know," said Buster, in what for him was a contemplative tone, "you piss me off, in a way."

Jack knew Buster wasn't serious; it was just his way of expressing something.

"I do? How's that?"

"Well, it's Bernice. Always yapping at me. 'Look at other guys. Look at Jack Kenton. *He* didn't stay around Ridgewood, Queens, hanging out and screwing around. *He* went on and got into college, and *he's* going to be somebody someday.'" Buster quieted, almost shyly. "You think so?" he asked, in the small voice of a dead-end kid who has just caught the glimmer of a greater world.

"I sure as hell hope so," Jack replied, offhandedly. He had an impulse to say, hey, Buster, forget this whole stupid Lipschitz business; it doesn't matter; avoid all the battles you can; you're going in the wrong direction. But the little park was directly ahead of them now. It occupied a small triangle of grass and bushes and trees that had been formed by a bizarre convergence of local streets. Oddly, the streetlights had been stoned out, which was unusual for a nice neighborhood like Ridgewood.

"I don't think Lipschitz is here yet," hissed Buster, hopefully. "Maybe he ain't coming."

The park had no formal entrance, just a place in the bushes through which so many people had pushed that now it was a common gateway. The leaves on the bushes smelled dry and dusty in the heat.

"Might as well go in and wait," suggested Jack. He turned sideways as he stepped through the bushes, and as he did so, Jack saw a sudden, strange look on the face of Buster Pauley, who was following right behind. Pauley was looking beyond Jack, toward something in the park, something unexpected . . .

Then Jack felt a blow, not quite on his shoulder, not quite on the back of his neck. He was down in the dust before the pain came, aware of everything that was happening, aware of Buster Pauley turning, running his ass off down the street. Jack could hear the big heels of Buster's combat boots thock and clatter on the sidewalk. And Jack was aware, too, of at least half-a-dozen old Canarsie grads and of Bernie Lipschitz standing over him with a baseball bat.

"So it's Kenton." Lipschitz snorted. "I didn't know you were a buddy of that asshole Pauley, but that's your problem."

Then the bat came down.

Mercifully, the first blow knocked Jack unconscious. Not so fortunately, Lipschitz, primed for mayhem, went on hitting for a while, and the rest of the Brooklynites decided that proof of manhood required them to give Jack at least a couple of kicks apiece. If it weren't for Jane and Sheila who had just arrived to see what was happening, Jack might have been killed. Instead, their screams were heard across the street by a man who came to the window of his apartment, looked out at the fight, and closed the window. Somewhere a siren started up. Sheila and Jane were yelling like crazy. Lipschitz and his buddies ran.

Jack Kenton was in the hospital for two months, and the doctors thought he ought to stay for a month more. But classes were due to begin at City College, and Jack didn't want to miss any school. Weak and tired at first, handicapped by cast and crutches, he enjoyed certain positive aspects. He was wiser and richer. Lipschitz's old man, who owned forty percent of a popular local brewery, had been willing to pay Jack in return for not pressing charges. It was a lot better than having his kid doing five-to-ten in Attica. So Jack had one hundred thousand dollars in the bank when he came out of the hospital.

And he was wiser because he had learned something he ought to have figured out on his own, long before: if you're going to fight, make sure the battle is your own. And make sure you win it.

After running from the fight, Buster Pauley felt like the biggest shithead in Queens, quite possibly in all of his known world, which extended from Mel and Irma's Tavern in Ridgewood all the way to Coney Island. The former "Foulest Mouth in Grover Cleveland" did not appear at the hospital to visit the wounded Jack, generally made himself scarce around the neighborhood, and—suffering from bittersweet self-accusations of "failure," "no-good," and "dip-stick"—allowed himself to acquiesce in certain decisions designed to transform himself into a responsible, mature man. So Buster and Bernice tied the knot and took a whole three-day honeymoon in a motel near La Guardia Airport. Buster had with him three-dozen Trojans, a French tickler with a tip shaped like a cat's head (whiskers attached), and a purloined copy of an outdated entrance exam to the New York Police Academy. Bernice wouldn't let him use the rubbers or the French tickler, but in between bouts of sex, sleep, double cheeseburgers, and bourbon-and-ginger, Buster started studying the exam.

3

"Twister?"

"Twister," replied Lieutenant Jack Kenton.

"Oh, Jesus Christ," mourned Colonel Wiley, Jack's superior at the U.S. Army's Military Intelligence Unit in Munich, Germany. "And he's a general. You're absolutely certain he's involved in the PX Plot?"

"He's not just involved *in* it. On the basis of my investigation, which you ordered, the results of which are in those files on your desk, he's the head *of* it."

"Oh, Jesus Christ," Wiley moaned again. "Do you have any idea how much trouble a general can cause? Even if he is a crook? *Especially* if he is a crook?"

"I suppose we're going to have to find out."

"There must be some way we can get ourselves off the hook, at least a little bit," Wiley hoped, getting up from behind his oversized desk in his oversized office. MI headquarters were located at McGraw Kaserne, Munich, a vast, blocky complex taken from the German army after World War II. It combined the functional utility of a dry-goods warehouse with the architectural beauty of a randomly selected correctional facility.

"We could give Twister a look at our evidence," Wiley speculated anxiously, pacing from his desk to the picture of Lyndon B. Johnson on the wall and back again, "before we turn the data over to IG." IG was the inspector general. When MI turned over the evidence Jack had secured, one thing was sure to happen: the PX Plot would blow sky-high.

"Sir?" asked Jack. "Wouldn't it be unauthorized for us to communicate with the general in any way?"

"Lieutenant, Lieutenant," replied Wiley tiredly, "the army has two sets of rules, one for generals and one for the rest of us. Moreover, this is Karl Twister! I do not doubt that there is a tertiary set of rules, just for him."

"But showing him the evidence would be unauthor—"

"Lieutenant," snapped Wiley, with the peremptory, half-guilty anger of a superior who knows he is in the wrong, "don't you care if you get promoted to captain or not?"

"No, sir," Jack Kenton said.

Wiley held himself in check. Angry denunciations or spurious appeals to loyalty would not sway Kenton. When Jack had first been assigned to Military Intelligence, Colonel Wiley immediately sensed his difference from the other young officers, who were either pedantic file-jockeys or half-baked cloak-and-dagger boys, forever trying to ferret Commies out of their footlockers. Moreover, Kenton seemed to know his own mind damned well for a man of twenty-six, and carried himself with the commanding air of a more sage, experienced officer like, say, Wiley himself. Curious, the colonel had called for Kenton's personal file: City College, New York, 1962, Bachelor of Arts in Economics and Model Theory; Columbia University, New York, 1963, Master of Arts in Banking; Commissioned a Second Lieutenant, U.S. Army and graduated from Military Intelligence School, Fort Devens, Massachusetts, 1964. First in his class. Assigned to Munich, Germany, November 1964 for two years of active duty. It was now June 1966. Jack Kenton's obligatory hitch was almost up. *Perhaps I can use that fact to my advantage*, Wiley reflected now.

"So," he began slowly, "if you aren't concerned about promotion to the captaincy, I guess you've decided not to extend your enlistment and make the army a career?" He put his hands behind his head and leaned back in his chair.

"That's correct, sir. I've decided to leave when my time is up."

"Shame. Damned shame. You're a fine officer."

"Thank you, sir. I appreciate hearing that from you."

It was the truth, for Jack considered Wiley a particularly effective officer. But Jack also appreciated the politics of the situation. Wiley wanted to make *very sure* he did.

"As I mentioned a moment ago," the colonel drawled, "generals have been known to cause a lot of trouble even in the best of times, to say nothing of situations in which they are crossed."

"Yes, sir."

Wiley shook his head, mostly in frustration. "Am I getting

across? A wounded general can be like a wild boar. Even a dead general has all kinds of friends who won't hesitate to take their pound of flesh in his name. You don't think that leaving the army will lay everything to rest, do you? *If* IG gets this evidence and moves on it?"

"Sir, the *Frankfürter Zeitung* has already run a small item," said Jack, and pulled from his briefcase a newspaper clipping, which he handed to his boss, "and our sources indicate *Der Spiegel* will have a piece in its next issue. If the story gets out and we're caught here sitting on the evidence, then nobody can save us, not a general or anybody else."

Wiley translated aloud from the German newspaper story:

> Consternation mounts among officials behind the Iron Curtain, as the black market booms. According to reports, a massive clandestine pipeline, the origins and operations of which have yet to be revealed, is literally deluging cities from Prague to Zagreb with American goods. Hundreds of empty crates bearing the markings of the American Military Post Exchange System have been discovered. The matter is now under investigation in Czechoslovakia, Hungary, Bulgaria, and Rumania. Red authorities have all but accused unnamed American military officials of "connivance in wrecking healthy socialistic economies." In Heidelberg, General Karl Twister, Commander of American Military Police in Europe, and, as such, charged with security over Post Exchange matériel, declined to comment on Red charges . . .

"Look here, the general declined comment," said Wiley, desperately hopeful, folding and refolding the clipping, "so why don't we just let him carry the ball?"

"While we're left holding the bag?"

Wiley grimaced. He was in real pain. So was Jack. Karl Twister had been one of his boyhood idols. Like Eisenhower, Twister had been an obscure staff officer when Japan attacked Pearl Harbor, but the war had given him three stars and a chestful of medals and ribbons. After the war, Twister administered the occupation of Bavaria, served at SHAEF under Eisenhower, fought the Chinese in Korea, and was now back in Heidelberg as head of Military Police.

"Lieutenant," said Wiley, in a tone that mingled compassion and resignation, "everybody's got something, right?"

"Sir?"

"Something in their past. Something they wouldn't want known. Some person or incident or mistake that, if it came out, would be embarrassing, or worse."

"I suppose so, sir."

"Do you?" Wiley demanded. "Have something like that?"

Jack considered it. Once, when he was seven or eight, a playmate on the block had received, as a birthday gift, a terrific horse, a miniature replica of Roy Rogers's Trigger on wooden rockers, complete with ornate saddle, sequin-studded stirrups, and a real rope lasso tied to the saddle horn. Just catching a glimpse of his friend's marvelous mount grazing there on backyard grass quickened Jack Kenton's young heart to hitherto unknown tumults of envy. At night, the horse was customarily stabled in the garage. Then one week, the neighbor boy went away on vacation with his parents. Hoping against hope, Jack drifted down the block, found the side door of the garage unlocked, and found the horse just sitting there waiting for him. Heart beating a mile a minute, he dragged the glorious beast back to his own yard, back behind the high hollyhocks where—he hoped—his parents wouldn't see it, and prepared for a week of joy. But it didn't work. There was no fun in it. He couldn't take the guilt, and so, next morning, he trundled the horse back to its rubber-tire and paint-can-smelling stall. The horse, along with a number of purloined cans of Coke from the machine at the Texaco station, pretty well described his life in crime.

"I can't recall anything, sir," Jack told Wiley.

The colonel shrugged. "Well, you're young yet. Or your memory's bad. No wronged girl friends? Doctored transcripts? Jack Kenton, Jr., hidden away somewhere?"

"No, sir."

"If there were something in your past, do you think you might feel more sympathy for General Twister?"

"It's not that at all, sir. It's simply that, from the look of the evidence, he's monumentally in the wrong. As we will be, if we don't bring this matter to the inspector general."

Wiley sighed audibly. It was less a sigh than a low moan. Young Kenton here would complete his tour of duty, go back to civilian life, and likely make a pile of money. Wiley himself had his heart set on making "Full Bird Colonel" before retiring to the family farm in North Carolina, and he could still retire there, all right, but if he moved against Twister, he could kiss that golden chicken good-bye. Twister's friends in the Pentagon, enraged by the sad fate of their hero and erstwhile protector, would shuffle WILEY, LaMar P., Lt. Col. U.S.A., to the bottom of every promotion list.

"Lieutenant," he decided, "you're right, of course. We can't sit on the evidence. But the general deserves more than this shot in the dark from me."

Jack straightened slightly. Did Wiley have one last feint in mind?

He did. "Lieutenant Kenton, since you conducted the investigation, I am sending you to Heidelberg. You will inform the general of the charges against him. Simultaneously, I will make my call upon the inspector general."

Wiley watched the lieutenant closely. He hoped Kenton would show reluctance to confront the general personally. Wiley himself, as a lieutenant or even now, would rather have parachuted behind enemy lines than be ordered to face Twister with the evidence. And if Kenton hesitated, Wiley was prepared to say, "Well, Lieutenant, you're not certain then, are you? So let's reopen the investigation." That would buy time, if nothing else. Fighting anxiety, Wiley was reminded of a medieval tale. A man was sentenced to death by his sovereign. "Majesty," pleaded the condemned, "will you spare me if, within a year, I teach your dog to talk?" Intrigued and amused, the king agreed. "Are you daft, man?" wondered a friend, after the king had left the trial chamber. "Not at all," answered the condemned man happily. "A year is a long time. In a year, the king may change his mind. Or he may die. Or . . . the dog may learn to talk."

Wiley felt like the condemned man, buying time. If Kenton hesitated now, or offered second thoughts . . .

But Jack didn't. "When shall I leave for Heidelberg, sir?" he asked.

*   *   *

Jack took the autobahn from Munich to Heidelberg, pushing his little red MG up to a hundred and fifty kilometers per hour. Twister's role in the PX Plot obsessed him throughout the trip. The plot was astounding, and driving much more slowly now on narrow old Heidelberg streets, Jack considered its darkest aspects. What would a man do—not just a man but a general—to hold off vast personal humiliation, the ruin of his life and reputation? What if, in Munich, Wiley was *not* taking evidence to IG? What if he had already spoken to Twister, had set up some kind of trap for Jack himself? But, no. Jack dismissed his suspicions. These were not the Dark Ages, when a man entered the throne room wondering if he would ever leave. These were modern times, civilized and restrained. He parked his car in the officers' lot next to Military Police headquarters.

"State your business?" demanded a burly MP on duty at the main entrance.

"Appointment with the CG."

The guard almost smiled. "So you're Kenton, huh?" he said, without consulting roster or list. He summoned another guard, who escorted Jack—speculating anew about throne rooms—to the office of the Commanding General.

Three leaf colonels and two majors glared at Jack, as he waited twenty minutes in an outer office. Then a lean, tall colonel, pale and gimlet-eyed, appeared at the door to the inner sanctum.

"The general will see you now," he said.

Twister looked up in good-natured curiosity when Jack walked in, came to attention in front of the desk, saluted, and reported. Twister's face, which in newsphotos appeared craggy and weathered, glowed with pink health; small, sharp blue eyes, frank and inquiring, suggested a confidence that had encountered nothing with which it could not contend. Instantly, Jack wished he were anywhere but here; he liked the general at first glance.

"Sit down, Kenton. Right here, next to my desk."

"Yes, sir. Thank you, sir."

Twister was in shirt sleeves, no decorations. The red, white and blue "Flaming Sword" insignia of USAREUR (United States Army, Europe) was on his left shoulder. A row of four small stars sparkled on both collar points.

"Have a nice drive up, Lieutenant?"

"Yes, sir."

"Clocked you at one-forty-six k's just north of Stuttgart."

Twister's expression remained friendly, open, even benign. But *clocked you at one-forty-six k's* . . . Had Jack been tailed all the way from Munich? He didn't know, and Twister didn't say.

"Just got off the phone," the general drawled. "Was having a nice chat with my old friend, LaMar Wiley. Served under me in Korea, LaMar did. Damn fine MI man. You could bank on his intelligence estimates of Red strength."

Jack thought fast. Wiley had spoken to Twister. But about what? Who had called whom? Jack had no way of knowing, and did he just imagine hearing the steely click of a trap being set? "It's been my privilege to serve under Colonel Wiley," he said.

"LaMar informed me that you've come up with some rather deplorable material. Involving the Post Exchange System, I believe? Naturally, I'll want to move quickly against any person or persons in the event of demonstrable culpability."

Jack felt queasy for a moment. Wiley had lied about going to the IG. He had tipped off Twister, and set Jack up for a fall. It was ridiculous to suppose a man as powerful and strategically positioned as Karl Twister could not maneuver his way out of a mess.

"Why don't you tell me exactly what you have," the general suggested, "and then we'll both know."

"I believe Colonel Wiley is turning over the evidence to higher authority, sir. Begging the general's pardon, I think it would be inappropriate for me to—"

"Colonel Wiley is turning nothing over to anyone," snapped Twister. It was the Twister dearly beloved by media correspondents and Patton fans: laser-gazed, jut-jawed, razor-tongued. Although the sudden change in the general's demeanor surprised Jack, it did not startle him.

"I'm sorry, sir. Colonel Wiley told me distinctly that he was going to—"

"That's all been changed, Lieutenant."

Damn you, Wiley, Jack swore to himself.

"And if you didn't understand me clearly, Lieutenant," Twister went on, his little boring eyes a blazing blue, "I want to know about this so-called investigation of yours."

Jack studied Twister. If the general was making this much of a scene, he probably did not know a great many details.

"How did you come by this information, Kenton?"

"Model theory, sir," Jack said.

"Say again?"

"Model theory. Patterns of probability. I devised a number of possibilities to account for fuel shortages in Southern Area Command storage depots, inconsistencies in Post Exchange shipments and inventories, and rise in black market activity behind the Iron curtain."

Twister's face was blank and impassive. He was unimpressed. Or was he? "And then what?" he asked.

"I matched the facts with each of the models I had devised, and then chose the model that explained what MI calls the PX Plot."

"You intelligence boys and your plots," sneered Twister. It was a momentary lapse, just a quick grimace of sarcasm. But Jack noted it, and the general realized he had made a mistake.

"So why not describe for me, Kenton, this—ah, model you selected to explain your putative plot?" His voice was controlled again.

"Sir, regulations forbid—"

"I *am* the regulations, Lieutenant."

Disobey the general or subvert legal procedure? Jack kept his eyes on Twister's face, to read every flicker there, and decided on a gamble. He would make Twister see the chain of evidence against him, without revealing any of that evidence. Maybe.

"Sir, have you ever heard of Sergeant Potts? Big Ben Potts, they call him, attached to Transportation Corps in Munich?"

"Can't say as I have," drawled Twister, leaning back in his chair, crossing his hard hands over a belly that was flat for a man his age.

"Major Adolph Olk, sir? Have you heard the name?"

Twister shrugged, and shook his head in amused bewilderment. "What is this all about, Lieutenant?"

Jack felt the faintest flutter in his heartbeat. Was it conceivable that he was *wrong?*

"My patience is evaporating with increasing rapidity," Twister said, his voice hard again. He leaned forward and glared at Jack. "What kind of happy horseshit is this, anyway?"

No choice but to up the ante. Mentioning the next name would implicitly reveal the linchpin of the case.

"General, I am aware of your acquaintance with Igor Kujnisch," Jack said flatly.

For a second, nothing, no reaction from Twister at all. But it was a stunned second of astonishment. When the general spoke again, he was no longer Karl Twister, legend, but just a man. A cornered, dangerous man, whose past had come crashing up to him out of the darkness.

"Kujnisch?" he asked, weakly. "Don't believe I know the name."

Jack's anger was fading now; he felt sorry for the general. But Twister did not encourage this burgeoning sympathy. When the history books were written, Karl Twister would not be numbered among those who advocated retreat.

"Lieutenant, let us hypothesize." He rallied. "I know a lieutenant colonel in Munich. I believe this lieutenant colonel would comply with my wishes, given certain assurances on my part. The lieutenant colonel has the complete file; the entire matter would die. Oh, sure, the Kraut media would blow off steam about us for a while, but we could ride it out. And, to speculate further, a junior officer working for the lieutenant colonel might wind up top aide to a general, or he might wind up humping an M-14 rifle in a Nam rice paddy. Tomorrow."

Kilowatt power was building again in Twister's glare. Leadership: juicy carrot or bitter stick. Power at the highest levels worked just as it did in a schoolyard feud, except that the stakes were greater. Jack was revolted.

"Sir," he said, "since I have no more than four months remaining in my tour of duty, I will initiate an inquiry into the reasons for any sudden transfer. To Vietnam. Or elsewhere."

Jack watched Twister consider his plight. German media stories were about to break. In spite of the general's bravado about "riding it out," the Pentagon was sure to show interest. Then too, if Twister succeeded in burying Wiley's files, how long could he hope to keep them quashed? Not long, and the very attempt to do so was illegal. Finally, if he shuffled this apparently incorruptible young officer to the other side of the world, the officer would instigate a legitimate inquiry, and the whole business would come out anyway. All bad, every possibility dark. But Twister was far from finished.

"My wife will take this very hard," he said, almost softly, looking away from Jack, as if his sorrow, his wife's future sorrow, was too great to contemplate.

Jack recalled a *Stars and Stripes* story—When had it run? Last March?—that told of Twister's marriage to a lovely German model, much younger than the general. Why was Twister introducing her into this discussion? To gain Jack's sympathy? To imply that he had needed stolen money to win or keep a beautiful woman? Jack said nothing.

Twister was studying him.

Jack said nothing.

"All right, then," the general decided. "If that's the way you want to play it, okay. See you in court, Lieutenant. And, just remember, you're no cleaner than anybody else. We can always dig up something. In fact, we already have some stuff on you. Things like this don't just wash away, Lieutenant. Think it'll all blow over when you leave the army? Forget it. Ripple in the pond, Lieutenant. Ripple in the pond. You get my drift?"

"Yes, sir. Ripple in the pond."

Twister laughed mirthlessly. "Go on back to Munich then, Lieutenant. Wiley will turn over what you call evidence. The matter will proceed. But just remember this: How far are you willing to go? All the way? You better be ready to go that far. Because if you aren't, I'll whip your ass. I'll ruin *you*. For good. You got that?"

"Yes, sir," said Jack, standing.

"Dismissed."

Jack came to attention, saluted, and held the salute, waiting for the general to return it. Twister's eyes were burning into his.

"I don't salute scum," said Twister, in an icy rasp.

It took a second for Jack to realize what he had just been called by this man, once his idol.

"I would advise you to drive *very* carefully, Lieutenant," General Twister called after him.

In the preliminary court-martial, Sergeant Benjamin Potts and Major Adolph Olk were convicted of conspiracy to defraud the United States Government and sentenced to the Fort Leavenworth Military Correctional Barracks in Kansas, for terms not to exceed twenty years. Yet, in spite of overwhelming evidence connecting them to General Karl Twister, neither Potts nor Olk admitted such a bond, and both refused to testify against the general.

So it was Jack who would bear the brunt of testimony and cross-examination at the hands of Twister's hired civilian attorney, urbane but relentless Frank Brewster, of New York. Brewster riffled papers at the defense table while Jack took the stand. The trial was being held in a small amphitheater at McGraw Kaserne, Munich. Neither spectators nor the press had been allowed to observe, and most of the tiered rows of seats in the small gallery were empty. The PX Plot was a worldwide embarrassment to the army now. Among those who regarded Jack sourly were five military judges, Potts and Olk, General Twister himself, and, from her seat beside him, Twister's stunning German wife, Gisela. Aryan in composure, her eyes never left Jack, and in her eyes was fiery hatred. She wore a tailored, lilac-colored suit, which matched the blush of restrained passion beneath a set of cheekbones God Himself had fashioned.

Lieutenant Colonel LaMar P. Wiley was also present. Wiley had watched the trials of Olk and Potts with growing alarm. "Their connection to Twister is only circumstantial," he wailed to Jack. "You'll . . . I mean *we'll* never connect Twister to anyone or anything behind the Iron Curtain. Have you watched those generals on the judge's panel? They're ready to hand down a not-guilty verdict right now."

"Don't be too concerned about it, sir," Jack had replied, with just the slightest edge to his voice.

"What? What's that? You've got something up your sleeve?"

"You might say that."

"You didn't withhold evidence, did you, Lieutenant? Because if you have—"

"Sir, I don't intend to say anything more about it."

"But if you have something, we could work out a plan. It's my neck too, now. If Twister gets off, I'm through."

"The last time I was part of a plan," answered Jack, "I found myself sitting in an office in Heidelberg, with nothing to back me up."

"I just thought I'd play it safe," said Wiley, still embarrassed at his delay in turning over the evidence.

"Well, that's what I'm doing too, playing it safe," Jack told him.

"Lieutenant Kenton," Frank Brewster began, "do you grasp, do you truly grasp, the enormity of your testimony against one of America's most famous generals?"

"I grasp it," said Jack, meeting Twister's eyes.

Brewster began pacing now, in front of all those stars on the shoulders of the military judges. *What a sad thing*, Brewster was suggesting to the judges, *what a sad thing it is that this inexperienced young officer has brought into disrepute so distinguished a career.*

"All right now," barked Brewster, turning back toward Jack, ready to go to work, "let's cover it all again. How did you first become involved in this case?"

"I was assigned to inspect records in the Transportation Corps."

"For what purpose? I thought Military Intelligence operated on a higher level."

"Inventories showed discrepancies in POL stocks. Petrol, oil, and lubricants. Strategic matériel. Spot checks demonstrated falsifications in reporting actual levels of POL available. A lot of it was missing, especially in Nuremberg and Regensburg, close to the Austrian border . . ."

And so Jack testified, item by item, playing out the rope and looping the noose for Karl Twister. When he'd first come upon evidence of POL shortages, the question had been where was the fuel going? Was it being dumped on the German economy clandestinely, by army black marketeers? Or were deliveries from suppliers significantly under amounts specified on invoices? No, to both questions. Dead end. He personally staked out various POL dumps, armed with an MI infrared camera, but his photos showed nothing but authorized Transportation Corps vehicles entering and leaving the sites. Then one Saturday morning, lying in bed with his girl friend, Pauline Yates, Jack had the answer. It was as strong and clear and bracing as an icy shot of Steinhager. The fuel was missing because it was being used as . . . fuel.

He left the little flat he shared with Pauline, and headed straight for the motor pool, checking mileage records of trucks and matching them with actual odometer readings. Sentries wondered what in hell that crazy young lieutenant was doing, running from truck to truck with a clipboard. Jack did not know either, at first, but he was on a trail that would lead to Sergeant Big Ben Potts, motor pool honcho. Potts's trucks were doing unrecorded roadwork.

Once intrigued by a problem, Jack was incapable of giving it up. Diagraming his models, each new insight, every new twist, led him on, with an occasional tilt of his head, as he encountered a surprising new piece of evidence. Once he had established the record-finagling of Potts, the next connection came: Major Adolph Olk, director of inventory at the massive supply depot in Giessen. All that matériel. All those supplies. While Olk controlled the inventory records, tons of commodities—appliances, furniture, clothing, foodstuffs—simply disappeared, their departures listed on neither inventory nor invoice. But further inquiry revealed that money did appear, in quantity, to line private bank accounts of Potts and Olk. Yet those sums, vast as they were, did not begin to account for the lost goods.

Jack could not determine where the missing supplies were going. But he did notice that a great deal of Transportation Corps activity was taking place down along the Austrian border, near Passau and Braunau. So he ventured out into the hills at night with an infrared camera and plenty of film. He got good shots. Shots of trucks by night, shuttling PX supplies to carefully camouflaged sites for transportation into Austria. Since Austria was a neutral country, intelligence sources there were assigned to work on the problem, and they did. The PX supplies did not remain in Austria, but were pipelined along to the Eastern Bloc, where many hungered for the decadent bounty of the capitalistic West . . .

Still Jack was puzzled. A sergeant and a major, no matter how well placed, seldom possessed international connections. Big Ben Potts was a hard, bluff man who did not so much lie as refuse to answer questions. Major Adolph Olk's intelligence was of an evasive, cunning kind. The two were operatives, not architects. No, there had to be somebody more powerful, higher up, somebody who knew a lot, and knew a lot of people, and could manipulate them, whether by money or power or guile alone. Somebody supremely confident of his capacity to cover every trail.

Karl Sherman McClellan Twister.

"Lieutenant," Counselor Frank Brewster demanded, "I have heard your talk of so-called model theory. But this is not a place for theory. It is a court of law. We cannot convict a man on *theory*. Now, in previous testimony, we have heard mention of a mysterious Igor Kujnisch, an international black marketeer, apparently, and you have asserted that Herr Kujnisch could in some way be connected to the defendant, General Twister."

"Yes, sir. Kujnisch gets the goods from Austria to Bratislava, and on to Békéscsaba. And the money goes back from Kujnisch to the military personnel who aid him. General Twister has, in the past several years, made massive investments—"

"I know that," Brewster shot back, and quickly abandoned the subject. Dwelling on money would not buy the general off; Brewster had to demolish this Kujnisch business.

Apparently born with the gift of making two shekels appear where only one had been, Igor Kujnisch was already thriving when he fled his homeland, Czechoslovakia, just one step ahead of the advancing Red Army. This was in 1945. Devious, brilliant, and totally without scruple, he was soon participating vigorously in postwar Germany's violent underworld. He was participating so successfully that some of his less adroit competitors caballed to put Igor out of business. They set up a trap. Kujnisch was arrested and soon found himself facing Major General Karl Twister, then in charge of the Occupation in Bavaria. Charges were made; the case dragged on; there were a lot of other things happening at the time, including trials of Nazis, and nothing came of the Kujnisch arrest. But an old newsphoto had survived, and it showed General Twister in a double-breasted civilian suit, and a dark, flashy Igor Kujnisch in a velvet-lapel dinner jacket. The photo was made at a small table in Maxim's, Paris. Both men looked slightly startled by the camera.

"This," cried Brewster, holding up the photo now, "this thirty-year-old photo is the *only* piece of evidence that *in any way at all* suggests a link between my client and Kujnisch."

It was a telling point, and Brewster put it over forcefully. Jack saw the faces of the judges; they were swayed. They were convinced. He could see the headlines in the *Stars and Stripes:*

TWISTER EXONERATED
Case Circumstantial, Court Concludes

Instinctively, Jack looked toward Twister. The general had allowed himself a slight smile, a taut, iron smirk.

"No, there is another photo," Jack told the court.

"WHAT?" shouted Frank Brewster. "Then why wasn't it introduced as evidence at the appropriate time?"

In the gallery, Lieutenant Colonel Wiley paled. This must be what Kenton had up his sleeve.

"And I have the photo right here," said Jack, taking it from the pocket of his uniform before Brewster or the judges could devise a stratagem to stop him. The photo was a long-range but skillfully enlarged shot of General Twister in the company of Herr Kujnisch. It was not three decades old.

"I took that photo myself, no more than two months ago," Jack explained. "General Twister and Kujnisch met at the General Walker hotel, in Berchtesgaden, and as you can see from the picture, they are seated at the outdoor patio, overlooking the Obersalzberg."

"Let's see that picture," ordered the chief judge, a three-star general. Jack gave it to Brewster who scanned it, scowling, then handed it over. The judges passed it among themselves, agitated, angry, and confused. Brewster leaned toward Jack, speaking to him privately.

"You're certainly no stranger to the Alps, are you, Lieutenant? But there's no point in bringing that up now."

Bringing up what? Jack wondered. Certainly, he and Pauline spent a lot of time in the Alps, only an hour-and-a-half south of Munich. They hiked and camped in the summer, and skied in the winter.

"I move for a mistrial ruling," Brewster was asking the judges. "This photo cannot be introduced now; the rules of evidence have been made a mockery here."

But the judges had no chance to consider Brewster's motion. General Karl Twister was on his feet. He knew enough about battle to know when a battle was lost. Conceivably, Brewster might win him a mistrial ruling. This time. But the photo existed. As did Twister's Swiss bank account, his massive investments, his failure to pay income taxes. So, if he would be doomed in a new trial, he was already doomed now, and he knew it. He had violated his sacred oath, and his betrayal was there, for all the world to see.

"Gentlemen, may I ask that my wife be escorted from the room?"

"No, Karl," Gisela Twister screamed, leaping to her feet and clutching his arm, his shoulder. "Don't do anything rash. Wait and see. You can fight again—"

"No, no," he soothed her, prying loose her fingers. He nodded toward two MPs, who gently led Gisela, now sobbing, to an adjacent room. Twister waited until the door was closed, then addressed the court.

"Lieutenant Kenton was right all along," he said, "for all the good it's going to do him. Lieutenant," he went on, turning to Jack, "I have to give you credit. You took it all the way, as you had to do to win, and it looks like you *have* won. Certainly, I have lost. But let me tell you one last thing. This isn't over and it will never be over. I may be wrong, but I don't think so. Every victor knows about defeat. I planted the seeds of my own vanquishment thirty years ago, at a table at Maxim's in Paris."

Twister paused. The courtroom was hushed, everyone in it caught and held by the general's words.

"That's all," Twister said. "I'm ready to give myself into custody. But first I request permission to have a few moments alone with my wife."

"Permission granted," said the chief judge who was embarrassed and appalled. Where was it written in army regulations that a great general be brought so low so hard so fast?

Karl Twister strode to the door of the room next to the ampitheater, opened it, and stepped inside.

There was a vast silence.

Then an explosion, followed by a howl of overwhelming rage and grief.

Gisela Twister flung open the door, and looked out into the courtroom. She stood there, red blood staining the lilac material of her lovely suit, red blood from breasts to belly and dripping down, possessed of an icy Nordic rage.

"You!" she cried, pointing at Jack. "You did this. And for this you shall pay!"

"Well," muttered Frank Brewster to Jack, as they were leaving the courtroom, "I guess the old man was one of those Roman-type generals who do themselves in when they lose."

The two men walked up the aisle. Sergeant Potts and Major Olk, in handcuffs, were standing among the benches, waiting for MP guards to lead them out.

"Listen to me, Kenton," Olk hissed, "when Potts and I get out of Leavenworth, you better already be dead."

"Hell, he probably *will* be," Potts allowed, guffawing, "after what he did to old Twister."

Jack walked on without responding.

"Got a minute?" asked Frank Brewster, friendly and relaxed now that the trial was over.

"Sure," replied Jack, curious.

"Come on, let's find a conference room. I've got something to show you."

Brewster opened the door to an office on one side of the corridor, saw that it was unoccupied, and shouldered his way in.

"Let me ask you something," said Jack.

"Shoot." Brewster slapped down his attaché case atop a table, and unfastened the catches.

"The threats. Gisela's. Olk's and Potts's. Do you hear that kind of thing often? After a trial?"

"All the time. Don't waste your life worrying about threats. Only one person out of a million will actually set out to do you in."

"But that's still one person. That's all it takes."

"You afraid or something?"

"I'm not used to being threatened."

"Trial's over now. Forget it. Here, let me show you this . . ."

He took from the attaché case a manila envelope and handed it to Jack. "I was going to have these destroyed, but you might as well do it yourself."

Jack opened the envelope, looking at first one photo and then another, as his anger and astonishment grew. There was a good shot of Jack and Pauline Yates entering a restaurant, Pauline looking up at Jack, smiling her shivery and oddly hesitant smile, full of love, yet incomplete. That strange aspect, a mystery to Jack, as if Pauline did not altogether believe in love, or herself, or even her beauty, which had a breathtaking effect upon Jack. In the picture, Pauline's reddish-gold hair was blown partway across her face, and Jack had his arm around her waist. There was another photo, taken outside the flat Jack and Pauline shared in Schwabing; Pauline was getting into the MG, showing her long slender legs, and Jack was fastening something to the luggage rack. Another picture showed the two of them leaving a small *pension* in Bad Reichenhall, down in the Alps, where they sometimes spent weekends. But there was one photo Jack would never forget. It was a long-range but extremely well-developed shot of Jack and Pauline making love in the mountains, and Jack knew just where it had been taken. Up on the Obersalzberg, in a meadow rich with wild gentian, edelweiss, and banks of lilacs where the meadow ended and the trees began. In the picture, Jack was upon Pauline, driving into her, tight and lean and thrusting. Her legs were drawn high, slender ankles crossed and locked upon his back, her hands clutching him, drawing him more deeply into herself. Pauline's eyes were closed tight, her mouth open. Jack could see the tip of her tongue. Her teeth were wet. The picture was that clear. Jack could even see the individual petals of the flowers!

"You son of a bitch," Jack said.

"Wait a minute," Brewster protested. "I didn't do this. The general had men tailing you. Jesus, what do you think I am, anyway? A Staten Island ambulance chaser? When I saw this stuff, I told him to forget it. It would have made him look terrible, to use these pictures. Besides which, it's an invasion of privacy. You've got a right to live your personal life as you choose. I didn't even know he was having you tailed until I saw the photos."

Jack was not convinced.

"It's the truth, Kenton, I swear it. Here, you've got the negatives and all. I made damn certain. Burn them yourself and it's all over." He handed Jack his gold cigarette lighter. "Be my guest."

Jack was about to touch flame to the photos when a *Putzfrau* entered, carrying bucket and mop. They were ubiquitous, these cleaning women. They maintained every room in Germany, and believed that they owned every room they maintained.

"*Feuer verboten!*" howled the *Putzfrau* in alarm. She set down her bucket and shook a finger at Jack. "*Feuer verboten in diesem Zimmer!*"

"*Ja, ja.*" Jack obeyed, "Okay, okay." He closed the lighter, gave it back to the lawyer. "I'll burn them at home," he said. "And thanks."

"Don't mention it. What are you planning to do when you leave the army?"

"Go back to New York and make some money, I hope."

"Well, *auf Wiedersehen.*" Brewster stuck out his hand and Jack shook it. "If you ever need a sharp New York lawyer, I'm down on Wall Street. Look me up."

Jack put photos and negatives in the manila envelope, left the room, the building. McGraw Kaserne was strangely quiet now; the news of Twister's suicide hung like an eerie pall above the gray cobblestones. Jack felt eyes on him, thousands of pairs of eyes, watching. What he had done in the course of the PX Plot and the Twister trial, begun as simple duty but building to shattering consequence, had made him a personage. The guards on duty at the gate saluted him more snappily than ever, when he drove out of McGraw, but their eyes were carefully blank.

Ripple in the pond, thought Jack, remembering Twister's words. The hell with it. One never knew what was going to happen. He would go home. Pauline would blot from his mind the image of icy blonde beautiful Gisela Twister with the general's blood spattered all over her.

4

Pauline Yates was afraid she would lose Jack Kenton. She was afraid he would find out that she did not deserve him. She was afraid he would meet a woman more beautiful than she.

It was all perfectly logical to her. That was how life worked. But naturally, she could not tell him of her fears because then he would find out how weak she was, and she would lose him too. Their love was too good to be true; she could not imagine a future for herself in which she did not somehow blunder and lose him. Every time he was away from her, she suffered the agonies of the damned.

Now, nervously, she lit another cigarette and walked to the window of their little apartment. Today, he had told her, was the final day of the Twister trial. It was a dangerous day for him, she knew. He had been controlled, but tense. She didn't want to think about the trial. He should be home now, with her. She looked out upon the narrow, twisting street below. Schwabing was artists' territory in old Munich, and that was one of the reasons she and Jack had sought a flat here. As an officer, he was permitted quarters off-base, or "on the economy," in the military phrase. And she, a Red Cross nurse assigned to Europe, could live where she chose. Schwabing was a perfect place. The actors and writers and painters left you alone, and Pauline would have been undisturbed to learn that she and Jack would spend the rest of their lives alone together.

Pauline had had little enough of love. Raised in a basement just off Pelham Parkway in the Bronx, raised with five brothers and four sisters, raised by a mother who venerated a plastic statue of the Virgin and a leather strap, and raised by a father who venerated bottle and bed and not much else—and who never got around to putting up the house he had planned to build over the basement— Pauline had never known a moment's peace. It was always crowded down in the dingy basement. Not too much room there for love.

She was unusually pretty, a fact which, in another family,

another neighborhood, another life, would have been an advantage, but which, in her own grungy milieu, only served to make her the target of envious tease and dirty trick. Too gentle by nature to grow bitter, Pauline became sad instead, a lovely little girl who could not hold back tears when her brothers and sisters and their equally mean-blooded companions pulled her hair or picked on her.

Yet the same natural beauty which had led children to abuse her in early years, later frightened away dull and loudmouthed teenage louts, leaving them free to harass, seduce, rape, and impregnate less comely girls in weed-rampant lots, abandoned warehouses, or the backseats of stolen cars. Left alone, Pauline stayed after classes and studied in the high school library, found a job as waitress in a diner, and only went home to sleep when her father was too drunk anymore to argue with her mother, who had, bearing a burden of martyrdom and misery, retreated to the hall closet, where Jesus often materialized and spoke of bargains at Kresge's.

After high school, Pauline won a two-year nursing scholarship to Pelham Community College. Equipped with nursing certificate, and wanting to get as far away from home as possible, she joined the Red Cross and went to Germany. There she met Jack Kenton by spilling half a glass of Coca-Cola on his green uniform jacket at lunchtime in the Munich PX snack bar.

"Oh, I'm so sorry," she cried, more flustered still when she looked from the blotchy stain on his jacket to his face, saw his dark hair and green, amused eyes. "I thought I saw some napkins over there . . ."

"So you're a New Yorker?" he asked.

"What? Yes. How did you . . .?"

"Only New Yorkers say *saw* with an *r* at the end of it. Now where did you say you sawr those napkins?"

That's how it started, their relationship, their love. Pauline could not believe it was happening. He was so handsome and so smart. He was fun and tender, interested in everything, and he seemed to have all kinds of money. Here she was, a Red Cross nurse with a certificate from Pelham Community College, and he was asking her to live with him. Her whole world turned upside down. It was all too good, she feared. To be true. He told her how lovely she was, but she didn't feel lovely enough for him. When he made love to her, she rose beyond herself; never had there been anything like the sensations he gave. She exulted in them; they made her frantic. He would go someday; he would leave, and never again for the rest of her life would she know such imcomparable joy. She would lose him; she would lose him; oh, God, she would lose him; she just knew it.

Naturally, she could not tell him of her fears, and when she thought of the future, it was always his, not her own. She always pictured him with a beautiful woman, sometimes blonde, sometimes brunette. Always the woman was exquisite, serene, someone who knew how to act and what to wear and just what to say every time.

But that woman with Jack was never Pauline Yates.

Smoking her cigarette, Pauline paced from window to wall to window again, waiting for Jack, trying not to think about the Twister trial. Whenever she was this agitated, she tried to imagine back to the most gorgeous day of her life. Jack had taken her hiking up on the Obersalzberg, and they'd stopped to rest where the flower-riven meadow met the forest. Below the meadow, rocky blue cliffs dropped forever into time. The sun was warm, the grass and leaves so sweet and green and gold. The world, the whole world, was a charmed cathedral of tenderness and love, and the lovemaking more perfect than ever. Pauline remembered the scent of edelweiss and lilac, the kaleidoscopic patterns made by the sunlight behind the closed lids of her eyes, the overwhelming rapture she'd felt as Jack played her body, as he distilled her very essence down to one keen fine point of pleasure trembling to explode . . .

Approaching outside, up the street, she heard the powerful, high-pitched growl of Jack's MG, stubbed out her cigarette, and raced to the window. A knot in her stomach loosened when she saw the car and Jack in it. But, where he had been tense this morning, he looked tired and troubled now. Instantly, she was worried again.

A moment later she heard Jack's footsteps on the stairs and opened the door to greet him. They embraced, and he kissed her, but Pauline pulled away to study his face. He was tired, but to her relief she saw that he was no longer held by the persistent special tension he had had to maintain throughout the trial.

"The general?" she asked, worriedly.

"Shot himself." Jack made half a headshake, half a shrug. "Dead." He gave her the details, told of Gisela Twister in her bloodstained dress, threatening revenge.

"*And for this you shall pay,*'" Jack said, capturing perfectly both Gisela's passionate desperation and the stiff precision of her English.

"Oh, how awful!" Pauline exclaimed. "The poor woman. She lost her husband. I can understand how she feels." And she meant every word of what she said, since she lived in constant fear of the loss of Jack.

"Do you think she means it? About revenge?" Pauline wanted to know.

Jack pulled off his uniform jacket and tossed it onto a chair. He sagged down onto the couch. "Oh, she means it, all right. But Twister's lawyer told me not to dwell on it. Threats are frequent when passions run high."

"I don't know," doubted Pauline, kneeling on the floor next to the couch and gently massaging his temples. "I know how I'd feel."

Jack had closed his eyes, but he opened them and looked at her now, smiling tenderly. "How *would* you feel?"

Pauline tightened her mouth and squinted, looking fierce. "If somebody did something to you, I'd get them. No, don't smile. It's true. I would. I'd follow them to the ends of the earth, just to get even."

"And how would you do that?"

"I don't know. But some terrible way, though. You can believe it."

"Nobody really gets even," Jack said drowsily. "People bent on revenge think they're going to finish something that started a long time before. All they really do, though, is to create a whole new mess."

"I don't care. If they did anything to you, I'd still get even."

"Anyway, it's over now."

"I hope so."

"Let's go out tonight. If I sit around here, I'll just replay the trial over and over. Once was enough."

"You know I'll always do anything you want."

Jack smiled and kissed her again. The completeness of her devotion unnerved him at times. Surpassing love, her feelings approached reverence. Her love was gift enough; he did not hope for more. Pauline was so easily wounded, a person capable of extremes. Jack was careful with her. He suspected that in her past, of which she never spoke, resided the key to the secret: why such a voluptuously beautiful girl was so fragile.

"Don't be alarmed, it's over now," he said, "but check the manila envelope there in my jacket."

Pauline quickly took the envelope from the pocket of Jack's uniform, and tore it open. Surprise overtook curiosity as she looked quickly from one photo to the next; when she saw the last shot, blood rushed to her cheeks.

"Oh, how could they?" she cried.

"With a camera. Twister was trying to get something on me. His lawyer wouldn't let him use it though."

"That *bastard!*" she exclaimed, meaning the general. Somehow, though, Pauline did not feel as angry as she might have. The most beautiful day in her life was no longer lost in memory and time. On the contrary, she held it right here in her hand to see and cherish.

"We'd better get rid of the photos and negatives," Jack was saying.

"Get rid of them? How?"

"Burn them in the kitchen sink." He yawned. "I feel like dozing off for a little. You don't mind?"

"Darling, of course not. You rest." She covered him with his uniform jacket, kissed his forehead.

Pauline took the pictures into the kitchen, looking at each one carefully before touching a match to it, watching flame and black ash curl and devour. Finally, only one photo remained: her and Jack making love beneath the lilacs. She remembered their perfume, the enfolding softness of a million tender petals. She studied her face in the picture, and saw how her spiritual feeling of love actually *looked*. She held the picture and considered what to do. If she burned it, she would never again be able to gaze upon proof of her union with the man she loved above all else.

Pauline glanced out toward the couch. Jack was fast asleep.

She walked to the bedroom, opened a dresser drawer, and slid the photo beneath her silky lingerie. Whatever might happen she would at least have the remembrance. And, Pauline was absolutely certain, disaster waited to swoop down and demolish the only happiness she had ever known.

Die Vier Jahreszeiten, or The Four Seasons, was a comfortably inelegant club not far from Jack and Pauline's flat. It featured good beer, the best goulash soup in Bavaria, and a mediocre floor show that was unfailingly amusing. Young comedians perspired freely, and old songstresses tried to be Marlene Dietrich one more time.

"New singer tonight," Jack observed, glancing at a glossy photo in the club's dim entryway. "Karyn Bari. Real name's probably Brunhilde something." He walked on, but turned to find Pauline studying the picture.

"I don't think so," she said. "This girl's not German. But whatever she is, she's beautiful . . ."

Jack walked back and looked at the publicity photo, behind its rectangle of streaked glass. The singer was not Nordic, but faintly Oriental; many bloodlines had commingled to forge her face. She *was* beautiful, but Jack knew if he agreed with Pauline, it would only upset her. He couldn't understand why she was unaware of her own beauty.

"Come along, gorgeous," he said, putting his arm around her.

They went into the small, familiar dining room, and Heinrich, the waiter, brought them, in sequence, a bottle of Liebfraumilch, tiny sausages with brötchen and butter, veal Cordon Bleu with asparagus, coffee, and Cointreau.

"At least Heinrich spared us his tales of the Russian Front this time," said Jack, trying to cheer Pauline, who had been unusually quiet throughout the meal.

"What?" asked Pauline, as if coming back from a place of dark distraction.

"I said—" Jack began again.

Then the seedy drummer produced a rattling roll.

The guitarist took a final drag on his cigarette and flipped the butt away.

The pianist banged a few bored chords.

And the jowly, over-the-hill comic who doubled as master of ceremonies stepped to the microphone and said, in a rushed, artificially excited voice: "Now here she is, all the way from Bombay, India, *Karyn Bari.*"

"All the way from East Orange, New Jersey, is more likely . . ." Jack started to say.

But then, against all expectations, Jack Kenton saw the most stunning girl he had ever imagined, saw the most amazing performance in his life. Karyn Bari appeared from behind a tawdry screen, exploded onto the tiny *Die Vier Jahreszeiten* stage, not so much taking the stage as *seizing* it for herself, seizing the entire place and everyone in it. The bartender, shaking a drink, paused to watch her. Waiters stopped in their tracks, trays teetering. Busboys and the chef gathered at the swinging doors to the kitchen. Even the jaded, motley little band came alive, *shocked* to life by this wildly exotic young woman, who lifted them to play as they had never played before, to play as they were musically *incapable* of playing. At what price had such a miracle of showmanship been acquired? And what seduction and sorcery lay behind the mystery?

Each of Karyn's songs was direct, unique, and driven by overwhelming personal intensity, so that no one could turn away from her. In "Blues in the Night," her voice held the wail of the sax and the tears of everyone ever alone in the night. At her singing of "Money Honey," the place shook, crashed, jumped, and blasted with the beat of it. And then Karyn sang a song, a tender song, delicate as the petals of a flower, a song in some remote Hindu dialect, by which she transported her audience to a blue range of far mountains, where a boy and a girl had once loved and lost.

"She is *sensational*," said Jack, as Karyn paused at the microphone, smiling between numbers. "Hey, why so gloomy?"

"I'm not gloomy," said Pauline, forcing a smile, not taking her eyes off the singer.

Nor could Jack stop looking at Karyn. She wore a gleaming white sari and a small white turban, fastened with a glittering red jewel. She was not a small girl, yet her body had a willowy Oriental lightness about it, and her figure, as she moved to the beat of the music, seemed seductively poised beneath the sari. Her eyes were large and black, like dusty onyx, her cheekbones wide and perfect. Her lips were full, and her hair was straight and black.

"You like that, don't you?" Pauline asked, in a strained voice.

Jack turned to her. Pauline's eyes were sad. It was that puzzling vein of insecurity that lay within her. Jack took her hand. "We can leave if you like?"

Pauline shook her head no.

"And now," announced Karyn Bari from the stage, "I shall tell you a secret." With that, the band recommenced, and Karyn began a driving, strutting, stomping rendition of "I'm Evil."

". . . *yeah, eee . . . eee . . . eee . . . vil, is my name . . . is my naa . . . aaa . . . aaammme!!!*"

"I'm Evil" ended her set. The lights went up, and the small crowd burst into prolonged applause. Karyn bowed and smiled from the stage, looking directly at everyone in the audience, taking her time about doing it. Then with a last bow and a small, graceful wave, she disappeared behind the tawdry curtain. The show was over. The band members looked dejectedly at one another. Where had the magic gone? Waiters scurried to fill drink orders.

"Well," said Jack, turning to Pauline. "I think we saw the beginning of something tonight . . ."

He had meant to express his surprise that a singer as good as Karyn Bari was performing in a club like this, but he saw in Pauline's eyes a sudden flicker of fear, hr gaze on something behind him. He whirled to see what had made her afraid.

"Hello."

The voice was rich and silky, sultry and mysterious, and utterly assured. Karyn Bari was speaking directly to Jack, as if Pauline did not exist. "Did we not meet in another time?" she asked. "May I join you for just a moment?" She sat down at the table.

"Why, of course, Miss . . . Bari," said Jack, half standing, dazzled by the closeness of this beauty. Pauline's face darkened in alarm.

"Bari is my stage name. I am really Rupal Lorimahal. But surely you remember. I told you that in Budapest . . ." She let her voice trail off, glanced discreetly at Pauline. "Oh, I'm sorry . . ." she smiled.

"Excuse me," said Pauline, getting up and heading toward the ladies' room.

Jack started after her, but then he decided to clear up this Budapest business before Pauline returned to the table.

"I'm very sorry," he said, in the face of Karyn Bari's dazzling, insinuating smile, "but I'm afraid I've never been to Hungary."

"No? Could I have confused you with another man?"

The tone of her voice, the light in her eyes, made Jack wish he had been that other man. Anyway, the matter was explained: mistaken identity.

"I really enjoyed your show," he said, glancing around for Pauline.

"Thank you," said Karyn. "By the way, your friend has left."

"What?"

"The pretty lady you were with. She has gone."

"No, she'll be right back."

"No. I mean that she has left this club. I just saw her go out the door."

"What? Look, I'm sorry." Jack got up, fumbling for his billfold. "There seems to have been some kind of misunderstanding, and . . ."

"Are you going to run after her?" Karyn Bari smiled.

"Yes." Jack pulled out a number of *Deutschmark* bills and tossed them onto the table.

"Perhaps you'll come to see me again?"

But Jack was already moving away, ·between the small dining tables, toward the door. He rushed out into the chilly Munich night, looked up and down the street. No sign of Pauline. He shivered. A wind had come up from the Alps in the south. The *Föhn*, the Germans called it. They believed that the *Föhn* brought sickness and trouble and psychological distress.

They were right.

It had finally happened. Jack was lost to her. Pauline left *Die Vier Jahreszeiten* and started to run back toward the flat. High heels slowed her down, so she took them off and ran in her nylons, feeling the concrete cold against her feet. She stopped in front of the door to the apartment building, fumbling with her keys. *No, don't go in. He'll come back. You can't face him now. He shouldn't see you with no pride left at all.* So she ran across the street and ducked into a darkened alleyway, sobbing dryly, soundlessly, half bent over and holding her stomach to keep from throwing up. In a minute, Jack arrived, entered the apartment building, and ran up the stairs. She saw the lights go on in the windows of their flat. Minutes later, he came down again, standing out under the streetlight, looking about. Then he got into the MG and drove off slowly. Looking for her, no doubt. Well, he wouldn't find her. He had that other woman now. He didn't need her. He had never needed her. Retching, Pauline stumbled across the street, entered the building, and went up to the flat. All the lights were on. She picked up the phone and dialed. "Taxi, *bitte.*" She gave the address. "I want to go to the Munich airport.

"*Ja.* Right now. *Schnell.* Lufthansa terminal." She slammed the phone down, washed in the bitter satisfaction of self-pity. When Jack did not find her on the streets or in the few other *Gasthaüser* they sometimes went to, he would probably go over to her Red Cross office, which always had someone on duty day and night. He would not think of the airport, not right away, perhaps not until tomorrow. And by then it would be too late.

It was already too late. She ran to the bedroom, pulled her luggage out of the closet, and began throwing her clothes into the bags. *Get out, it's over. Hurry. He has her now. Get out, don't give her the pleasure of gloating.* Pauline's mind worked furiously. She would pay for her ticket by check, at the airport. She would resign her Red Cross job by letter, from the States. Another thought struck her, and she began to cry out loud. Jack and that singer would probably live together now, right here in this little apartment, that had been so lovely a time . . . *Don't cry now. Pack and get out. Cry later.*

She threw her things into the bags. Yanking open the dresser drawer, grabbing her lingerie, she saw the picture of herself and Jack making love. Her heart stopped and the tears poured. It had been so beautiful, so gorgeous and so beautiful. Pauline tried three times, but could not bring herself to rip the photo into shreds. Finally, she sat down on the bed, took out her ballpoint pen, thought for a long tearful moment, and wrote on the back of the picture what her heart told her to be true.

> *John Tyler Kenton*
> *and Pauline Yates*
> *were once in love.*
> *Germany, 1966.*

Then she slipped the picture into one of her suitcases.

In the taxi on the way to the airport, she tried not to cry, but with little success. The Bavarian driver kept turning around, soothingly saying, *"Ach, Fräulein, Fräulein,"* as if that would help. It didn't help. Nothing could help.

The plane left at dawn. Left the only place on earth in which Pauline Yates had ever been happy. Maybe she would be happy again, someday, with someone else, but never in the way she had been happy with Jack. The big jets thundered as the plane rose, wheeling in the sky. To the south were the glittering snowcapped peaks of the Alps, and all beneath lay the lush green plains of Europe. The past. Her past now. Pauline watched Munich grow smaller and smaller until it disappeared in distance and morning mist. She wept, listening to the rumbling whisper of the engines that bore her away, and then she reached America and sank untraceably, without wanting to be traced, into the swirl of New York's eight million lives.

Jack spent a desperate night, hunting the streets of Schwabing, trying to find Pauline, calling the Red Cross office, calling again, phoning the flat half-a-dozen times only to hear the instrument ring on and on, unanswered. Slanting rays of dawn light cast shadows of cathedrals upon ancient cobblestones. He must check the *Bahnhof*. Perhaps she had taken a train somewhere? To that little hotel in Bad Reichenhall, where they had spent such happy weekends? Maybe that was it! But driving back to the apartment, he saw a big jet rising from the airport on the outskirts of the city. Maybe it was just worry and fatigue, but his heart sank, and he already knew. She had gone. Checking passenger lists later in the morning confirmed his premonition. Possessed of her own private demons, Pauline had arisen from the maelstrom and touched him and loved him, and he had loved her. But now she had disappeared. Three days later, Pauline's superior at the Red Cross office called to tell him they had received her letter of resignation. She had given no address. They did not even know where to mail her final paycheck.

That night, while Jack sipped a cognac at The Four Seasons bar, he heard a silky voice beside him.

"I see that you are sad," said Karyn Bari. "It is about that girl, is it not?"

"Because you and I met in Budapest," he replied dismally.

"Ah," she said, easing onto the barstool next to him and ordering a dry vermouth, "but we might have met there, don't you think? Who can say? In any case, we have met now. Already I know two things about you."

Her smile was conspiratorial, insidious, bewitching; in spite of his depression, Jack felt himself responding to her. "Two things?" he asked. "What are they?"

"Your sadness will disappear more quickly than you think," she told him, "and you will not sleep alone tonight."

5

Another June had come, and Carol Jean Atwood's semester of student teaching was over. In a week, she would graduate from Bryn Mawr, her four years of college over too. Many things had ended in this doleful 1968: Martin Luther King, Jr., had been killed in April; Bobby Kennedy had been shot just the previous week in a Los Angeles hotel kitchen; and Carol's love affair with Vic Brand III lay in terrifying ruins.

Carol sat at the battered desk in the decrepit classroom and entered final grades in the record book. Mrs. Rigoletti, the regular teacher with whom Carol had worked, a sympathetic but realistic veteran of South Philadelphia's Abraham Lincoln Elementary School, had just called out the year's final "class dismissed." All of the children had immediately pounded out, screeching and roaring. Not one had remained to say a final good-bye. Carol was hurt. Alone among Bryn Mawr's future teachers, she had chosen to do her student teaching in a tough South Philly school, to help out where help was really needed. The rest of Carol's college classmates had opted for Main Line suburban schools, rich, safe, tidy, and genteel.

Mrs. Rigoletti noted Carol's crestfallen expression. "You've done just fine," she told the younger woman. "I couldn't be prouder."

"Thank you. But not one of them stayed to—"

"Say 'thank you'? You can't expect that. If it happens, consider it a bonus. But someday, years from now, one of them might remember something good you did."

"I guess that'll be thanks enough. *If* they remember me as good."

"Well, you are, so why shouldn't they? Do you have a teaching position for the fall?"

"Yes, I do," said Carol brightly. "In Royall Beach, on Long Island, New York. I'll be teaching fifth grade."

"Royall Beach?" Mrs. Rigoletti exclaimed, as if her prize soldier had gone over to the enemy. Royall Beach was a far cry from South Philadelphia.

"I know how it sounds. But I'll be close to my family in Connecticut. And the Royall Beach School has a very good pilot program for underprivileged kids from other neighborhoods."

At mention of the pilot program, Mrs. Rigoletti's faith in Carol seemed restored. "I'm happy to hear that—"

She was interrupted by a timid knock at the door. A worried little black face peered through the thick glass pane.

"It's Lonnie Jefferson," said Carol. "I wonder if he forgot something?" It was standard safety policy at Lincoln to keep classroom doors locked, so Carol went over and slid the bolt back. Lonnie eased shyly into the room.

"I have to tell you something, Miss Atwood."

Mrs. Rigoletti smiled and Carol waited.

"Alone," Lonnie managed.

"Oh," cried Mrs. Rigoletti, as if remembering something she had to do. "Must dash. I'll leave you two. Carol, will you turn the grade book in at the office when you're finished? Lonnie, you have a terrific summer, okay?"

The boy nodded. Carol and Mrs. Rigoletti traded glances, and the older teacher went to the door. "Keep this locked, Carol, all right? The only person coming by this afternoon will be Luigi, closing up the place for the summer. And you have a good one."

"You too, Mrs. Rigoletti. Thanks for your help." Carol glanced out the door as the other woman walked away, checking the corridor to see if Luigi, the school custodian, was anywhere around. She didn't see him, so she closed and bolted the door again.

"What is it, Lonnie? Forget something?"

The little boy shuffled nervously. "No, it's not that, Miss Atwood."

Poor Lonnie. His clothes were dirty, and he was rapidly outgrowing them. Looking at him, Carol's consciousness was nudged by something dark and fearful, and she remembered Renfrew Watts, the pathetic boy killed on the dirt road south of Stamford, Connecticut, all those years ago. Lonnie was attentive and bright, but what real chance did he have to thrive in a neighborhood of anger and hopelessness and bleak, mean streets?

Now he was rummaging in the pocket of his threadbare jeans.

"My ma has these old magazines," he said, "and I found your picture in one of them."

"But I don't think I've ever had my picture in a—"

Lonnie thrust a folded piece of glossy paper at her. She took it, opened it. A page ripped from *Look* magazine in the 1950s, it had to do with the filming of *The Bridges of Toko-Ri*, starring Grace Kelly and William Holden.

"There's you," said Lonnie, pointing to a picture of Grace Kelly. "But my ma, she doesn't believe me. She says you haven't been in a movie."

Carol was flattered and touched by the boy's eager mistake. "Why, thank you, Lonnie," she said, "I'm happy you think so. But this isn't me."

He stared doubtfully at the photo. "It isn't?"

"No. Sad to say."

He looked at the picture some more, then he turned his face up to Carol and studied her for a moment.

"You're right," he said. "You're a lot prettier than this other one."

With that, he took the magazine page back, stuffed it into his jeans, and headed for the door. She unlocked it for him, and watched him go on down the corridor. Then she stepped back into the classroom, smiling to herself. Lonnie hadn't come out and said "thank you," not in so many words, but that's what he had done all right. Prettier than Grace Kelly. Not bad. Exactly what she had needed to hear. Since Vic Brand III, Carol hadn't been feeling too pretty, or smart. In fact, she hadn't been feeling much of anything at all.

It was funny. Carol had always believed that she would never be fooled. "I'll know when the right guy comes along," she confided to her closest friends. "He has to pass three tests. Body, heart, and mind. Not necessarily in that order. But if he rings three bells, I'll know he's okay." So when she met Vic Brand and not long afterward averred that he had scored splendidly on her private tests, Carol's sisters at Kappa Kappa Gamma attached a "III" to Vic Brand's name. "CiJi, Vic was one in a million, so how could you have known?" Carol's father had said, attempting to comfort her later. "It wasn't your fault." Maybe not, but how could her three tests have failed so utterly? How could she herself have botched so badly? It wasn't funny at all.

The disaster had begun last September, just after Carol returned to Bryn Mawr for senior year. She was in the library, working on a bibliography for her school and community course, when Samantha Ralston, a sorority sister, rushed in. Samantha was looking for action. She had just returned from a summer in Rome, which had offered a few more males than Bryn Mawr on this fall weekend. "Let's go *somewhere* and do *something*," she pleaded, "they could give me Extreme Unction for horniness right now."

Carol's own situation was not quite so severe, but she was less than ecstatic about studying the weekend away. A mood of poignant sweetness lingered from the summer. Randall Jayne, the boy from Princeton whom she had dated fairly regularly all last year, was studying economics in Berlin on a Fulbright Scholarship. And Jeff Gimbel, who had been at Wescott Cove in August for three weeks, was way out at UCLA.

"There's a football game up at Cornell," informed Samantha, "or there's Jim Morrison and the Doors at Fillmore East in New York."

"Football game."

"Right," affirmed Samantha. "We're not a bunch of rock-mad hippies here. We're from Bryn Mawr. We've got class."

Samantha had a Corvette, which she drove like a madwoman northward to Ithaca, New York. They missed the game—Cornell 13, Dartmouth 6—but arrived in time for the parties just getting started along Fraternity Row. Phi Delta Theta proved to be no great shakes, the crowd lackluster and the drinking too obviously frenzied. But Sigma Alpha Epsilon was something else again. "This is more my style," Samantha announced, putting herself in the direct path of an appealing jock type in a Davy Crockett hat. He took the bait and was soon telling her about his prowess in surfing and with Coors. Carol felt a hand on her shoulder and turned to see a marvelous-looking guy, tall, with a rich swatch of dark hair curving down over his forehead, and the clearest green eyes she'd ever seen on a man. Carol even felt a small thrill from his touch.

First test, Body: Pass. For a day begun dully in the Bryn Mawr library, things were moving along just fine.

"Enjoy the game?"

"Missed it," she told him.

"So did I."

They both laughed. "I was in—in Pittsburgh," he said. He seemed about to say more, but then he either decided against it or had nothing else to tell about Pittsburgh. He looked strong and forceful, but she sensed in him a sweetness, maybe a shyness. She liked that, and she felt rather sexual and motherly at the same time. Second test, Heart: Pass. He was also well on his way toward hurdling the Mind test, with a serious, mature manner, accentuated compellingly when his smile dazzled her at intervals.

"I'm Vic Brand. Cornell."

"Carol Jean Atwood." Giving her name like that seemed so formal, and she was so attracted to him, that she gave her private nickname too, something she hadn't done in years.

"CiJi? Oh, of course. From *C* and *J*."

"*Magna cum laude!*"

Again, his brilliant smile. "Why don't we get out of here?" he suggested.

They went outside. He took her to his car, a yellow Maserati, and they went for a drive. Carol felt drawn to Vic, as if she'd known him forever. Then she realized she didn't know anything about him at all.

"I'm just Bull Brand's kid," he sighed, when she asked him about himself.

"Bull Brand? Who's Bull Brand?"

"You don't know?" he asked, in happy astonishment. "I thought everybody in the country knew my old man. The Chicago Wheelers?"

It sounded familiar, but Carol wasn't sure. "Is that basketball, or something?"

"Oh, my God, I love you. No, that's football. My old man owns the team. And I've always been Bull Brand's kid, you know, son of the guy who owns the football team. I usually wind up telling people, no, I don't have tons of free tickets to give away. You like me, don't you?" he asked suddenly.

Later, Carol would remember not so much the inquiry itself but how he had made it. His manner and tone were so much at variance with the way he'd first seemed, it was as if another person had asked the question. But Carol interpreted the lapse as a part of the shyness she'd sensed in him.

"I think you'll do," she answered, laughing. But she was serious, too. Serious already. Because Carol had heard the third bell, and she was convinced that Vic would be just fine in every way there was.

"You like football?" he was asking.

If you do, she thought. "Yes, but I don't get to many games. Always too busy, I guess."

"Tell you what. Being Bull's kid has some perks to it. How'd you like to fly out to Los Angeles next Saturday? We'll stay over, see the Rams game Sunday, and then fly back."

"What? Well—"

"Of course." Vic was enthusiastic. "I do it all the time."

Things were going pretty fast, but Carol didn't mind at all.

"And Carol?" he asked, in a voice she had heard other men use before, and so she was not surprised to hear the words other men had also used, "let's find a place and spend the night together."

Her girlhood passed before her eyes, as if she were sensually drowning. There comes a time. The first time. This summer at Wescott Cove with Jeff Gimbel, it had almost been right, but not quite. Jeff had sensed in her not doubt exactly, and certainly not unwillingness, but a delicate hesitance, and the moment had come tenderly to nothing. But with Vic Brand now, given his desire and her piercing inclination to yield, everything was different. Besides, he looked almost exactly like the image of the man she had always thought of as "ideal."

"Only if it's a nice place," she told him.

He smiled, his teeth glittering in dashboard light as he reached out and took her hand. "It will be," he promised.

Carol's head was spinning a little. No, more than a little. Senior year had certainly gotten off to a resounding start.

Carol had been naked with men before, and she enjoyed the freedom and mutual exploration of it. But when Vic turned out the lights, she was too shy to tell him she would have preferred them on. Despite her excitement in wanting this night, her mind was filled with impressions of adventure and wonder, pleasure, and loss. Nor would her body move, respond as she expected it, and certainly not as she commanded it. When Vic came in hurried, thrusting spasms, he apologized. "I just wanted you too much, that's all. Here, I know how to do some other things . . ."

"No, it's all right," Carol told him. And it was. She didn't mind. The first time was over, and that was history. Something to build on. Anyway, she was tired. The last thing she heard him say was, "I know Mother would have liked you very much."

When she awakened in the morning, Vic was leaning on an elbow, watching her, his expression one of unbelievable intensity.

"You're mine now," he whispered, "you're really mine."

Beautiful words, and eerily unsettling in the first moment between sleep and waking, but in another moment words did not matter as Vic turned his attention to her, long and lovingly, kissing her everywhere, everywhere. Carol loved it, but neither his kisses nor caresses were enough. Even when he made love to her again, nice as it was, it didn't work. Was something wrong with her? How awful *that* would be! But Vic did not seem to mind. If anything, he was almost too solicitous and attentive. "I love you," he kept saying, "you're mine now, and I love you." Not that Carol minded the words, but she had been used to a little more personal space. She felt *crowded;* that was what it was, and when he put her on a plane back to Philadelphia, she felt guiltily relieved to separate.

"I'll call you at school tonight," he told her, his arm tight around her waist at the boarding gate. "And I'll have Clancy, our chauffeur, pick you up at the Philadelphia airport, and take you back to Bryn Mawr."

"Vic, you don't have to. I'll just take an airport limo or a cab."

"No, no, I want to. I have to take care of you now, because you're mine."

Before she boarded the plane, he gave her a kiss that was almost desperate in its intensity, releasing her just an instant before she would have decided to struggle away from him.

"Are you all right?" asked the stewardess, as Carol buckled on her seatbelt.

"What? Sure. Why?"

"I thought you looked a little worried. Sorry."

Worried? Carol thought about it. *No,* she tried to convince herself, *it was your first time, and that's a big step. Vic is wonderful.*

But by the time the plane landed in Philadelphia, Carol was asking herself a jittery question: *My God, have I made a great big sappy mistake? Maybe my heart and mind erred, and was my body trying to tell me something?*

Bull Brand lived on a country estate outside Doylestown, in Bucks County, and, just as Vic had promised, Clancy, the Brands' chauffeur, was waiting to drive Carol back to Bryn Mawr. He looked at her—she thought—a little more closely than was polite as he held the door for her. Maybe "doing it" the first time left a visible sign, like a mark on the forehead. Or maybe, she thought—not liking the feeling at all—Clancy had been called to pick up a lot of girls, put on airplanes by Vic in some distant city. They drove off, and Carol tried several times to start a conversation, but Clancy didn't venture beyond yes and no. Riding along in the ensuing silence, Carol remembered old Rufus, their family chauffeur, dead now, remembered how pleasant he had always been. But the thought of Rufus led her back to the Connecticut roadway and the accident. No, she didn't want to think of that: *A life for a life.* It was strange. Considered in years, Miss Blaisdell's School was a long time in the past, but memory was a living thing, and *The Waltz of the Dead* seemed like a song from yesterday. Carol suppressed a shudder. She didn't want to think of that, either.

Carol felt immensely relieved when the car drew up in front of the Kappa Kappa Gamma house, more relieved still when she saw Samantha Ralston's Corvette in the parking lot. Home safe, as was she. Clancy went around and opened the car door for her. "One thing, miss," he called, after she had started up the walk toward the house.

"Yes?" she asked, turning.

He looked apologetic, almost worried. "I'm afraid I'll have to tell Bull about this."

Carol didn't know what to say. Without knowing why, she felt on the verge of trembling. "Fine, you do that," she told him, as coolly as she could.

But whatever worries she had seemed to be totally dispelled a bit later that evening. A huge bouquet of flowers arrived for her, and attached was a card that read:

"CiJi, I love you."

Signed by Vic Brand. She was thrilled again, and told everyone about him. That was when they made him a "III."

Vic caused no little stir at Kappa Kappa Gamma when he arrived the Friday evening after he and Carol had met at Cornell. "He's not just a *three*, he's a *ten!*" Samantha exuded.

"I thought we were flying to Los Angeles tomorrow?" Carol wondered, since Vic had told her that he'd arrive Saturday morning.

"Oh, we are. It's just that I couldn't stand to be apart from you. Did you get the flowers?"

"Yes, thank you. And something funny happened. Your chauffeur, Clancy, said he'd have to tell your father."

Vic looked nonplussed for a second, then: "Tell my father what?"

"I don't know."

"Well, I certainly don't know either. Forget it. Let's go out to dinner."

That was the way the pattern went. Vic would arrive, they would go out to dinner, dance until early Saturday, and grab a jet to wherever the Wheelers were playing that weekend, Miami or Houston or Minneapolis. They'd stay overnight Saturday in a hotel, catch the game, then jet back to Philadelphia, where Vic had left his car in the airport lot. The only odd thing was that they would make a trip every other weekend; during intervening weekends he wouldn't come to Bryn Mawr at all. "Had to go to Pittsburgh," was all he would say. "Family business."

Family business, indeed! Carol began to suspect his absences each fortnight had to do with the Saturday nights they spent together in distant hotels. Because in spite of the most tender, protracted bouts of love, she had not fully responded to him physically. That might explain, too, why he was so tense and restless on Sunday nights when he dropped her back at Bryn Mawr. "No," he told her. "I love you. I seem a bit hyper because I have to leave you now. I don't want to go back to Cornell. Maybe I'll just stay down here." Carol would pass it off as a joke, because by the time she got back to school after a weekend, with all the rush and the increasing tension borne by her private inability, all she wanted was a little time alone.

Was this love?

She began to wonder.

Maybe she ought to pick up some strange guy, make it with him, and see how her body did then.

No.

But what did Vic *do* in Pittsburgh every other week?

Moreover, since his father's home was nearby, why hadn't he taken her out there? Why didn't he go out there himself? He always stayed Friday nights in a motel close to campus.

"Dad's on the road this time of year, anyway," he explained. "No point driving out to the house."

Something unusual was going on, Carol figured. And, at times, Vic's intensity was upsetting. Coming back from New Orleans in late November—again she had not been able to come the night before—he thrashed about in his seat on the plane, face dark and taut.

"What's the matter?"

"You know."

"Vic, I don't know. But I hate to see you so distressed, I—"

"I'm not distressed. Don't say that. I'm perfectly fine."

"Then why are you so tense?"

He looked her full in the face, his expression oddly twisted. "What do *you* do on the weekends I'm in Pittsburgh?"

"Family business," she snapped, irritated by both the question and his manner. She meant to explain, then, telling him she got caught up on work left unattended during her time with him, but his hand shot out and caught her just above the elbow, his fingers digging into flesh.

Involuntarily, she cried out. Passengers turned to gape, and a stewardess craned her neck over the high seats.

"It's okay, it's okay," Vic told everyone, with his best smile.

That was when Carol decided to ease up on the relationship a little. She was glad when the next weekend was his Pittsburgh trip, or wherever. She would have some time to think things over.

Vic was subdued the rest of the trip, and when he stopped in front of Kappa Kappa Gamma to let her off, she heard the same tone in his voice that she'd heard back in September, when he'd asked if she liked him. Except this time he said, "I know you don't love me anymore."

Truthfully, Carol didn't know anymore if she loved him or not, but he seemed poised on a treacherous, private precipice of his own devising, so she forced a fabrication.

"Of course I do," she said.

He roared away, unconvinced. Carol went into the sorority house, almost dreading the Chicago trip two weeks thence.

"Hey," cried Samantha, "you got a male call while you were out."

"Who from?"

"Somebody named Jeff Gimbel, from UCLA. Said he'll be passing through here next weekend, and wants to see you. He'll call again later tonight."

Jeff Gimbel. After this trip with Vic, the thought of Jeff was welcome. Jeff was witty and irreverent, and Carol remembered with affectionate delight his tender necking at night on the Wescott Cove beach last summer.

Samantha read her friend's happy expression. "Does this mean VB III has competition?"

"If he does, I certainly won't be the one to tell him," Carol replied, still feeling the place Vic had squeezed her arm.

Jeff showed up the following Friday night, wearing blue jeans, his blond hair halfway down his back.

"Shhhhhh," he warned, to Carol's laughter, "Ronald Reagan

personally ran me out of California. Quite a costume, hey, for an ex-preppie from Andover?"

They sat down in the lounge, prepared to get reacquainted a little before deciding where to go out that night. Carol was called to the phone.

"It's my night," Jeff said, as she excused herself.

The voice on the phone was deep, peremptory, and worried. "Miss Carol Jean Atwood? Is that you?"

"Yes, who—"

"Bull Brand. I think you know my son."

The Famous Father. He didn't mince words.

"Is he there with you now?" Bull demanded.

"No, he's—"

"You're sure he's not? This is very important, Miss Atwood."

"He told me he was going to Pittsburgh this weekend. Has anything happened?"

She pictured Vic and his yellow Maserati wrapped around a telephone pole along a snowy roadway in western Pennsylvania. She pictured—she didn't know what she pictured.

"No, he's not in Pittsburgh. I've checked. And I don't know if anything's happened. He was very upset, and I thought you might know something about it."

"Me?"

"Miss Atwood, perhaps we ought to talk. I can't explain it over the phone—"

"Explain what?"

"About Vic. I thought he was getting better, and I felt you were a good influence on him, but . . . Tell you what, can I send a car for you tomorrow morning? Let's have lunch here at my place. I'll explain things to you then."

It sounded like a command.

"I don't know—" Carol began.

"Miss Atwood, *please.*"

She heard a note of desperate urgency replace the faint, underlying worry in Bull Brand's voice.

"All right, Mr. Brand."

"Good. Clancy will be there at about ten, ten-fifteen. And if you hear from Vic tonight, call me right away, okay?"

He gave her the number, and they said good-bye.

"Trouble?" asked Jeff Gimbel, reading Carol's face as she came back into the lounge and sat down next to him.

Then the front door crashed open. Vic Brand stood there, looking at them, green eyes blazing, face darkened and distraught.

"Yes," Carol said.

"So this is what you do when I'm in Pittsburgh," snarled Vic, advancing. "I knew it all along." Vic had at least thirty pounds and three or four inches on Jeff, who was further disadvantaged not only by being seated but also by having absolutely no idea what was going on.

"What the hell—" he cried, trying to get to his feet, but there was no chance. Vic Brand jumped on him, biting, kneeing, and pummeling like a man gone berserk. Carol screamed and jumped on his back, trying to pull him off Jeff, who was yelling as the blows fell. Samantha, who had phone duty that night, looked on in momentary horror, then dialed the campus security office, and a couple of young men, waiting in the lounge for their dates to come down, jumped up from their chairs and came forward tentatively.

"Help!" Carol implored, still clawing at Vic's back.

Vic's knee rammed upward, and Jeff Gimbel's head snapped backward, blood spouting from his nostrils, red blood luminous in the air.

"Vic, stop, please stop—"

"I'll take care of you when I finish with him," Vic yelled, flinging her onto the floor. He grabbed Jeff's long hair with one hand, and drew back a fist. Dazed, Jeff struggled to raise his arms, trying to protect his face. Carol, on the floor, lunged forward and grabbed Vic's ankle, pulled hard. Vic went down. The two other men, emboldened now, jumped on top of him. Jeff collapsed, howling, on the blood-spattered couch. Vic tossed, clawed, and bit, struggling with the two. A campus patrolman appeared at the main door. "Stop it!" he yelled. "That's enough." Nothing happened. Vic kept on battling, and the two men fighting him were afraid to let him go, fearing what mayhem he might do if he ever got up.

"Call the office again," the patrolman shouted to Samantha, "tell 'em all to get over. Fast."

According to policy, the patrolman carried no firearm, but he did have a small truncheon, and he took it from his belt, prepared to use it. But the patrolman, unused to such incidents on the serene Bryn Mawr campus, delayed too long. Vic hurtled forward, drove the patrolman halfway across the lounge, and knocked the truncheon from his hand. It struck the floor, spinning away, and rolled under the couch upon which Jeff Gimbel moaned and bled. Vic dropped to his knees, animallike in his frenzy, and reached for the club. Carol sobbed and yelled. The patrolman was choking and holding his gut. Samantha was crying, and the two men bested by Vic were crawling toward the door. Then Vic's hand grasped the truncheon. With a mad light in his eyes, he pulled it from beneath the couch, jumped to his feet, and fixed Carol in his awful glare.

"You shouldn't have left me," he gritted, slowly, with unspeakable menace. "You shouldn't have dumped on me . . ."

"Vic, I didn't, I didn't," wailed Carol, backing away.

It was strange, but she looked at him now, this man who had been her first lover, and knew that the wild light of craziness had been in his eyes all along. She ought to have seen it, but she had not.

Now her blood chilled utterly, and the core of her soul went cold. Because she heard the first woeful chord of a phantom organ, prelude to *The Waltz of the Dead*.

Vic raised the truncheon and came toward her, leering slackly.

The presence of death. *Her* death.

Carol screamed.

Five campus security men saved her, bursting in through the door. To their credit, they did not wait to gauge the situation, but rushed Vic en masse and slammed him to the floor. It took all five of them to pin him down, and they had to do it until a doctor got there and administered a shot of sedatives, triple-strength. Still, strapped to the stretcher, in legal custody—town cops were there too, by now—Vic Brand mumbled and raged, jerking his head this way and that, trying to find Carol in the crush.

"Nobody leaves me," he vowed, in a strangled moan. "Nobody leaves me until I say so."

Next morning, shaken and pale, Carol climbed into Bull Brand's car.

"Sorry to hear about what happened," Clancy offered, settling behind the wheel. "Bull will explain, though. He's a good man, Bull is. In spite of his reputation as a tough nut."

This time, it was Clancy who seemed to want to talk and Carol who could not find responses. Her perspective on life and reality had become dislodged, and Carol felt herself adrift. Shattered as her confidence was at having so completely misjudged Vic Brand, she was, if anything, even more troubled by the resurgence of that half-buried nightmare music, *The Waltz of the Dead*. The past came boiling back and did not require a genius to interpret. Carol had heard the music once, and Miss Blaisdell died; she'd heard it a second time for little Renfrew Watts, killed by the car. And last night, yes, last night she had heard the deathly music for herself. Only the timely arrival of campus police had forestalled the end Vic had intended for her.

I couldn't be crazy, she thought, feeling weirdly disembodied. Indeed, how could she be? It was very logical, wasn't it? When she heard *The Waltz of the Dead*, somebody was going to die. But why was she hearing it? Again? Why had she not heard it for all these years?

The answer to that was much easier than she wanted it to be: Miss Blaisdell and Renfrew Watts had been the only two people to die *in her presence*. Had Vic succeeded in killing her last night, Carol herself would have been the third.

Oh, my God, she thought, as cold currents shot up and down her spine, *there is some power inside me that tells when death is coming!*

"You okay, miss?" asked Clancy, glancing around.

"Yes, I just feel a little chilly."

"I'll turn up the heat."

And he did, but earthly warmth could not ameliorate the kind of cold by which Carol had been stricken.

The Brand estate, set in the lovely, rolling Pennsylvania hills, was an old comfortable house of fieldstone and tudor, and Bull Brand, in spite of a severe, iron-gray crew cut, hard eyes, and a thick, intimidating body, put Carol at ease.

"Thank you so much for coming," he said, leading her to an overstuffed chair. He had tea served, and a maid poured as Carol looked around. They were obviously in the trophy room. The glitter of massed cups and statuettes could not have been less startling than that which surprised the plunderers of the tomb of Tutankhamen. Photos of a younger Bull Brand, lean, trim and taut, padded and helmeted, were everywhere. Bull with Knute Rockne. Bull with Bear Bryant. Bull with Bobby Kennedy. Bull with Connie Mack. Carol could see where Vic had gotten his looks.

"Time took care of me," Bull said now, a little shyly. "One day you can do the hundred in seven point two, and the next day you're an aging jock, getting a shot plugging lite beer on TV."

The manner in which he said it was so old-shoe rueful, so easily familiar, that Carol laughed. Her misgivings about coming here faded, and Bull began to speak.

"What happened to you last night, what Vic tried to do, well, I'm afraid a lot of it's my fault."

"Your fault? How?"

"Well, you see, Miss Atwood . . . may I call you Carol? You see, Carol, my son Vic is the product of a misspent past. *My* misspent past. When he was little, I was always away playing football, or getting ready to play football, or recovering from having played football. Didn't get to see much of my boy. I figured there'd be time for that later." He sighed, smiling sadly. "I guess that's life. We always figure there'll be time later on to do what we ought to be doing right now. Well, anyway, Vic was bothered a lot because I was never around. I didn't recognize the signs. When he cried, which was every time I had to go on a business trip, I'd yell at him and tell him to grow up, stop sniveling. You know, that he-man crap—oh, I'm sorry."

"That's all right, Mr. Brand. I hear a lot worse than that around campus."

Bull laughed. "Yeah, I forgot. You're part of this modern free-speech generation, aren't you? Well, that's okay, and no crazier than anything that's gone before. Now, as I was saying, I kind of neglected my son all along, and he developed a very close relationship with his mother. Wasn't her fault. It just happened. I noticed it, and so did she, but again we figured time would just sort of take care of it, he would grow out of it, that sort of thing. You hope for the best . . ." His voice trailed off for a moment, but then he recovered. ". . . you hope for the best, but there are some things that require a hell of a lot more than hope.

"But to make a long story short, my wife died about six years ago. When Vic was fourteen. Amyotrophic lateral sclerosis. Lou Gehrig's disease, they call it. Takes about two years. Your muscles disintegrate, is what it is. Can't walk, lift an arm, sit up. Finally, can't breathe. It tore Vic apart. He cracked up, when she died. Had a breakdown." Bull grimaced at the memory. "Threw himself on the coffin, 'Don't leave me, you can't leave me.' That sort of thing."

Carol stiffened in her chair. Last night at the sorority house, Vic had screamed: *"Nobody leaves me until I say so."*

"I had no choice," Bull told her. "I signed him into the Mellon Clinic in Pittsburgh."

So that was why Vic had to go to Pittsburgh! What the Mayo Clinic was to medicine, the Mellon institution was to psychiatry.

"He still has to go back a couple of times a month," Bull said, "and I thought he was getting better. They did manage to pull him together quite a lot over the years. But now since this new attack—"

"What new attack? You mean the one last night? Have there been others?"

Bull nodded. "Five. Last night makes six. In a way, you were lucky."

"Lucky?" Carol cried.

It took an effort of the will for Bull to meet her eyes.

"That's why I asked you to come here. So I could explain and apologize in person. What happened to you is, really, my fault, and so were his other attacks. I should have insisted that he remain at Mellon. The pattern is always the same. He'll develop a fondness for a girl, and it's usually reciprocated. He's a good-looking guy, and when he's not in the grip of the sickness, he's perfectly fine. But the people at Mellon have told me time and again, he's caught in a kind of compulsive psychosis. If he could work through relationships at a superficial level and gradually get more deeply involved, there might be some hope. But, no, he has to jump right in, all the way, right away."

"I know what you mean," said Carol. She recalled Vic, the morning after they'd first made love, saying: *"You're mine now."* Yes, it had been true in a way, but . . .

"And something bad always happens. He gets to worrying, feeling jealous, feeling whoever he happens to be in love with will leave him, just like his mother did."

"Where is he now?"

"Back at Mellon. High security. Restrained, in fact."

"Is—is that all necessary?"

Bull gave her a straight look. "Miss Atwood, last year he attacked a girl, and left her paralyzed. She came out of it after a couple of months, and the case is still going on. My lawyers found out the girl was more or less an amateur hooker, and Vic's psychological background made it possible for us to stall, but . . ." He lifted a hand and let it fall, a gesture of futility. "But that was my fault. I should have recommitted him then."

Now Carol was angry. Bull saw it. "Yes, Carol," he said, explaining his behavior but not excusing it, "I was wrong, and it is my fault, but you haven't had a child yet. Don't judge me too harshly until you know what it's like."

The big man looked so sincere that Carol let her anger slip away.

"He's my son. What else can I say?"

"It's all right, Mr. Brand. And I really do hope Vic gets better."

Bull shook his head. "Oh, he won't. Barring a miracle, Vic will never be able to leave Mellon without constant supervision."

When Carol was alone, memory of her affair with Vic settled over her like an angry cloud, making her frightened and depressed. Her self-confidence was sullied, her underlying romantic nature a little marred.

"Don't blame yourself, CiJi," her father had said, "Vic was one in a million. One in a million. How could you have known?"

"I should have been able to see the signs," she had replied. And now, all these months later, completing the grade records in an empty classroom at Lincoln School, she told herself again: *I should have been able to see the signs.*

The greatest pain was in knowing that, for a time, she had really, truly, deep down *loved* Vic.

I wonder if I'll ever love anybody else again? she thought, entertaining a poignant despair.

Well, the school year was over, anyway, even if her life wasn't. Since the custodian had not shown up yet to check and lock the classroom, Carol got up from her desk and yanked down the large windows, and then she erased the blackboards. Tyrannical old Luigi was death on unerased blackboards. Carol was just in time, too, because outside the classroom, far down the corridor, she heard approaching footsteps, heels clicking on the tile floor. Carol sighed. There was something bereft and gloomy about the big old school.

Luigi's footsteps came closer, a sharp *click click click* on the ancient tile.

Carol started toward the door; she would have to unlock it.

She saw the bolt was open; she had not locked it after Lonnie Jefferson left.

She remembered that old Luigi always wore rubber-soled loafers, easy on aging metatarsals. Virtually soundless.

And above the syncopated click of those advancing footfalls, Carol heard, within the cavern of her mind, that first doomed chord of *The Waltz of the Dead.*

She leaped toward the door, fumbling with the bolt. Too late. The door was pushed open brutally, and she went spinning, almost falling, back into the classroom.

"Oh, no!"

"I'm afraid so," snarled Vic Brand, standing there in the doorway, breathing hard. Superficially, he was the same Vic she had known. Tall, well-shaped body, dark hair, striking green eyes. But he was altered in a deeper sense. His private madness had transformed him. His mouth was tight, with a dangerous set to the lips, and sadistic malevolence glittered in his eyes.

The organ of hell swelled to a second lingering chord, higher on the scale. A phantom audience gathered for the fateful dance, and Death advanced down a corridor of Carol's memory.

"You left me," Vic accused, with quiet menace. His beautiful green eyes were slits of angry light.

"Vic, no—"

He started toward her. Carol backed away. He was blocking her path to the door. *Think,* she commanded herself, *you have to get him to talk.* He came on. She backed around the desk, toward the windows along the opposite wall.

"All right, Vic," she said. "I made a terrible mistake. But can we talk about it? Please?"

He shook his head, grinning. "Too late for talk. You should have thought about that before you left me." He began to skirt the desk, step by slow step, coming after her.

Desperately, she tried another tack. *Details. Get him to talk about practical things.* "Vic, how did you get away from Mellon? How did you know I was here?"

He gave her a canny leer. "After a few months, they let me out on the lawn for exercise. I was 'improving,' you see. I waited for weeks, but one day they didn't watch me, and here I am." He laughed, a terrible cackle. "Then at Bryn Mawr I called your house, asking where you were student teaching. I said I was Jeff Gimbel. Clever, huh?"

Vic was all the way around the desk now, and Carol was close to the wall. Should she scream? *Could* she scream? She didn't know.

"Vic," she said, gambling on talk again, "if you hurt me, I won't ever love you anymore."

He paused, thinking it over. But he was too far gone. "When you're dead," he answered, "you won't be able to love anybody anymore."

Backed against the wall, Carol heard the quivery, discordant third note of the prelude; now the waltz would commence. And she would die.

Vic lunged. Carol felt his strong hands close around her throat. His body was against hers, pushing her into the wall. The stately dance music resounded in her mind; she was swept up in the swirl of it, carried along with it. The organ throbbed, the classroom darkened. Everything swayed and wavered. No air in the world, only the howling music of demise. Carol's heart thrashed in alarm, battering against her rib cage. She was fading, fading . . .

And then she was on the floor, choking and gasping. Vic Brand lay sprawled across a child's desk, blood dripping down from a cut beneath his hair. And Luigi, his wrinkled face violet-pink, was bending over her, babbling in alarm. In his big, work-hardened hands, he gripped the broom handle he'd used to smash Vic Brand. Assuring himself that Carol was all right, he inspected Vic with a chary touch.

"He's not dead, Miss Atwood. I don't think he's dead. Oh. I saw him by the office, ten minutes ago. I said to myself, Luigi, he looks okay. Such a fine-looking young man." The custodian shrugged. "But you never know," he said.

Carol slumped against the wall, and put her hands over her eyes. The music was gone now, tantalizing precursor of disaster, omen and herald and prophet all in one. Blood dripped, from Luigi's broom handle, dripped from the desk onto the worn wooden floor of the classroom. Vic was not dead, true, but for a dark moment Carol almost wished Luigi had hit him a little harder.

6

Rupal Lorimahal loved to wander about the sleek East Side apartment Jack Kenton acquired in late 1967, after he resigned his army commission and returned to New York. The apartment was on the thirty-second floor, and from its windows Rupal could see the East River; the United Nations complex; the flag of India tall on a UN staff; dozens and dozens of great buildings; Manhattan; and beyond it the overwhelming expanse of America, stretching westward as far as she could see. Rupal loved New York and America in the same way she loved Jack Kenton. They were nice and good to her. They thrilled her and excited her. She needed them for now. But she was just passing through. Rupal stood at the window, naked except for a coat of peerless sable. The coat was turned inside out; she luxuriated in the feel of the fur against her skin. When she was alone and happy—and she was almost always happy, passing through—she would hum an American folk song:

> *Are you going away with no words of farewell?*
> *Will there be not a trace left behind?*
> *I could have loved you better,*
> *Didn't mean to be unkind.*
> *You know that was the last thing on my mind.*

But, as Rupal walked about in the sable coat, humming the tune, the words that ran through her head were subtly altered:

> *Am I going away with no words of farewell?*
> *Will I leave not a trace left behind?*
> *You could have loved me better,*
> *Didn't mean to be unkind.*
> *I know that was the last thing on your mind.*

The song was not so sad that way, and more true. She would

walk and hum, look out the windows, hug the wondrous fur next to her body. Now and then she would move to the mirrors—mirrors in the bedroom, bathroom, hallway, entryway, living room—and study her image in the glass.

"I am Karyn Bari," she would say aloud. "I am Karyn Bari." And then her eyes would darken, harden, and that incomparable skin would grow taut and lovely over cheekbones that the Queen of Sheba must once have possessed, and Rupal Lorimahal would cry, "I want!" Such wisdom was the birthright—the only birthright—of one born in a gutter in Bombay.

The mother of Rupal Lorimahal had been a Brahman, the highest caste in India. Her family had not lived in the teeming milieu into which little Rupal was born, but rather in a great white house on a vast estate behind guarded walls, north of the city. Walls and guards kept beggars away, and thieves, and all the other riffraff whose hearts beat with fine hatred for the remote, unfeeling rich. Sanji Lorimahal, Rupal's maternal grandfather, had amassed a tremendous fortune while dealing with the British during two wars, and he saw no reason to give India over to the loinclothed likes of Mahatma Gandhi. The man did not understand money; he was a dreamer and a fool. He loved his fellowman. Such men are dangerous.

Lorimahal money was found in the pockets of the young man who shot the sainted Mahatma on the tear-riven day in 1948. Lorimahal guile and planning was discerned within the plot. His British friends deserted him; they would have to do business with the government of free India. And the government of free India sent him to the gallows, and took from the Lorimahal family every last rupee, every piece of silver in the big white house, and the house as well.

Rupal's mother, unfamiliar with anything but the genteel life, drifted toward Bombay with her brothers, sisters, aunts, and uncles, trudging on foot over dusty roads they'd once traveled in the finest European motorcars. It was hot. The crowds were maddening, human swarms of flesh and stink. It had been their plan to go to a distant uncle who dwelt in the city. Some of the family may actually have reached the uncle's home, but not beautiful Vashali.

She became separated from the others somewhere among the dark, narrow streets that led to the marketplace, and while wandering about, trying to find her way, she drew much attention due to her grooming and a last fine sari she'd been allowed to retain. She caught the eye of a man known as Haru, sometimes called "The Tartar," a thief, thug, and killer-for-hire, in whose veins beat the blood of Britons, Saxons, Russians, Mongols, and Chinese, and who lived a violent existence between rich and poor in the great cities of India. Haru abducted the helpless Vashali, took her to a waterfront hovel, held her there for many months, and raped her whenever he felt like it. During the course of one such attack, the child who would become Karyn Bari was conceived.

Haru was killed by the Bombay police while attempting to flee a food shop he'd just robbed, and when he did not return to the hovel, the pregnant Vashali worked desperately for two days, finally succeeding in undoing the knots by which he held her during his absences. Disoriented and half mad, not even quite sure what was happening to her body—she was scarcely more than a child and had led the stringently protected life of a Brahman princess—Vashali roamed and begged for several months, sleeping at night, like a million others, in the streets. On one such street, two-thirds of a mile from the British hospital, she gave birth to her child. The chance passing of a Red Cross ambulance was all that prevented an increase of two in the death statistics for that night.

Many years may go by and for no apparent reason luck is very bad. Then, for no apparent reason, the sun breaks through and all is green and golden. At the hospital, Vashali and her child were tended by a shy British doctor, who fell in love with them both, eventually marrying the mother and adopting little Rupal, and thus Rupal acquired one of the two discrete entities that would direct her fate: a British passport. She had been born with the second: a cold indomitability that would have gladdened the soul of Haru, the Tartar.

Rupal was educated at an English school in the "foreign" sector of Bombay, and as her beauty bloomed, so did her talent. Not only did she have a voice rare in range and power, she seemed instinctively to grasp and retain lyrics and melodies. From the most ancient of Bengalese poems to the most jarring and blatant of the British popular tunes that came over the radio, once Rupal heard them, they were hers forever. Music became her passion. Music became her life. And music, too, would become her pathway out of India. There was no place in her homeland for what she wanted to do, and over the radio she heard Cliff Richard and Tommy Steele and Shirley Bassey, and all the American rockers. She was not an American, however, so one day, with her British passport and the supply of money she'd stolen over a period of years from her mother's handbag and her father's wallet, the beauty who was Rupal Lorimahal bought a ticket and boarded a BOAC jet for London. During the long flight, she saw an interesting name on a button pinned to a flight attendant's blouse, and when the plane stopped to refuel at Istanbul, she heard a woman address her husband with a name she had never heard before. And so it was that Karyn Bari stepped off the plane at Heathrow airport, England.

Her beauty got her inside the offices of agents. None of the talent managers who interviewed her had ever seen a young woman as frighteningly beautiful as Karyn Bari. Nor had they heard a voice like hers. Unfortunately, for all her apparent maturity, Rupal had led a sheltered life in the house of the British doctor. She was signed on immediately by an agent she correctly judged to be honest, but one whose connections in the entertainment business were less than the best. Mainly, he booked talent for clubs on the Continent that wanted English acts. So Karyn Bari appeared at the *Prinz Hohenzollern* in Cologne, the Florida Club in Frankfurt-am-Main, the *Mausloch* in Nuremberg, and finally at The Four Seasons in Munich, where she met Jack Kenton. By the time she appeared there, she realized that she ought to have started at the top in London, and that she wouldn't make the same mistake in America.

She complained, via trans-Channel phone, to her British agent. "This is nothing, give me more," she told him.

"What do you want?" he pleaded. "You're just starting out. What on earth do you want?"

Karyn Bari considered the question. "I don't know," she told him, in the mysterious, compelling voice that made men and women shiver. "I don't know. I just know that I want."

"I want to go to America," she told Jack, the first time she was in bed with him, in his little Schwabing flat. "Why don't you marry me?"

"What?" he asked. He had found her to be an incredibly skilled lover; now he was learning that she was simply incredible.

"Yes," she said. "It doesn't have to be anything personal. Just marry me. As the wife of an American, I'll automatically be a citizen. There won't be trouble with passports, visas, and work permits."

"What do you want to do in the States?"

"I want to be a Broadway star. Just marry me and take me to the United States. You can divorce me as soon as the boat docks."

"Karyn," he said, studying the beautiful face behind which lay something he did not understand, "you're a darling, but I'm not sure if—"

"If you love me?" She laughed. "I don't ask that you love me."

"But what if I did?"

"Then you would."

"Wouldn't that be important to you? In some way?"

"Not really. Should it be?"

"You fascinate me."

"Do you enjoy that?"

"I think so. Yes."

She shrugged, lifting slightly and dropping her lovely naked shoulders that were the color of ripened wheat under sun. "If it makes you happy to be fascinated, that is very nice."

"And you don't appreciate it that I spend time wondering about you?"

"Should I?"

"You're a Jesuit. A question to answer a question. What made you the way you are?"

Karyn didn't hesitate. "I was born with a desire to get what I want. Any way I can."

"And how's your luck been?"

"Not bad," she said, running her hand down his belly. "I have you, don't I?"

Much later, she suggested he find an army chaplain to marry

them before he was due to transfer back to the States.

"Karyn, no," he said, serious now, "I just can't marry you. Not now. Not yet, anyway. After Pauline, I feel sort of strange even to be with you here in this apartment."

"Oh, well," she said, "I guess I'll have to settle for one of those ninety-day tourist visas then. You will show me New York, though, won't you?"

After they arrived in the United States and got settled into the East Side apartment, Jack prepared a job-hunting campaign, and Karyn pored over issues of *Backstage* and *Variety*.

"I thought you said you were going to be a Broadway star," he kidded her, while drafting his résumé.

"Give me a few days, will you? And what are your plans?"

"When I was in Europe, I had an idea to set up my own company. Financial advisement. I've done very well with my own money. But New York looks bigger than I remember it. So I guess I'll start with a banking job."

Karyn looked up from *Backstage*, disapproval in her eyes.

"Why waste your time?" she asked. "Do what you want to do. Right now."

"Sure," he said. "And you be a star."

Karyn just smiled. "I start tomorrow," she said, mysteriously, tearing a page from the trade paper.

Jack interviewed for a position as portfolio manager with Brown Brothers, Harriman, a commercial investment bank on Wall Street.

"Familiarization lasts for six months," he was told, by the personnel vice-president, "after that your duties gradually increase."

Jack considered this, from his chair in the Partners' Room, with its antique rolltop desks. He felt dispirited. Having been a military intelligence officer, risking virtually everything during the Twister trial, and having parlayed the original Lipschitz one hundred thousand dollars into a cache that, today, stood close to four hundred thousand, he had been totally and successfully in control of his own life. Did he *want* to put in six months looking forward to duties that would "gradually increase"?

Karyn was right. Do what you want to do now.

There were a lot of things to do in life. Pay your money and take your choice.

"Sorry to put you to the trouble," he told the bewildered VP. "But I just don't think it's for me."

He returned to the apartment, his mind roiling with plans for his own business, to find Karyn lying on the white shag rug, listening to Barbra Streisand records.

"Going out today?"

"I've been out," she said, smiling.

"For records. I see."

"I also got a job." She got up, turned down the volume, and came over to him with that animallike stalk of hers. She put her arms around his neck. Her eyes were dark and dusky. "Sort of a job," she said, nonchalantly.

"Go ahead."

"On Broadway. Rehearsals start in two days. It's a musical called *Guinevere*."

"Terrific!" Jack was very enthusiastic. He was happy for her. The role might not be much, but at least it would be a start. She certainly had the talent.

"I'll be Guinevere," she said casually.

"I don't believe it."

"You don't have to. It's true."

"But how . . .?"

"I just sang a few songs for a nice man, and he liked me."

Jack read her face. It *was* true. She had the lead. Never had he seen anything as powerful in her expression as the pride and delight he perceived now, like just the right amount of champagne, a perfect cocaine high, the precise millisecond that orgasm struck.

"I got the son of a bitch," she said, grabbing him furiously, ecstatically. "I got everything I ever wanted. Until I find something else to want!"

Jack held her tightly, saying nothing. Wordlessly, he was aware of the fact that he held in his arms an anomaly, something unique and wild. He wondered what she would want in the future.

Karyn had prepared shrewdly, too, for her assault on stardom. In the trade papers, she read the chaotic story of producer Hoyt Merritt and singer Deanna Rubicon. Merritt had the rights to *Guinevere*, which everyone knew would be a smash, but only if the lead role was played by a woman who not only was a fabulous performer but also projected what Merritt termed "angelic, tormented wantonness, great purity mingled with overwhelming sensuality." Deanna Rubicon was actress enough to project those qualities, but she hated Merritt, and he hated her. Negotiations were undertaken, only to collapse and be undertaken again. Karyn Bari arrived in New York just at the moment Rubicon walked out on what Merritt had considered a final deal. He was—*Variety* reported—"fuming." But what could he do? Who else but Rubicon could portray Guinevere?

"*Angelic, tormented wantonness,*" Karyn read aloud, sable coat inside out upon her naked skin. "*Great purity mingled with overwhelming sensuality.* Well, all I have to do is fake the purity part."

Then she took the longest bath of her life, soaking in hot water, fragrant bubbles, and a special oil she'd once found in a Bombay shop, which contained obscure herbs to pleasure and tingle not only skin but nerve endings too. After dressing in one of her simple glistening-white saris, she placed on her forehead the Brahman caste mark, which was part of her heritage in spite of the intrusion of Haru the Tartar. Studying herself in the mirror, Karyn wondered how Queen Guinevere would have worn her hair. She had never been an especially devoted student at Bombay's English school, but she remembered fragments of boring class discussion regarding *Morte d'Arthur* and "Lady of the Lake." So: her lush black hair must fall about her shoulders, and that meant the white turban she sometimes affected would simply not do. Karyn had little jewelry— some necklaces, a few inexpensive rings, and the fake ruby she used in her act. She wanted jewelry, just as she wanted wealth, but not with a crucially urgent wanting. They would come in time. She was sure of it. But she did need something for her hair . . .

Taking an elevator down to the street, and leaving the building, Karyn almost inspired a traffic accident on Third Avenue, and four taxis pulled to the curb. She gave Merritt's office address, which she'd looked up in the directory, and the cab pulled away, with the driver turning around every three seconds to stare at her.

"From India, huh, miss?"

"*Verstehen sie nicht*," Karyn said. It had been her way of discouraging conversation in Europe. "I do not understand you."

"Oh, yeah," said the cabby, nodding sagely, "French, huh?"

Merritt's office proved to be in a tacky, dirty building, midtown on Broadway. Karyn did not mind. Two doors down was a junk and trinket storefront shop. She went inside, to the astonishment of the stubble-cheeked, potbellied proprietor, one marginally sane shopping-bag lady, and a wino who had wandered in for reasons known only to God. "I need a headpiece," Karyn told the owner, who chewed that request awhile until he realized the apparition before him was real and a paying customer as well.

Karyn found a headband of fake silver, demanded that it be polished, and put it on. Then she marched back to Merritt's building, walked through the outer room, in which nineteen aspirant stars were cooling their heels, strode into the office of Martha "Mad-dog" Shipley, who protected the sacred portals to the producer's inner office. Martha, startled and openmouthed, as if an Archangel had suddenly materialized, did not have time even to take a breath. Karyn threw open the producer's door. He was behind his desk. She recognized him right away, from pictures in *Variety*. He was talking to three men in business suits, going over scripts or contracts and numerous long forms. They all looked up, shocked as Mrs. Shipley had been.

"I am Guinevere," Karyn proclaimed.

And, beholding the bold, exotic, quintessentially feline animal who stood before them in sari and silver, who were they to deny her declaration?

Karyn auditioned. She sang, danced, read lines. *Enchanted* would have been far too mild a word to describe the reaction of Hoyt Merritt and his talent coordinators.

"Cable that Rubicon bitch," Merritt ordered Mad-dog Shipley, "and tell her I don't need her to *play* Guinevere. I've found the *real* Guinevere." He laughed maliciously, then added: "You can also mention that rehearsals start in a couple of days, if she wants to try for a part in the chorus. Young lady," he said, turning back to Karyn, "1968 is going to be your year. You can write your ticket. You can have anything you want."

"I know." Karyn smiled.

"I want to celebrate," she informed Jack, after telling him of her coup. "Go into the bedroom and get undressed."

On the night table beside the bed, Karyn had placed a small candle-powered warmer, and heating on it was an antique copper-colored decanter. "Hurry and get naked," she ordered, doing so herself. "I have a surprise for you."

Her body aroused him as it always did: exquisite skin; firm, uptilted breasts, not too large; powerful yet perfectly shaped behind; long, smooth legs, sleek thighs, and a triangle of hair glistening like the pelt of a wild animal. But no mere animal, however wild, knew the things that Karyn knew. After kissing, touching, fondling him to readiness, she took from the copper receptacle a swallow of warm, delicately scented oil of Bombay, went down upon him, and carefully worked him between her lips, deeply into her mouth. The mysterious properties of the oil were as maddening as her gentle, sliding kiss, and against his will, before he knew it, Jack was shuddering and shuddering with ultimate pleasure.

"I didn't know I'd be that fast," he said, sated for the moment, but disappointed that it was over so soon.

"You didn't have any choice," she replied, with a sly smile of pleasure at her skill. "Now, it's your turn."

"We could have done it together." They had before.

"That's too distracting," said Karyn, handing him the vial. "You're working so hard on the other one, you miss half your own pleasure. Good lovers know to take turns."

Slowly, Jack oiled her body with the tingling liquid, caressed her until she moaned for it to end. But he was just beginning. The oil was warm, faintly stinging his tongue, and he traced with his kiss the delicate lips which had so often given him ecstasy, until finally he bestowed the gift of ecstasy in his turn.

"Tell me something," Jack said, when they lay afterward in each other's arms. "On the night we met, why did you think you'd seen me in Budapest?"

"Budapest?" Karyn asked, her cat's eyes glittering in the darkness.

"You came to our table at *Die Vier Jahreszeiten*, remember, and said you thought we'd met in Budapest?"

Her soft laugh was silky and rich. "Darling, you are not an unattractive man, as Americans go. I wanted to meet you, so I asked the manager about you. He told me something of that trial you were involved in, and how you won it by talking of a man from Hungary, or someplace."

"Yes, Igor Kujnisch. Twister's accomplice. A Czechoslovakian, though."

"What does it matter? Budapest was good for a conversation. I assumed you'd been there."

"No, I never was. Were you?"

"No," she answered, laughing again, pleased with her maneuver and the way things had worked out. "By the way, whatever became of the girl? Pauline, wasn't that her name?"

"I don't know. She took a plane from Munich to New York, and that's about all I know. I tried calling her once."

"You did? Naughty darling. I'm jealous."

This time it was Jack's turn to laugh. There was probably no woman in the world beautiful or sexy enough to make Karyn Bari insecure. "I tried calling, though," he explained. "I wanted to make sure she was all right. I remembered she'd come from the Bronx, up along Pelham Parkway. There was a listing in the directory for a Yates family up around that neighborhood."

He remembered the conversation with distaste.

"Yeah?" a young voice had answered, dumb and mean.

"This is Jack Kenton. Is Pauline Yates in? I'm a friend of hers, from Europe."

"Huh?"

"Miss Pauline Yates. Is this her residence?"

Then a woman's voice in the background, demanding to know what in hell was going on and who in hell was on the fucking phone.

"Some dude callin' for Ina," the kid told her.

Another moment, and a coarse female voice, dripping suspicion, asked Jack: "What you want Pauline for?"

"I'm a friend of hers. Jack Kenton. I knew her from the Red Cross, in Europe."

"Well, she ain't *in* the Red Cross no more, and Europe neither."

"Then where is she?"

"You married?"

"Why, no," Jack said. "What does that . . .?"

"Well, Pauline is, so you can drop dead." And, with that, Mrs. Felix J. Yates had slammed down the phone.

"She wasn't right for you anyway," Karyn told him now, in bed, deftly running warm, oil-slick fingers over and over and over the tip of him.

"And you are?"

"For the time being," she cooed. "For the time being. Now, come in me. I want to make an aura."

"An aura?"

"Yes, so we will always be one, in a special way, no matter what happens. You must be in me all the way, but you mustn't move. You must be absolutely still."

"What?" It sounded impossible to Jack, just then.

"Yes, for twenty-four minutes exactly. You cannot move in me and you cannot come in me. It takes that long for an aura to arise from us. After twenty-four minutes, you may have your delight, and any other delight you care to dream or name."

Strange and wild she was, but Jack was intrigued. She opened to him, and he felt her all around, felt her cunning sex and mystery more fully than he ever had. She did not move for him, nor did he move, in spite of a need that built and built and built to piercing want. Yes, that was the essence of it: to have and not to have, at the same exact moment. She did not speak, nor did Jack. Time itself rose up, glowed, and spread out upon the earth. Light danced in the room, burned within their bodies, iridescent sheets of red and gold and amber, a rainbow of heaven born in tender flesh.

"Now," she cried, lost with him there at the end of forever, "*now.*"

And all that he had been, was, would ever be leaped from him to her, dazzling electric current of ultimate pleasure. It was true. With eyes closed tight, and body burning, Jack sensed and felt and even saw the ghostly aura rise from their mingled bodies, brilliant and fantastic and sublime.

"Yes," she whispered to him, as he lay gasping beside her, "now even when I leave you, I shall not have left."

He wasn't certain he'd heard correctly. "Leave?"

"Oh, hush, and don't be silly. Nothing is forever, and one should not worry about it."

7

Broadway producer Hoyt Merritt might well have been a prophet. 1968 became the year of Karyn Bari. While Jack set about establishing Kenton Diversified, a high-risk, high-profit venture that applied his military intelligence background to the investigation of corporate skullduggery, the girl who had been born Rupal Lorimahal in a Bombay gutter took the entertainment industry by storm.

NEVER IN THE HISTORY OF BROADWAY MUSICALS . . .
New York Daily News

BARI IS MAGNIFICENT . . .

NBC

Those who have suggested, perhaps even believed, that tremendous new talent can no longer be found, or, if found, cannot find its way to the public, ought immediately to see *Guinevere* . . .
The New Yorker

KARYN BARI: ENIGMATIC SENSATION
New York Post

Whatever you plan to do or not to do this year, do see Karyn Bari in *Guinevere*, and do not miss Karyn Bari in *Guinevere* . . .
Village Voice

GANDHI NIECE CONQUERS BROADWAY

New York (UPI) Miss Karyn Bari, niece of the legendary Indian leader Mohandas K. Gandhi, and currently star of *Guinevere*, Broadway's most successful musical in four decades, said yesterday that she owes her determination to succeed primarily to her sainted uncle, the Mahatma, or "great soul," who was assassinated in 1948. Miss Bari's family once lived in splendor, she said during an interview at Hoyt Merritt's publicity suite in the Plaza, but eventually gave all worldly goods to Gandhi's cause. "My mother, whose name was Vashali, left my ancestral home barefooted," Bari told a visitor, "and humbly served the riffraff who swarmed in the streets . . ."

"Karyn, what the hell *is* this stuff?" asked Jack, in some confusion, as he laid aside the *Enquirer* he'd picked up at the market.

Karyn's picture was on it, but the information given in the story about her matched nothing he knew. "Did they quote you right?"

"To the comma, darling. Would you like a drink?"

It was a little after six in the evening. Jack had just returned from his Wall Street office, and Karyn would soon leave for the theater to effect her nightly incarnation, becoming once again King Arthur's faithless, loving, passion-driven queen. Now she came in from the kitchen, where curried shrimp simmered, and glanced at Jack's *Enquirer*.

"I don't understand why people are so critical of this poor little newspaper," she said innocently. "They reported every word I said."

"But Mahatma Gandhi wasn't your *uncle*, for Christ sake."

"Oh, darling, you know I must have meant it in an affectionate sense, that nice old man in his *dhoti*, and the spinning wheel. He is good copy in America. Can I help it what American journalists will believe?"

"And I see here that your family *gave* its worldly goods away. I thought they were expropriated?"

"*Somebody* got them. That's for sure. My mother had nothing left when she was kicked out of the big house. I told you. This is a good interview. This is *publicity*, darling. Look, my mother even served the riffraff, or *serviced* would perhaps be more accurate."

She leaned over his shoulder, skimming the article, and Jack saw her eyes go dusky and far away, as if she were lost in sex or daydream. Her usual demeanor was one of self-possession and occasional wry amusement.

"What are you thinking?" he asked suddenly, taking an impulsive stab at finding a secret, unguarded side to her.

He found it, as surely as if an iron door had unexpectedly sprung open.

"Those filthy rich bahstuds," she swore, in her British-Indian accent, "those rich bloody muckety-muck bahstuds who run every-thing and make all the rules! They took away my family's home and took away the big white walls that kept us safe. They took everything away, and if there is one thing I want more than any other in my life, it is to be behind big walls like that, to be an enemy of the bloody fuckers *behind their very own walls*. Oh, wouldn't that be sweet though, to get even for what's been done . . ."

She caught herself, saw Jack studying her, his head tilted slightly sideways, which he did when something surprised him. But Karyn was not embarrassed by her sudden, uncharacteristic excess. She simply closed the iron door again, upon the plunder of passions there, and touched his face gently.

"But you don't have to care about that, darling," she said, Bari the Star now, not little Rupal Lorimahal, who had come across three continents to fame. "My father was a thug and a rapist and a thief." She tapped the *Enquirer* with a lacquered nail. "And I am grateful for it. Such blood makes me a success in New York, don't you think? Now, do you want that drink?"

"Yes. Jack Daniel's and ice. I'll get it."

"No. You sit down. Any news on that Connecticut contract you were working on? Did anything dangerous happen?"

Karyn always asked about danger, as if fascinated by it or by Jack's proximity to it. She fully approved of his business when he explained to her the object of Kenton Diversified: to investigate criminal activities within businesses that contracted him to do so. Fiscal manipulation, embezzlement, white-collar crime, union strong-arming: whatever hindered the smooth functioning of a corporation.

Now he answered her question with pleasure.

"Yes, we cracked that Connecticut case today."

She brought him a Jack Daniel's on ice and sat down beside him.

"I came up with five possible models to explain what I thought was happening," he told her. "Number four was the most far-fetched, but it turned out to be right on the money. It goes to show you. Crack criminals can be as creative as anybody."

"Except you," she said, putting her cheek against his, "now wasn't I right?"

Indeed, Karyn had been right. Jack was cut out for bigger things than working for a bank. His reputation was spreading, and he had not been reluctant to publicize his most singular success.

This Kenton is the guy who brought down General Twister? And that

PX Plot was an international scam, wasn't it? Let's invite him in to the next board meeting, and see if he can give us some ideas why our import operation is going to hell in a handcart."

Such a comment was made by John Delano Atwood, of Darien and Wescott Cove, Connecticut, owner and operator of Atwood Industries, with offices in Hartford, New York, and Boston. Atwood had, two years earlier, signed what promised to be a lucrative trade agreement with a Hong Kong–based cartel, to bring high quality but relatively inexpensive fabric into the United States through the port at Boston. The whole deal promised to be a substantial money-maker for Atwood. But it didn't turn out that way. Alarming printouts showing lack of any profit at all led to an internal investigation. Half the shipments of fabric seemed never to have arrived, though the shipments were registered as having been off-loaded and shipped by rail from the warehouses. A phantom cargo is more than just a mystery when it costs 14.5 million dollars.

"Twenty-five percent," Jack told Mr. Atwood and his board of directors. "That's my fee for a solution to your problem."

John Delano Atwood, patrician in background and bearing, found it impossible to contain his astonishment. "Mr. Kenton," he pointed out, "one-fourth of our loss is over three-and-a-half-million dollars. Perhaps, for a fee, ten percent would be more . . ."

"Twenty-five percent," Jack said again. "If you had any idea where your fabric was going, you wouldn't be almost fifteen million in the hole now. And here is my statement of services. If I don't bring you a solution within two months, there'll be no fee at all, not even expenses."

Two months. A guarantee. No fee, no expenses. Or, in the event of success, Jack received one-quarter or the amount of the original loss. That became the Kenton formula, and Kenton Diversified was a name spreading fast in the corporate community.

It had taken him six weeks to crack the Atwood problem. Operating from Boston, using computers and sophisticated patterns of statistical probability, he had formulated five models to explain who was hijacking the fabric and how it was being done. Once a model was complete, he would assign field agents to confirm the method already postulated in the theoretical model. It was the same strategy that had led from Sergeant Potts to Major Olk to Igor Kujnisch and General Twister.

Mr. Atwood himself had come to Boston, early in June, while Jack was at work on Model Four, which eventually cracked the case. The main feature of Model Four posited an offshore rendezvous point, at which the cargo of fabric was transferred from one ship to another, diverted to an alternate port, leaving certain unknown Atwood employees to doctor invoices and bills of lading in Boston. Thus, by the time losses showed up on Atwood ledgers, the money itself—and many of the employees too—were long gone.

"But how can that be?" Mr. Atwood wanted to know, over crabmeat salad at the Back Bay Brasserie. "Offshore waters are heavily patrolled by the Coast Guard. We're not talking about smuggling a little shipment of marijuana. We're talking bolts and bales, *tons* of material. Why, ship cranes would be necessary to transfer the stuff. No, I don't see how we could be losing the fabric at sea."

Jack took a moment to formulate a response. He was somewhat distracted by Mr. Atwood's daughter, Carol Jean, a recent Bryn Mawr graduate who had accompanied her father to Boston. She was very lovely, but a little quiet, and she seemed sad. Why such a beautiful girl should be sad intrigued him more than who was sidetracking her father's cargo.

"I feel it's got to be happening offshore," he said, after a long sip of Moselle. "We've already eliminated the Hong Kong model, the Boston Harbor model, and the warehouse–rail yard model—"

"You said you had a fifth model, Mr. Kenton," Carol Jean spoke up, looking at him. Her eyes were a deep, striking blue; he met her glance and held it. A long moment passed.

"A fifth model," he said.

"Yes."

"Oh," he replied, breaking the moment, and they both smiled. "Yes, a fifth model. I call it the Gallimaufry Special. I throw all the available data into a computer and hope for the best."

She laughed. The trace of sadness disappeared for a little while. Mr. Atwood, who had been watching his daughter and this bright young man, turned the conversation back to business.

It turned out that supply ships bringing food and equipment to offshore oil-exploration stations met the Boston-bound Hong Kong ships on the high seas, took on the shipments of fabric, and shuttled them back to New York, where they disappeared into the maws of the Garment District. The scam was larger and more complicated than anyone had anticipated, but Jack had solved it, and his reputation was rising as fast as his bank account.

"And tomorrow," Jack told Karyn, as she served spicy curry over fluffy white rice, "I'm meeting my most important potential client yet."

Karyn glanced at her watch. It was almost time to leave for *Guinevere*. "Oh? Who's that?"

"Rudolf Bennington. He's the ranking son of a bitch in the Western World. And there are a lot of people who wouldn't limit him to just one hemisphere."

"Oh, darling, be careful," Karyn said.

The Bennington Building, located on East Fifty-third Street in New York, was flying its royal standard when Jack's driver pulled to the curb. Rudolf Bennington, less monarch than dictator of his empire, had a personal flag that he ordered raised on every house, building, skyscraper, mansion, yacht, or ship on or in which he happened to be present. The flag, funereal black with silver border and a huge, Gothic, silver *B* in the center, hung limply today in the humid June air. Rudolf Bennington had not had much fun in life.

Except for revenge. Were he to have added a cherished belief or motto to his flag, it would have been:

"Shaft me once, and you're never safe again."

"Sit down, Kenton," he ordered, as Jack was ushered into a sprawling office, decorated grotesquely in red and black. The room was crowded with bodyguards, secretaries, clerks, flunkies, and several beautiful young women, but Bennington waved his hand, and in a moment Jack was alone with Bennington and an old man in a wheelchair. Bennington was burly, hawk-nosed, silver-haired. He looked like an American Indian in a Savile Row suit. Indeed, he had been born on an Oklahoma reservation, and was half Osage. The man in the wheelchair was thin and wobbly, with little hair left, and less vigor.

"This here's Jim Taggart," Bennington pronounced. "He was my first and only partner. That's why you're here, Kenton."

Taggart forced a feeble nod.

"Sit down, goddammit, Kenton," said Bennington to Jack, who had not yet absorbed the bizarre setting, or Bennington either. "Sit down. You the kind of asshole who likes a drink in the morning?"

"No, not actually, I—"

"Well, I am. Jim? You?"

Old Taggart shook his head.

"That poor fucker," Bennington said to Jack, jerking his thumb toward Taggart as he poured himself five fingers worth of scotch, "all he can drink is water, and all he can eat is mush. Ain't that right, Jim?"

Taggart only nodded.

"The poor old son of a bitch," Bennington said, taking a long gulp of the whiskey. "But he's why you're here, Kenton. And also I read about you in the papers."

Jack expected to hear something about the Atwood case he had solved, but Bennington surprised him.

"I see you're hanging around with that new singer in *Guinevere*. I never go to any of the shows; they're all phony and bore me to death, but I saw that picture of the two of you, and it caught my attention . . ."

Now Jack remembered. Two weeks ago, there had been a fundraiser for out-of-work actors, and he had accompanied Karyn. Photographers were everywhere, and photos of the two of them had made all the dailies and trades.

". . . so then I learned what line of work you're in, and I think I have a job for you."

"I'd be glad to hear about it," Jack said, wondering who on earth would be reckless enough to put his fingers in Rudolf Bennington's till.

"Jim here," said Bennington, jerking his thumb at Taggart again, "ain't got long for this world. Rheumatoid arthritis, and now a stroke too. I want to make him happy before he shuffles off to the great treasury in the sky. He was my first and only partner, and the only man in the whole world who ever got the best of me in a trade."

"Now, Rudy, that ain't true, and you know it," Taggart protested, in a voice that sounded like air gasping through a loose valve.

"The hell it isn't," Bennington told him, with what might have been interpreted as rough affection. He turned to Jack. "See, Kenton, the two of us started out as wildcatters, you know, oil hunters, down in Oklahoma in the early days. Well, we found us some likely acreage—I was sure there was oil under it, and so was he—and we commenced to try and come up with financial backing. Neither of us had shit or shinola for security, unless you counted our mules, wagons, and a couple of those early-model drills held together with baling wire. But there was this one bank in the little town of . . . what the hell was it, Jim?"

Jack had the feeling that Bennington remembered the name of the town all too well.

"Pawnee," Taggart gasped.

"Pawnee. That was it. Anyway, there was this one bank, and the banker said he was willing to gamble on one of us, but not two. So I went in to talk to him, and Jim went in to talk to him, and he looked at me and saw my Indian blood, and Jim got the money. I never have been so pissed again in my entire life."

Bennington was laughing, or making a sound something like the sound of human laughter, and Taggart was wheezing away, but Jack received the keen impression that Bennington was *still* outraged over the ancient slight.

"But as luck would have it," Bennington continued, "Jim hit oil right away, and I had to struggle on for another year. Never forget it, I had it tough. And him living it up in Tulsa, with the girls. Tell me something, Kenton," he asked suddenly. "What's it like? With that singer?"

Jack looked into cold, black, implacable eyes. He was torn

between the desire to tell Bennington it was none of his goddam business and the impulse to make a deflecting remark, when the tyrant dropped the matter.

"As I was saying," he said, "Jim got the money and the well, all because I was Indian. Part Indian. And I had to move on down the road and sweat some more."

There it was again. That raw current of ineradicable anger. Jack recognized it very well, having heard the same vein of rage in Karyn's voice when she'd talked about her family's dispossession.

Then Bennington snickered. "But Jim's well gave out and ran dry in a couple of months, and when I hit, I hit not one but twenty-two wells. And he's sitting here in that contraption like a sack of shit, while I'm one of the richest, meanest sons of bitches on the face of the earth. You believe that, do you, Kenton?"

"I certainly do," said Jack, who did.

"Smart boy. Let's see if we can put you in the way of making a little serious money. Like I said, I want to make my old partner happy before he croaks. He has had him some fair luck, got a little string of businesses with what he tells me is a net worth of about a hundred million, but he is not international in scope, and that's what he's always wanted to be. Right, Jim?"

Taggart nodded. "I want Taggart, Incorporated, to have a foreign operation."

"And," said Bennington, turning to Jack again, "I've got just the thing to sell him."

Bennington stopped rambling then, and explained the matter coldly. Taggart had a modest net worth, but he was in potential trouble. Having divested himself of several operations in the early sixties, he bought stocks. Then they started to drop and showed every prospect of dropping further. "He wants to haul ass out of the market now," Bennington said, "and buy a likely money-maker . . . a business. And I believe I have just the thing for him."

"So where do I fit in?" asked Jack, who had been wondering what use Kenton Diversified might be to these two men who'd known each other so long.

"I want Jim checked over with a fine-tooth comb," Bennington said. "He knows that's the way I operate, and he knows I'm not selling him a business out of charity. I want to see that he's good to pay me the thirty million I'm asking, and an outsider has to do it, because nobody in his right mind would let himself be scrutinized by my own men."

"Why me?" Jack asked.

"I like your taste in women," Bennington said, his cold eyes glinting. "And you're not exactly unknown after that Atwood business."

"My fee is—"

"Twenty-five percent of nothing is nothing. You want the job, you better get cracking."

"It's too simple," Jack told Karyn that evening. "There has to be a catch to it."

"Then find the catch," she said. "That's what Bennington's paying you for."

"That's what it *seems* like."

"Well, build one of those fancy models of yours."

"I would. But there's a problem. A reliable model replicates reality. Not even a mirror reflects illusion. And I have the feeling that Rudolf Bennington is a purveyor of illusion."

"But so am I, darling," Karyn said.

Jack began work on the Bennington-Taggart contract in early July of 1968, an extremely hectic and busy time for him. Requests for information about Kenton Diversified flooded the mail each day, in the wake of the successfully concluded and now well-known Atwood case. Jack had to interview and hire several associates and spend time choosing a legal firm to handle his business. In the end, he reached back into his past and retained Frank Brewster, who had defended General Twister at the PX Plot trial. "You've made a wise decision and a fair one," said Brewster, accepting the retainer. "Especially fair. You beat me in Munich, but wait until you see my fees. All things come out even in the end."

"Just get to work," Jack replied. "I'm swamped. Bennington insisted that I, personally, audit Jim Taggart's operation."

It was mid-August, with two weeks to go on his guarantee, when Jack sat down and began to examine the Taggart stock portfolio. Jim Taggart had been hospitalized with another slight stroke, which delayed Jack further, and Bennington was always yelling on the phone.

"Goddammit, Kenton," he complained, "I thought you were supposed to be some kind of whiz kid. If you are *one day late* presenting that shit to me, you are out of a fee, you got that?"

"Got it," Jack said. He would have been tempted to drop the whole matter, fee or no fee, but the situation was intriguing, and he was unable to resist challenge or mystery. And the prospective Taggart-Bennington deal began to appear puzzling.

In the first place, except for a meat-processing operation in Chicago, Taggart, Incorporated, was in poor shape, managerially and financially. Roughly thirty million that Taggart planned to yank out of the stock market, if lost in a business venture, would utterly swamp the company.

In the second place, was it not excessively convenient that Bennington should own a newly built meat-packing operation, in Venezuela, that he was willing to sell Taggart? For, again, most conveniently, thirty million dollars?

In the third place, sentiment was not a characteristic associated with Rudolf Bennington. When Jack analyzed it on a personal level, it seemed extremely atypical that Bennington would break the misanthropy of a lifetime to make Taggart's dream of owning a foreign operation come true. If anything, would he not try to get revenge on old Jim for having gotten that Pawnee bank loan fifty years earlier?

Late in August, with only days to go on the contract, Jack was lounging on the couch in the apartment, looking over data on the Venezuelan meat-packing plant. New York was sweltering through another August of violence, smog, and jungle heat, and the air conditioner whirred and droned in irritating constancy. Karyn was late in returning from her evening performance, and although her tardiness did not trouble Jack—she often attended small parties after the show—it was on his mind.

Once again, he studied the meat-packing prospectus. Located in the cattle-raising state of Apure, the blueprints were extensive, the photos professional, the data voluminous. Records were so detailed they showed the precise quantities of lumber used in the construction of each cattle-holding pen. Every meathook, knife, power saw, and lard-rendering vat were accounted for. Jack rechecked prices, made calculations, allowed for inflation and depreciation, extrapolated on the bases of market, demand, potential and actual competitors. Everything fit. It would be a sweet deal for Taggart. By exporting meat and meat products, he could quite conceivably—in unison with his Chicago plant—recoup his floundering fortunes. Yet one part of the "Specifications of Transaction" paragraph gnawed and niggled:

> In the event of purchase, Taggart, Inc., accepts responsibility for transferring thirty (30) million dollars, American, to Venezuela, via John Tyler Kenton, authorized agent of Taggart, Inc., converting currency to Venezuelan bolivars, and making payment in person to Rudolf Bennington, at Bennington International Headquarters in Caracas. Completion of the payment, and acceptance of the cash by Mr. Bennington shall render the transaction final and irrevocable.

Well, naturally it would be final and irrevocable, Jack reflected.
Why wouldn't it be?
Why use the words?
Unless they were nails, final nails to be driven into a coffin fashioned long ago?
Jim Taggart's coffin.
What the hell, give Bennington a break, Jack told himself then. *Maybe he is doing the one good deed of his life.*

But still the matter of Bennington's vicious and vindictive persona could not be dismissed. Yet the deal looked good. More than that, it looked perfect . . .

He picked up the phone, dialed, and made reservations to leave JFK airport for Caracas at ten the next morning. If he moved fast, he would be able to check out the meat-packing plant in person, and return to New York in time to make his report to Bennington. Booking the flight amused Jack in a mild way. He would be flying aboard one of Bennington's planes. The tycoon, who had long owned a vast ranch in Venezuela, also owned sixty-four percent of the national airline.

Then Karyn's key clicked in the lock, and she came in, radiant as always after a performance.

"*What I do for you, I do for loooove,*" she sang, from the lyrics of "Guinevere's Song," "*if love be evil, evil be my naaame . . .*"

She bent down and kissed him, as he lay on the couch.

"You look tired, darling."

"I am. How was the show?"

"Terrific. Raoul Cosannon, of Omega Records, came to my dressing room. He's desperate that I do an album for him."

"Why don't you?"

"In another week, he'll offer more money."

"A girl after the heart of the IRS."

"But that isn't why I'm late. Want to know?"

"Okay."

"I went out for a drink with one of your clients. Rudolf Bennington. Surprised?"

"Slightly. He told me he didn't like shows."

"Well, he's changed his mind. Darling, he looks like I imagine my father, Haru the Tartar, must have looked. But he is a dangerous man. Fascinating, but dangerous."

"So they say."

She knelt down beside the couch, looked at him closely, and said: "He wants to see me again."

Jack went on breathing, his lungs continued to empty and fill, but for a moment it seemed that there was no sustenance in the air. Karyn had said, from the start, that she wanted to be free. No permanent ties. That was how she was, and he had accepted it. But accepting it intellectually was quite different from understanding it in his gut.

"I think he's in a position to cause you a lot of trouble," Karyn said.

"Forget about that. It's no reason to go out with him. I know that you will if you want to, of course."

"Of course." Karyn smiled.

Jack shook his head slightly and kissed her. She was an enigma he would never understand. Far back within those strange dark eyes of hers, he saw so many things he could not name.

"What's there?" he asked, touching her eyelids gently. "What's behind these eyes?"

"All you have to know is that you are. For now. Is that enough?"

"More than enough," Jack said.

Jack was in social studies classroom at Grover Cleveland High School in Ridgewood. Mr. Hartman, the teacher, was droning unintelligibly. There was a picture of Abe Lincoln on the side wall. Buster Pauley, from the football team, was talking to a girl with big breasts. He talked and smirked; she cracked gum and giggled. Then Buster turned to Jack and started to say something. But the bell rang, ending the class, and Jack couldn't hear him. "What?" he asked, but the bell rang again, obscuring Buster's words. "What?" But again the bell rang.

Then Jack was sitting up in bed, groping for the phone. Beside him, Karyn stirred and covered her head with a pillow.

"Hello?"

"Kenton? You can skip that trip to Venezeula."

It was Rudolf Bennington. How did he know? Bennington anticipated the question.

"I own the damn airline, that's how. You got as many enemies as I have, you make it a point to check things out. Anyway, reason I'm calling is that the deal's off. At least for now. That bastard Taggart dropped into a coma. It doesn't look good. So let's just put everything on hold."

Jack was happy to agree. He had other things that needed attention.

"Anyway, you wouldn't like Venezuela this time of year," Bennington said. "It can get unhealthy."

The tycoon's tone, never light at the best of times, was not light now. "By the way," he added, "I met your girl friend last night."

"Yes, she mentioned."

"Fine woman," Bennington said, *"real* fine."

8

After the November chill of New York, the Caracas heat was deadly. Jack left the plane, cleared customs, and headed immediately to book a charter flight inland, to Apure.

Venezuela. The very air smelled strange, funky, half sweet, like funeral flowers of the long-dead.

Dead, like Jim Taggart.

Taggart had succumbed in mid-September. Reading the *New York Times* obit, Jack recalled the old man's dream of owning a foreign operation and felt a little sad. What was it like, dying? Did one have time to mourn dreams unachieved? Or was there a bequest of wise peace, in which the folly of all dreams became known, and dreaming itself renounced? Hadn't mattered for Taggart; he'd never come out of the coma. ". . . preceded in death by his wife, Elvira," Jack had read, "and survived by a daughter, Nancy, of Kalamazoo, Michigan . . ."

A week later, working in his Wall Street office, Jack's intercom buzzed.

"A Miss Nancy Taggart, sir," said his secretary. "She claims it's urgent. Shall I schedule an appointment?"

The whole Bennington-Taggart business was still troubling Jack. "No, send her in right now."

Miss Taggart was fifty, but solid and well kept, the kind of woman who knows her mind.

"I don't want to buy a meat-packing plant in South America," she told him. "I want to sell the one in Chicago that Dad left me and sell everything else, too. And since you're getting that monstrous fee, I just want to tell you in person. If I have to spend every last cent suing you, that's exactly what I'll do . . ."

"Whoa. Hold it. Wait a minute," cried Jack in self-defense.

Miss Taggart gave him a shrewd, calculating look, and apparently decided in his favor. Her story came out in a rush. Rudolf Bennington was claiming that, as sole heir to her father, Nancy must go through with the deal to purchase the Venezuelan plant. Moreover, a large fee owed to Kenton Diversified, of New York, must be paid by Nancy but turned over to Bennington, who would hold it in escrow, pending the outcome of a suit brought by Bennington International against John Tyler Kenton . . .

Jack was amazed. *This* was the Rudolf Bennington he had heard so much about. Compared to Bennington, General Karl Twister had been Peter Pan! Even *after* Taggart's death, the thief was going after everything: Taggart's legacy. Jack's fee. Jack's *girl!*

He calmed Miss Taggart and told her to go back to Kalamazoo. He would straighten things out as best he could, if he could. She did not owe him a cent and wouldn't. It was a matter he wanted to clear up for his own peace of mind.

"Bennington was planning to do all that?" asked Frank Brewster later, when Jack phoned him with the news. "I'll call him right away."

"What'll you say?"

"To get off our backs. We don't scare so easily."

"Neither does he."

Brewster called Jack later to report. "Bennington told me to tell you to forget about it. He was just having a little fun. He never liked Taggart, he said."

"Forget about what?"

"Your fee, for one thing. You missed your two-month guarantee period. Is that right?"

"Yes, but—"

"Want to sue for it?"

"No, forget the damn fee."

"He's taking Nancy to court though," Brewster said. "It's none of your affair. You can't do a thing about the fact that Bennington still hates a dead man."

"But I promised Nancy Taggart I'd look into it."

"Well, you have, haven't you? Forget about it now. You don't want to get your ass in a Bennington sling just when things are starting off so well for you. Everybody hates him, but he's very well connected. He spreads tons of political money around, legal and otherwise."

Brewster had a point, Jack reasoned, and so for a month or so, he merely followed the matter from a distance, reading an occasional *Wall Street Journal* piece about the pending Bennington-Taggart court battle. Accompanying one of the articles was a photograph of the Apure meat-packing plant, which, the reporter asserted, was a "bone of contention" in the suit. Then Nancy Taggart called him from Kalamazoo.

"Mr. Kenton, you lied to me."

"No, I didn't. And I'll tell you what I'm going to do."

"What's that?"

"I'm going to Venezuela to make an on-site inspection."

And so Jack was in South America, approaching a small hangar some distance from the main terminal. Three diminutive planes crouched in the sun, two fairly new Cessnas and a decrepit old Piper Cub. Seeing no one, Jack banged on the metal hangar door a couple of times, and a short, sleepy-looking man ambled out of the hangar's depths. He had a round brown face, with teeth haphazardly missing. He looked like a brown jack-o'-lantern.

"Hi! I'm Ramón. You want a plane? Where do you want to go?"

"Palmarito, in Apure."

Ramón did some calculating. "Yiyiyi," he said, "no, too far, too far." He waved his arms in alarm. "No, never. Cost you five hundred dollars," he added casually.

"Four hundred."

Ramón waved his arms some more, and stamped his booted foot. "Too far. Never," he said again.

"Four-fifty," Jack said.

"Okay, get in the plane." Ramón shrugged.

"You fly this route often?" shouted Jack some minutes later, as the tiny Piper Cub leaped and lurched and dropped in the air currents over Caracas.

Ramón did not reply, his knuckles white. They were flying toward the mountains to the south of the city, and the mountains looked a lot higher every minute. The little plane rose encouragingly, then slammed into a downdraft.

"You can turn around if you want to," said Jack. "I'm sure there's a train."

But the pilot showed his gap-toothed grin. "Chicken, eh?" With one last jerk of the stick and the luck of wind, God, or Devil, the plane rose and sailed over stony peaks.

"We did it!" exulted Ramón.

"Have you done this often?" Jack said, breathing again.

"Not for four-hundred-fifty, *señor*."

Eventually, they left the mountains behind, and the Piper headed out over the vast Portuguesa River Valley, swinging southwest where the Apure met the Portuguesa. Jack, who had known and loved the rugged beauty of the Alps, nonetheless gazed in awe at the trackless miles of wilderness sliding beneath the wings. Then Ramón sailed out over magnificent grasslands, and great ranches came into view. One, in particular, caught Jack's eye. No remote cattle station, even from the air it bore the mark of money, luxury, style, and the main house was surrounded by an immaculately whitewashed wall or fence.

"What's that?"

"That big ranch? It belongs to a *norteamericano*, like you. *Mucho dinero*. Calls himself Bennington. You know him?"

Bennington. And the meat-packing plant was located just a little farther on, in the village of Palmarito. Well, that made sense, didn't it? He could raise and slaughter his own cattle. An efficient operation, all around.

"Palmarito coming up now." Ramón pointed toward a collection of houses and small buildings on the horizon.

They landed on a pasture outside the little town. It consisted of one hotel, a petrol pump, two grain elevators, a church, houses, and a narrow-gauge railroad passing through. It had just about everything its provincial residents might want, but it did not have a meat-packing plant, and had never had one.

"You're not performing tonight?" Jack asked in surprise.

"No, darling," Karyn said. "I want to spend the time with you. I am sure my understudy will not be too upset."

"I suppose not. But the audience will."

"It is their sad fate. But I have not seen much of you since your return from South America, and . . ." She seemed about to say something more, but did not.

What she said was true, though. Karyn had been occupied, as always, with *Guinevere*, film producers, and recording executives. United Artists had signed her as the lead in a movie version of the Broadway hit, and she was selecting material for a projected Omega Records album titled *Eros and Enigma*. She had not, she said, seen Rudolf Bennington since Jack's return from Venezuela, although she volunteered that he had phoned her several times, and sent orchids to her dressing room at the theater. "He hates you now, darling," she had warned Jack. "You must never forget that."

It would have been a fact hard to ignore. Having been involved in the Taggart audit, and having definite knowledge of fraud on the part of Bennington, Jack had no legal choice but to blow the whistle on the tycoon. Bennington was soon to be called before a New York State grand jury, faced investigation by the Securities and Exchange Commission, and—business-district rumor contended—was planning to flee the country. "I don't flee nothing," Bennington was quoted, after slugging an inquisitive reporter outside Sardi's. "When I leave, you'll know it. I got scores to settle here first."

Scores to settle: Rudolf Bennington's motivation for life.

Jack did not dwell on the matter. What would happen, would happen.

"I've got tickets for the *Firebird* ballet," Karyn was saying. "Let's go. Why don't you hurry and get dressed?"

"Did you keep your doctor's appointment this time?" he asked, as they were being driven over to the New York State Theater at Lincoln Center for the ballet. She had been complaining for some weeks of fatigue, although she looked as radiant and stunning as ever.

"Oh, darling, no. I've been so busy. I had to cancel again. It's probably just nerves."

"I've got a great idea."

"What's that, darling?"

"Why don't you take a couple weeks off the show? In January or February? I'll rearrange my schedule. We can go somewhere and rest. Anywhere you want."

"Oh, that would be sweet. But I don't know . . ."

"Please think about it." He took her hand, locked fingers with her, lifted her hand and kissed it.

"I will," she said. "I'll think about it."

Carol Jean Atwood, Royall Beach Elementary School's new fifth-grade teacher, rode the Long Island Rail Road into New York that night to see the *Firebird* ballet. She went alone. She could have gone with Stan Walsh, who was constantly asking her out. But the experience with Vic Brand had taught her a lesson, and she sensed a dark core to Stan Walsh, partially evidenced by the patent instability of business schemes he was always dreaming up. Carol could have gone to the ballet with Blanche Dunphy, another new teacher, but she had begged off due to the pressure of work. The pressure of work was why Carol had decided to go into the city anyway, even if alone. Preparing her lessons, dealing with students and their parents, and attending faculty meetings left her much in need of relaxation.

Now, at intermission, she was glad she'd made the trip, in spite of the discomfort of the Long Island train. The performance was spectacular, and it was always exhilarating to experience the cold, arrogant glitter of New York in the night. Carol sipped a plastic tumbler of white wine and watched the people moving about, chatting, smoking, getting drinks at the bar, forming and reforming until it was time to drift back into the theater before the curtain rose again.

"Miss Atwood, isn't it?"

Carol turned. To see a familiar and most appealing face, dark hair, green eyes, broad tuxedoed shoulders.

"Jack Kenton. We met in Boston last June, at the . . ."

"Back Bay Brasserie! Yes, I was with Dad. How *are* you?"

"Fine. I saw you standing here. Enjoying the ballet?"

"Very much." She noted that he seemed to be unaccompanied, and that was encouraging. Now what were those three tests she used to have, when she was a silly schoolgirl?

"How is your teaching coming along?"

He remembered. "It's hectic. But I really like it. And you? I have to thank you personally for saving the family business," she said lightly.

"My pleasure." He smiled. "But I knew the heat was on when your father brought you up to Boston. You looked very severe. I hate to think of your judgment, had I failed."

So he remembered, too, her mood that day at lunch, when she had still been psychologically reeling from Vic Brand's attack on her.

"It wasn't nice of me," she said, acknowledging his comment. "I'm even human sometimes."

"That's not a bad recommendation." He laughed.

The intermission was ending, and people were going back inside. She would have liked to remain with him, talking. Maybe later. She was just about to fabricate an excuse for them to meet again when, approaching them across the now-deserted lobby, Carol saw the most dazzling female she'd ever imagined, let alone seen. Dressed in a gown of glistening white satin, which set off her perfect olive complexion and rich, piled masses of black hair, the woman's smile was white as radium, cold as ice. Carol had seen the face in newspapers, magazines, playbills, billboards, and poster ads along railroad platforms coming into the city. *Guinevere.* Karyn Bari.

Carol stiffened, as if getting ready to be measured. Curiously, she also felt jealous, and her social smile seemed stiff on her face.

"Jack, darling," said Karyn, in her low, infinitely suggestive voice, nodding politely at Carol, "it's time to return to our seats."

Jack, darling! Oh, hell, Carol thought.

"Karyn," Jack was saying. "I'd like you to meet Carol Jean Atwood, the daughter of one of my clients . . ."

The daughter of one of my clients!

". . . Carol, Karyn Bari."

"Miss Bari. Of course," Carol said. "You've had such wonderful reviews. I'm so looking forward to seeing *Guinevere.*"

Was it just Carol's imagination, or did the singer look, for a fleeting instant, startled, nonplussed? Why? But the instant passed, and the three of them walked back into the theater together, the women on either side of Jack Kenton. Before they parted, Carol to her orchestra seat, Jack and Karyn to a private box, Jack said he hoped he'd see Carol again, and she said she was glad to have run into him. Back at her seat, Carol could see Karyn Bari. Her presence was so striking, so powerful, that simply being there she seemed one of those mysterious stars that emanate fire forever but are never consumed.

"Karyn," Jack asked, on the drive back to their apartment, "you said you had tickets to *Firebird*. But we wound up in someone's box?"

"People are always giving me things and doing favors for me, darling."

Bennington! thought Jack. *That bastard.*

Angry, hurt, he felt like having the matter out with her, right then, but as if sensing his intention, Karyn touched his hand gently. "Don't talk," she told him, "it's important not to talk."

"Why?"

"Because tonight we are going to create an aura again, and it will speak for us."

Endless aching sweetness, timeless and all-obliterating, all-encompassing, later with Karyn in the bed, never had Jack experienced anything so lustfully carnal, shiningly pure. She was everywhere around him, clutching him with herself, wordless, that he might never leave. Yes, wordless, until the very end, and beyond. In the aura of flesh, glow of love, no words were required, because flesh itself found tongue, and passion moved from spirit to substance. Jack and Karyn were more than themselves now, a holy trinity of stunning pleasure.

"Now," she said, after forever, "the twenty-four minutes are gone into time. Go out of me, and then come in again, just once, but all the way. It is all we will need."

She was right.

When Jack awakened in the morning, Karyn was already up and gone. She'd had so many meetings lately; no wonder she felt tired.

He made himself some tea and drank a couple of cups, while eating a pear and some Brie. The *New York Times* occupied his mind for a while. Lyndon Johnson was not about to end the war in Vietnam, and President-Elect Nixon was vacationing in Key Biscayne. Some good news, though: Hoyt Merritt reported that *Guinevere* was totally sold out for months in advance.

Morning at the office passed uneventfully, until about 10:45 when Frank Brewster phoned.

"How would you like to get sued for wrongful death by Gisela Thuringer?"

"*Who?*"

Brewster laughed. "Don't worry. Remember Gisela Twister, that gorgeous hunk of Aryan womanflesh? General Twister's tearful widow? She's apparently married now to a Prussian landowner with a lot of *Deutschmarks*, and she's decided to use some of them against you. Won't get anywhere, though. It's strictly harassment. Be thrown right out. How about lunch?"

They made a date for Fraunces Tavern, at one o'clock, and Jack returned to his work. The image of Gisela Twister kept intruding, however; he could not shake the memory of her, standing there in the amphitheater, blood dripping, and Gisela saying: *"For this you shall pay!"*

"For that I shall pay my lawyer, at least," he muttered to himself, walking toward Fraunces.

Brewster was already at his regular table. He had a funny look on his face when he rose to shake hands with Jack, a look people often have when they meet you after learning that someone in your family has either died or knocked over a filling station.

"Sorry about it," Brewster said, "but, like they say, there'll always be another one coming down the road."

"What the hell are you talking about?"

Now the expression on Brewster's face changed to one customarily worn by a bearer of bad news. "You don't know?" he asked. "You don't know," he said. From the briefcase on the floor next to his chair, Brewster withdrew the *Post*, just out on the streets, folded it open to page six, and handed it to Jack. The headline said:

BARI QUITS GUINEVERE
Gives No Explanation

A newsphoto showed a familiar man and a most familiar woman climbing some stairs. "Singer Karyn Bari and Industrialist Rudolf Bennington board the latter's private jet for a flight to Venezuela," read the caption. Bennington was smiling broadly. He had his revenge. Karyn's face could not be seen clearly. She was, Jack realized, going away. With no words of farewell.

Some weeks later, gossip columnists reported the marriage of Karyn Bari and Rudolf Bennington. ". . . in a picturesque chapel in the tiny Venezuelan village of Palmarito," one of them wrote. *How sweet*, thought Jack.

A child was born to the happy couple in July of 1969. The news hurt—how could it not?—but by that time Jack was in love with someone else.

9

Roses exploded in the arbor. Azaleas, gladioli, and orchids of a dozen colors decorated the little altar that had been erected on the glistening lawn. And clouds of pink-and-violet lilacs covered the hedges that surrounded the vast white Atwood "cottage" on Wescott Cove on the bright day Carol Jean Atwood married John Tyler Kenton, in May 1970.

Carol and Jack made their vows in open air, surrounded by women in bright dresses, men in colored jackets and frilly, luminous shirts. To a sailor far out on the water, the wedding party must have seemed like petals of a gorgeous flower, gently stirred by wind.

Some months after Karyn had fled with Bennington, Jack felt a loosening of the bitter grip in which he had been held. Little could be done to relieve the intense emotional pain he felt. He could only wait for the moment when the burden would begin to lift. Moreover, Jack had had no bargain with Karyn, no promise, no deal. She had always told him she would do what she wanted, go after what she wanted, *get* what she wanted. And so she had. But it still hurt, until one day he reached for the phone and dialed information to learn the listing for an Atwood, C. J., in Royall Beach, on the North Shore. When Jack made the call, he knew he was alive again.

Jack and Carol Jean told each other everything.

He told her about the time he had taken his little friend's toy horse from the garage and dragged it back to his own yard, and how he had been too guilty to enjoy it. She told him her special nickname, "CiJi," was the result of her own early inability to pronounce Carol Jean properly. He told her about working in the gas station for tuition money, told her about Ridgewood, Queens, his old neighborhood, told her about Buster Pauley, "Foulest Mouth in Grover Cleveland," and the fight Buster had dragged him into. She told him about bucolic Miss Blaisdell's School, about summers on Wescott Cove, about the madman Cleophus Watts trying to break into their car back in 1960, and his subsequent threatening messages. He told her about working in Military Intelligence, formulating the model that solved the PX Plot, and about Gisela Twister's vow of vengeance, standing there in the courtroom, soaked in her husband's blood. She told him that she had been thinking of going on to earn a doctoral degree, to become more effective in her educational work. He told her that Kenton Diversified was fine, but that he wanted to do more as well, get involved in public affairs, and that he had been thinking lately of politics. She told him about her three tests, that he had passed every one with flying colors, and that when he touched very lightly the small of her back during intimacy it drove her wild. He told her he had never met anyone who had affected him the way she did, and when she squeezed around him just as hard as she could at the exact instant of orgasm, it just drove him wild. She told him she wanted to have his child, and that she had never felt that way before. He told her about making an aura, but she held back and did not want to, thinking of Karyn Bari and asking: "You've done that with somebody else before, haven't you?" Then she told him about Jeff Gimbel, exaggerating the role Jeff had played in her emotional life, and saw that he was jealous and a little hurt. So she did not tell him about Vic Brand. He saw that she was upset and probably would always be bothered about his relationship with Karyn Bari, and so he did not tell her about Pauline Yates at all. She did not tell him about *The Waltz of the Dead;* it was a hard thing to explain if you did not want someone to think you were a little crazy. And she did not want him to think that, when everything was going so terrifically between them.

So Jack and CiJi told each other *almost* everything.

Two years later, in May of 1972, Jack and Carol Jean left their Park Avenue duplex and crossed the street very carefully at the corner, heading toward the Central Park Zoo. Jack pushed the stroller proudly and not at all self-consciously. After all, the healthy, rollicking fifteen-month-old in the stroller was John Tyler Kenton, Jr., firstborn son and only child.

There could be no more.

Carol had gotten pregnant during their wedding trip to Curaçao in the Netherlands Antilles, off the coast of Venezuela. It proved to be a difficult pregnancy, caused by a tropical fever she had contracted in the Antilles, and so Carol took a leave of absence from her Royall Beach teaching job and spent her time and energy hoping for a healthy baby. When Johnny was born, Carol and Jack were ecstatic. But the fever, caused by the virus *metasporamacea*, did its damage. She could never conceive again. But Carol was not one to dwell on darkness when so much of her life was blessed. She devoted her time to the baby, to the Park Avenue apartment Jack had bought, and to her doctoral courses at Columbia University. When Johnny was a little older, she planned to return to her teaching job at Royall Beach.

Jack, in the meantime, had begun to get involved in local politics. Appalled by a decline in metropolitan services even as taxes shot skyward, he and half-a-dozen other young professionals had founded the Independent Citizens Committee, to analyze tax intake and cost outgo on a scientific rather than a political basis, and to put pressure on Borough Boss Charlie Kiefer, an ambitious pol of the you-scratch-my-back-I'll-scratch-yours species. Just last month, the *New York Times* had sent reporter and photographer to the Kenton apartment, and a story lauding the "new scientific-modular approach to political analysis" had appeared in the paper. "Charlie Kiefer won't appreciate this," Carol had said, after reading the piece. "Too bad for him," replied Jack. "What can happen?"

"Park's crowded today," observed Jack, as they made their way toward the zoo. The stroller rolled easily on its little rubber tires. Johnny gurgled and waved his arms, alarming several pigeons. "Where should we go first?"

"Something dramatic," said Carol. "His attention span isn't that great yet."

"How about the bears? Dramatic enough?"

"Big enough, anyway."

They headed toward the bears' enclosure, moving slowly in the ebb and flow of the Sunday crowd. The mood was festive, so many people out today after a long winter and a rainy spring. Carol walked along beside her husband, loving the warm sun, and wondering whether to go back to teaching in the fall, or to wait another year. If she went back, they would probably decide to move out to Long Island. But if she waited, she would be that much further along toward her Ph.D. degree when she did return to the classroom. And she missed the classroom, the school, with the professional challenge, the sweet murmur of children at work discovering themselves, even the often outrageous faculty politics. Well, no need to decide right now . . .

They walked on and came to a small crowd surrounding an amateur juggler, his hat on the ground next to him, collecting tossed coins of appreciation. Johnny's eyes were drawn to the whirling brightly colored balls spun by the juggler, and Jack stopped the stroller to let his son watch.

"There's a vendor," Jack said. "Want an ice cream bar, or a toasted pretzel?"

"Sure. A pretzel. Johnny can gum part of it."

Jack walked off to get pretzels, and Carol stood next to the stroller. Johnny gawked and chortled. The juggler pulled the balls in and, surveying an acceptable scattering of coins around his hat, lit three small torches and prepared to flaunt his skill. The sight of fire attracted more people.

"If I don't do this right," the juggler winked, setting the torches into a threatening trajectory, "my girl friend will be disappointed."

The crowd laughed, and above their laughter, inconceivably, Carol heard the first throbbing organ note of *The Waltz of the Dead*.

She looked around in panic. Jack could not be seen, lost in the crush around the pretzel-vendor. The group surrounding the juggler milled and jostled, ooohed and aaaahed, watching the ring of fire.

The Waltz of the Dead. Why *now*? What possibly could happen, out here in public, surrounded by thousands, in Central Park? But Carol heard it again, and once more the horror was upon her. Time blurred, and she was in third grade, when the girls of Miss Blaisdell's and the boys at neighboring Springfield Academy had dance class. "The Vienna Waltz." But the song was altered now, no longer that whipped-cream-chocolate waltz. The second chord of the awful prelude sounded in Carol's brain. Still seeking Jack, jostled by the people, she reached for the handles of Johnny's stroller.

The stroller moved easily beneath her touch. Very easily. Johnny wasn't in it.

Carol screamed.

"Hey, lady!" cried a startled man standing next to her.

"Carol!" Jack shouted.

"*My baby!*" she screamed, and a black pit opened, with Carol at the edge, ready to plunge . . .

"What's wrong?" Jack shouted, rushing up to his wife.

Everything seemed to stop, and in the zoo in Central Park time itself froze solid, violating universal law. The juggler's astonished face was framed in a ring of fire. The man next to Carol lurched away from her, frightened. Jack's face was just beginning to register shock. He held a half-chewed pretzel.

Then time smashed out of abeyance. Jack's hand was on Carol's arm, his eyes on the empty stroller.

"Where . . .?"

"I seen a guy pick up the kid," yelled a jogger with a blue headband.

Everyone was shouting now, fear and alarm transmitted from person to person like a primitive pulse of danger.

"You saw him?" shouted Jack, grabbing the jogger by the shoulders.

"There he goes now!" the man said, pointing at a dark-suited figure racing up the path toward the bears. Johnny's stunned little face could be seen over his shoulder.

"Stop!" yelled Jack, already running. He knocked down a little old lady, upset the stroller, and collided with one of New York's finest, who'd come running in response to Carol's first scream.

"My kid's been taken!" Jack cried over his shoulder. He was running again, in pursuit of the dark-suited man. The cop stood there for a split second, registering what he'd been told, deciding on a course of action. A half-dozen people in the crowd were yelling at him. "The guy in the dark jacket! That guy! The one up the path there, with the kid!"

The cop turned and ran after Jack.

Carol started running, too. People were scattering before her, getting out of her way. People were yelling, "What's wrong? What happened?" She didn't feel herself breathing at all, didn't really feel herself *running* at all. The cop was ahead of her, Jack was ahead of the cop, and the man with Johnny was ahead of them both, running toward the bears. Carol saw the great beasts, up on their hind legs, sniffing the air with their dull plodding wonder.

"Stop!" Jack was yelling. The cop pulled a black pistol out of his holster.

Johnny was screaming at the top of his tiny lungs.

Jack almost caught up with the man, who was just abreast of the agitated bears. Most of them had turned away from the chaos, seeking shelter among the big rocks in their compound, but one beast lumbered toward the high stone wall, fangs bared.

The dark-suited man stopped, lifted Johnny, and prepared to throw him over the wall.

Carol could not even scream. She sank down on her knees. The organ of death blasted its terrible chords.

Jack lunged forward, only a few last yards . . .

The man's arms were moving with the child in them. His fingers were releasing the cloth of Johnny's little jacket. Johnny was screaming.

The cop fired.

Jack saw the man's cheekbone explode before his eyes. He lunged toward his son.

The gun blasted again, and a huge chunk of the man's skull spun into the air, a glimmering sheet of blood in the air as well. He was falling . . .

Jack Kenton seized his son and fell with him to the ground.

"Holy Jesus," said the winded, panting cop. "Holy Jesus, holy Jesus."

Johnny was screaming.

After what seemed like a very long time Jack got up, soothing Johnny, crooning to him. Carol struggled to her feet, staggered over, and Jack put his arm around her too. The cop was bending over the dead man, gingerly checking out his pockets. Carol took a quick look, then averted her eyes from the burly black man with half his face, half his head, blasted away.

"Newspaper clipping," said the cop, holding it up. It was the article from the *Times*, telling about Jack and the Independent Citizens Committee, complete with a photo of Jack, Carol, and Johnny in their apartment, which said—among other things—that Carol was the daughter of John Delano Atwood, head of Atwood Industries, Connecticut . . .

Then the cop pulled a battered billfold from the dead man's pants pocket, opened it, and fumbled through the papers and bills and cards.

"You people know a Watts, Cleophus?" asked the cop.

The Waltz of the Dead ended in quivering cacophony, and Carol remembered that long-ago warning: NEVER GOING TO KNOW TIME OR PLACE.

"It was one in a million," Jack told Carol, days later. Johnny was fine again, but his parents still lived with the horror of what could have happened.

One in a million, Carol thought. That was exactly what her father had said about Vic Brand.

"Jack, I have to tell you something. I should have told you a long time ago. I don't know how or why, but I seem to be able to tell when terrible things are about to happen."

She saw, with relief, that he took her seriously. "Then you knew something was going to happen in the park?"

"Not while we were on our way there. But just moments before Watts grabbed Johnny. I heard this—this music. Organ music playing a kind of demented waltz. It gives me cold flashes just to talk about . . ."

"And this has happened to you before?"

"Off and on since I was at Miss Blaisdell's. In fact, it started there. But every time I've heard the music, someone has either died or been in danger of death."

"Ever you?"

She nodded.

"Want to give me specifics?"

She thought of Vic Brand, her first and only lover until Jack. "Honey, it isn't important. Not to us. Not anymore."

"Of course it's important. Everything in the past is important, where acts of revenge are concerned. That's the whole point."

Carol was still reluctant, but he embraced her, told her to go ahead. "It couldn't be that bad," he said. "I'd love you in spite of everything, no matter what."

"You would?"

"How could you doubt it? Wouldn't you me?"

Yes, she thought, she would. He was right. Briefly, she told him how her relationship with Vic Brand had flared, then died, then gone awfully awry.

"And he attacked you twice?" Jack asked.

"Both times I heard this music, this horrible parody of a waltz. It started in chapel at school, and the very moment she died Miss Blaisdell looked at me and said, *'You knew!'*"

Jack thought it over, his face taut with concentration.

"Jack," she said, "I swear I'm okay. Sane, I mean. Sane as anybody. I think."

"I think so too," he said. "It's just that you have some heightened form of intuition. Death is an emotional crisis for everyone involved, victims or survivors. Apparently, something passed between you and Miss Blaisdell that evening in the school chapel. She was dying, and in her last breath she was aware that you had known. Somehow. In some way. You associate the feeling with the chapel, and with its organ. See what I'm getting at?"

"Yes, but—oh, Jack, I hate this!"

He held her closely.

"I wouldn't worry about it. A lot of people would give their eyeteeth for a built-in radar device."

"I'm not so sure. What good is sensing disaster when you can't do anything about it?"

"But we *are* going to do something about it. Starting right away, we're going to be more careful. I never thought about it much, but in both business and the army I've made enemies. I didn't want to. It just happened. Any definite action is bound to attract somebody's attention. And if they happen not to agree with that action, or if they are harmed by it, or just think they've been harmed, then you have an enemy. And I don't want you or Johnny suffering at the hands of some maniac who might emerge from my past."

"Jack?"

"Yes?"

"Tell me something. Really. I know you've had plenty of girl friends who didn't mean a whole lot. I've had boyfriends like that too. But besides that—that singer? Was there anyone else besides her?"

"Yes," he sighed, "there was." And he told her about Pauline Yates, the Red Cross girl in Germany. "Karyn scared her away, though."

"Scared her away?"

"Pauline was beautiful, but very insecure. Much more insecure, it turned out, than I had ever suspected."

"Unstable, would you say?" Carol asked.

The question was mildly shocking to Jack. "Why—yes," he admitted, thinking about it after all these years. "Yes, she was unstable. But nowhere near the degree Vic Brand nust have been. Must still be. I mean, Pauline isn't in the high security section of the Mellon Clinic."

"How do you know?" Carol asked. "Jack, honey, let's drop all of this. It *is* the past, that's true, and it won't ever go away, but we don't have to let it ruin our lives, do we?"

"No," he agreed, "we don't. And we aren't going to. Tell you what. Let's move out of the city. Too many people here. Too easy to be anonymous, to strike at will. Chances are that Cleophus Watts was one in a million . . ."

"Two in a million," Carol amended, thinking of Vic Brand.

"Two in a million, okay. So our odds are better than they were. But just to make sure, we'll build a house in the country, with every possible safeguard. Johnny will need a yard pretty soon anyway."

A big *safe* yard, they both thought.
Because you never know what can happen.
It could be anything.
Anyone.
Anytime.

Book Two

DARK BLOSSOMS

1

In May of 1981, nine years after Jack and Carol Kenton built their magnificent home in Royall Beach, Long Island, and moved out of New York, Charles G. "Charlie" Kiefer, former Manhattan borough boss and now chairman of the New York State Democratic Party, stuck a big brown Monte Cristo in the corner of his mouth and jumped out of the limo as soon as it stopped, not waiting for the chauffeur to hustle around and open the door. Charlie had nothing against chauffeurs doing their jobs; he had nothing against anybody in the world, not the monkey-suited doorman to whom Charlie waved and flashed his cap, and not the fat redheaded guy at the security desk inside who gave him the old "yessir, Mr. Kiefer, sir." No, Charlie had nothing against *nobody* today, because he'd finally gotten the summons. He entered the Park Towers a very happy man, enjoying everything from the subtle bite of expensive tobacco on his tongue to his tailored suit with the *fleur-de-lis* print-on-silk lining to the massage and workout-hardened tone of his new flat gut. Higgins had told Charlie to drop twenty pounds for "image" purposes. Charlie had dropped thirty, to show how eager he was. Charlie reached the bank of elevators, received and accepted a deferential nod from a security man stationed there, and climbed aboard, heading up. Ever since his early days on the Lower East Side of Manhattan, Charlie Kiefer had always headed up.

The private elevator shot Charlie right up into Higgins's vast apartment, and the governor himself was waiting as the doors slid open.

"Charlie! Charlie, my boy! Come in. Come in. You're looking good. Here. Let me take your hat."

John Higgins accepted Charlie's pearl-gray homburg and flipped it to a cute girl in a tiny uniform.

"Drink, Charlie? Say, you really do look good."

"Thirty pounds," Charlie proclaimed. "Sure will. Scotch, with maybe a little soda on top."

Higgins waved away the comely servant and personally fixed Charlie's drink.

"Well, Charlie," said Higgins, sitting down next to him and handing over the drink, "what have you got planned for the weekend?"

"Spendin' it with Ma, of course."

The governor nodded. Sunday was Mother's Day, and Charlie's devotion to his ma was legendary. Charlie himself still lived in a little West Side apartment, in the ward that had given him a political start, but he'd bought his mother a big place out in King's Point, a fancy North Shore suburb right next to Royall Beach.

"Soon as we finish our business here," Charlie said, "I'll head on out there. Beat the Friday traffic."

Higgins nodded and sipped Dubonnet. He leaned back against the velvet cushions on the couch and crossed his long legs, a patrician at ease. The crease on his Bond Street pants could have split a hair, and his Johnson and Murphys glistened. Charlie was in awe. Not too much, though. Higgins was a man, but so was Charlie, and next year he was going to get his chance to run for governor of the Empire State.

Nor did Higgins beat around the bush. "Charlie, I've got one hell of a job cut out for you."

"I know that, Governor, and I'm ready."

"You look ready."

"Thirty pounds."

Higgins put his hands behind his head. Leaned way back. "Now I know I haven't actually sat down with you for a one-on-one about this matter. We hadn't cleared all the details with Kenton."

Kenton? Charlie sat up straight. What the hell did that young guy, that tax-reform champion with his Independent Citizens Committee, have to do with Charlie getting a shot at the governorship? Kenton wasn't even a Democrat; he was a goddam independent! Higgins was winding up his second term, had chosen not to run again. Charlie had his heart set on succeeding him. But *Kenton?*

"Charlie, you and me, our type of politician, is not what the people will vote for anymore," Higgins was saying.

"Aw, Governor, c'mon. What are you talking?"

"No, it's true. The last twenty to thirty years have been growth years. For most people. And government, local government, served mainly as a provider of services. More and more services, costing more and more money."

"Right as rain, there, Governor." Charlie thought he understood.

"But that era is over now," Higgins said. "We both belonged to it, advanced with it, thrived on it. But it's over."

Behind the cigar smoke, Charlie Kiefer blinked once. Twice. He felt a tremor pass from the center of his world, up through the bedrock of Manhattan, up through the steel girders, the New England granite, and Italian marble of this shimmering tower, up through the parquet floor and the Oriental rugs, up through the soles of his Ballys, and into him. Charlie felt a queasy jiggle—just a little—in the reworked sinews of his gym-hardened gut. What the hell was going on here, anyway?

"The new era, the new spirit," mused John Higgins, "is economy, conservation, retrenchment. Exactly the qualities Kenton projects so well. Plus he's photogenic, and that tax-reform movement of his has chapters in every county in the state. Charlie, he's got—he's already got—a name-recognition factor of seventy-seven percent."

Charlie ducked his chin to hide a gulp. His own name-recognition factor, a crucial political measure of how many voters have even heard of you, was only forty-two percent. But, after all, that was because he'd mostly worked in New York City politics. The election was over a year away; he'd have plenty of time to build name-recognition. But something had gone terribly wrong. Now, it was true that Higgins had never actually *said*, not in so many *words*, that he'd back Charlie in the fight for candidacy, but never in a million years would Charlie have suspected something like this!

So then what was this "big job" the gov had in mind for Charlie?

Had he sweated and strained to lose all those pounds for nothing?

"We got to consider all the angles on this," Charlie heard himself saying. There was a flicker of desperation in his voice. He had heard that same quaver when he was six years old, late January it had been, in their one-room, walk-up, cold-water flat down there on the Lower East Side. Little Charlie awakened, practically frozen to the sheets, and Ma was talking real funny, like to herself, and pouring sweat came off of her, even in the cold.

He hadn't known then about pneumonia. Or delirium. But he knew somebody had to help Ma or something terrible would happen.

Pa would help, of course.

But Charlie couldn't wake Pa! "C'mon Pa!" he remembered pleading, with that quaver of suppressed terror in his voice. "C'mon, wake up! Oh, please, you got to wake up . . ."

Yet something told him, even as he shook and pounded and pounded and shook that rigid body in the frozen bed, that his father, a fruit and vegetable pushcart vendor, would not wake up anymore. And the shiver of dread in his voice had told Charlie that he and Ma were alone and unprotected, somewhere out in a world that would always be arctic, with a future as unreadable as wind.

So Charlie had fought; he had grown; he was tough. He had made it "on his own," as he liked to say, made it mostly in the Garment District. If people mistook Charlie Kiefer, or read him wrong and tried to pull a fast one, they learned not to do it again. There was Merklewicz, that shyster, his thieving ex-partner. He was rotting now up in Attica. Charlie had had to ruin him. And Guapino Campa, he'd never try extortion again, the cold dead guinea prick. Buster Pauley had helped Charlie with that one when Buster was still a cop. And then there was that so-called intellectual, Ray Logan, who had tried to block Charlie for state chairman. Don't think *he* didn't know who'd put those hungry *Daily News* schmucks onto Logan's youthful membership in that Workers' whatchamacallit Socialist Alliance!

People respected Charlie Kiefer, damn right. And many feared him. That was okay, too. They feared him because they *knew*. They knew he was just a little *too* intense, would do the extra thing to make sure that he won. Well, fuck them. It never hurts if your enemies think you are a little crazy.

Despite the dawning vision of personal disaster, Charlie could not help but *marvel* at Higgins's air of command. You came from aristocracy, like him, you saw the world from on top, you said *I want it thus and so, I want this and that*. You saw things from the

World Trade Center Towers downtown, or Wall Street, or the Plaza Hotel, across the way there, or from this apartment, high in the clouds. *Au contraire* (one of Charlie's three Frog phrases), you came from the Lower East Side, with a view of limp laundry and alleys and dogshit, you said *Please, may I have* and then *Please, give me*, and then *Give me!*

Charlie's cigar was dead. The scotch was sour on his stomach, bile in his mouth.

"Now here's where you come in," declared Higgins with his glittering grin. God, where did those people get such *teeth!*

"At your service," Charlie barked. He thought it sounded all right; he couldn't hear the quaver, anyway.

"Charlie, the reason I summoned you . . ." *(I summoned you!)* ". . . is to tell you we're . . ." *(we're!)* ". . . going to make a move that will accomplish all my . . ." *(my!)* ". . . goals. We're going to preempt tax reform, the biggest issue the Republicans have, by nominating Jack Kenton for governor."

"And you said this was all cleared with Kenton?"

"That's right. I have it arranged so that he'll make his announcement declaring candidacy on the Fourth of July. That's a reasonably bipartisan date, don't you think? And your job, Charlie, will be to work on the county chairmen, get them behind Kenton. Name-recognition or no, he's not—hasn't been—a party man, and he's got to be sold to the regulars."

Charlie was beginning to feel angry, instead of just kicked in the balls. Kenton! Christ! The kid couldn't be more than forty. (Charlie was sixty-one.) And so what if Kenton was a tax-reform Lochinvar? What about the traditional requirement of paying your dues? Charlie felt like fighting back.

"Why the rush to have him announce, Governor?" he asked. "Fourth of July's coming up pretty quick."

"Two reasons. Kenton needs time to get really rolling for next year's campaign. And . . ." Higgins inspected his manicured fingernails. ". . . and if he flops, *we'll* have time to get somebody else."

Higgins, the Machiavellian now. Charlie's heart enjoyed a couple of optimistic beats.

"I don't think he'll flop, though," the governor observed.

We'll see about that, Charlie thought, shaping his ploy. "What if there's something in his past that'll embarrass us? Shouldn't we take the time to make a thorough check?"

"No problem there that I know of," Higgins said confidently. "Jack Kenton is as clean as a hound's tooth."

"I see," said Charlie, thinking hard. *Clean as a hound's tooth, huh?* A lifetime of rough-and-tumble had taught him that time was an excellent weapon. Maybe, before the Fourth of July, Kenton could be sidetracked, sandbagged. There had to be something that could stop him, and simultaneously put Charlie Kiefer in the vanguard of potential candidates.

"Naturally, if you want me to sell the guy, I'll have to run a check on him myself. In my capacity as party chairman."

"Charlie, I'd be amazed if you didn't. But Kenton's all right. There's not a thing in his past to worry about."

Charlie frowned. There was *always* something. You just had to know where to look. *How* to look. Charlie was already making plans. He would assign Buster Pauley to the job. Buster was very effective on stuff like this. Buster, the ex-cop, had had plenty of hard knocks in life, just like Charlie. He could be foulmouthed and crude, and he had had no end of trouble with Bernice, that complaining wife of his, but if he knew you were loyal to him and would stick by him, there was nothing he wouldn't do for you. He'd proved it already.

Charlie looked a little more cheerful now. His cigar was cold and dead, and the meeting was over. Governor Higgins stood, and so did Charlie.

"Tell Mrs. Kiefer happy Mother's Day from me," Higgins said, as he showed Charlie to the elevator. The elevator that went down.

"Where to now, Mr. Kiefer?" asked the chauffeur.

"King's Point. Ma's place."

The big limo crawled through Manhattan, over to the FDR Drive, up across Triboro Bridge and onto the Long Island Expressway. Usually Charlie sat tall in the saddle so people might recognize him and know a personage was passing, but today he hunched in the backseat, fretting and worrying. That goddam Jack Kenton, coming from nowhere. Again. Like nine years ago, when Charlie had been riding high as Manhattan borough boss, had had every salary, contract, payoff, and kickback arranged, with a little something left for Charlie himself, along had come Kenton with that Independent Citizens Committee study group. Out of fucking *nowhere!* Suddenly, analyses of borough budgets were in all the papers. Radio and television had picked it up. Charlie had sweated and backpedaled that one for over a year. The only thing that had saved him was the fact that the cops, sanitation workers, syndicate boys, and party hacks were just as scared as he was, and had, out of self-preservation, agreed to cuts in their "take." Kenton!

"Our time is past, Charlie," Higgins had said.

"But I don't *want* my time to be past," Charlie mourned to himself. Problem was, what could he do? Without even *talking* to Charlie about it first, the lordly Higgins had already told Kenton he would support him in his shot for the nomination. And Higgins would do just that unless Charlie found a compelling reason—something in Kenton's past—to make the governor change his mind.

But what if Charlie couldn't find any such damning thing? By July 4? Then what?

Charlie had always told his cronies that the governorship was something he would "kill for." It was the highest rung he could hope to achieve on his ladder of life. Anything in the national arena was out. Charlie was a New Yorker. It was in the blood. Take him out beyond the Hudson, and they would laugh his ass back to the Lower East Side. And Charlie knew it. So, for him, the governorship was the top of the heap.

And now it looked like the top of the heap wasn't for him either. Kill for it?

Naw, c'mon. When Charlie and Buster Pauley had killed extortionist Guapino Campa, well, that had been different. If they hadn't done it, Campa would have killed them! Kenton wouldn't kill anybody. He wasn't the type. Yet he was obliterating Charlie's greatest goal in life and taking it himself, *noblesse oblige*, sort of. That was Charlie's second Frog phrase.

He lit up a fresh cigar, but it didn't taste good, and he felt some heartburn start up, down there under his toned gut muscles.

A new era, Higgins had said.

Charlie spat out his third and pithiest Frog phrase.

"Merde," he said.

"What?" the chauffeur inquired.

Usually, Charlie took the Lakeville Road exit off the Expressway and then drove on up through Great Neck and into King's Point where Ma's house was. But he just didn't feel up to seeing Ma yet, since he wasn't bringing the good news he'd rashly promised. If only he hadn't bragged to her about getting the governorship. So many times he had seen pols—shrewd, hardheaded, longtime pols—see assent where there wasn't any, see support where there was nothing but words. *Join the group*, he thought, a fool who'd seen a nod in John Higgins's wink.

"Go up to the next exit," he told the driver, "let's take a look at Royall Beach."

King's Point was at the tip of one lush peninsula, about fifteen miles from New York City, on the North Shore of Long Island. Royall Beach was out on the edge of an almost identical peninsula, a few miles east. A sailboat-dotted bay separated the two.

"Find Cove Drive and swing me up there," Charlie grunted. "It must be someplace close to the bay." He wanted to have a look at Kenton's house. Surely it couldn't be as classy as the one he'd bought for Ma.

But he was wrong, and he knew enough to know it at a glance. The farther north they drove, the bigger were the houses, the more spacious and well-tended the grounds. The whole area was like an enclave; you had to drive through a big iron gate in a high stone fence, with a police car and a couple of local cops on duty there.

And then he saw Kenton's house. Charlie had never seen anything like it. Ma's house, over in King's Point, was an old stucco Georgian that Charlie had had painted a bright yellow. In contrast, Kenton's was ultramodern, unique but subdued, all boxes and angles and steel and glass. Hell, you couldn't even see where the *doorway* was. How could anybody get in there? Besides that, the place was pretty well obscured by lilac hedges.

Aw, hell, Charlie thought. "Ma's place," he told the driver.

Ma knew him like the back of her hand, always had. "What's wrong, Charlie?" she asked, as soon as he came in.

She hoisted herself up on her steel "walker" and peered at him. The male nurse he'd hired for her stood up too, but Ma waved him away. How Charlie regretted the stroke that had slowed her down! He saw her round, kind old face, framed by iron-gray hair. She couldn't get around much anymore, but her eyes were sharp and clear. Now her eyes were on her son, because she could tell he wasn't feeling right.

"Aw, Ma," Charlie said, going over, bending to her, putting his arms around her, "Aw, Ma."

He felt a tear slide out of the corner of his left eye.

"What is it, son?"

"They beat me. They beat me, Ma."

He felt like he was a kid again, back on the Lower East Side, that terrible January morning.

Ma's gnarled old hands patted his shoulder, patted his head. "Charlie," she advised with love and warmth, "then you have to fight again. Don't let them beat you, son."

Charlie hugged his ma for a little while, and she hugged him, and he felt better. She was right, of course. He had always fought before, and he would do it again. He would be governor, by God. *All right, Kenton. No holds barred.*

He needed Buster Pauley, and Buster wouldn't be hard to find. Since his wife, Bernice, had thrown him out, the ex-cop was practically living at Mel and Irma's Tavern, down there in Ridgewood, Queens.

2

Carol had made several attempts to leave her office, but one thing after another kept cropping up, demanding her attention. So she stayed. It was part of her job as principal of Royall Beach Elementary School. She enjoyed the variety and responsibility of the position, although for the last few years, she'd begun to feel that teaching had been a lot more fun. This Friday afternoon, however, all she wanted to do was drive home, because Jack had promised the family a Mother's Day *cum* wedding anniversary at Gurney's Inn, on Long Island's Atlantic shore. She could certainly use the rest, and so could Jack and Johnny. But mostly they needed a quiet time to bring Lisa Walsh into the family, the six-year-old for whom they'd just been named foster parents. Lisa was still haunted by her mother's death—if simple death is what it had been.

Carol didn't think so.

She glanced at her office clock. Three-forty-five. The Royall Beach Teachers' Union was holding a crucial meeting in the teachers' lounge, just down the corridor. Its members were yelling and screaming, which was fairly typical and might or might not be a good sign. They were debating the budget proposal for 1982 fiscal year that Carol had recently circulated among the faculty. No, admitted Carol, facing reality, the hullabaloo was not a good sign. When it came to budgetary matters these days, few things augured well.

Mrs. Crispus, the school board president, had been in for her weekly appointment earlier in the afternoon, to restate and reaffirm the board's opposition to any increases in spending.

"Not only for teacher's salaries, Carol," Mrs. Crispus had said, "but also, especially, for your pet, the pilot program."

That had hurt. The pilot program, which had attracted Carol to Royall Beach in the first place, way back in 1968, provided funds so that children of poorer neighborhoods might attend certain activities in a community more privileged than their own. Carol had always considered the program a success, but times had changed, and people were no longer willing to see their tax dollars go for "bizarre pseudosociological schemes that don't work anyway."

Mrs. Crispus had used exactly those words.

"Carol, let me be frank," she had also said, picking up her Gucci bag and preparing to leave. "We all respect your commitment. Everyone on the board does, and so do most of our taxpayers. We admired your grit, commuting to Columbia all those years, getting your doctorate and all that. It was one of the reasons we made you principal. But the pilot program is passé. Your husband is very much in favor of tax cuts. What does he think of the program?"

"I haven't asked him."

"What?"

"Jack and I have a rule. Unless asked, we don't interfere in each other's jobs."

"Well, I'm sure that's a good rule," Mrs. Crispus smiled, "but why don't you ask him and see. The time for tax reform has come, and if it doesn't happen at the local level, how can we expect it to occur higher up? Charity, my dear, begins at home. Have a pleasant weekend, Carol, and think about what I've said."

How could Carol not think about it, with the union members screaming right down the hall? Carol's budget called for continued full funding of the program, but only cost-of-living increases for the teachers. Her proposal was preliminary, of course, and she did not have the final say. Such a decision belonged to the community and the school board. But her version of the budget was a clear sign that she would fight for the pilot program. The sound and fury in the teachers' lounge was an equally clear signal that opposition was massing.

Stella, the school secretary, poked her head in the doorway.

"Dr. Kenton?"

"Yes, Stella."

"Anton Semlac just arrived and went into the lounge. I thought you'd want to know right away."

"Yes, thank you, Stella."

Oh, great, thought Carol, when the secretary withdrew. Semlac's name was synonymous with "work stoppage," and if the RBTU had invited the union's statewide coordinator, it did not require a Columbia University Ph.D. to deduce that the thought of a strike had entered the minds of some teachers.

Anton Semlac was not unknown to the Kentons, either. In Albany last year, both Semlac and Jack Kenton had testified before the legislature—Jack in his political capacity as head of the Independent Citizens Committee, and Semlac as union representative. Testimony had led to conflict, conflict to charges and denials, charges and denials to what the *Albany Union Leader* had termed: ". . . a verbal brawl. Antipathy between the principals was impossible to overlook . . ."

"I don't hate a single person on this earth," Jack had said later, telling Carol about it, "but that Semlac is one of the meanest, most vindictive bastards I've run across yet. Sort of like Rudolf Bennington playing in the minor leagues. I hope he doesn't think up a way to give you trouble at school."

So much for hope, reflected Carol, sitting in her office. If Jack didn't hate Bennington, Semlac had certainly rubbed him the wrong way. Certainly the union coordinator remembered the Kenton name and would not pass up an opportunity to give Jack some grief, even if he had to resort to embarrassing Carol to do it.

Carol packed her briefcase. Something to do. She didn't plan to work this weekend, but there were plenty of items that needed attention: the budget proposal printout, a federal grant request, the state curriculum bulletin, and a letter from a parent whose child had been beaten up by one of the kids in the pilot program. "To have outsiders come in here to Royall Beach is bad enough," the letter read, "but when violence is done to our own children, it is time to stop deluding ourselves about helping the riffraff of the world . . ."

Slightly angry parent, lawsuit in the works. Carol wondered if the writer's attitude would have been different had she been an alumna of Miss Blaisdell's School. Would fifty lectures about "being of service to your fellowman" have given that parent empathy for those less fortunate than herself?

"Your son and—ah, daughter," announced Stella, her head poking around the doorjamb.

Johnny rushed in then, ten, tall, and sturdy, with dark hair like

Jack's but Carol's own blue eyes. Following slowly and shyly was Lisa Walsh, six and in the first grade. Even though she had been with the Kentons for only a few weeks, Carol thought she noticed an improvement in the little girl's mood, a lessening of gloomy silence. Lisa was a member of the family now, even if she did not yet grasp the fact fully, and she certainly looked it. With her golden blonde hair and fair, radiant complexion, several people had already taken her to be Carol's natural daughter.

"Mom, let's go home," Johnny urged. "You ready to go yet?"

Although the Kenton house was within walking distance of the school, Carol had always made a habit of driving Johnny—and now Lisa too—back and forth. It was—well, it was *safer*. The Kentons were wealthy, and Jack was, increasingly, a public figure. You never could tell.

"I've got to stay a little while longer," Carol told the kids. "Sorry. Why don't you go down to the library and look at some magazines?"

"Oh, Mom, we were just there."

Lisa nodded a glum corroboration.

"Try the gym then. The coach should still be there. Why don't you show Lisa how to kick a soccer ball?"

"Sure," Johnny agreed, "that's a good idea." He was working hard to make Lisa feel at home. Carol was so proud of him. "Come on, Lisa," Johnny said, "I'll show you how to do an instep kick. That's real easy."

The children left for the gym, and there was Stella's head in the doorway again, her eyes big and round. "Ms. Dunphy and Mr. Semlac would like to have a moment."

"Thank you, Stella. Send them in. Then, if you've finished the state attendance forms, you might as well go home. I'll see you on Monday."

"Yes, they're finished. Thanks. And you have a nice weekend. Want me to stop by the gym and check on Johnny and Lisa?"

"Oh, you don't have to—"

"It'll only take a minute. I'd be glad to."

Stella moved away from the door, and Blanche Dunphy came into the office, followed by Anton Semlac. They didn't just walk in, they *stalked* in, possessors of powerful secrets as yet unknown to

Carol. Blanche, Carol's old friend from her early days of teaching at Royall Beach, had a full figure, rich brown hair cut short, and a strong lovely mouth that seemed to grow just a little bit harder each year. She had once wanted to be principal, but her lack of an advanced degree had counted against her. Now she was president of the RBTU, which carried considerable clout.

Semlac was thin in a strong, wiry way, and so dour he seemed to have no expression except a morose and concentrated watchfulness, punctuated randomly by a twitchy grimace that might, on another person, have been mistaken for a smile.

Blanche wore a smile and, as always, her lilac scent, the smile nervously and the scent heavily. But behind the slight quiver of her lips, Carol read a sense of vindication. Blanche had gotten what she'd wanted at the union meeting; they'd voted her way. And what was going to happen now could be labeled under the rubric "Confrontation with Principal." Semlac's attitude confirmed this impression; he regarded Carol sleepily.

"Sit down," Carol offered.

"Thanks," said Blanche, moving toward a chair.

"We'll stand," Semlac pronounced. Blanche changed her mind.

"This won't take long." Semlac grimaced, with that strange horizontal tightening of his mouth. "Go ahead, Ms. Dunphy."

"This is official business," Blanche began. "According to article ten, paragraphs seven through twelve of the current contract, we're informing you of a decision reached today by our union."

"Of course, you'll be receiving a copy in writing too," Semlac added. "We always do things exactly by the book."

"So do I," Carol offered.

"I'm *sure* you do," said Semlac, with infuriating piety. "It's gettng late. I 've got to get back to the city. Blanche, tell your leader what we'll do if she doesn't come out full and foursquare to raise salaries."

"We're going out on strike," Blanche said.

Although she ought to have expected it, Carol was a little alarmed. It would be the first teachers' strike Royall Beach had ever had. The residents of Royall Beach would not be too pleased to have the honor.

"Next fall, I assume."

"Hell, no," Semlac said, with relish. "We'll strike this place just before state *exam* week."

Now *that* was a stunner. Exam week, at the end of June, was the culmination of the school year. A strike then would jeopardize the legitimacy of the entire academic year. Final tests could not be administered. There was also a personal concern: Jack's fate. He was known throughout the state as a tax-reform leader. Some friends of Governor Higgins had approached him with talk of the gubernatorial race. He wanted to run, and the possibility seemed genuine, but Carol did not trust John Higgins. Moreover, a strike here at school, which Semlac could all too easily manipulate, would lead to disastrous media coverage. Exactly what Jack did not need. Exactly what Carol did not want.

"Think it over until Monday," Semlac was saying . . .

When, somewhere inside the school, a child screamed.

Before the three in the office had time to think or move, the scream came again.

Semlac was first out the door, followed by Carol and Blanche. For a moment, they stood out in the brightly lit corridor, trying to determine the source of the shrieks, which echoed down the halls of Royall Elementary. The building was modern, a sprawling one-story structure of steel and brick and glass.

"The gym!" cried Carol, and began racing down the corridor, kicking off her high heels for greater speed.

"Mrs. Kenton! Mrs. Kenton!" Stella was calling. From inside the gym. "Johnny! Lisa!"

Semlac was pounding along behind Carol, gaining, and together they reached the gym. Its big double doors were wide open; the highly waxed floor gleamed in afternoon light. Stella stood just inside the door. Johnny and Lisa were near the bleachers at the far end of the gym. Oh, thank God, they looked okay, except Lisa was crying hysterically . . .

"Mrs. Kenton—I mean, Dr. Kenton," Stella gasped, her right hand at her breast, "Lisa screamed. Just when I got here. It scared me half to death."

Blanche Dunphy came puffing up, red-faced and breathless.

"What happened?" she wanted to know.

But Carol, Semlac, and Stella were already trotting across the basketball floor toward the children.

Johnny had his arm around little Lisa, but his solicitousness wasn't doing much good. She was wailing, crying, and in her eyes was a look of terror.

"John, what happened?" Carol asked, bending to take Lisa into her arms.

The boy was startled too, and he fought to retain his composure. "I—I don't know. I kicked the ball over here . . ." The soccer ball was visible, wedged beneath a bleacher seat. ". . . Lisa ran to get it, and then she started screaming . . ."

"Might have seen something," Semlac suggested, looking around. "Hey, the exit door's open back there!"

"Not something, *someone.*" Carol thought she knew just who he had been.

"Johnny, did you see a man under the bleachers?"

"No, no Mom, I—"

But Lisa cried louder and nodded frantically. Anton Semlac ran for the exit door.

"Was the coach here?" Carol asked.

"No," Johnny said, "just us, I thought."

An intruder in the school! Carol realized, all too vividly, the dangerous ease with which a person might enter Royall Beach school, with its many doors, sliding glass panels, and a part-time security man who worked only after classes were over. Royall Beach was safe and serene. This was not South Philadelphia. Carol remembered, too, the sound of Vic Brand's footsteps on the tiled corridor. But wait! She had not heard *The Waltz of the Dead* this time. Maybe Lisa was imagining, or hallucinating . . . or *remembering* something from the night of her mother's death, something the doctors believed to be temporarily blocked from her conscious mind.

Semlac came back, shaking his head. "Nobody out there that I could see."

"Lisa," Carol said, holding the child tightly. "Lisa, this is very important. Try and calm down. Please. *Did* you see a man? Here in the gym?"

The little girl gasped and choked, tried to speak, failed, choked some more. "Yes," she managed finally, nodding.

"Who was it? Did you recognize the man?"

"Yes," she said, beginning again to wail and twist reflexively in Carol's arms, "it was my—it was my *daddy!*"

"What the hell is going on here?" Anton Semlac asked.

At Royall Beach High School in the fifties, his classmates had voted Stan Walsh "Most Likely to Succeed." It was hard to see how he could miss. Good-looking in a manner more cute than handsome, he was bright, glib, and according to an expression then current, he "could talk you right out of your pants." In Stan Walsh's case, conventional wisdom was correct. His wealthy father paid for two abortions and settled a paternity suit against Stan out of court in order to avoid the publicity of a trial. But Stan wasn't worried; he was destined for the top; his classmates had told him so.

Nobody paid much attention to the mean streak that appeared whenever something didn't go exactly the way Stan wanted it to. Anger in the face of obstacles was only natural, wasn't it, when one was so obviously marked for success? Take the time Biff Tugwell, the football player, asked Licia Allen for a date. Stan was "going" with Licia then. But he had slapped her face during a disagreement about which movie to see (she wanted *Gidget Goes Hawaiian*, and he preferred *I Was a Teenager from Outer Space*), and so to punish him she accepted a date with Biff. When the doorbell chimed at the Allen home that night, Licia ran to greet her new jock beau, and Biff was there, all right. Dressed in a bloody blanket a gang of guys had thrown over his head and body, prior to kicking and beating him senseless. He recovered, but it had been a moonless night, and he hadn't been able to identify his attackers. Well, two people can keep a secret as long as one of them is dead, and after a time it became known sub rosa that Stan Walsh had paid four or five high school hoods to "do a little job for him."

Stan was always talking about his "connections" and about the "big deals" he was going to make. After college, of course. Sturdily built, but not a big guy, he had spent most of his high school years lifting weights in the gym, not studying, but his father was a Yale alumnus and that "connection" got him into New Haven. For one semester. He either flunked out or didn't bother to try at all, and in later years it surprised some to see a Yale class ring on his finger, as well as to learn that Stan was also a member of the Harvard Club in New York.

Strange things happened when Stan Walsh was around. He was so good at being glib and charming, so smooth at talking up a storm, that it seemed he could rearrange the past, or at least his own past. "When I was up at Yale," he would say, "Bill Buckley and I—you know, William F. Buckley? The commentator? Well, he and I . . ."

And so on.

Stan didn't need a college degree anyway, because his father was sitting on top of a gold mine, an East Coast factory that produced an item for which the demand was inexhaustible, inner tubes for automobile tires.

Stan's father died not long after the major automobile manufacturers opted for the new tubeless tire, leaving Stan an aging, useless factory, a minimal amount of cash, and a lavish but heavily mortgaged home on a big piece of Royall Beach property overlooking Long Island Sound. "The estate," Stan called it. "I wouldn't part with one square inch of that land, not for a million bucks."

Master of appearances that he was, Stan Walsh showed no outward concern about his drastically reduced horizons, and over frequent and interminable business lunches at Adryan's, a local watering place, he fashioned a variety of schemes to recoup his staggering fortunes. He would market—on a national basis, of course—a revolutionary new kind of pizza: an ethnic pizza, taco-flavored for Puerto Ricans, sauerkraut-flavored for Germans, borscht-flavored for Russians, fried-chicken-flavored for blacks, haggis-flavored for people of Scottish extraction, etc. He had it all worked out. Couldn't get funding, though, and meanwhile his indebtedness mounted, but he counterattacked by buying on time a new Cadillac Eldorado with tubeless tires and inventing a revolutionary new clothes dryer that operated on a principle used in refrigerators. If Freon, a cold substance, can circulate in freezers and make things icy, then why not circulate something hot in coils, surround the clothes dryer with these hot coils, and thereby dry clothes? "I'll make the tumble dryer extinct," he declared, to the wondrous regard of the regulars at Adryan's Bar, where his tab was mounting. Stan actually borrowed from some of these eager, bewildered regulars, and had the local high school shop instructor make a prototype of the "Walsh No-Spin," but the test load of laundry burst into flames, and the project had to be abandoned.

"I needed a loss leader," Stan told his backers at the bar. "You always got to be thinking, get it? Now I write off the loss on my tax return. I suggest you fellows do the same."

Carol Jean Atwood met Stan Walsh just after she arrived in Royall Beach to teach school, and at the time Stan was working on a project to make a lot of money "going public" with a company that would revolutionize the garment industry by using inexpensive, imported fabrics.

"I think that's already been done," Carol offered, sipping her plastic glass of sticky Sangria at the school board's Welcome to Our New Teachers night. (Stan attended every function at which he could get free food and drink.)

Unexpectedly, because they had been talking with the superficial good humor required by the occasion, Carol saw a dark flash of anger in Stan's eyes, a momentary *Who-the-hell-are-you-and-what-do-you-know-about-it?*

He noted her disapproval and made amends by asking all about her. Learning that she was one of *the* Atwoods, Stan became absolutely gallant. He asked her out. She refused as politely as she could. The next day he phoned. She refused again, this time more definitely. When she saw him driving past her apartment in his Eldorado, time and again, Carol thought, *"Oh, my God, no. Not another wacko like Vic Brand."* Her antennae were supersensitive now; she didn't need to learn the same lesson twice. Stan's next request for a date was refused courteously, but not without some private trepidation. Carol need not have worried, though. Stan Walsh learned his lesson the third time. He decided that he was unlikely to succeed with Carol.

Royall Beach was a small place, and so Carol saw Stan around town from time to time. They said hi and exchanged opinions about the weather. His Eldorado had a dented fender now, and he wore the same gray suit a lot. Once, in a gloomy conversation at the A & P, he mentioned selling part of his peninsula property. That would make him a million, at last.

He was desperate for a million, too. Carol heard stories that Stan had invented an atomic-powered boat-train for Long Island commuters, rumors that he had founded a genetics lab to make family pets immortal, and tales that he had gone partners in a Success Unlimited Spa, where members sweated and listened to tapes of Norman Vincent Peale at the same time.

Less savory were the women's room stories. Weight lifting had made Stan a strong guy, and the girls he took to his big house in Royall Beach, with the glassed-in, heated pool out back, swore they would not go there again. "If he doesn't get his way," one explained, "you'd better be prepared to move fast. He slapped me once for no reason at all . . ."

Then Carol married Jack, moved into the city, had Johnny, and didn't see Stan Walsh for quite a while. But the ad in the *New York Times* real estate section brought them together again.

> 2½ wtfrnt acres, for bldng, rsdntl only, refined nghbrhd, must sell, will brgn, No. Shore.

"Looks like you and I can't get away from each other!" cried Stan, when Carol and Jack bought the Royall Beach peninsula property, choicest part of the Walsh estate. The new modernistic Kenton house, with all its elaborate electronic security devices, went up right next to Stan's home. Carol and Stan Walsh became neighbors.

Several years later, Stan married a voluptuous blonde who thought Stan had hung the moon and who herself—she let it be known—had been "Miss Lobster Festival" in Kennebunkport, Maine, some years earlier. Carol saw Valerie frequently, but she was too busy with her job and family to dine and dance at the Royall Beach Yacht Club, which the Walshes did regularly. Stan was riding high now, on money made selling his land to Jack and Carol, and Valerie told Carol that Stan was making a real killing, or that is, would be making a real killing soon with a couple of racehorses he had purchased.

Everything seemed to be going well for the Walshes, although there was a rumor that Stan had slugged Valerie one night at the club, reason unknown. When they had a baby, Lisa, it was the idea of parenthood that appealed more than the reality. Valerie hired a series of nurses who quit, complaining about being inadequately paid or not paid at all.

"I think Stan Walsh is in big financial trouble," Jack observed one evening at dinner. "He didn't buy racehorses. He bought pigs in a poke. The papers were forged. The so-called trainer he hired was in on it. It was all a scam, stabling charges, track rentals, everything. The horses ran, all right, but they ran as if they had terminal emphysema."

"Poor Stan."

"Poor Valerie. He knocked her down in the parking lot at the Royall Beach Yacht Club, the night of the Halloween Ball."

"What on earth . . . ?"

"There's a girl who hangs around the bar there. Vanessa. She took on three guys Halloween night, and one of them was Stan. Valerie found out."

"How do *you* know, hmmmm?"

"Look, I was home in bed that night with you. There's just a lot of talk about Stan, and none of it good."

There was more talk as the years went by. During summers, the trees and hedges prevented any view of the Walsh house, but in winter, when the leaves were gone, Carol occasionally caught a glimpse of Valerie and little Lisa coming or going in the old Eldorado, or of Stan coming or going in the Jaguar he'd bought after selling his two-and-a-half acres. When Lisa started first grade, just last September 1980, Valerie brought her into Carol's office at school. Valerie looked wan, and facial powder did not quite obscure a bruise on her cheekbone. Mrs. Boureg, the first-grade teacher, came for Lisa, and when the child had gone, Valerie burst into tears.

"Why don't you pay us?" she wailed. "How can you be so cruel, you with all that money? Stan's had to quit the yacht club because of you and Jack."

"Because of *us?*"

"Yes. He's desperate. That's why"—she touched her bruise—

"this. He's at the end of his rope, and he's taking it out on me."

"Valerie, as far as I know, we don't owe you anything."

The blonde woman knew her facts, though, and she shot Carol a withering glance. "The rent," she said simply.

"The rent?"

"Oh, come on. You live over there in our other house and don't pay the rent. Stan's thinking of having you evicted."

Stan had told his wife that he owned the Kenton house!

"The guy's sick," Jack said to Carol, when she told him. "There's not much we can do. Try and keep contacts at a minimum."

The year 1980 ended. Stan cracked up his Jaguar on New Year's Eve. He was in the North Shore Hospital for six weeks. Once in February and twice in March, Valerie called the police, and Chief Detzler, of the little Royall Beach force, drove out to the house to quell "family disturbances." Then in early April, just a little over a month ago, Stan disappeared.

"He just took off," Valerie explained to Carol, having called her over to the house to ask advice. Lisa had the flu, and Valerie wasn't sure what to do. Valerie had her right arm in a sling, and there was a cut on her forehead. "He just took off, when everything was starting to go so well for him."

"It was?"

"Yes. He invented an electronic game. Ecumenical Bingo. Catholic churches all over the country will snap it up. He'll make a million."

"You poor thing," said Carol to little Lisa, lying dazed and feverish in her bed. The girl wasn't getting much of a start in life. Mother a bubblehead and father a charlatan, or worse.

The crisis came to a head one night in mid-April. Carol and Jack—and Johnny too—awoke to the sound of shattering glass, screaming. Roar of engine. Shriek of tires.

"That came from the Walshes'," Jack decided. "I'm going over. Carol, call Chief Detzler right away. Just to be safe."

"I'm coming with you."

"Call first. Come over after."

He was out of the house, running down the long drive, between the budding lilac hedges. Carol called the police, told them something had happened at the Walsh place, grabbed Johnny's hand—she couldn't leave him alone in the house, no matter how well protected it was—and hurried over to the Walshes'. She and Johnny got there just as the police roared up, sirens wailing. Jack was coming down the front steps with Lisa in his arms. She looked perfectly calm, and Carol breathed a sigh of relief. Everything was all right. But then why did Jack look so stricken? Carol took a closer look at Lisa in the dim glow given by the light at the front door. The girl's eyes were far away; she stared trancelike into an eerie middle distance.

"Jack, what's wrong with her?" cried Carol.

He shook his head, sad, angry, shaken too. "I'd hate to tell you what I think she saw," he said. "And if she saw all of it, well . . ."

Carol went into the house before the police could stop her. She wished they had. The big master bedroom at the back of the house was a chaos of broken lamps, shattered mirrors, and overturned furniture. The French doors open onto the balcony were broken too, and so was the glass roof below that covered the swimming pool.

In the swimming pool, drifting near the bottom, blonde hair rising like a brilliant sea plant, hands moving in strange languid grace, was the nude body of Valerie Walsh.

Stan was the prime suspect, and an all-points went out immediately, authorizing his arrest.

Stan was the prime suspect, but whether he was his wife's real killer or not was a secret locked in Lisa Walsh's mind.

No relatives of Stan or Valerie came forward. Carol told Jack what she wanted to do. He thought it over for a couple of days, saw what it meant to her—she being unable to have another child—and agreed. They became Lisa's foster parents.

Now, in the gym, with Semlac, Blanche Dunphy, Stella, and Johnny looking on, Carol did all a mother could do to calm her new daughter. Had Stan Walsh come back to kill his daughter, sole witness to her mother's murder?

It seemed likely.

Yet something troubled Carol about that conclusion, and in a moment she knew what it was. *The Waltz of the Dead.* She hadn't heard a note of it. Did that mean she was just as inexplicably free of the curse of premonition as she had once been inexplicably burdened with it? Or did it mean Stan Walsh had intended his daughter no harm?

Maybe Stan hadn't killed Valerie.

"Stella, call Chief Detzler," she said to the secretary. "Tell him Mr. Walsh is in the area."

Lisa cried louder.

"It's all right, honey. It's all right. We'll try to help your daddy. We really will."

3

He came at Carol out of the sun. One moment he was not there, then he was, the outline of his body against the sun. Then he had turned and was already striding away from her, up the beach and up the steep, narrow concrete driveway that led to the parking lot at Gurney's Inn. He appeared and departed so quietly, and suddenly, that for a long moment Carol was unaware that he had been there at all, or that he had handed something to her. The man climbed the driveway quickly, a dark silhouette against the sun, soon lost in the shadow of overhanging trees. Then he was gone.

In Carol's hand, when she glanced down, was a sprig of lilac in full bloom, sweet-scented, violet-pink.

Carol was standing high up on the beach, near the lower tier of Gurney's comfortable, rustic units. She could see Lisa and Johnny searching for shells down along the Atlantic shore. Jack had been called to the phone, up at the inn, just as they'd finished Sunday brunch. Governor Higgins was on the line.

She looked from the flowers in her hand up to the parking lot, in which a few cars were backing and turning. Beyond Gurney's, other cars moved slowly along Montauk Highway, their occupants out for a Mother's Day drive. Later, Carol would struggle desperately to recall the makes and models of those cars. But, at that lost moment on the beach, the rational part of her mind was as mystified by the lilac-bearing stranger as her senses were drugged by the fragrance of the flowers.

Down within the delicate core of her being, Carol felt a tremor of fear, felt it the more because nothing alarming had happened. The weekend had been great, and for the first time in a long time she and Jack had had a chance to talk without the interruption of calls or messages, without one or the other of them having to rush away to some meeting or appointment. Jack was happy, keyed-up, psychologically "high," and ready to go after the gubernatorial nomination. Kenton Diversified was thriving; the Independent Citizens Committee had increased its influence over the years; political office seemed the next logical step.

"What can happen?" he asked.

"I don't trust John Higgins," Carol replied. "He's too smooth by half. If things don't work out just so, it'll be you, not him, with egg on your face."

"I doubt that, but even so, so what? This is a great opportunity. I'd kick myself all the way up the Hudson River if I didn't take it."

"Oh, Jack, I know. I'm sorry. It's just that . . ."

"Just that what?"

"Well, I guess a lot of my reaction to your running for office is personal. Sometimes—sometimes I feel that I'm just spinning my own wheels."

"That doesn't sound like you. You were happy when you won your doctorate and when they made you principal. Want to do something else? Be a professor? A consultant? Write books? Just go ahead."

"It's not that. I mean, I feel responsible for the school, but I miss teaching. I think I got lost somewhere."

"You don't look lost to me," he said, putting his arms around her. "You're right here."

Carol smiled. The children were asleep. Faint strains from the Saturday night dance band drifted down from the inn to their beachfront unit. Outside the dark Atlantic rolled again and again and again upon the shores of night. "It's not that I can't deal with dilettantes like Mrs. Crispus on the school board, or even thugs like Anton Semlac. It's just that I don't think I want to."

"Don't then," he replied, his voice husky with tenderness and want, "deal with me."

And so she did, and he with her, and it had been a glorious night. All morning Carol had luxuriated in the glow of well-being, the residual aura of their lovemaking. Indeed, she'd felt the glow until that stranger had handed her the lilacs.

Jack came down the narrow driveway now. "Governor Higgins wants me to fly up and see him in Albany tomorrow, and—"

He looked at her, saw something in her expression. "Something wrong?" he asked sharply. His glance fell to the sprig of blossoms, and his head tilted slightly to the side, that unconscious reaction he had when struck by something unexpected.

"I—I don't know," Carol replied, surprised at the uncharacteristic quiver in her voice. "A man just walked up and handed me these flowers."

Jack looked helpfully up and down the vast white sweep of beach, still pristine and virtually unmarred here on Long Island's East End. The day was sunny, if not yet warm in mid-May, and the people out taking the air could readily be counted on a couple of hands.

"He's not out here," Carol said. "I saw him go up the driveway."

"He just handed you the lilacs and walked away."

Carol nodded.

"What did he look like?"

"I can't say. The sun was in my eyes. It all happened so quickly. I was just standing here, watching the kids. And then this man put some flowers in my hand, didn't say a word."

"Stan Walsh?" Jack suggested immediately. If, as Lisa had said, her father had really been in the school, neither the Royall Beach nor the Nassau County police had been able to locate him. He was "At Large"; he was "Wanted."

Carol shook her head. "No. Stan's stockier, more solid. I'd have known."

Jack shrugged. "So it was a random act. Guy probably just liked your looks. Good judgment on his part, too, if you ask me."

And the lilacs were forgotten, crushed between Jack and Carol, as they embraced on the cold, bright beach.

"You were saying about Albany?" Carol asked, as they walked hand in hand down to the shining shore.

"Yes. Higgins said he talked to Charlie Kiefer Friday afternoon. Charlie has some ambitions toward candidacy himself. He seemed a little miffed to learn that I'm Higgins's first choice . . ."

"Charlie Kiefer does not get 'a little miffed.' He gets really steamed."

"Well, that's what the phone call was about. Charlie's taken it into his mind to give me a full field inspection, check everything from my tonsillectomy at two right up to what I had for brunch today. I'm supposed to give Charlie a call when we get home tonight, stroke him a little, and then the three of us, Charlie, the governor, and myself, will meet in Albany tomorrow. Higgins wants to get his measure of control on Charlie's so-called investigation . . ."

"Higgins wants to get his measure of control on just about everything, if you ask me."

"Oh, hell, Carol. What can happen?"

"I'm sorry. It's terrific. It really is. I wonder if I'll like Albany, though."

"I could get beat," he laughed.

"Come on. You've never been beaten in your life."

Not since that time with Buster Pauley and Bernie Lipschitz in the park, he thought. *Not since Bennington and Karyn Bari.*

"Dad! Mom!" cried Johnny, down by the water. "Come over here quick and look at these. A whole bunch of really neat shells."

He was digging happily, furiously. But Lisa just hung back, watching glumly. One weekend, no matter how tranquil, hadn't helped her much. One couldn't expect that it would. But what a burden the little girl carried with her. Did Lisa, at six, know how important the knowledge she had locked in her mind could be—the identity of her mother's murderer?

"Dad! Mom! Hurry up," Johnny called again.

Jack released Carol's hand, and trotted on ahead, over to the children. Carol followed, burying her hands deeply in coat pockets. A blast of icy air, too cold for May, swept across the wide Long Island beach. Far up on the sand, where Carol had dropped them, the crushed petals of the lilac trembled in the wind, and the bright, ruined sprig skidded away into the lonesome, rolling dunes.

The stalker did not think of himself as the kind of man who would intentionally harm another, but he had been so severely and cruelly hurt that he now had difficulty remembering how it felt to be the gentle, considerate individual he'd always tried to be. He knew he wanted to hurt the Kentons, and he knew why. So he was following them, watching them, stalking them. He had not imagined how easy it would be, or how deftly he would be able to improvise.

The stalker had not intended to hand the lilacs directly to Carol. His plan had been to slip them inside Jack Kenton's white Lincoln while the family was at brunch and then to wait nearby to see what their reaction would be when they found the flowers. The stalker hoped to see pain, the pain of memory. *Then I'll be satisfied*, he told himself. *Then I'll leave them alone.*

But the Kentons had not gone from the dining room to their car. Jack had been called to the phone. Carol and the children had gone out on the beach, and when the kids went down toward the water, she stood alone in the sun, and the stalker stood nearby, the sorrowful lilacs in his white-knuckled hand.

He had stepped over and given them to her. The startled expression on her lovely face! She was lovely, too; he had not realized how much so.

And the stalker was almost certain she hadn't seen his face clearly. Because of the sun.

If I were a truly violent man, he told himself, *she would be dead now. They might all be dead now. But I am not really violent.*

He was parked now off to the side of Montauk Highway, a short distance east of the driveway that led to Gurney's Inn. This was as far as he'd been able to drive before the trembling started. He was shaking all over. He waited for a break in traffic, wheeled into an illegal U-turn and stopped the car, facing west, the direction he would have to drive in order to go home. If he could only stop trembling.

If you're dead, you don't hurt, he thought. But he had passed that stage. At first, just after he'd suffered the terrible blow—he thought of it in those terms, "a terrible blow"—the stalker had thought seriously of killing himself. But he could not bear the idea of people thinking that he had been a coward, and gradually the hurt had begun to transform itself, a transmutation within his psyche akin to the metastasis of black cancer, so that now a portion of the pain had turned into hatred, and he was stronger. If anyone died, it would not be stalker.

But I am not a violent man, he thought. *If only the Kentons remember and suffer, I will be satisfied. I don't want more than that.*

Then he realized that, by handing Carol Kenton the lilacs

personally, he had had to turn away before he could study her reaction. Nor had he been able to see Jack Kenton's reaction to the flowers, and that was the most important thing of all.

But when Jack sees the lilacs, surely he'll know what they mean, won't he? the stalker asked himself, trying to make things right in his mind. *His memory and conscience can't help but know.*

His fingers, though he tried to tighten them around the steering wheel, reminded him of someone with palsy. It reminded him, too, of the way he had shaken and shivered upon learning that his wife, his beautiful, tender wife, was dead. If only the car hadn't crashed. If only she had not taken their child, their son, along into death with her. If only. The stalker had always wanted a child, especially a son—Jack Kenton had a son—but now his wife was dead, and the stalker's world along with it.

The stalker's wife and child were dead, but Jack and Carol Kenton lived, and they had Johnny, a son, and now Lisa Walsh too, a daughter. *They* had family. *They* had everything. *They* could celebrate Mother's Day, but not the stalker, undone by lilacs and memories, by the deceit of time, by death itself. Hot tears of rage and betrayal welled up and stung his eyes, but he fought them back, and reached for the ignition, didn't find it. A borrowed car: nothing was where it should be. He was used to his old one, which had been wrecked in the crash. Then he looked, found the key, and turned it. The engine growled into life. He glanced up into the rearview mirror, ready to pull out onto Montauk Highway and head back toward New York.

"Oh, my God, no—"

The stalker saw his own eyes, wide and terrified, staring out at him from the rearview mirror. And, pulling up behind his car, he saw the two-toned Suffolk County patrol car, its lights flashing.

What had he done? The illegal U-turn? That was five minutes ago, or more. The patrolman couldn't have seen it. Or had Carol Kenton recognized him, in spite of the sun in her eyes. But how could *that* be?

"How could they have called the police so fast . . . ?" he said aloud.

The policeman, just a young kid, was already climbing out of his cruiser. The stalker's first impulse was to jam his car into gear and scream the hell away, but the obvious lunacy of such a response sobered him. He would have to sit there and handle the situation, and at least he could draw upon his experience to do it. Besides, even if the Kentons had called a cop, what had the stalker done, really? Nothing, right? Just handed some flowers to a pretty woman. Nothing wrong with that, if the meaning of the flowers was unknown.

The officer was approaching now, coming up on the driver's side. The stalker did not reach into his pocket for his driver's license. To do so abruptly, without being asked, might suggest that tiny subliminal flicker of unease which good cops notice as readily as they notice the steel lump of weapon where nothing but a ballpoint pen should be. Also on stalker's side, he was dressed professionally in suit and tie. Respectability. It was important. One was generally perceived to be what one appeared to be—and the stalker *had* been what he appeared to be until the great catastrophe had hurt him so . . .

"Trouble, sir?" asked the patrolman, glancing around inside the car the way he was trained to do. Body in the backseat? Firearms on the floor? Open booze bottles?

"Oh—what . . . ?" The stalker feigned surprise, as if he hadn't already seen the cop drive up. "Oh, I'm sorry, officer. You startled me." He smiled. He had learned to use his smile professionally. "Is something wrong?" *No, don't ask questions. Don't let him do the talking.* "I just stopped here for a moment to admire the view of the ocean."

And then stalker did something he hadn't intended, but which—he gambled—would disarm the policeman. Thrusting his hand out the window toward the faintly suspicious young officer, he gave his true name and real address. Veracity rang in his voice. "Just out for a Sunday drive," he added cheerfully, and the startled trooper, unaccustomed to such congenial receptions from motorists, took his hand and shook it. Firm grip. That was important, too.

"Didn't I pull far enough to the side?" the stalker asked.

"Oh, sure," said the cop, reacting warmly to such easy acceptance of himself as a member of the human race. "I just thought your car might have stalled, or something."

"Well, I certainly appreciate your concern. And I'll be moving along now. If that's okay?"

"Sure," agreed the officer. He remembered the address the motorist had given him. "You don't have too far to drive, if you're heading home. But traffic's moderate-to-heavy today." He enjoyed using technical terms like "moderate-to-heavy" and "condition red" and "alleged."

The patrolman stepped away from the car. The stalker put his car into gear, looked back carefully, and pulled slowly out onto the roadway. He wanted to say something more to the cop, something warm and friendly, so, remembering the day, he called out "Happy Mother's Day" with a slight wave and a steady smile.

"Jesus!" groaned Officer Bruce Toole, recent graduate of the Suffolk County Police Academy, as he climbed back into the patrol car he liked so much. Bruce was disgusted with himself. He'd forgotten all about Mother's Day. Lucky that man had reminded him. Bruce made a mental note of the harmless roadside encounter, radioed the car's make, Chevrolet, and license number, New York 413 QFH, back to precinct, and remembered that there was a florist's shop in Montauk Village.

The stalker was just about to drive past the entrance to Gurney's when Jack Kenton's big white Lincoln pulled out in front of him. There was no danger of a collision, but it seemed to the stalker that Jack Kenton had intruded upon the roadway. He got a good look at Kenton, his beautiful wife, and the two kids in the backseat. All of them looked as cool and unconcerned as anything!

Stalker's heart fell, and he knew that he had accomplished nothing. His puny little branch of lilacs, which signified everything to him, anguish and heartbreak and disaster, had meant nothing at all to the Kentons. They'd probably dismissed the whole incident as some odd gesture of chance or circumstance, some random quirk of a mooning loony!

Then another thought came to the stalker. Jack Kenton moved freely, and he did not have to worry about anything. Money made that possible.

The stalker thought it over. There *was* one way he could get a lot of money, but it would be a very risky job, and if he was found out, he might lose everything.

What am I thinking about? he admonished himself. *I've lost everything already.*

Because of Kenton!

He felt sick, impotent. He had been a timid, little pip-squeak with a handful of flowers, like some half-cracked mooncalf of a teenager on his girl friend's front steps. Kenton was where he was in life because he'd taken risks, chanced things, *seized* the day!

Stalker might do that too, but did he have the nerve, the inherent hard-eyed gut-taut impulse of will?

I do, he told himself.

4

The Kentons arrived home at dusk. Jack turned up the drive, which ran toward the house between lilac hedges. Their two-and-a-half-acre wedge of land was surrounded by foliage, except on the beach side, which faced King's Point across Manhasset Bay.

Jack drove into the yard, and swung the car toward the side of the house. He pushed a button on the dashboard, engaging an electronic mechanism, and a panel on the side of the house slid upward. Rows of fluorescents came on in the garage, and Jack drove in. He pushed the button again. The wall slid down behind them, and locked into place.

Jack had commissioned a house as safe as human ingenuity and modern electronics could make it.

They got out of the car, and Jack opened the trunk, removing their luggage. At the kitchen door, Johnny addressed a voice-code device, and the lock clicked open. Besides the sliding wall that led into the garage, the house had two doors: this one from the garage, leading into the kitchen, and the front door on the beachward side, that opened into a vast living room. Both doors were activated by voice coders, programmed for Jack, Carol, Johnny, and Mrs. Wenthistle. She had been their housekeeper since Johnny's birth, but she was now back in England for several months, visiting relatives in Yorkshire. Carol had decided to manage without Mrs. Wenthistle, rather than to engage a new servant at the same time that Lisa was joining the family. Lisa's voice had not yet been programmed into the mechanism. Having that done was on Carol's "Things to Do" list.

Only those whose voices had been programmed could legitimately enter the house. Except those who were invited inside.

Carol flicked several switches on a master control panel in the kitchen, and the house exploded in light. She also checked the burglar alarm, which was tied into the headquarters of local Police

Chief Darby Detzler. Detzler boasted that he and his men could reach any house in Royall Beach within two minutes of an alarm. But the red light on the panel was off; the alarm had not been tripped while the Kentons were away.

The children went into the television room; Jack carried luggage upstairs, and Carol slid sirloin tip and wild rice casseroles into the oven. They were her most succulent creation, and she had a supply in the freezer. She was setting the dining room table when Jack, who had gone into his study, called to her.

"What is it?" she asked.

He was sitting behind his desk, yellow legal pad before him, and a puzzled look on his face.

"I was playing back the phone recorder, to see if anyone called while we were gone. Got some funny ones."

He flicked the rewind button, and a voice announced:

"Mr. Kenton, this is Ed Peters, your agent at Stuyvesant Mutual. Sorry not to catch you in, but . . ."

Jack pressed the rewind some more, and the machine whirred.

"What's so odd about that?" asked Carol. She knew Ed Peters. He'd been their agent for years.

"No, not that," answered Jack. "He just wants to update our coverage to include Lisa. I'll do it this week. Stan didn't have insurance, either, among other things. No, here's one . . ."

First there was a raspy sound, then a voice—ancient, defiant, and feminine. "Jack Kenton? You listenin' to me? This here's Gertie Kiefer, and I want to tell you a thing or two . . ."

Then another voice in the background: "Oh, Mrs. Kiefer, no . . ."

"Ma! Don't do it . . ."

Then the click of the receiver and silence.

"*What* was *that?*" Carol asked.

"That was Charlie Kiefer's mother."

"She didn't sound too happy."

"No, and I've got to call Charlie tonight. But listen to *this* one."

He adjusted the instrument once more. Ring of phone, followed by a long, long listening silence, then something like a gust of wind against dry branches. The strange sound seemed unhuman at first, eerie and unsettling, but as it continued, Carol realized what it was. A man, weeping.

The machine clicked, and the weeping ceased.

Carol and Jack looked at each other. Carol felt something that was not quite fear, but rather the anticipation of fear. Whoever it had been on the phone, his tears had been real, desolate, and desperate. She thought immediately of the man on the beach.

Perhaps Jack did, too. "Let me give Charlie Kiefer a quick call," he said slowly, dialing. "Maybe Charlie is more upset about this gubernatorial thing than I thought, but, Jesus, he's not one to bawl over the phone . . ."

He flipped a switch so that Carol could hear the conversation. The phone rang and was answered by a young male voice, not by Charlie or his fabled ma.

"This is Jack Kenton. Mr. Kiefer in?"

"No, I'm sorry, Mr. Kenton. He left this morning . . ."

That was odd. Charlie hadn't spent Mother's Day with the number one favorite person in his life?

". . . I'm Stu Inkspell, Mrs. Kiefer's nurse, and . . ."

In the background now, Carol and Jack could hear the *thunk . . . thunk . . . thunk* of the steel walker as Gertie Kiefer approached the phone.

"Stu, you gimme that phone!"

"Now, Mrs. Kiefer, please—"

"You gimme that there phone right now, young man . . . Jack Kenton? That you?"

Jack smiled. It was Charlie's ma all right. "Why, hello there, Mrs. Kiefer. I hope you had a nice Mother's Day, and I just wanted—"

"Shut up!" the old lady shrilled. "You come calling like this! You! Why, you ruined it for my boy!"

"Come on now, Mrs. Kiefer," Stu Inkspell was pleading, trying to calm the woman, who wasn't having any of it.

"How could you do this to Charlie? How could you do this to my boy?"

Then, apparently, the male nurse got hold of the phone again.

"Sorry about that, Mr. Kenton. Look, I'll have to hang up. I don't want her throwing her walker at me. You might try Mr. Kiefer at his apartment in the city."

Jack said he would and hung up.

"I think Charlie's mother wants him to be governor," observed Carol dryly.

Jack shook his head. Was it possible that the weeping man *had* been Charlie Kiefer? No, couldn't be. Charlie was emotional as hell, but he was also tough. If you dealt him dirt, under-the-table stuff, you could be certain to get it back. In spades. Jack remembered something about the time that gangster Guapino Campa had been killed in Charlie's office, during the days Charlie was making his money in the Garment District. But that had been accidental, hadn't it? If Charlie wanted to be mad at anybody, he should be mad at John Higgins!

"Well, let's have some dinner," Carol suggested, feeling a vague distress that did not lessen at all when Lisa wouldn't eat a thing.

"I'm afraid she's going to get sick," Carol worried later, as she and Jack prepared for bed. "Maybe when she gets a little better acquainted at school . . ."

"CiJi, you know that's not the problem. The problem is that she's blocking the memory of the night Valerie was killed."

"What'll we do when she does remember?"

"Hope one of us is around. Hope Stan Walsh isn't."

"Jack, do you really think . . . ?"

"Yes. Frankly, I think it was Stan on the beach this afternoon, and we're pretty damn sure it was Stan at school last Friday. He can get in and out of this town. He grew up here, remember? He knows every lane, every bush. He knows Royall Beach a lot better than some of these cops, with the exception of Chief Detzler, who's too old to move fast anyway. *Are* you coming to bed?"

Carol slipped out of her dress and gave him a sultry look. "Impatient, are we?"

She hung her dress in the closet, took off her slip, and wiggled out of her panties, beginning to feel excited. But some things on her mind had to be settled before she let her body enjoy itself.

"Jack," she said, sliding into bed beside him, "no, not yet. I just thought of something. You said Charlie Kiefer is going to run a check on your past?"

He put his arms around her and drew her very close.

"I forget. Did I say that?"

"Jack, this is serious. Hey. Stop that . . . ummmm, stop, no *fair*. Listen, I have something to—"

"I'm not listening."

"—just a *minute!*"

"Oh, you poor thing. I didn't know it was your first time. I'll be gentle, I'll—"

"Jack! Just a minute. This is important. *Is* there anything in your past that could be considered really dangerous?"

Jack raised himself up onto an elbow, studying her.

"Carol, I don't think I'd lose money betting that you just thought of something that might be," he said.

"That . . . singer. What was her name?"

"I know her name. What about her?"

They never spoke of Karyn Bari. Jack did not speak about her because she was a part of his past that hurt. Why dwell on disaster? Carol did not speak of her because she wanted Karyn Bari consigned forever *to* the past.

"I've been thinking of her husband."

"Bennington?"

"Hasn't he always been a major financial contributor to the Republican party?"

"Aren't most big businessmen?"

"Jack, I know this might sound a little weird. Maybe even paranoid. But Bennington's reputation is terrible. If you do get the nomination and run, don't you think he'll try to mess it up for you? For spite, if nothing else? You and . . . his current wife were once . . ." She didn't finish.

"Honey, they've been in Venezuela for years now. The extent of Bennington's political participation has been to write checks. I really don't think there's anything to worry about on that score."

"Did you reach Charlie Kiefer at his apartment tonight?"

"No. I tried several times. No answer. What's the connection to Bennington?"

"None. That I know of. But I was also thinking about that strange call from Charlie's mother."

"Why don't you just stop worrying about all these things?" He took her into his arms again. "For Gertie Kiefer, that was a standard call. Charlie and his mother are a legendary team. Everybody knows them like they know Gaston and Alphonse, Laurel and Hardy, Cheech and Chong . . ."

He was right. At this moment, he was very right. Carol let herself forget about the other things, and pressed against him. ". . . like Jack and Carol Jean?" she sighed.

"Exactly. A legendary team like Jack and Carol Jean."

But they were more than a team. They were lovers, friends, allies, everything. They knew the extent of their luck, guarded it, cherished it. "You're the best thing that ever happened to me," he told her, caressing her body which he had learned so well, "the very best."

"And you to me," she replied, feeling the glow of need build in her, holding back, holding him back too, to make it be the sweeter, last the more. "We'll have to be good to keep it."

"If anything were to happen to you," he told her as she opened to him, and he came upon her, "I think it would be all over for me."

"Nothing will happen," she said; "nothing will . . ."

Except the love then, wordless and enchanting, feeding the hunger and teasing the hunger and holding the hunger at bay. Their years together had enhanced the tenderness of intimacy, the keenness of sensation. She knew him, and he knew her, from first lingering touch to breathless final gasp and everything in between. They could make time stop, if they wanted, and make it rush, and make it climb as high as they wanted whenever they wanted, and make it sing to them if they so chose. And they could be joined with it, against all the world and everything, wreathed in delicious wonder, shot through with ecstasy and splendor, charmed and fine and safe.

"Darling, darling," she was saying, cradling his head, her fingers brushing aside the sweet perspiration on Jack's forehead, both of them riding the soft afterglow, when the phone on the night table rang, an intrusion into heaven like a doorbell in a dream.

"Damn," Jack murmured, fumbling for the receiver. "Hello?"

He listened, and Carol heard too the pathetic croaking, the desperate weeping on the other end of the line.

"Calm down now," Jack said, in a quiet voice. "Calm down. Who are you? What's the matter? You called before, didn't you? What can I help you with?"

Then he listened, and Carol heard the caller gulp and cough and try to recover. Finally, a few quick words were spoken—words Carol didn't catch—and the caller slammed down his phone. Jack waited a moment more, listening, then hung up too.

"Who was it?" she asked, pulling the sheet around her shoulders and breasts, an unconscious, protective gesture. "What did he say?"

"He said," Jack answered, "'You've got my daughter, you bastard, and you're all going to pay for that.'"

"Stan Walsh?"

"Stan Walsh."

"Where was he calling from?"

"He didn't say. But I doubt if he's too far away."

"'*You're all going to pay,*'" Carol said, repeating the words. "Do you think that means Lisa too?"

"I don't think it would be safe to assume otherwise."

"But who could hurt his own child?"

"Someone who knew his own child could prove he was a murderer. You wait here."

"Where are you going?" Carol asked, as Jack got out of bed and pulled on his robe.

"To double-check the doors and turn on the outside floodlights."

Later, with Jack asleep beside her, Carol tossed and turned. She was haunted by a dim hypothesis. What if Stan had not killed Valerie, but was simply strung out at the end of his psychological rope, unable to deal with his life? If so, wouldn't his actions seem bizarre, no matter how well intended? Wouldn't it seem to Stan that she and Jack had robbed him of Lisa? Maybe Stan was no threat.

Maybe that was why Carol had not heard *The Waltz of the Dead* at school.

The thought drifted away. A wavering image of the man on the beach took its place.

A random act.

One in a million: Vic Brand.

Two in a million: Cleophus Watts.

Three in a million: Stan?

Four: The man on the beach, with the lilacs?

Stop it, she told herself. *This could go on and on.*

Because there is always someone.

5

Buster Pauley, ex-cop and current unemployable, parked the fucking car next to a fucking fire hydrant. No sweat, this time of day, and wasn't even his car. He had borrowed the clunker for free, and it was no deal even at that price. Then he slouched on into Mel and Irma's Tavern and sailed his hat onto a hook next to the cigarette machine. He had to wait a whole fucking minute while old Mel ejected some dim-witted son of a bitch who didn't know he had his ass on Buster's favorite stool, where he could see the ball game on the TV real good. Shee-it. Already the fifth inning in the second game of a doubleheader. No chance to relax all day. Buster had had to do that job for Charlie Kiefer. He stared at the tube. The Mets were getting their ass whipped five-to-two up at Shea Stadium there, and Buster might have gone to see them in person if he hadn'ta had to work.

"Hey, nice suit you got on there," grunted Mel, coming over with a bottle and a shot glass. "It don't match the expression on your face, though."

"Shee-it," said Buster. Now on the TV that new kid just up from the minors, the one they'd given about ten million bucks to be the great white hope, hell, the green punk just hit into a triple play! How many triple plays a year? Four? Five? Buster figured he could of done just as good as the rookie with one eye closed even.

He took a healthy jolt of the booze, shuddered, knocked back the rest, and put the glass down again. Mel poured with one hand and drew a beer with the other.

"So you're working again?" Mel asked hopefully.

"You might say that," said Buster, sliding off the question. "Hey, I heard a good one," he said. "Polack comes into a bar, says, 'Gimme a fifteen.' 'Fifteen?' bartender says, 'What the hell is that?'

'Geez, are you dumb,' Polack says. 'It's a seven-and-seven.'"

"Haha," said Mel. "I'm Polish. Hey, I heard a good one about ex-cops . . ."

"Shove it, hey? I had a tough day."

Mel backed away. "C'mon Buster? What's eatin' you? I didn't mean nothin'. Hell, you're a regular. You an' me go back. Here"—he slid the beer across the tobacco-burned bar—"this one's on me."

Buster nodded, poured down about half of the second double shot, and took a gulp of the beer. He started to feel more normal. He finished the rest of the booze.

"Okay, hit me again here. Oh did—oh shee-it! God double damn! Did you see *that?*"

The first Cincinnati shithead at bat in the top of the sixth, that catcher they had there, had slammed a home run. *Six* to fucking two now. A glimmer of a thought came to Buster. Why was he always rooting for losers? Naa, naa. That wasn't it. That wasn't it at all. The fucking Yankees were from the Bronx, and Buster was from Queens like the Mets, and once you were from Queens there, it was sort of like in the blood.

How come not for Kenton then? How come he got out in the world and made it big?

The insight hit him like a jolt of bad booze, unbidden and unpleasant.

"You okay?" asked Mel.

"Sure," said Buster. But he wasn't, not really. It seemed like life was getting away from him, if it hadn't left a long time ago. Seemed like just a little while ago he was walking tall around the neighborhood; people would say, "Hey, there goes Buster Pauley; he's a real pisser, man," and he was putting it to Bernice every chance he got and going to cop school. Now he was split from Bernice, the bitch, and she was after him for dough, and the cops had thrown his ass out. Sheee-it. Guys like Kenton had all the luck. That's all it was, really. Just luck. Anybody could see that.

Jack Kenton was on Buster's mind again, after all those years, because Charlie Kiefer had called Friday night. Had had a little job for Buster. Well, he'd taken the job. Had had to, from Charlie. And had done it professionally, just like always, just like the old days. Sheee-it, he didn't want to think about the old days. He'd have himself a few more belts here, get him a buzz on, go home, and sleep.

So he was just watching the game there and slipping easy now and starting to relax when a guy came in the door wearing a uniform jacket and a fancy billed hat. "Mr. Pauley here?" the guy called, as heads turned to look.

"I'm Buster Pauley," Buster said, wondering what the fuck now to add to a perfect day.

"Mr. Kiefer would like to speak to you outside, sir."

Sir! Not bad. Buster dumped down some bills on the bar, grabbed his hat from the hook, and barreled out of there with the chauffeur bringing up the rear.

Inside the Rolls, it was real nice. Charlie was huffing the cigar, just like usual, but they put some special kind of exhausts in a Rolls that drew the smoke out so you didn't even notice it. Buster appreciated the mechanism, not that cigars bothered him but because he was pretty handy himself. Charlie motioned the chauffeur to stay outside.

"Did you do it?" Charlie grunted, not looking at Buster.

"Yeah. It's taken care of."

"Any reaction?"

"Not that I could really tell. Not yet, anyway."

"Anybody see you?"

"Well, I . . ." Buster had been prepared to lie, but it was better to let Charlie know just what the situation was, so he didn't overreach himself in this. They had both overreached themselves that time with Guapino Campa. Too bad it was Buster who had had to pay the price. Well, Charlie had stuck with him through it all, right up till now, so Buster told the truth. "A cop did see me," he admitted, "but he didn't seem to think nothing about it. And I had a borrowed car, so even if they trace, it'll slow them down . . ."

"How close did he see you?"

"Eyeball to eyeball, almost."

"And you think it's okay?"

Buster made his observation as a professional. "I'd put money on it," he said.

"Well, you should know. You were a cop. Birds of a feather, and all that . . ."

Charlie sat there puffing and thinking. The chauffeur was scratching his ass out on Queens Boulevard.

"What do you want me to do now?" Buster asked, to break the silence.

"Well, you'll have to go back, of course. I need a reaction—almost any kind of a definite reaction—by tomorrow afternoon. I got to meet the gov and Kenton up in Albany."

"Okay, I figured I'd have to go back anyway. Soon's as good as late."

"Okay. Go again. I'll call you tomorrow, about noon, at your place."

"Gotcha. I'll be there."

"You seem a little low, if you don't mind my saying so."

"Oh, that goddam Bernice."

"Say, how you makin' it?"

"You never have enough, but . . . okay, I guess."

Without a word, Charlie Kiefer pulled out a fat roll and peeled off a number of pretty hefty bills. He shoved them into Buster's not exactly unhappy hand and motioned the chauffeur back into the Rolls. Buster got out, and the big limo pulled away. Charlie did not wave, nor did Buster. *What the hell,* Buster thought, heading into Mel and Irma's again, doing a crazy thing like this to Jack Kenton, after all these years.

"If you'd apply yourself a little, like that Jack Kenton does," Bernice used to say, "you might make something out of yourself. But the way you're going, I doubt it, I really do."

You know something? It looked like Bernice had been right about that.

Or was it too soon to tell? That's what the screaming announcer was saying when Buster got back up on his barstool. Everybody in the bar was yelling and jumping fucking up and down. That new great white hope rookie had just hit a grand slam home run, and the score was all tied up at six-and-six. Too soon to tell, and you damn well better believe it, babe. Go Mets!

It made Buster feel so good that he was only just a little bit "p.o.'d" to have missed the big moment when the kid cracked the ball. He didn't mind too much. There had been a really big moment in his life once, and he would just as soon have passed it up.

*   *   *

Charlie Kiefer had had his office in a wire cage on the second floor of an old building at Seventh Avenue and Thirty-third Street. The place was a honeycomb of lofts and sweatshops, and Charlie's operation used space all over the building. But his office—such as it was—was on the second floor. Buster met Charlie there, and although Charlie did not look flat-out scared, Buster could tell he was not a very happy man.

Buster knew why.

Their first meeting took place during the days when Charlie was starting to make big money, when Charlie had just become ward leader in his old neighborhood, and when Guapino, a.k.a. "Woppo," Campa was riding high in the extortion business. Well, Charlie had a little clout, even then, and he wanted the precinct to send a man over just to "look around." He sure as hell wasn't going to get specific. How was he to know how many boys in the precinct were getting regular kickbacks from Woppo? Some must have been, though, because the cops didn't send anybody over.

Buster was working undercover in those days, and he laughed to think of it now, but, Jesus Christ, he had believed fair was fair. Woppo Campa was not fair. It galled Buster to think about Woppo gouging those District guys, even if ninety percent of them did live on chopped chicken liver and matzo ball soup, wash it down with Maalox. So when he heard that Charlie had gotten Woppo's best offer—"fire protection" at a grand a month—Buster made the move. He went up to that wire cage on the second floor.

"Yeah? What the hell do you want?" This was Charlie.

"Police. Can we talk?"

Charlie regarded the street clothes. "You don't look like no cop to me."

"I'm undercover on the extortion racket, here in the District."

Charlie thought that was pretty funny. "Didn't they tell you over at the precinct? There ain't no extortion around here. It's only our imagination. Your chief told me that himself, the greaser goombah dago. I think he's married to Woppo Campa's sister, for Christ sake."

"I hear Woppo's been to see you," Buster put in. "Tell me, did he barge right into that locked cage there, and set his fat ass down? How did you feel when he did that?"

Charlie looked him up and down, and Buster saw a complicated wave of emotions pass across Charlie's broad, strong face. It was as if he had been personally violated by Woppo's trespass, his brutality and arrogant presumption. The same things Buster hated, and he believed in sticking up for his buddies. Although he tried not to remember that time with Jack Kenton in the park near Grover Cleveland High School, that time he'd tucked tail and run, the memory had proved hard to lose.

So now when Charlie said, "Okay, I'm with you. Let's put that goombah son of a bitch out of business," Buster was not about to back down.

"You figure out a way to square it with the precinct," Charlie said.

"The precinct don't even have to know," grunted Buster, with a big grin.

Charlie pushed a little button somewhere in back of his desk, and a mechanism clicked in the lock on the door of the wire cage. Buster opened the door, which was made of heavy steel wire too. Buster looked that wire cage up and down. He knew what he would do. And he had access to all the latest electronic tools. Trouble was, he had to get them from the precinct office, but nobody thought much about it at the time.

"You sure this is gonna work?" Charlie demanded on the morning of the big day, watching Buster set things up, the cage strewn with tools and wires.

"It will if you don't fuck it up. See, you press the button just like usual when Woppo comes in. He does his business, such as it is. Then he gets ready to split, see? This is your big moment. You have to press the button again to unlock the door and let him out. That second time will do the trick. The *second* time, and don't even breathe in the direction of the button otherwise."

"I won't."

"You sure you're up to doing this? It ain't gonna be pretty."

Charlie gave him a cold, level look. "I'm more than up to it. Where'll you be?"

"Back there in the dress racks, out of sight. I wouldn't be surprised if Woppo knows me."

Charlie grunted.

Campa showed up on time, just before lunch. He was shortish, overweight, with a big prowlike nose, square horse-teeth, and little mean eyes. He regarded Charlie in the locked wire cage, with the desk, file cabinets, and in the corner a squat, iron safe.

"You got something for me in that matchbox?" he sneered.

Charlie just nodded, and pushed the button. It was right next to his middle desk drawer, and his hand had to disappear out of Woppo's sight for a second. The hood didn't even blink; he was that contemptuous of his victim. The lock on the steel door clicked, released, and Woppo entered the wire office. The door swung shut automatically, and the lock clicked again.

"Make it snappy. I got a lunch date over in Red Hook with Captain Smedley. You know, the one what runs this precinct."

He laughed at his own joke, showing his teeth. Charlie suppressed a surge of angry disgust, held back his excitement as well, and spun the dials on the safe's combination lock. Down along a warehouse aisle, obscured by thousands of imitations of other imitations of Parisian creations, Buster followed the action. The fabric of the dresses whispered around him, but in Charlie's office the safe opened with a clunk. Charlie removed a white envelope and handed it over. Woppo grabbed it, grinned, and kind of saluted Charlie with the thing, a debonair flick alongside his right temple.

"See you next month, *schmuck*," Woppo snickered, grabbing the latch on the steel door, jiggling it. "C'mon, open up. I ain't got all day. Me and Captain Smedley's got a big appet . . ."

Charlie pushed the button. He was grinning.

Woppo was half-turned away from Charlie. Did he have time, during that final millisecond, to see the pure look of scornful triumph on Charlie Kiefer's face? Maybe. But he didn't have all that much time to reflect on it, because a raw current yanked him upright, sent him to his toes, and slammed him against the steel door. Frozen against the door, his hand bonded to the latch, the voltage jolted into him. He gave a little grunt or cry—he had no time to scream—and the red electricity flashed through his body, crackling his skin like a roast pig's. His carefully barbered hair stood on end, like a kid's Halloween fright wig, and his tiny eyes were big as silver dollars now, blood surging red into the whites as vessels ruptured inside his head. The smell of cooked meat rose to mingle with the dusty textile scent of the warehouse.

Charlie Kiefer, still grinning, stood there in the incandescent cage. He let the current run for a full minute, watching Woppo jerk and twitch. It was about fifty-eight-and-a-half seconds more than necessary, but Charlie wouldn't begrudge Con Ed its going rate. Then he pushed the button a third time, resetting the mechanism that Buster had installed, cutting off the current. There were a lot of things that could be done with electricity, if you knew how.

That was the end of Charlie's problem with Campa, but only the beginning of grief for Buster Pauley. The death was ruled an accident, freak accident, because Buster took care, making sure nobody could figure out how it happened. Nobody was all that sorry about losing Woppo's contribution to society, except Smedley and some of the other muckety-mucks at the precinct, who'd been in on the take, and there wasn't much they could do without opening a great big can of worms. But they checked and found out about certain precision electrical equipment checked out to and later returned by Buster Pauley, and a couple of years later they railroaded him out of the force—a dishonorable and no pension—on some totally unrelated charge. That was when Charlie showed what kind of a guy he was and started helping out. He paid off the guys who stuck up for him just like he paid off the guys who tried to shaft him. Trouble was Bernice couldn't take the new life, if you could call it a life. She didn't. Buster tried to go into legitimate investigative work, but his dishonorable nixed that. Law says a bad cop can't be a registered private spook, and no way around it. There followed some odd jobs: security guard at a factory, until his past caught up; delivery man for a dry cleaner; part-time house painter. And now and then some dirty work for legitimate investigators who needed this or that special trick. Buster knew a lot of them, most illegal, but if he got caught at the trick, he'd have to take the fall. That was the deal.

"*What?*" screamed Bernice. "First you screw up a perfectly good job out of your own stupidity, and now you're trying to get yourself into prison? Count me out, I'm leaving. But don't think you can get out of supporting me. I never wanted to marry you in the first place, and now you're going to learn a lesson. You're going to *pay* for your mistakes."

She was right. Buster was paying. If he was a day late with his check, Bernice called, threatening the law. What a fucking fix Buster's life had turned out to be, and it didn't look like it was gonna get any better any too soon.

Hell, Buster thought, sitting there knocking 'em back at Mel and Irma's, *at least I had the guts to go through with the Campa thing. If I'd backed up Kenton that other time in high school, like I should have, I probably wouldn't feel the way I do about him.*

The game was long over, Mets lost her seven-to-six in the tenth, on a fucking error, of course, and outside on Queens Boulevard the streetlights had come on. Mel waddled over and asked if Buster wanted another hit, but Buster said no, and paid the fucking bill with one of Charlie's hundreds. That sent old Mel's eyebrows up.

"So you really are working?"

"What'd you figure, I'd lie to you?"

Buster went out, thinking, *Work, hell, if I get caught, harassment'll be the least of the charges. Good old Jack Kenton.*

Outside it was gloomy, and a chill had come into the night. Buster slid behind the wheel of the borrowed car and realized he had a pretty good buzz on, so he took it easy as he started back to his dumpy little apartment. On the way, he had to drive by the damn park. That's where it had happened, the thing between Jack and him. It was their shared secret, their memory. Buster was sure Kenton remembered. A man didn't forget something like that, didn't forget a buddy tucking tail and running when the chips were down. Hadn't even been Kenton's fight. Buster was sure, too, that Kenton hated his guts, and the knowledge alternately angered and depressed him. Buster still carried a pretty big chunk of guilt about the whole thing—it was one of those unfinished things in life that you have got to get settled in some way, at least if you expect to have any peace. He just didn't like the idea of Kenton going around the world carrying in his mind the thought that Buster Pauley was just a jerk-off coward. Which Buster was not. But then Buster remembered he hadn't even had the guts to go visit Kenton when he was lying all beat up in the hospital. Sheee-it. Once, years after the fight in the park, while he was working as a cop, Buster caught Lipschitz drunk in a whorehouse raid in Rockaway and kind of accidentally managed to break up his face and several other bones with a billy club, but not even that had made Buster feel good about himself for too long. It seemed to Buster that Jack Kenton still thought he was the kind of person Bernice always claimed he was, a complete jerk. Which Buster was not. Someday he'd show everybody. Don't forget, he'd had the guts to help Charlie take on Woppo Campa, and . . . Sheee-it. He parked the car, locked it, walked to his place and let himself in. What a dump. One big room with a bed in it and three closets off to the side. One closet was a kitchen, one was the crapper, and the third was an actual closet, with Buster's valuables in it. Such as they were. Buster looked at his place and felt shittier than ever. He had seen Jack Kenton's mansion today. Maybe it was written down somewhere that if you ever ran out on a buddy, you had to eat dirt for the rest of your life.

Buster thought he was real tired, and threw himself down on the bed without undressing. But he couldn't sleep, lying there, restless and tossing, looking up into the blackness where the ceiling was.

6

Churning memory did not permit the stalker much sleep. His room was dark, and there was nothing to look at except the blackness where the ceiling was, and beyond it the greater blackness of the night, and in that night Jack Kenton. The stalker knew where Kenton's big house was, knew too that it was virtually impossible to break into. Tactics would have to be used, wile and cunning and stealth. But that was why the stalker had planned everything carefully. Revenge is no good unless it comes as a surprise, and the avenger can fade back into the night out of which he has emerged.

So the Kentons had been away for the weekend. Wasn't that nice? A little treat for them, and a surprise of flowers for the wife. They had had their little vacation, received the first message. How would the stalker proceed now? He knew. By letting the tension build. By giving them a little nudge of memory from time to time, and then, when they were taut, when they were as taut as a violin string, the stalker would play upon their very souls a delicious Godforsaken melody of utter fear!

Night was the time to dwell upon such sweetness.

So much hurt. So much time.

Don't think. You have work in the morning. Sleep.

Did she show him the lilacs, though? Did he know what they meant?

The stalker did not know, neither did he sleep.

Memory. A shaft of pure pain streaked down out of the blackness and buried its raw ragged point into the stalker's cold heart. No sleep. He swung his feet over the edge of the bed and onto the cold wood of the floor. He felt the chill; he was alive; it was such pain to be alive.

To be dead and heaped with flowers? No. Not that. Not yet. He had passed beyond that desire.

Kenton, then? Dead? Any of the Kentons? All of them? Little Lisa too?

No, the stalker was not a violent man.

Yet he was possessed by the beast of vengeance. A red flash, a rolling wave of fire, passed behind the stalker's tired eyes, and imposed against that fire for one subliminal instant was the shape of the beast itself, atavistic and profound. By feeding it one tiny sprig of lilac today, the stalker had intended to satisfy the beast; with one tiny morsel of memory, he had sought to kill the monster that hungered in his heart. He did not know that vengeance wants more, demands more, will not be satiated until it has everything there is, mind and heart and body, soul too.

The stalker tossed, sleepless, feeding the beast. Not long before dawn, with his brain cold and clear, the stalker's rush of nighttime thought slowed. As the sun rose out of the Atlantic, he reconsidered his past and distilled from it a syllogism:

My wife and son are dead.
Jack Kenton has a wife and son.
Therefore, they should be dead too.

7

First thing every morning, in his house in Garden City Park, Long Island, Edward L. Peters awoke and checked his daily calendar. He always knew what was on it anyway, but he was known—not inaccurately—as a "detail" man by his colleagues at Stuyvesant Mutual Insurance Company, and routine habits gave him satisfaction, if not pleasure. Besides, Ed Peters had "come up the hard way," as he liked to say—poor family, worked his way through college, CPA via night school—and "getting the job done," any job, required planning, attention to detail. Such discipline had won him promotion to vice-president and treasurer at Stuyvesant, in downtown Manhattan. He was proud of that; he had "arrived." Without discipline, he might still be just another agent, flogging policies on the Island.

He swung out of bed, stepped into slippers, and pulled on his robe. The first item on his desk calendar read:

> Drive by Kentons on way to work. Drop off policy info additional coverage re: Lisa Walsh.

In spite of Ed's promotion, he'd let it be known that he wanted to retain important clients on a personal basis. And Jack Kenton was important. Ed knew the family. He had also belonged to Kenton's tax-reform association a few years back, and the fact that he and Jack had both gone to City College—although they hadn't known each other then—was almost "old school tie." Ed had always been pleased about that; he was sure it had helped him to sell Kenton policies.

Ed went into the kitchen, put some water on the stove for instant Maxwell House, poured himself some orange juice, and dropped two slices of bread into the toaster. He picked up the *New York Times* from the doorstep, and glanced through it, drinking coffee and eating toast in the little den he'd built onto one side of the house. He'd done it all by himself, cabinets and shelves included, and he'd also built a small greenhouse in the backyard and put an extension onto the garage for a workbench. Do the job yourself, and you not only save money, you "learn something new every day."

He showered and dressed, choosing this morning a brown pin-striped Botany 500. He dressed conservatively and well, always had, and it was a definite requirement, now that he was treasurer. Sometimes he took the train into Manhattan, but since he had to stop at the Kentons', he took his new gold Oldsmobile—a sharp-looking car, too, even a guy with Kenton's dough would appreciate it—and headed north to the Expressway, exiting on Searingtown Road, through Port Washington and up into the Royall Beach enclave. One of the cops on duty at the gate waved to him. Respect. Ed liked that. Probably it was the new gold Olds.

Heading up Kenton's long hedge-lined driveway, approaching that magnificent house—maybe he could afford one like it, some-day—Ed was sure he saw a man, or a woman, or *something*. Crouching there among all the lilacs. Maybe it was the gardener. Then he saw Carol Kenton standing in front of the house, next to her little BMW—now *that* was a money car for you—and she looked lovely, a dark blue suit setting off her long blonde hair. Ed pulled up next to the BMW and braked his Olds. Carol turned toward him. She looked confused, as if something had just surprised her.

Carol's day had begun in a hectic rush, and it seemed to be getting worse.

First, no one had remembered to set an alarm, so they'd all overslept. Jack had had to rush off without breakfast to La Guardia airport where Governor Higgins's Grumman Gulfstream was waiting to fly him up to the conference with Higgins and Kiefer in Albany. He'd had time for half a cup of coffee, just about half a kiss, and a "See you tonight, I think."

Then Lisa complained of being sick. Carol felt her forehead, which was cool, took her temperature, which was normal, and tried to convince her that a good breakfast would do wonders. Johnny, all the while, called, "I can't find my schoolbag, Mom," and "Where's my brown pants?"

Finally, when they were just about to leave for school—Lisa

whimpering, but with a boiled egg and half a cinnamon roll inside her—the phone rang.

"Mrs. Kenton? This is Jeff Doobey of Techtronic Electronic over in Port Washington. Mind if we come over and program that new voice this morning?"

"This morning?"

"Got a man free. Can come over and do her right away. Won't take more than fifteen minutes."

"All right," she agreed.

"Okay. The man'll be over in a half hour."

"I don't want to be programmed," said Lisa, in a little voice, after Carol had hung up.

"Honey, it'll just take a minute. The man will be right over . . ."

Then Carol saw that Lisa was sinking away, her consciousness moving from this bright kitchen to another place, another time. Her face seemed to darken with the effort of concentration, as if trying to fit together the pieces of mixed puzzles.

The murder night! Carol thought. Jack had been sure the memory was very close to the surface.

"What are you thinking, Lisa? Why don't you want your voice programmed? What is it?"

"Because—because . . . somebody will come . . ." She drifted off for a second, then came back. "Come up the stairs, and . . ."

"Yes? Yes? Go on, it's all right."

Lisa's little face was screwed up now in a terrific effort of recollection. ". . . and all the glass is breaking, I'll get—I'LL GET CUT!!!" she cried, in sudden terror.

Carol put her arms around the girl. Lisa was back in the murder house now, on the night of Valerie's death. The mystery would be revealed.

"Hey, Mom! Aren't we ready to go to school *yet?*" cried Johnny, dragging his schoolbag into the kitchen.

Lisa's expression went blank for a moment, and then she relaxed, the memory flown.

"Oh, *Johnny!*" said Carol, instantly regretting the sharpness in her tone.

"What'd *I* do?"

"Nothing. I'm sorry. We'll be waiting for the voice-coder man.

Check over that report you did for your teacher, Mrs. Pilaf. Lisa, why don't you see if 'Sesame Street' is on?"

Carol went into the garage, climbed into her car, and started the engine. She pushed a button on the dashboard, and behind her the great panel of wall slid up. She backed out in the BMW, pushed the button again, and the wall of the house slid down. She switched off the engine and sat there a moment, admiring the hedges of flowers, the clear blue sky, drawing into herself the perfume of this perfect May morning. No sign of the Techtronic man.

I'll get a little sun, she thought. The lawn chairs were stored in the garage, and she pushed the dashboard button again.

Nothing happened.

A little flicker of fear burst into life down where her stomach was. She pushed the button again. With no result. The big panel of garage door didn't even jiggle. All of a sudden, the house loomed stark and impenetrable before her, a fortress from which she was barred. Inconceivable that the device had malfunctioned! The apparatus in the house itself simply *could not fail!* Even in the event of an electrical blackout, a special generator in the basement was programmed to kick in within thirty seconds after the current ceased.

Wait! She knew what was wrong. The dashboard button wasn't working, for whatever reason. She'd have the Techtronic man take a look at that when he showed up.

Dismissing the idea of sunning herself on a lawn chair, Carol decided to go back into the house and have a second cup of coffee. She walked around to the front door on the beachfront side of the house.

"Open up," she said, into the speaker.

And nothing happened. The lock did not click open; the door held fast.

Impossible! This could not be happening. Then, in an instant, she recalled Lisa's words in the kitchen—*"somebody will come."*

Had Lisa been thinking of the past, the night of her mother's murder? Or was she thinking of the future? Of today? Of *right now!*

Reflected sunlight struck Carol's eyes, and she turned to see a car speeding up the drive.

". . . *somebody will come* . . ." Lisa had said.

"Oh, my God!" Carol cried.

The front door had a chime, and Carol slammed her hand again and again upon the doorbell button, but nothing happened. It was an electric device, and the electricity was off. The children, somewhere in the house, could not hear her. What on earth had happened to that fail-safe auxiliary generator? Then another thought came to Carol. What if someone had gotten into the house?

She pounded on the glass of the door. No response from inside. What to do? The car came on, approaching fast, a bright, new, shiny car. Not the Techtronic van. She thought fast. *If I can't get in the house, neither can whoever is in that car. But I might have to go for help.*

She hurried to her BMW and reached it just as the new Oldsmobile pulled into the yard. The glare of the sun on the windshield obscured the identity of the driver, but then he opened the door.

"Mr. Peters!" cried Carol, with vast relief. Of course. He'd left a message on the phone recorder about bringing over policy information for Lisa.

"Mrs. Kenton," he began, "I thought I saw somebody down . . ."

He had meant to say "down there in the lilacs," but inside the house, Lisa screamed, suddenly, piercingly, as if nails were being pounded through her palms.

Peters raced with Carol toward the front door. They rounded the corner of the house. Lisa was just behind the thick, shatterproof glass of the door, banging on it with her small fists. Her face was streaked with tears, and her eyes looked strange.

"Open!" Carol shouted, but the mechanism did not respond.

Lisa was pounding on the door, trying to get out. Carol saw Johnny coming down the stairs, coming fast, alerted by all the noise.

"Has this ever happened before?" asked Peters, jiggling the door handle.

"I don't know what's wrong—" said Carol.

Lisa screamed again, and Johnny reached her, tried to grab and hold her. She fought him briefly, wriggled out of his grasp, and began again to pound on the door.

Then, as if nothing had been amiss, the lock clicked, and the door slid open. Lisa hurtled into Carol's unready embrace.

"I couldn't get out," Lisa was sobbing. "I couldn't get out, I couldn't . . ."

"I'm scared, Mom," Johnny admitted.

That makes two of us, Carol thought.

"I—I saw my mommy flying," choked Lisa, holding on to Carol for dear life. "He is—he is making her fly. The glass—" she sobbed "—my mommy is flying in the broken glass—"

But that was all Lisa remembered, just then.

"Make her stop talking, Mom," Johnny pleaded. "I don't want to hear that stuff."

Ed Peters looked on in wonder. "Is she all right?"

"No."

"Anything I can do to help?"

"Just a moment." Still holding Lisa, Carol went to check the panel in the kitchen, which monitored the household security apparatus. There had *not* been an electrical outage. That was why the generator hadn't kicked in. Yet the red burglar alarm light *was* on. Chief Detzler or his men should already be on their way.

"Strange," Carol murmured, soothing Lisa.

"Mrs. Kenton," said Ed Peters, "I saw somebody down in the hedges as I drove in. Do you have a gardener?"

"He isn't due until the end of the week," Carol replied, as two Royall Beach police cars came up the drive.

"I'll have some explaining to do," Carol said, heading for the door. Chief Detzler tended to be more than a little choleric, and the fact that Jack Kenton's tax-reform influence had cut his last pay raise in half did nothing to improve his disposition.

Four officers jumped from the cars, guns at the ready, and started to fan out around the house, stopping when they saw Carol.

Chief Detzler climbed slowly out of one of the cars, scowling. He looked like a stringbean version of Colonel Sanders, with a wispy Vandyke and soft white hair.

"What seems to be the problem here?" he grunted.

Carol explained. Ed Peters affirmed. Detzler kept on scowling. Then Peters mentioned the man he thought he'd spotted in the lilacs. Everyone walked down the drive, a couple of cops in the lead, pistols loose in their holsters. There was no sense of alarm. The whole episode now seemed to have been a fluke, and it was too nice a day for trouble.

Peters estimated the approximate place he thought he'd seen the figure, and a policeman ducked into the hedges, slapping at a few curious bees.

"Hey!" he cried, after a moment. "I found something."

Everyone gathered around, and two officers held back some flower-laden branches. Around one of the bushes, the earth was scarred and gouged by numerous footprints, and tied to branches that formed a particularly large lilac bush was an odd netting of some sort, made of intersecting ropes and leather thongs.

"What the hell we got here?" Detzler grunted, leaning forward to inspect it, fingering his little beard. "That belong here?" he asked Carol.

"No, it doesn't."

"You mind if we take it in for evidence?"

"Evidence of what?"

"Don't know yet. You mind we take it in?"

"No, go ahead."

Two of the cops untied the knots by which the curious netting was fastened to the branches. Then the police checked the house.

"Seems okay to me," Detzler pronounced. "I wouldn't worry about it. Any gizmo can go wrong. And the more gizmos you got, the more things you got to go wrong. Probably never happen again. One of them one-in-a-million things, know what I mean?"

"I certainly do," Carol said.

Detzler and his men drove off. Ed Peters gave Carol the insurance information Jack could use to plan coverage for Lisa. He lingered a bit, making sure everything was all right, studying the house, too.

Peters left when the Techtronic van rolled into the yard. The technician made some adjustments within the circuits of the control panel, inserted a small microphone into one of the outlets, and held it in front of Lisa.

"Say a few words now, honey," he said, and pressed a switch.

"I don't want to."

"Good girl," he told her, unplugging the mike. "That's it, Mrs. Kenton. She's programmed for the doors."

"As long as you're here, we've had a few problems this morning."

"Oh?"

He checked, and found her dashboard device in good order. The auxiliary generator tested out too. "Must have been one of those two- or three-second outages. The generator won't kick in for about thirty seconds after current from the main line is cut off—"

"But it was off much longer than thirty seconds."

"You're sure?"

"Absolutely."

"Beats me," said the technician, scratching his head. "Must have been one of those flukes."

"Right. One in a million," Carol agreed.

"Okay kids, let's go," Carol called, after the Techtronic man had gone. She herded them into the car and raced over to the school. Lisa looked pale, like someone just after a fit. But she was calm now. Johnny was his usual self.

"If you're the principal and you're late," he calculated, "and I'm your kid and I'm late because you're late, then that means I don't have to go to the office for a pass, right?"

"Wrong," said Carol.

Ed Peters drove through Royall Beach, admiring the big houses, the gorgeous lawns, and, on impulse, decided to drive over to Mrs. Kenton's school. She was a smart lady and a very pretty one. Just the type of woman a sharp guy like Jack Kenton would pick to marry. A guy like Jack Kenton could probably have his pick of women, just about anyone he happened to want.

Royall Beach Elementary School was set on a beautiful green overlooking Hempstead Harbor. Behind the school, a thickly wooded bank ran down to the water. Ed, who was an alumnus of a crumbling brick public school in the Bronx, figured Royall Beach was a great place for a kid to go to school. If he ever had a kid, he would want a neighborhood like this, a school like this.

Still, the Kentons had their problems. Lisa Walsh, for one.

Everybody has their problems. With the excitement at the Kenton house, and the impromptu drive around the village, Ed had uncharacteristically let time get away from him. He got back into his Olds and decided to make tracks toward his Stuyvesant Mutual office in New York.

The cop on gate duty at the entrance to Royall Beach threw up a hand and flagged him down.

"Driver's license, please."

Ed experienced the slightly jittery feeling that comes with an unwanted encounter. But it never made sense to hassle a policeman. He handed over his license and his registration too.

"I drove in about an hour ago, and no one stopped me then," he said mildly, as the cop studied the two documents.

"That's true, Ed," replied the officer, with a presumption of familiarity that is a part of the breed, "but you don't have a sticker, and I'm supposed to check all cars that don't."

"A sticker?"

"That's right. We got to be careful. So these North Shore villages give out stickers to their residents, so we can tell at a glance who belongs and who doesn't. You don't have VRB on your bumper. Village of Royall Beach."

"That's because I don't live here," said Ed, with an edge to his voice.

The cop made a show of being satisfied with Ed's papers, and handed them back. "Sorry for the inconvenience, but somebody spotted a trespasser up at Jack Kenton's place, and Chief Detzler said I got to stop all unknowns."

Ed breathed a sigh of relief. So that was all it was.

"*I'm* the guy who spotted the trespasser," he informed the cop.

"What? Oh, sir, my apologies. You can go now. Sorry. But you never can tell."

"No," said Ed, "you never can."

Ed took the midtown tunnel into Manhattan, and headed downtown to the Stuyvesant Mutual Building, just a stone's throw from the World Trade Center. He liked the building, and he liked the area; they gave him a feeling of power, of connection to bustle and vitality. Stuyvesant was the very center of his life these days, and he did not know what he would do without "the company."

One of the most exciting things about his new job as treasurer was "access." His rank, along with the scope of his new duties, gave Ed Peters access to every facet of Stuyvesant Mutual, and this morning he had scheduled a block of time to gain greater familiarization with the computer operation. The computer area was off limits to all but authorized personnel, because someone who understood both finance and computer operation could push the right buttons and, in the space of minutes, transfer millions of dollars from one account to another.

The head of computer operations, overweight but grinning Norm Glowers, hopped up from his battered chair when Ed entered, a welcome sign of respect for an executive, and introduced Ed to Ms. Bambi Bush. Bambi, an expert computer programmer, was to show Ed how new accounts were entered into the computer banks, and how receipts were electronically deposited, transferred, or withdrawn. Ed, who had not met Ms. Bush previously, was momentarily startled at her innocent beauty. In appearance, she reminded him of his wife. Not in personality, however. Bambi was very direct, even brash, and the fact that Ed was vice-president and treasurer didn't seem to impress her very much.

"You want to see how I do this stuff, is that right, Mr. Peters? Okay, watch closely and don't miss anything. I'm going to run through the procedure now . . ."

Bambi sat down at the computer console, and Ed leaned over to watch her work.

Bambi patted a pile of papers next to the console. "Here I got a stack of new applications," she said, and picked one of them off the top of the pile. Then she began to punch keys on the terminal console.

"What are you doing?" asked Ed, mystified.

"Policy type, amounts of coverage, significant variations, and all that other stuff."

"Oh," said Ed, watching her. He would catch on quickly.

"And now here on this application we have a check attached," said Bambi, pointing. "This check has to be programmed with a different code . . ."

She proceeded to punch more keys. "What I just did was to notify the client's bank to transfer the money to our bank. When the check clears, the policy will go into effect."

"So you do that all right here?"

"All it takes is pushing the right buttons," observed Bambi, giving him a frank look. He was a VP and VP's made pretty good money. Was he interested in her at all, or just in her work? Just in her work, she saw. Too bad. He wasn't too old, wasn't bad-looking, and might be—she had heard—available. He looked too serious, though, she thought. But then you probably had to be serious if you wanted to be a VP. Oh, well. If he kept coming in here to learn computer stuff, something might develop. She would be here. She would wait and see.

Suddenly Ed yanked a policy application right off the top of the pile.

"Hey!" said Bambi. "What's the matter?"

"Oh, nothing," Ed managed, putting the paper back after staring at it for a long moment. He had been astounded right down to his socks by what he'd read. One of Stuyvesant's Long Island agents had innocently approved the application. How was he to know?

It was an application for insurance on the life of one WALSH, LISA ANN, aged six.

The applicant was WALSH, STANLEY J. He had given as his address the Harvard Club of New York.

A check of substantial amount was attached, to pay for the policy.

"Enter the check, please," Ed told Bambi. "I want to see how that procedure works. And, by the way, I'll need a list of all our account codes, first chance you get."

8

I *may not be the dumbest fuck-up in the whole world*, thought Buster Pauley, *but I gotta rank in the top ten.*

Up at dawn, he had a hangover that was like a Mack eighteen-wheeler diesel backfiring in his brain, and he had to get out to Royall Beach to recover the apparatus before anybody found it. He gulped a whole container of orange juice and felt a little bit better, but not much. He was going to have to swear off beer and balls.

Nobody had stolen the car, big surprise, but Buster got out to Royall Beach a hell of a lot later than he'd planned. The same cop who'd spotted Buster yesterday was on duty at the gate, but he barely glanced up as Buster rolled on through. It was taking a chance to come in like this again, but Buster hoped it'd be the last time, and the only other way to get into the place, not counting by parachute, would be to take a boat, and Buster didn't have no such fucking boat.

When he got into the hedges, he was happy to find the machine still there and working well. The machine rested on the netting, a webbed affair of leather and ropes, and Buster was pleased to see that it was still aimed directly at Kenton's house. Hadn't moved at all, but now he had to undo all the knots, and that proved to be a real bitch, especially since his hands were shaking. All he had to do was loosen the netting and put the netting and the machine in a leather bag he'd brought along with him, but he wasn't functioning at top speed. Time passed, and then it seemed the whole area turned into the Indy Speedway on Memorial Day.

First, Jack Kenton drove out in his big white Lincoln. Except for the newspapers and on television, Buster hadn't actually seen Kenton since that night of the fight in the park, and from what he could see in a quick glimpse from the hedge as Kenton went past, he hadn't changed a whole hell of a lot. Christ, he looked young! That was how you stayed if you were rich and lucky and had the brass ring in life. *Au contraire*—that was some French talk Charlie had taught him—if you were like Buster, you showed the wear and tear, with a gut getting fat and pouches under the eyes.

Buster turned back to his work, and that was when he fucked up really royal. He slipped, and his elbow nudged one of the sensitive dials on the machine, the latest thing in remote surveillance gadgetry. It could pick up conversations inside a building with a bombardment of microwaves. If, say, somebody in a house that was under surveillance had a conversation about money or politics or getting a good piece of ass, the pattern of the microwaves would be disturbed. A decoder, reading the disturbance in the pattern, could tell you what the conversation had been about, right down to the exact words used. But nudging the dial, like Buster had so stupidly done, would increase the power, and likely screw up every electrical device in the Kentons' house. He twisted the dial back as quickly as he could, switched off the whole machine, which he should have done right away—What a fuck-up! What a hangover!—and stuffed the machine in the leather bag.

Then a guy in a gold Oldsmobile had shown up. Buster was sure as shit that the guy saw him there in the lilacs.

And then the damn cops came!

What the fuck was going on? Buster didn't wait around to find out. He left the netting where it was, hightailed it back to his borrowed car, and got the hell out of Royall Beach.

Heading back to Ridgewood, the damn car had run out of gas, and by the time Buster got home, it was almost eleven o'clock, and he still had to do the decoding and get ahold of Charlie. He hauled the decoder out of the closet, where he'd stashed it behind the crate that contained his whole life. Some ancient bubble gum cards, a couple of old first baseman's mitts, a cracked baseball bat, with which Buster had once hit a grand slam, shoulder pads and a helmet from his football days, a moldy assortment of French ticklers in the shapes of a cat's head with whiskers, Mickey Mouse with huge ears, Popeye with a long, long rubber pipe, and one that looked like a dinosaur or a razorback hog, take your pick. Bernice had never let him use any of them.

Also in the crate was Buster's old NYPD uniform, bereft of buttons and insignia. Captain Smedley had yanked them off in a little ceremony at the precinct, with all Buster's ex-colleagues looking on. Buster shut his mind off about that. There would be plenty of time to settle scores with Smedley when Charlie got to be governor.

Buster's head throbbed and his hands were still shaking, but he managed to connect the male decoder plug to the female opening in the microwave monitor he'd retrieved from Royall Beach. Then he turned a switch, and the two machines, symbiotic in purpose and design, hummed like a couple of teenagers sixty-nining on a hot Queens night. The machines hummed and clattered, producing a lengthening printout that told everything spoken in the Kenton house from the time they had gotten back from Gurney's Inn to the time Buster switched it off this morning. Buster read as the machine spit it out: not too fucking interesting. Great little machine, though. Buster'd borrowed it from Zykra Security Systems, up in Astoria, for whom he did some dirty work now and then.

Reading along with the printout, Charlie noticed that the names *Kiefer* and *Higgins* stuck out here and there, and then the transcript got real interesting.

> *Jack! Just a minute. This is important. Is there anything in your past that could be considered really dangerous?*
>
> *Carol, I don't think I'd lose money betting that you just thought of something that might be.*
>
> *That singer. What was her name?*
>
> *I know her name. What about her?*
>
> *I've been thinking of her husband.*
>
> *Bennington?*
>
> *Hasn't he always been a major financial contributor to the Republican party?*

"Hot dog!" yowled Buster, convinced he had something important here. Every red-blooded American boy worth his salt knew Rudolf Bennington, just like they knew John D. Rockefeller and

· 199 ·

Babe Ruth and Howard Hughes and John Wayne. And right here on the printout, Mrs. Kenton was concerned about Rudolf Bennington's wife. Buster searched his mind, which didn't take long, and could not for the life of him figure out who Bennington was married to. But Charlie would know. Charlie always knew who was screwing who.

"That's that what's-her-name, yeah, Bari, Karyn Bari," Charlie said, when Buster phoned him. "She was real big in show biz some years back. Then she married Bennington, just when he got in hot water and ran off to South America. So Kenton's old lady is worried about her, eh?"

"Talking about her, anyway."

"Often the same thing."

"What do we do now?" Buster wanted to know.

"Two things. First, I'm meeting Kenton and the gov this afternoon. I'll broach the subject. See how Kenton reacts."

"And second?"

"You ever been to Venezuela?" Charlie asked.

9

"Y̶ou look tired, Mom," observed Johnny, as they drove home from school. "What's gonna be for dinner?"

"I'm not hungry," whined Lisa, in the backseat.

"Is Dad gonna be home from talking with the governor?" Johnny asked.

"I certainly hope so," Carol said. She drove into the yard, pressed the dashboard button. To her relief, the garage opened. She drove in, braked, turned off the engine, and just sat there. What a day. She'd spent hours getting Blanche Dunphy and the teachers' union to agree to a community open forum, in order to discuss the budget and the pilot program. Carol calculated that such a meeting would defuse the problem and avert a strike. Blanche had agreed to the open forum, then she had called Semlac. Semlac told her not to agree to anything; he himself wanted to come back out to Royall Beach and "negotiate" with Carol. So, everything considered, Carol had spent all day detouring from square one to square one.

"Talk in the speaker, Lisa, and open the kitchen door," urged Johnny, as he got out of the car and held the door for the girl.

"I don't want to."

"John, you forgot your schoolbag," said Carol, but the kids were already entering the house. She picked up the schoolbag, got out of the car, and made sure the garage was locked. She wished that Jack were home. She didn't know what to have for dinner. She wondered what Anton Semlac was planning now.

Carol heard the television going when she entered the kitchen. Mrs. Boureg, the first-grade teacher, gave little homework, but for the fifth grade, Mrs. Pilaf piled it on.

"Homework first, young man," Carol called.

"Aw, Mom, I don't have any."

"That doesn't sound right."

"Mom, it's *true*," he maintained, over the laugh track of a "Happy Days" rerun. "The weather was so good Mrs. Pilaf had science day down by the water. We got back late, and she didn't have time to give out homework."

"You didn't even turn in your report?"

"No, we'll do that tomorrow."

Carol decided to check Johnny's homework sheet. The schoolbag was a colorful arrangement of cloth and leather, decorated by R2D2, C3PO, and Darth Vader. She opened it, reached inside. And almost cried out. Her fingers touched something yielding, something cool and soft and fragile. It was as if she had touched a living thing. Jerking her hand away, she looked. And saw a sprig of lilac there, the petals slightly wilted, but still vibrant, pink as a maiden's blush.

Carol stood there transfixed in the bright kitchen of her safe house. The lilacs blossomed up at her from Johnny's schoolbag, as they had glowed in her hand on yesterday's beach. No reason. There was no reason. The vaulting blue sky outside the house came down like a shroud, and her heart beat fast. Something was very wrong. She did not so much hear *The Waltz of the Dead* now, but she remembered it, a hallucinatory recollection of doomed note and eerie cadence. It was all she could do to keep her voice even.

"John?"

"Yeah, Mom?"

"When you went down to the harbor on the science outing? Did you take your schoolbag with you?"

"No, I left it in the classroom all day."

Jack's words came back to her. How Stan Walsh had been born in Royall Beach. How he knew the village like the back of his hand. Yes, he had been weeping on the phone, and Lisa had seen him in school last week. And he had been there again today. Somehow, in the troubled, demented corners of his mind, lilacs meant . . . what? Signified . . . what?

And why had he left them in *Johnny's* schoolbag?

Carol fought a tremor of cold fear and checked the control panel. According to the little row of lights, all was well.

But Carol knew it wasn't. *Jack*, she thought, *call or come home. Fast.* Because Stan Walsh was clearly deranged. She understood everything now. Stan could have *hired* somebody to hand her the flowers on the beach, if he hadn't done it personally. But he was behind it. Carol knew.

"Lisa, are you all right?" Carol called.

Jack finally phoned just after dinner.

"Where are you? La Guardia?"

"No. Still up in Albany. I got delayed. Don't forget to catch the news, though. I think I'll be on. You don't sound quite right. What's up?"

"Jack, I'm scared. Something went wrong with the security system this morning, and I think Stan Walsh got back into the school today. There were lilacs in Johnny's schoolbag."

Silence from his end of the line. She knew what he was thinking. Lilacs on the beach: random. Lilacs in a schoolbag, in *his son*'s schoolbag: not random at all.

"That goddam Walsh. The cops had better get him pretty soon. Were the kids upset?"

"I didn't tell them."

"Call Chief Detzler if you get jittery," Jack advised. "Don't hesitate."

"I'm getting to know him pretty well," she replied, and told of the strange netting in the hedges that morning: "Do you think that was Stan's work too?"

"Has to be, doesn't it? He's gone crazy. Why couldn't he have stayed in the get-rich-quick business? He could have established a franchise operation to market the Brooklyn Bridge by now."

"Jack, it's not funny."

"Honey, I know that. Look, you'll be okay. Just be extra careful."

"What are your plans?" asked Carol.

"I've scheduled a speech in Buffalo tomorrow afternoon. The Independent Citizens Committee wants me to get together with Congressman Kemp. I figure I'd better do it. After today."

The Albany meeting! "What happened with Charlie and the governor?"

"I don't want to get too specific over the phone. But do you remember last night—"

"I surely do."

"No, not that. Last night just before we went to bed? We were talking about a certain man and a certain woman . . . ?"

Rudolf Bennington and Karyn Bari. "Yes, I remember," Carol said.

"Well, it so happens that they're on Charlie Kiefer's mind too."

Carol had a strong impulse to say, *I told you so. I told you Charlie would dig up those particular bones in your past.* "What did he say?" she asked evenly.

"Charlie learned the essentials of direct communication from his mother. He asked me how well I'd *known* . . . the singer. I told him. He wondered if Bennington knew how close we'd been. I said I thought so. He reminded me—and John Higgins—of Bennington's vindictive personality, and he allowed as to how it might cause the party a little trouble were I to become the nominee."

"Oh, Jack. What did Higgins say?"

"It hardly comes under the good news heading."

"Tell me anyway."

"Higgins agreed to let Charlie have it checked out. He says we have to be absolutely certain that neither the woman nor her husband will cause trouble. Right now, Higgins is still supporting me, and I'm still prepared to announce candidacy on the Fourth of July. It's planned for evening, in the Waldorf-Astoria, by the way. Put that on your calendar."

"How is he—how is Charlie going to check it?"

"Apparently he's sending one of his men down to Venezuela to talk to Bennington and . . . her."

"What do you think she'll say?"

"I honestly have no idea," Jack responded. He wanted to add, *I never really knew what lay at the heart of Karyn's personality.* "Bennington could cause a lot of trouble, though, if he's so disposed. There doesn't have to be any dirt. He could easily invent some. And if he does—"

"If he does?"

"If he does, then no further support from Higgins, and I think we'll see Charlie Kiefer declaring candidacy."

"You could withdraw now and forget all about it," Carol

suggested. "Then there wouldn't be any problem."

"That's the one thing I won't do. It would look awful, and I'd be disgusted with myself."

"I knew you'd say that."

"Okay. A kiss for you and the kids. Watch the news now."

"I will. Love you. Bye."

Carol hung up. The brief conversation with Jack had made her feel safe and secure, but now that the connection was broken she felt uneasy.

She busied herself fixing dinner and was glad for the activity.

"I feel funny," complained Lisa, sitting down at the table.

At first, Carol thought the little girl was not going to eat, but Lisa proceeded to finish a bowl of tomato soup, almost all of her tuna sandwich, and a fair-sized serving of salad. Occasionally, she stared off into a middle distance, and cocked her head slightly, as if listening for something. This was unusual, but at least she ate.

"Since I don't have any homework," Johnny bargained, "can I watch that movie that's on tonight?"

"What movie?"

"The House at the End of the Road."

"It doesn't sound especially educational to me."

"Aw, Mom, c'mon. It's not too scary. Some of the other kids are—"

"I'm not concerned what the other kids are."

"Awwww."

"We'll see. By the way, your father might be on the news."

"That's something, at least," Johnny said.

Carol put the dishes in the washer, pressed a button on the console, and all the draperies in the house closed, blocking out the falling night. She pushed another button, which turned on the outside lights, illuminating the entire house and grounds. That made her feel a little safer, but not much. She joined the kids in the television room, where they were watching an update of *The Scarlet Letter*, starring Donny Osmond as the tortured Reverend Dimmesdale and Farah Fawcett as Hester Prynne.

After the movie, New York Metro news came on, and then it was state wrap-up time.

". . . and now here's Marv Kubitz with the day's events in Albany. Go ahead, Marvin."

A reporter appeared on camera in front of the governor's residence.

"Thank you, Roger. It was fairly quiet here in the capital today. Earlier this morning there had been vague rumors of an important political announcement from Governor Higgins, but this never materialized. Late in the afternoon, however, John Tyler Kenton, the highly popular tax-reform proponent from Long Island, met with the governor and state Democratic party boss Charles Kiefer . . ."

Jack appeared on the screen then. Jack was poised and smiling, as he always was when on camera, but she knew him well, and she could see faint traces of tension and disappointment around his eyes and mouth. The meeting with Higgins and Kiefer had been even less successful than he had led her to believe in his phone call. The reporter, Kubitz, thrust a microphone into Jack's face, and asked:

"Mr. Kenton, how goes tax reform?"

"We are making substantial gains all around the state, and hope to . . ."

Carol had heard it all before. She watched her husband speak, realizing at the same time that either Kiefer or Higgins or both of them would have wanted to appear on screen with Jack if things had gone smoothly.

"And what is an independent like yourself, Mr. Kenton, doing in a secret meeting with a Democratic governor and the Democratic party leader?"

· 206 ·

"Well, there was nothing secret about it, and, after all, tax reform is nothing if not a bipartisan goal. I'm reliably informed that Republicans, Democrats, and even independent citizens pay taxes . . ."

And so it was over, with a good line. But. *But that Karyn Bari thing has come back to haunt you,* Carol thought. Kiefer would use it against Jack, even though there was nothing really to use. He was already doing so; he'd convinced Higgins that a man ought to be sent to Venezuela.

The House at the End of the Road came on right after the news.

"All right, you can watch it," Carol told the kids. "But if it gets too gory . . ."

"It won't, Mom. Thanks, Mom . . ."

The phone rang. Probably Jack calling to see if she'd watched the news. She picked up the receiver and answered.

"Carol?"

It was Stan Walsh. Well, at least he wasn't bawling tonight.

"Carol, I've got to come over. I've got to see my daughter. I'm coming for her. She's going with me—"

"Stan, where are you?"

His laugh was hard. "Don't you want to know, though?"

"Stan, you need help, and—"

"DON'T YOU SAY THAT! I'M PERFECTLY ALL RIGHT. IS THAT WHAT THEY THINK? THAT I'M NOT ALL RIGHT?"

Mistake. Wasn't there some sort of unwritten rule that you weren't supposed to tell a crazy person he was crazy? *I ought to have known better,* Carol admonished herself, *after my previous experience with Vic Brand.*

"I have to talk to Lisa," Stan demanded. "I'm worried about her."

Carol felt like saying, *You weren't too worried about her when you killed her mother right in front of her eyes and then ran away for almost two months.*

"I'm afraid that's impossible," she said instead.

"Then I'm coming over."

"Don't. Jack will call the police."

He laughed again, laughter with a cunning edge. "I just saw Jack on TV, sweetheart. He's in Albany."

"That—that was taped earlier," Carol fumbled. But too late and to no avail. Stan knew Jack wasn't home.

"*I'll* call the police," she told him, trying to keep her voice low.

Stan began to sob. "How did it all happen?" he choked, "I just don't know how it all happened."

"Stan, just be a man for a minute, will you?" she demanded. "What am I supposed to do? You threw Valerie off the balcony into the pool, and she died . . ."

"No, no," he said, feebly.

". . . you ran off like a damn coward, and your child had to have responsible care . . ."

Stan blubbered.

". . . and now you're sneaking around town like some idiot—*please* pardon my saying so—doing the intruder bit at school last Friday and today . . ."

"Today?" he managed to say.

". . . and what in hell is that stupid business with the lilacs?"

"Lilacs?"

Carol knew. She knew at that very moment. She heard the genuine surprise in Stan Walsh's tone. Stan was so phony so much of the time, it was impossible to miss a sincere reaction on his part. Nor did Carol miss it. And she knew Stan had had nothing to do with the lilacs.

And that meant *someone else* was out there, had been on the beach, had been in the school, and was right now . . . where?

But her immediate problem was Stan Walsh. "I'm going to hang up now," she told him, "and then I'm going to phone the police and tell them you called here."

"No, Carol, don't. Don't. All I want is my little girl. You can't do this to me . . ."

"You're doing it to yourself. You've done it to yourself. Give yourself up. Please."

"But I didn't do anything!"

This was absurd. "Stan," she asked him, "do you know what your daughter saw? Do you know how much she saw that night?"

Stan stopped talking. Nothing on the line now but thin electric wind.

"Stan, she did see something. That's why you want her, isn't it? Isn't it?" she demanded.

He gave one final desperate sob, and hung up.

Carol was just about to dial the police and tell them Stan had called, when she noticed Lisa looking at her from the couch.

"Why don't we go upstairs and get your pajamas on?" Carol suggested.

Lisa looked right through her.

"Let's go upstairs, okay?"

"*Shhhhhhhh!*" Johnny admonished, as the movie sound track swelled and trembled. "Here comes the good part."

The people in the factory where the film had been put together knew how to hold audience attention. In the movie, the night was dark. Wind howled. Chains clanked. Strident violins were screaming. Johnny, Carol, and Lisa watched the screen and saw the shadowy figure of a man approaching an old and weather-battered house.

"Are you sure this isn't too scary?" Carol asked.

"Mom! It's too silly to be scary," pronounced John, Jr., all suave maturity, suppressing a shudder and curling into his corner of the couch.

Lisa looked on blankly.

"I'm not so sure . . ." said Carol.

Now the man reached the house. His back was toward the camera as he clumped up the rickety porch steps, and staggered toward a massive, ornate door, with swirls and dim figures carved upon it. It had a big doorknob, which the man grasped and turned.

"He's the bad guy," Johnny advised, "and . . ."

Now the camera moved inside the house, moved upstairs to show a lovely young woman in a sheer negligee. She was terrified. She rolled her eyes and gnawed hungrily on her fingers. She looked down a long staircase with an unimpeded view of the front door opening. The man entered and looked up at the girl, his cruel face twisting into a smile that promised pain.

"Let's switch this off . . ." Carol started to say.

The girl at the top of the stairs screamed.

And so did Lisa. She screamed and began to fling her little body around on the couch.

"He's coming!" she cried.

"John, turn it off!" ordered Carol, reaching for the child. Lisa struggled in her arms, twisting and fighting, not so much resisting Carol's embrace as attempting to escape an unwanted memory that came flooding back.

"Lisa, it's all right," Carol told her, "it's all right to remember. You're safe and we're right here with you."

In her heart, she did not want to know what Lisa might tell her, but she knew it would be best to free the memory.

Johnny turned off the television set and stood next to the couch, frightened and uncertain.

"He's coming up the stairs!" Lisa cried, her eyes wide with terror. *"Mommy! Run!"*

"Who's coming up the stairs?" asked Carol, holding the girl closely and trying to stay calm. "Who?"

Lisa screamed again. *"Run. Run, Mommy. Oh, Daddy, don't—don't do it . . ."* She seemed to be trying to struggle with someone. Carol knew who it was. *Oh, Daddy!* Stan Walsh. He *had* been the killer. That worthless, unspeakable bastard!

But the memory was free now, and Lisa with it. This time, the night of her mother's death surged upward through caverns of memory, pressed toward the bitter surface of consciousness. This time, she went all the way into the past and came all the way out, carrying a burden far more painful than forgetfulness.

Then she was crying in Carol's arms, and the tale poured out.

"My mommy—my mommy and my daddy were fighting. She said he didn't make enough money. He ran out. He ran out of the house. Mommy and me were upstairs—upstairs. Then Daddy came back in. He was very angry. He came up the stairs. First Mommy yelled at him some more. Don't fight, I told them. Don't fight. But she stopped yelling at him. She got scared. I was scared . . ."

Lisa choked back her sobs, while Carol wiped away some tears.

". . . then Mommy ran into the bedroom, and tried to hold the door shut. I tried to stop Daddy, but he didn't—he pushed open the bedroom door, and then he—and then he . . ."

Carol knew the rest. And then he pursued Valerie until he caught her. And when he caught her, after making a shambles of the bedroom, he smashed through the doors leading to the balcony and flung her out into the darkness, down into the glass roof over the pool. Then he'd fled, tires screaming, into the night.

Lisa cried softly. Carol held her. "What are you going to do now, Mom?" Johnny asked.

"Let's get ready for bed," Carol said, as calmly as she could. Now that Lisa's memory was out in the open, she would have to give her account to the law, but not tonight. Carol would put the kids to bed and call Jack at his Albany hotel. Jack would probably call Chief Detzler.

They were climbing the stairs when the mail chime sounded.

At night? Impossible.

The mail chime was a final flourish to the house. When the postman dropped a letter into the mail slot at the front door, a chime sounded.

But the postman did not come at night.

Someone was right outside the house.

"John, take Lisa upstairs and stay with her."

"Yes, Mom."

Carol held her nerves in check. The draperies were drawn tight, yet she felt observed, watched, naked. To reach the mailbox, she had to cross her wide, brightly lit living room. Was it better to have the lights on, or off?

The house was silent. Silent also, outside, was whoever had slipped something into the mail slot. Carol moved quickly to the main control panel, switched off all the living room lights, lest her silhouette be visible to a watcher in the shadows. She slid along the wall, and reached into the mailbox.

The yielding softness against her fingertips told her this was a lilac night.

"Jack, Jack, is that you?"

"Yes, what—"

"It's not Stan. It's not."

"What? Honey, slow down—"

"I mean, Stan killed Valerie. We know that. For sure. Lisa remembered. But it's not Stan with the lilacs—"

"Carol!"

· 211 ·

She knew his voice. He was trying to snap her back into control, even as the effect of her message was making him jittery. "Now one thing at a time," he said, "go ahead."

"I thought I should phone you first," Carol explained, astonished at how rational she sounded, "before I called Chief Detzler."

She told him about Lisa remembering. She told him about the lilac in the mailbox.

"And whoever put it there might still be—"

"Outside," he finished. "Carol, go to the control panel. Push the burglar alarm. Don't ask questions. Just get the cops out there right away."

"I think you ought to have called us earlier," Chief Detzler opined. "Walsh is skulking around here for sure. If he killed his wife, he'll kill his kid to keep her mouth shut about what she saw."

"I don't think so," Carol disagreed.

"Come on. What are you talking? You don't know crooks. You come from a whole 'nother background."

"Chief, Stan killed his wife, but he's not a murderer, if you see what I mean. He's just—"

"Nuts?"

Carol nodded. "And I know he didn't put the lilacs in the mailbox or in Johnny's schoolbag, or . . ."

Detzler was tired and cranky. He'd been sleeping. The cottony white hair was matted down on the right side of his head, and a faint imprint of patterned blanket or ridged cushion had left its trace on his cheek. "What the hell have lilacs got to do with this? You talking about that netting in the hedge? And who in the hell left that big branch out there by the door?"

"What branch?"

"I almost tripped over it and broke my neck."

Carol went to the front door. There, where Detzler had kicked it, was a branch from one of the lilac bushes. The floodlights shined down upon it. Thousands of frail petals shivered in the cool night air.

10

If a man wills himself to put aside the superficial restrictions of civilization, then he is capable of anything. The stalker had heard it many times before. Not until recently had he given the concept much thought.

But now, in a waterfront bar in Glen Cove, across Hempstead Harbor from Royall Beach, he was considering the idea seriously for the first time in his life. He was frightened and exhilarated.

If I just *will it*, he thought, steadying his hand to gulp some scotch, if only I *will it*, I can have money *and* revenge.

The rented outboard was checked in at the marina, paid for in cash. He had used a false name for the rental too. Nobody asked questions of a prosperous, trustworthy-looking guy. He swallowed some more scotch, slower this time, and smiled to himself. The false name he'd used to rent the boat was "Walt Stanley." That ought to give Kenton and the cops something to think about.

The scotch was making him feel calmer. He ordered another, and thought about what he'd done tonight.

It had gone so well. A well-handled job.

But, no, something was not right about it. Something did not go down well.

What was it? The stalker wasn't sure.

He replayed the evening step by step in memory. A simple boat rental. An uneventful trip across the calm bay to Royall Beach. He had beached the little boat in the wooded area below the elementary school and headed on foot to the Kenton house. If he'd been spotted by anybody, the stalker didn't know it.

It was dark by the time he reached the Kenton house. Their outside lights were on. Good. That might mean they were scared, or at least apprehensive. *I'll give them something extra to think about*, he vowed, breaking a lilac branch off a bush where the netting had been. He worked his way toward the beachfront side of the house, taking care to stay outside the circle of light cast by those big spots. Taking a deep breath—not so young anymore—he made the dash, raced across the illuminated lawn right up to the front door. He meant to slam the door with the branch of lilacs—they might have ignored him on the beach, might not even have *found* the flowers in the schoolbag—but they couldn't very well fail to wonder about an entire branch. Then the mail slot caught his eye. Terrific! Pressing himself against the side of that magnificent house, he broke off a little sprig, and slipped it into the mail slot.

Hadn't counted on that chime! Christ, they even had a doorbell for the mail! The sound startled him and made him aware of his own tension. Racing down the drive, his heart pounding in his ears, he was blinded by the lights. He hid in the hedges for a little and collected his thoughts, regained his breath. The door did not open, and the house loomed before him in all its impregnability. *Apparent* impregnability. The stalker knew he could get in, when he needed to, when the time came. He just *knew* he could.

Rested then, he skulked through Royall Beach, back to the shore where the boat was. The little outboard motor purred into life, and the stalker hummed back across the harbor to Glen Cove.

Everything had gone well. He had thrown down the gauntlet, and it was Kenton's move now. The stalker had thrown down the gauntlet, but he wasn't even certain Kenton knew it *was* a gauntlet.

That was what bothered him. So did other things, now that he reflected upon them. He'd *ducked* alongside Kenton's house, *skulked* through Royall Beach.

Ducked and *skulked* like a jerk out doing dirt on Halloween.

A feeling of humiliation came down upon the stalker, and with it a sense of impotence, which had afflicted him since the terrible blow had fallen. What good was it even if the Kentons were getting worried about his lilac messages? He was not a violent man but there must be justice in this world! Those who seek the rare and bloody recompense of retribution cannot go ducking around hedges with flowers in their fists. No, those fists must be filled with steel . . .

Drinking, the stalker became morose, then angry at himself for his own irresolution. Death for death. What did he have to live for anyway, except revenge?

Get the money. Plan the revenge. Execute. Then escape. These were the requirements. Simple things. If he would but *will* them. All he had to do was get inside the house, at exactly the right time. And the stalker was sure he knew how to do it.

The stalker slept that night in a strange wavering land of fever and dream. The time would come soon enough, but it must be the right time. He would have to wait, perhaps, and plan, but his moment would come, his night.

Lilac night.

11

$\mathbf{H}$is parents had made Buster go to Sacred Heart of Jesus Grammar School, so he hadn't picked up much geography. In the first place, Sister Mary Stanislaus dismissed much of the world as "pagan" and, therefore, wicked to consider, and in the second place, she had Buster in the front row where she could keep an eye on him. There was one big map at the school, and it got transferred around from classroom to classroom whenever one of the nuns got it into her head to teach a little geography that day. If Sister Mary Stanislaus got it into her head, she would hang the big map on the blackboard in front, take her pointer, rap it on the map and say, "Class, this is Jerusalem. What is this, class?" And all the poor bastards in class had to answer, "It is Jerusalem, Sister." Then Sister Mary Stanislaus would point to another place and say, "Class, this is Queensborough, where we live. What is this, class?" "It is Queensborough, Sister." "And what do we do there, class?" "We live there, Sister." That was her hotshot way of teaching geography. It had been approved by the Pope and Cardinal Spellman, and Buster would at least have learned where Jerusalem and Queens were, except that every time Sister Mary Stanislaus asked her question of the class, she would rap Buster on the head with the pointer. It was a kind of nervous reflex on her part. She did not dislike Buster. She thought she saw the makings of a priest in him.

But Buster learned too little geography, even for the priesthood, and when Charlie told him he had to fly to Venezuela on a political assignment, well, Buster had no real idea where in hell Venezuela was. Buster, in fact, had been outside New York only twice in his life: once to take a vacation trip to Florida, and once when he took it into his mind to get away from Bernice's nagging—this was before the divorce—and spent two nights in a motel in Hoboken, New Jersey. He had a vague idea that Venezuela was farther from Hoboken than it was from Florida.

"Can't you send somebody else?" he asked Charlie.

"Buster, I *trust* you," Charlie returned.

You own *me, is more like it,* Buster thought.

"I trust you and we got to have total control. I want my man on the spot to talk to Bennington."

"Isn't something like this going to be a little, ah, sensitive? I mean, isn't Bennington going to get a little pissed if I go in there and ask, 'Hey, man, did you know Jack Kenton planked your old lady regular back in New York?'"

"Buster, it's not going to be that way. Things are all set. Higgins told me to check out the part of Kenton's life that deals with Karyn Bari. I've already contacted Bennington's headquarters in Mantecal, Venezuela. They know you're coming, and they know it's about the campaign, even though I didn't talk personally to Bennington. All you really have to do is ask him whether he'd consider contributing to Jack Kenton. But I want you to watch his face, listen to him, even meet his wife, if you can. I want to know his gut reaction to Kenton's name, if you think he knows or cares or feels animosity toward Kenton. Jesus, I hope he does."

Since it was summer in New York, Buster naturally figured it'd be winter in Venezuela—he thought he remembered that from some bleak afternoon at Sacred Heart—but luckily the travel agent told him about the equator, so Buster arrived in Caracas wearing a snappy tan polyester. He was real proud of being an American among oily foreigners and only momentarily disconcerted when he discovered Caracas to be a modern city. He hadn't quite known what to expect, but skyscrapers had not been prominent in his vague imaginings. After clearing customs, he humped around until he found a place to hire a private plane.

The charter pilot had a round brown face and missing teeth. He looked suspiciously at Buster.

"Mantecal? Why do you want go there?"

"None of your business, if you don't mind my saying so."

"Long way. Cost you plenty of dollars."

Buster remembered something about these foreigners always wanting to haggle about everything. It was a game for them because they didn't have much entertainment in life, except getting laid, and you couldn't do that all day. At least Buster couldn't. He didn't feel like haggling either.

"You have a plane that'll go over these mountains?" grunted Buster, looking at the peaks to the south of the city.

Ramón, the pilot, was insulted. He pointed to a dilapidated two-engined Cessna. "Are you going, or not?" he demanded.

"Going."

"Then get in the plane," said Ramón.

Two engines and Buster's muttered incantations to every saint he'd ever heard of got them over the mountains, and then Ramón had the Cessna gliding smoothly out over a vast sweep of rich land. Buster had never seen anything like it in Florida or New Jersey, and it surprised the hell out of him to see country like this in a drippy third-rate backwater place.

"Why do you want to go to Mantecal?" Ramón tried again.

"To hunt jungle-bunnies and flat-nosed spear-chuckers," said Buster, to shut him up. Ramón didn't figure that out, but he did figure out that he was being made fun of, and he started muttering about gringos.

"Rich *norteamericano*, he lives in Mantecal," Ramón offered later. "Señor Bennington. He is filthy rich."

"Yeah, I'm going to see him," Buster said.

Ramón was so impressed that he shut up.

The Bennington ranch looked huge from the air but even more imposing when one was driven toward it on a wide, paved roadway that ran through a rolling field of high, green prairie grass. Cattle grazed alongside the road and right up next to the great white wall that surrounded the compound. Buster had called the ranch from the little Mantecal airstrip, and Bennington sent a car to pick him up, a car Buster didn't enter until he'd made Ramón promise to wait, not leave him stranded out here in the parrot-talking boonies.

Inside the compound, the driver, who had not spoken to Buster at all, braked to a stop before a cool white house, and Buster was shown inside. Somebody dressed up in a butler suit like in an English movie took him through half-a-dozen rooms, gestured that he was to be seated, and left. Buster looked around and saw that he was in some kind of a porch. The furniture was all rattan; the tables had glass tops, and beyond the screen was a jungle that Buster figured had to be the garden. A lovely, dark-skinned girl in a white uniform brought out a pot of tea and a cold stone pitcher of daiquiris. Buster pointed at the pitcher, and the girl, smiling, poured him a huge drink. Goddam, this was living, he thought. Charlie should send him on more assignments like this.

Then the girl left, and Buster sat there, drinking, getting slightly high. This place certainly had it over Mel and Irma's Tavern. Bennington didn't seem to have been alarmed by Charlie's introductory letter. Buster wondered what Charlie had put in that letter. Then Buster was aware of a presence in the doorway. He turned, thinking it must be Bennington, and started to rise for the handshake.

But Buster did not stand up, not right away. His brain perceived and absorbed the vision standing in the doorway, and his first bizarre impulse said *genuflect*, said *on your knees*. Buster had seen the pictures in the paper, but they had not given one-tenth of one percent a suggestion of Karyn Bari's beauty, nor any indication of the power of her presence. For the first time in his life, Buster felt himself in the company of a woman for whom he would do anything, and he hoped she would ask. He had to struggle to his feet, gulping for air. He couldn't take his eyes off her: that flawless skin beneath which beat not simple blood but the essence of all life, those strange dark eyes that held him like the cobra its victim, the body that had been in God's mind when He fashioned Eve.

"Will you sit down, please?" said Karyn Bari, taking a seat near him. *Near* him. He could smell not her fragrance, although she wore something delicate and faintly vexing, but the heat of her living body. She struck old Buster to the marrow of his soul, pierced him to the source of all rut, all lust. *Lucky I'm here on business*, Buster thought, his insight jerky and disjointed. He couldn't have gotten it up in a million years. Sitting here with this woman was like sitting in the presence of a strange and wild Madonna. Gradually, he became aware that she was holding something. It was oddly familiar. He'd seen quite a few like it in his time; he had several himself.

"You don't need that gun," he croaked.

"I suppose not, you moronic pig," she said, in a voice that was soft depth and throaty resonance. She was still smiling.

Buster's eyes flashed from the barrel of the pistol to her sleek brown leg, exposed by a thigh-high slit in a white satin skirt. He ought not to have looked, Buster decided, when Karyn called *"Tie!"* or something in a clear tone of command. Buster had visions of himself trussed up and tortured—why, oh why, had he ever done any work for Charlie Kiefer?—when another person came into the room. And Buster knew for sure and all he'd wandered off into the twilight zone.

"Tyler," said Karyn softly, with the gun still on Buster, "this is Mr. Pauley, from New York."

"Pleased to meet you," said the boy, in faintly accented English, and held out his hand. Buster took it, shaking hands in the process with the precise, perfect replica of a boy who'd lived in an apartment in Ridgewood, Queens, just right down the street from Buster's place, and whose name had been Jack Kenton.

Tie? No, *Tyler*. Kenton's middle name.

Oh, shit, thought Buster, in his first lucid moment since Karyn had appeared. Random flashes shot like tracer bullets through the bewildered beer-and-ball-scarred furrows of Buster's brain. Would dying take long? How much would it hurt? Would somebody ship his carcass back Stateside, or would they leave him out on the plains for cows to shit on, buzzards to eat?

"Coming here wasn't my idea—" he stammered.

"I can tell that just by looking at you," Karyn said, smiling in amusement. She slipped the gun into the waistband of her skirt.

"This is Tyler Bennington," Karyn told him. "He is my son by Jack Kenton. That's what you came here to find out, isn't it?"

Buster went ape, right there in his head. What broad would admit something like that? Either she was the most honest woman he had ever come across—although that wouldn't be a hard title to win, considering the broads he had come across—or she was crazy. And if she was crazy, his ass was surely grass. No way she was going to let him go back to the States with that bit of news.

"You may go now, Ty," said Karyn, touching the boy's face

gently. Buster shook his head, as if to clear it of Jack Kenton's youthful image.

"I received an introductory letter from a New York nonentity named Kiefer," Karyn was saying, "telling me you'd be arriving. I assumed my son would eventually be pawn to some ambitious fragment of scum."

Nonentity! Scum! Charlie would go flat out crazy to hear what he was being called. But wait a minute. If Karyn thought Charlie was those bad things, then how much worse did she think poor old Buster was? He felt like he had the time Sister Mary Stanislaus wouldn't let him clean the erasers because of remembering only two of the Ten Commandments. His feelings were hurt.

"I sure didn't mean to cause no trouble," he heard himself saying. "We—ah—Mr. Kiefer just wanted to know how—ah—Mr. Bennington might view certain potential candidates in the New York election."

"Namely Jack Kenton?"

"Namely."

"Have another drink," Karyn offered, quite cordially.

Buster's hand shook a little as he poured from the big pitcher; that gun was still in her waistband.

"Do you think my husband did not know the boy is Jack Kenton's son? You have heard of my husband's reputation?"

Buster gulped some booze, and nodded.

"Cruelty is not the word for Rudolf Bennington. He enjoyed more than anything the domination of human beings and the control of their destinies. But I beat him at his own game."

Buster took a big swallow of daiquiri and said nothing.

"You may tell Mr. Kiefer that the entire concern is mine and Jack Kenton's. And Tyler's too, of course," Karyn said.

Not Rudolf Bennington's? Buster wondered.

She read his mind. This woman was a witch. Either that, or his mind was disappointingly easy to read.

"It is no longer of any concern to my husband," Karyn said. "Would you like to meet him? You must. After coming all this way."

Oh, God, now the ax falls, Buster groaned to himself. Bennington had the reputation of a rough, uneduated motherfucker who'd broken a lot of heads in his time, or ordered a lot of heads broken. Scared half shitless, Buster followed Karyn Bari through more rooms, up half a flight of stairs to what must have been another wing of the house. Buster was sure he was going to die. And yet, oddly, he made no move to escape or even to postpone his probable fate. When Buster passed through a glass door and smelled ammonia, he knew he was a goner: they were planning to asphyxiate him.

"My husband," said Karyn Bari, as they rounded a partition and entered a large, sunlit room. "You and your friend might have saved yourselves the cost of the airplane ticket."

Buster gaped. She was right. There was Rudolf Bennington. Buster recognized him from the old photos. But it was a Rudolf Bennington altered by the fate of man, the will of eternity. The famous man was in a case of glass and steel, his features visible through an icy, drifting fog, a chemical mist fashioned to hold back the deterioration of flesh and muscle. From the store of his vast wealth, Rudolf Bennington's last desperate purchase had been a cryogenic chamber, to preserve his body against the chance that future medicine would find a way to make it quick again.

"Nobody knows," muttered Buster, at once fascinated and revolted by the spectacle.

"That's right. He's been dead for almost a year now. I am free. I have been considering what to do for my son and myself. And I thank you, because your visit has helped me to decide."

"It has?"

Karyn just smiled.

"What about the companies? All the businesses? You run them?"

"My husband, my departed, unlamented husband lying there, had a weakness. Everyone has at least one weakness. I was his. He left me everything. What he thought was everything, at any rate. It is not what I want. Do you know something? Business is very boring, and businessmen are even worse. They remind me of circus pigs who have learned to balance a ball on their snouts. They think only how fine their trick must be, while the audience sees merely the ugliness of the pig."

Buster gaped.

"So you may tell your Mr. Kiefer that he is a fool. He will get no cooperation from me."

"Then I can leave?"

"May and can."

"But—" worried Buster, with a last look at the cryogenic chamber, and Bennington's frozen corpse within it . . .

Karyn read his thoughts again. "But what if you tell people my husband is dead?"

He nodded glumly, not without fear. Perhaps her invitation to depart was a new kind of trap. She was beautiful, true, but in her glittering onyx eyes, he saw the limitless patience and spirit and guile that had deceived and outlasted Rudolf Bennington.

"You may tell anyone you want anything you want," she told him. "It won't matter. The beauty of the corporation is that it lives on, no matter who else dies."

Buster turned that over in his mind. He had a lot of things to turn over, and he left the great house bewildered, as if he had come out of a dream that receded from him faster than his memory could race after it. He wanted to figure things out. Buster had the feeling that he had heard something in that house, had learned something very important, but hadn't quite put his finger on it yet.

"You see him?" asked Ramón, when they were airborne again, on their way back to Caracas. "What is he like?"

"Well," said Buster, sensing that here, at least, was someone he could impress with inside info. "I'm not at liberty to say much, you understand, but I can tell you this: Rudolf Bennington is one hell of a cold guy."

"Ah!" Ramón said knowingly.

"Ty?" said Karyn Bari, later that night, as she sat on the edge of her son's bed. "Ty, we ought to see more of the world. I have been putting it off, but now I think the time is right."

"Yes," the boy agreed sleepily. "Where will we go?"

"New York," she answered. "Then India."

Tyler turned over, yawned, and looked at his mother with Jack

Kenton's green eyes. "What will we do in those places, Mother?"

"Anything we want," she answered softly, bending down and kissing him on the forehead. "Anything we want."

Sister Mary Stanislaus of Sacred Heart had always maintained, against considerable opinion to the contrary, that Buster was not "slow for his age." "He's just deliberate," she had pronounced. "He thinks things through very carefully and cautiously. That's a quality to make him an excellent priest, don't you agree?"

Few did. No one, in fact. But Buster always had a soft spot for Sister Mary after that, and when something puzzled him, her long-ago judgment about his thinking ability kept him plugging on after some other dumb shit who was honest-to-God "slow" would have given up. So he got on board the plane back to New York, and just kept plugging away. He had his big idea somewhere over the Caribbean Sea.

Was it possible that Jack Kenton had a kid he didn't even know about?

Book Three

THE PETALS OF TIME

1

Buster Pauley arrived back in New York on Memorial Day, 1981. A seasoned international traveler now, he even experienced a combined thrill of importance and nostalgia as the big 747 skimmed low over Queens, where he'd grown up, and landed at JFK airport. *Screw you, Bernice,* he thought, *I got out of Queens at last, just like Jack Kenton.*

He ignored, for the moment, the fact that he would have to go right back to Queens again.

Buster cleared customs and hustled out onto the street in front of the International Arrivals Terminal. There was Charlie Kiefer's big limo, and Charlie was in it.

"I am going to treat you to a feed," Charlie said. "You just start telling me the whole story, real slow. I intend to enjoy the hell out of it."

Buster remembered Karyn Bari's words for Charlie: nonentity, scum, and fool. He decided to omit a few things from his report.

At Charlie's direction, the chauffeur drove them to the Lower East Side, Charlie's old neighborhood, to a place called Gregorio's. Charlie always had a thing about going back to where he'd started out whenever a big decision had to be made, or a shrewd coup celebrated, and he especially liked the out-of-the-way but excellent old restaurant where they fawned all over him. Funny the way things went. People talking about change all the time. But nothing really changed. The tenement in which Charlie's father had turned into a human icicle was still doing business, but housing Thais and Laotians and Koreans now instead of Irish and Jews and Russians and Italians and God knows who, like in the old days.

"Bring me a double Chivas," Charlie told the waiter, "and my friend here'll have a beer and a ball."

"No thanks, I'll have a daiquiri."

"A daiquiri? What the hell. You getting delusions of grandeur or something?"

"A daiquiri is a very classy drink," Buster explained, thinking of Karyn Bari. "The best people drink them."

"Well, they say travel broadens everybody." Charlie shrugged, and he ordered a couple dozen oysters on the half shell, fettuccine Alfredo, a tureen of minestrone, and medallions of veal so tender you could slice them with a sideways glance. Buster devoured a rack of lamb and several small loaves of bread, telling Charlie—between mouthfuls—what he'd learned down in Venezuela.

"No kidding," Charlie said, when he learned that Bennington's corpse was frozen stiff.

"Just like there's gonna be a resurrection after all," Buster expanded, "except not exactly the way it was planned. And, Boss, this is hard to believe, but that Bari pulled a gun on me. Not even Bernice pulled a gun on me."

"A gun," said Charlie. "Jesus Christ."

"And even the kid *looks* like Kenton. She didn't even go through the trouble to deny he was the father. In fact, she made a point to tell me he was."

"Holy absolute *shit!!!*" chortled Charlie. "This is like being in hog heaven."

"But, Charlie, she says she won't cooperate with . . . us."

To Buster's surprise, Charlie wasn't disappointed at all. He called for coffee and Cognac and lit up a Monte Cristo. It was a big fat one. Charlie started the day with a little bitty cheroot, gradually increasing the size of his stogies all day, until now, after dinner, he had this Churchill thing sticking out of his mouth like a length of dynamite.

"It was your feeling Kenton doesn't even know the kid is his?" insinuated Charlie, blowing smoke.

"I'd say. And Bari won't have nothing to do with us."

"Anything. But she doesn't have to."

"She doesn't? But I thought Governor Higgins wanted to know if there was any incriminating evidence against Kenton?"

"Buster, you and me have been through a lot, and you should know by now there's more than one way to skin a cat. There's this reporter I know at the *New York Times*," he said, leaning forward and speaking real low. "Seymour Hochzeit. He was on the balls of his ass, once, and I helped him out. I'll just leak a few little suggestions to him. He might not actually go and *print* anything, but you bet your life he'll do some phoning. To Kenton. To Higgins. To Bari too. It'll be beautiful. Higgins and Kenton will *know* there's going to be a problem, but they won't know exactly where it's coming from. I'll be in the clear. Hochzeit can't reveal his sources, see. It's a matter of—uh—ethics." Charlie leaned back contentedly and blew a big cloud of cigar smoke. "And I just thought of something else, too. I'll tell Hochzeit that Kenton plans to announce candidacy at the Waldorf, on the night of the Fourth of July. That's Higgins's big plan. Big surprise. Mucho press. All that crap. So on top of the news of a bastard kid, Higgins and Kenton are going to have to lose their big media surprise or deny there is going to be an announcement of candidacy!"

Charlie was glowing. He was altogether beside himself with joy.

"If they suddenly got a free ballroom there at the Waldorf on the Fourth of July, hell, it might be just somebody named Kiefer who makes a little announcement!"

Buster sipped some coffee and thought it over. Truth to tell, he was getting a bit uneasy.

"I want you to go back out to Royall Beach," Charlie was saying. "I want you to set up that dojiggy microwave machine again. Pick up anything you can. I want to know every *word* Kenton says. I want to know how he reacts to the stuff Hochzeit is going to hit him with. I want to watch him twist."

"Hold on a minute," said Buster, stalling for time to get some sense into Charlie, "the cops out there might remember my car. It's the only wheels I can scare up, a loaner from old Kohler at the Texaco station. I'm not sure it's safe to—"

"You workin' for me or you workin' for *me?*" demanded Charlie, giving Buster a hard glare.

"Yeah."

"So what you do is rent a Mercedes or a Jag. One of them fancy cars that won't get noticed out there in Royall Beach. Go ahead and rent one. I'll foot the bill. But I want that machine in place PDQ, make it yesterday, and telling me every word that comes out of Kenton's mouth. You got that?"

"Yeah," said Buster again.
"Jack Kenton is not going to know what hit him."
"Just like that time in the park," said Buster.
"What?"
"Oh, nothing," Buster said.

2

Memorial Day weekend was over,
and the last stretch of the school year had begun. Carol would have
given a lot to be head of a school in a state having only a nine-month
academic year, but this was New York. Vacation was a whole
month away.

"Hey! How come Dad's home so early?" asked Johnny, as Carol
drove into the yard and saw the white Lincoln in front of the house.

"Don't know," answered Carol, but she had the feeling that it
spelled trouble.

"How about if I take Lisa down to the water?" suggested Johnny,
as the three of them got out of the car.

"Wait outside a second. I'll ask your father. If he's home this
early, maybe he has plans."

"Jack?" Carol called, entering the house, "Jack?"

For just an instant, the house was deathly silent. Carol was so
jittery these days that an unanticipated moment of quiet made the
fine hair on the back of her neck stiffen in alarm.

"In the den, honey," he answered.

She knew already, from the tone of his voice. More bad news.
But she could not have dreamed how serious it was, nor how it
would alter the pattern of her life.

"I'll have to talk to you alone for a moment," he told her, with a
slight sidewise tilt of his head and an expression she could not read.

"What's the matter?" she asked, as he drew her inside the den and
closed the door. "Jack, what's wrong? You look—"

"You can't tell what I look, because I'm not sure what I feel.
Honey, let's sit down. Telling you what I have to tell you is going to
be the hardest thing I've ever done."

He looked so absorbed, so perplexed, that all of Carol's feeling for
him welled up. They sat down, and she took his hand, caressing it.
"Just tell me. Whatever it is doesn't matter . . ."

"It does matter."

"Yes, it does matter. But there's nothing that will affect my loving you. That's what makes us *us*."

He looked grateful. He looked right into her eyes. She could see the pain. And she felt the pain when he said, "Carol, I think I have a son by Karyn Bari. I just found out about it."

There are probably no more than half-a-dozen great moments in life, whether for good or ill. Some of them are common to everyone: the first time you know that you are in love; the death of someone dear to you; a first glimpse of your own living child; the moment you know you are going to die. But each life has, too, such devastating moments unique unto themselves, that arise out of time and chance alone. Now Carol had one of those moments. She felt everything, and she felt nothing. She felt hurt, anger, outrage, confusion, betrayal. Even disbelief. *Stay calm*, she told herself, *you can handle this*. She looked into Jack's eyes and felt his hand in her own. *I'm staying calm*, she told herself, remembering what she had told him mere seconds ago: ". . . *there's nothing that will affect my loving you . . .*"

Carol couldn't speak but only remember: the first time she'd seen Jack, with her father at the Back Bay Brasserie in Boston; the time they'd made love on the beach at Wescott Cove, with broad daylight all around; the pride and love on his face the day Johnny was born. Now there was another son. Another son. His, too.

The cold, beautiful face of Karyn Bari regarded Carol across time and the years.

"Jack," she said, "there's nothing that will affect my loving you, and there's nothing we can't handle."

Then he was holding her, and she was crying a little, but it was all right, because they were not bad tears, and because he was holding her.

"You said you *think* you have a son," she managed, after a time. "How did you learn this? Exactly what do you know for sure?"

I stayed pretty calm, she told herself proudly, wiping her eyes with his silk pocket handkerchief.

"CiJi, I . . ."

"Hey! Can we go down to the water or not?" shouted their son, banging on the door.

"Just a minute or so more," Jack said. "I'll go with you. Get some buckets and shovels for Lisa, okay?"

"Okay, Dad."

"I got a couple of phone calls at the office today," Jack said. "The first was from a *New York Times* reporter, one Seymour Hochzeit. He'd 'heard' a few things, he said, and he wanted to get my reactions. One, Rudolf Bennington has been dead for over a year."

"What?"

"Apparently so. And Karyn Bari told someone she has my child, whose name is Tyler, by the way. Did I have any knowledge of that, Mr. Hochzeit wanted to know. I told him no, but later, after he'd hung up, I put some things together. You know how readily you can recall things that happened long ago? Especially if you tried to forget them?"

"I know," Carol said sadly.

"Well, some things happened then that I didn't understand. My abortive contract with Bennington about that Taggart business. Karyn seeing Bennington. My trip to Venezuela. Her sudden departure. With him. *And* the time she started not feeling well. I figured it out. If she has a child, he could be Bennington's, but he is possibly mine."

"And the second call was from . . . Karyn Bari," said Carol, without expression.

"No. From John Higgins."

"Oh, Jack . . ."

"Well, no cause for alarm yet. Higgins hasn't made any new decisions or rescinded any old ones. Besides, two and two aren't so hard to put together. Charlie Kiefer denies leaking anything, though."

"Charlie Kiefer? He talked to the *Times?* But he's the party chairman."

"He also wants to be governor. A big part of Higgins's plan was the surprise of my announcement. If the story comes out in dribs and drabs, there's no effect at all. It'll be like having ringside tickets to wait for Godot."

"What did Higgins tell the reporter?"

"Bought him off, in effect. Promised him a big exclusive just as soon as all plans are set. That'll buy some time, anyway. Higgins is one smooth operator."

"Too smooth by half."

"You may be right. No choice but to wait and see. I'm not going to be intimidated."

"Did—did Higgins—had he heard about the boy? Tyler?" Carol asked.

"He had. Mr. Hochzeit is not a reticent man. But the governor's not particularly concerned, unless Karyn makes an issue of it, or if the supermarket tabloids do."

"How will anybody know what Bari plans?" Carol wanted to know.

"I guess we'll ask her. She's on her way to New York."

"How do you know?"

"I tried calling her in Venezuela."

"Hey, Dad! Mom!" Johnny called. "There's a car coming up the driveway."

"Expecting anyone?" Jack asked.

Carol shook her head.

They left the room, and crossed to the big windows. The approaching car was big and black, shiny but old, a limousine retired to private use. The car pulled up next to the house, but neither driver nor occupants could be distinguished behind the smoked glass.

Then a trim, well-muscled young man climbed out from the driver's door and nodded at someone inside the car. He glanced doubtfully at the house.

"Who is it?" asked Lisa fearfully, watching with the rest of them inside the house.

"I don't know," said Jack. "But I'm going out and see."

"Jack—" worried Carol.

"It'll be okay," he said, and it looked as if he were right, because by now the driver had gone around the car, and opened it for an elderly woman who struggled out, leaning on a steel walker used by the partially handicapped. She was glaring balefully at the Kenton house.

"It's Mrs. Kiefer, Charlie's ma," said Jack, going outside. Carol and the children followed him.

Charlie's ma, her companion-*cum*-nurse beside her, had started to chug toward the front door. She stopped when she saw Jack approaching.

"Mr. Kenton, I'm Stu Inkspell," said the young man, not looking too happy. He nodded toward Mrs. Kiefer, as if to say, *Don't blame me, she made me drive her here.*

Gertie Kiefer was a chunky, solid-looking old lady, wearing a flower-print dress, a string of pearls around her veiny throat, and a 1950s Mamie Eisenhower hat with a little film of veil on it. After squinting at Jack for a long time, she addressed Carol.

"You'd best get them kids in the house, missy. I still got some sense of decency, even if nobody else has, and I got some hard things to say they oughtn't to be hearing."

"Come now, Mrs. Kiefer," cautioned Stu Inkspell hopefully.

"Shut up, young man. You just keep taking orders from me, and we'll get along fine."

Johnny and Lisa, fascinated by this creaking, indomitable apparition, had not moved.

"Go in the house for a minute, kids," said Jack, "this is just big-people talk anyway."

"You damn well better believe it," gritted Gertie Kiefer, as the children retreated. Bracing herself on the walker, she pointed a bony finger at Jack. "Charlie knows about your bastard kid," she croaked. "He knows about it, and I told him to use it against you, unless you do the right thing by everybody, tuck tail and run. You are a disgrace, do you know that? Why, my boy Charlie is as pure as the driven snow . . ."

Stu Inkspell looked away, embarrassed; Carol could not take her eyes away from the fierce old woman.

". . . pure as the driven snow, I tell you, while you, Mr. Kenton, with this fine, lovely girl for a wife, have to go around poking your thing into—"

"That'll be enough, Mrs. Kiefer. I get your point," said Jack.

"Can't take it, huh? Well, this is only the beginning, let me tell you—"

"Please, Mrs. Kiefer," pleaded Stu.

"Shut up."

"Did Charlie send you?" Carol asked.

Gertie swung her glance to the younger woman, eyes filled with pride and fury. "Why, no," she said, a parody of sweetness. "Why, no, my dear. Charlie didn't send me. Gertie Kiefer is capable of doing quite a few things on her own, thank you very much. And I do a lot of things on my own, ain't that right, Stu?"

The young man nodded glumly.

"Mrs. Kiefer, I know there's no point discussing this," Carol began.

"You're damn right, young lady."

"So why don't you just leave."

She said it with such calmness, such authority, that old Gertie gaped and blinked. "Suit yourself," she said, with a mean look, and turned back toward the car. Stu Inkspell shrugged apologetically, and helped her into the backseat.

"Sorry," he muttered to Jack and Carol, before getting behind the wheel and driving off.

"You were splendid," praised Jack. "But I can't tell you how sorry I am, all this—"

"If somebody goes to all that trouble to let you know she's your enemy, the best thing to do is let her know you're ready."

"Ready for what?"

"That's what I *don't* know," admitted Carol, taking his hand as they walked back toward the house. "Jack!"

"Yes?"

"I just had a thought. Stu Inkspell!"

"What about him?"

"He could have been the man who gave me the lilacs on the beach! It was someone with a build like that. And he could have gotten into the school easily, to put them in Johnny's schoolbag. He looks like any young father from around here. No one would have given him a second glance if he showed up at school. And you saw how Mrs. Kiefer bossed him around. I wonder . . ."

"Oh, Carol . . ."

She pulled his hand. He stopped. They faced each other. "Maybe you're right," she said. "But I just don't know anymore. Things are coming at us from all sides, and Stan Walsh is still out there somewhere, on the loose . . ."

They embraced, an imperceptibly strained embrace. He was still Jack, her husband, but he was also the father of a strange boy who had just come into their lives.

"I've got a feeling that June is going to be one hell of a month," said Jack.

3

The New York summer can come at any time. Some years the mercury will shoot into the nineties in April, and almost always there will be a hot spell in May. For the Kentons, along with everyone else, summer came just after Memorial Day. Morning after morning, the sun rose hot and hard out of the Atlantic, burning the new grass and the leaves, wilting the flowers and the vines. The pretty pink petals fell from the lilac hedges along the drive, until not a blossom remained.

Carol was glad to see them go.

But there were other things to worry about. She had to prepare her statement for the community open forum, which would take place just prior to state exam week at the end of June. If she took exactly the right tone, played just the right note, might a strike be averted? It was worth a chance.

A less obvious but more ominous problem was Karyn Bari. She was no longer in Venezuela, but apparently not yet in New York either. Jack had tried to reach her daily, with no success. Perhaps, just perhaps, she did not want to be reached at all. If that were true, then Karyn and her son could be anywhere in the world, but most assuredly out of the Kentons' lives!

Carol did not allow herself to hope too hard, lest this possibility be jinxed.

Yet not knowing what Bari was up to was like sleeping beneath a sword.

Carol was looking forward to a reasonably peaceful weekend, when Jack announced he had to make an out-of-town trip.

"Oh, honey!"

"I'm sorry. But I have to. You know that federal contract I have to monitor illegal alien traffic across the Mexican border? Well, I wasn't as clever as I thought when I formulated the model," he continued. "Where gain is concerned, bribes are water and human nature a sieve. I've got to go down to El Paso. Just for a day. I'll be back tomorrow night."

Tomorrow night was Saturday, so there was only tonight to spend at home alone. The children were here, of course, but it still seemed alone without Jack. She got them to bed at a little after nine, came downstairs, and fixed herself a brandy and water. What to do? Write her speech? Not on a Friday night, strike or no. The television listing revealed another exciting summer sequence of reruns. She was looking through a stack of records when the phone rang.

"Mrs. Kenton? Ed Peters here, of Stuyvesant Mutual. I hope I didn't interrupt your dinner."

Oh, good grief. She and Jack hadn't even discussed coverage for Lisa, with everything else that had been happening.

"Mr. Peters, I'm sorry, but we just haven't had time to get around to that yet."

He laughed pleasantly. "I've heard that before, in my business. But I wouldn't press the point if it weren't important . . ."

"Would it be possible," asked Carol, "to have Lisa insured just the way Johnny is now? I'm sure that would be fine."

"Why certainly. If you want to go that route, just let me prepare the forms, and I can drop them off at your home for signature. Even so, it'll take a little time. The paper mills grind slowly. That's why I wanted to make sure we're in agreement on principle, so to speak."

"I think we are."

"Is your husband in? Perhaps I might speak to him about it?"

"Oh, he's—yes, he's here. But he's busy right now. Could I have him call you back?"

"No matter. It's a Friday night. Have him call me at my office Monday. Or I'll call him, just to confirm what we've discussed. Have a nice weekend, Mrs. Kenton."

"And the same to you."

She hung up, sipped some of her drink, and put Mahler on the stereo. The record was just about to drop, when Carol thought she heard something, out by the front door. All the draperies were drawn shut, so no one could see inside the house, but racing imagination made her fearful. The vast living room, empty and austere, lay between Carol and the front door, a cold open space in which, it seemed, *something was destined to happen.* But how could that be? The door was locked; the house was secure.

Push the alarm. Detzler and his cops are just moments away.

Then the phone rang again. She picked up the receiver, hungry for a human voice.

"Hello? Is this the residence of Carol Jean Atwood? Or Kenton?" A man's voice, distant and doubtful.

"This is Mrs. Kenton," she said.

"Mrs. Kenton, you might not remember me. I called your parents' residence in Connecticut to track you down. You knew me a long time ago. Bull Brand."

Vic Brand's father! What on earth . . . ? "Mr. Brand, of course. How are you?"

A welter of memories came back to her, eddies and currents and waves of angry sadness. Why was Bull Brand bringing back all those things? Still, he had treated her with kindness and understanding. She remembered their long talk in his glittering trophy room.

"I'm fine," Bull told her. "Just older. Look, let me get right to it. I believe you ought to know. About six months ago, the doctors at the Mellon in Pittsburgh decided Vic was well enough to begin making trial visits home, here to Bucks County. The visits went well, and became more frequent . . ."

Carol followed his words, and wondered. If Vic had been leaving the Mellon Clinic regularly for half a year, then was he in some way behind the lilac business?

"Did he take trips, or anything?" she asked Bull. "Where did he stay when he left the clinic?"

"Right here with me. Until today. He sometimes went for long walks in the country, so I didn't know he was gone for certain until dinnertime. But he's not here. That's why I'm calling."

"I don't understand."

"Last night at dinner, for the first time in years, he mentioned your name. I just want to tell you that he might try to get in touch.

I've alerted the police in Pennsylvania and New Jersey to be on the lookout, because he *is* a mental patient. I think you should do the same, with regard to the police in your area."

"I *certainly* shall. You can count on—"

"And Mrs. Kenton? I don't like to have to say this, but I think you should know. Vic did not remember the past, how shall I say, happily."

"Then, Mr. Brand," she told him, half regretting her words even as she spoke, "he and I finally do have something in common."

She hung up and stood there a moment, not so much thinking of what Bull Brand had told her, but instead trying to let the flood of memories wash over her, wash over her without touching and leave her in peace. But how could she relax with Vic Brand on the loose? The man first to pass her three tests—body, mind, and heart! What a terrible joke. Vic Brand III!

Carol was just about to call Chief Detzler when she heard a sound, less than a rattling, more than a scraping, at the front door. And she heard something else, too, woeful and mesmerizing and forlorn, a sound composed by Satan, *The Waltz of the Dead*.

I am not hearing this! she told herself, as the first note throbbed within the temple of her soul.

This is not happening! she declared, as the second swooping note of that terrible prelude rose up within her being.

"I can't bear this imaginary lunacy," she cried, reasoning shakily that the waltz was being caused now by her own nervous apprehension, not by any objective threat.

As the third note sounded, the note that had accompanied death before, Carol rushed to the door, thrust aside the drapery, and looked.

Into the demented, accusing eyes of Vic Brand. He had not changed greatly. He still wore his hair down across his forehead. But there was something monstrously altered about him. He was empty, a human husk, all fires burned out save one: his sick belief that Carol had betrayed him.

She pressed the alarm button, and pressed it again, and again.

*　　*　　*

· 241 ·

Then Detzler and the police were at the house. Carol, on the verge of a nervous jag of tears, and cursing herself for it, opened the door. The chief came in.

"Wasn't any false alarm this time, I guess," he drawled. "We nabbed the alleged perpetrator down there on the driveway. Right where that netting used to be. I think we caught the guy who put it there."

"I'm not so sure . . ."

"You know, Mrs. Kenton, it's none of my business, 'cause I'm a paid public servant, sworn to run out in the night after all manner of craziness, but have you and your husband considered hiring a private guard? Not that me and my boys don't get *paid* enough, you understand, to come running out here every other day—"

Outside the house, someone shouted, then others, and a pistol snapped like a whipcrack in the dark. Detzler, in spite of his age, made it out of the house fast. Carol closed the door, but watched through the window. The chief walked far down the drive where dim cones of flashlights arced like tiny airport beacons. In a minute, he slouched back toward the house. Carol let him in. He looked every year of his age, and then some.

"What—what happened?"

"Did you know the guy?"

Carol caught the past tense and nodded fearfully.

"He pulled a knife on one of my men, wounded him. Officer Grafft shot him then. He's dead."

Vic Brand. Back from all those years, back from the past, burning with hate, dead in Carol's own driveway. But Carol knew that Vic could have had nothing to do with the netting. Or the lilacs. She knew it as clearly as she knew that *The Waltz of the Dead* would be her millstone forever.

"Well, it's over," Chief Detzler was saying, "for whatever that's worth."

"No," replied Carol, "it's not."

4

Governor John Higgins gave a press conference in Albany on June 18, and Carol read about it next morning. The Kentons had the *New York Times* delivered to the house, but, except on weekends, Carol seldom got a chance to read it there. She usually took it with her to school and looked it over in her office before the daily battle began, paying special attention lately to political news. Today's story was by Seymour Hochzeit, friend of Charlie Kiefer, and he was doing his best to put some pressure on the governor.

> When asked if he intended to run again next year, the Governor replied, "That's a long time from now, isn't it?" Pressed further, he would neither confirm nor deny reports that State Party Boss Charles G. Kiefer, Assemblyman Arthur L. Salzman of Buffalo, and Long Island Tax Reformer John Tyler Kenton were actively seeking his backing for the job. "As far as I know, I'm still Governor," he said, clearly irritated, "and I might have something more to say about that on the Fourth of July." A query as to whether there might be more dark-horse possibilities in the closet led Higgins to reply, "The last time I checked, I had one Harris tweed, three or four pinstripes, and a dinner jacket with a mysterious red smudge on the lapel."

Very witty, Governor, thought Carol, unimpressed. She glanced at the wall clock. Union "coordinator" Anton Semlac was due in twenty minutes. Carol took a sip of coffee that Stella, the school secretary, brewed every morning—she was suspected of using pencil shavings for added flavor—and turned to the Arts and Leisure section of the *Times*. She wished she hadn't.

BARI RETURNS TO AMERICA:

SINGER IN SECLUSION AT PIERRE HOTEL.

Rumored Bennington International Heiress
Travels with Son.

There were pictures, too. Carol did not know if it was more

unnerving to look at the cold, silken beauty of the woman, or to stare at the striking boy beside Bari herself. *"Karyn Bari and her son, Tyler,"* said the caption. Tyler! The gall! Even more unsettling, the boy looked almost like her own son, Johnny.

"Mr. Semlac is here to see you," announced Stella, sticking her head around the side of the doorjamb.

"Show him in," said Carol.

"Down to business," Semlac announced. "The community open forum is three days away. Next week is exam time. Blanche has spoken to you. If you don't renege on your support for the pilot program and come out in favor of teacher salary increases, we will strike your school."

"I believe that's an accurate representation of the situation to date," Carol agreed.

"Seems you're the one person, the central agent, so to speak, who can avoid all that trouble for everybody. Including yourself."

On sudden impulse, Carol asked him: "Mr. Semlac, are you partial to lilacs?"

"Lilacs?" he asked, seeming genuinely puzzled by her question. "No, why? I kind of like lilies myself."

"Nothing," she began, "it's just that—"

They were interrupted by a sudden electronic snarl from the intercom: "Dr. Kenton! Dr. Kenton!" It was a woman's frantic voice. "Dr. Kenton," she cried again, "this is . . ."

Her next words were garbled in panic. Carol was on her feet behind the desk. Semlac stood up. Stella was in the doorway, her mouth open. Then the voice came on the speaker again.

"This is Mrs. Boureg in classroom one-twenty-one. There was a man. He was just here. Dr. Kenton, *he took Lisa!!!"*

Stan! thought Carol. But this time Royall Beach Elementary was ready for an intruder. Carol pressed a button that had been installed at her desk. A red light would begin flashing at Chief Detzler's headquarters, and the police would be on their way. She pressed a second button, and a whistling blast came from every speaker in the school. All classroom doors were to be locked immediately—shades of Abraham Lincoln School in South Philly—while the custodians raced to cover the exits. The coach was to get out to the parking lot, to intercept the intruder, and to keep him or her from fleeing the school grounds.

"Anything I can do?" offered Semlac, recalling the suspected intruder in the gym.

"Yes," said Carol, "answer the phone if it rings."

It took her a minute to decide what to do. Already she could hear police sirens shattering the still June air. *If Stan has Lisa,* she reasoned, *he must have a car to get away* . . .

She was just about to leave her office when Semlac yelled, "Hey, wait!"

"What is it?"

"Here! There's a guy with a kid, just went down the slope through the trees, heading for the bay. Right outside your office window!"

Down to the water! Stan was planning to take Lisa away in a boat! Everyone else would expect a getaway by car.

The police cars screamed up outside the school. Carol heard the sirens wind down to a thin, pale moan. "Get the cops," snarled Semlac, jerking the window open and climbing through it, "I'll do what I can." He jumped from the low ledge, landed in a half-crouch, scrambled to his feet, and started down the steep embankment after Stan Walsh and Lisa.

Two officers pounded into the school then, and panted up to Carol in front of her office. "In back. Down toward the water," she told them, leading the way to an exit door. "It's a man. Stan Walsh. He took one of the children, she's—be careful . . ."

They disappeared into the trees, and two more policemen flashed past Carol, following their comrades.

Chief Detzler came up in a wheezing dogtrot.

"It's Stan Walsh," she told him, before he could make one of his underpaid-overworked cracks.

"Walsh!" he grunted enthusiastically. "I've had to eat crow from the Nassau County boys ever since the Walsh woman's murder, on account of we couldn't catch Stan. By God . . ."

Detzler ran out, and Carol followed, losing a heel, ripping her skirt on a branch, ruining her pantyhose. She came out of the trees on the run and halted at the water's edge. Hempstead Harbor was blue and still today, and a rowboat with an outboard motor drifted about fifty feet from shore. Anton Semlac was sitting on Stan Walsh's back, with one of Stan's arms twisted into a hammerlock. Stan was crying. Lisa was crying too, breathlessly. One of the officers was holding her. The others stood with guns drawn, watching Stan, waiting for Chief Detzler to tell them what to do.

"I forgot to take the anchor out of the boat!" mourned Stan Walsh, striking his forehead with the heel of his hand.

"Pretty sharp of you, buddy," Chief Detzler said contemptuously.

The chief, Carol, and two cops were with Stan in the principal's office, holding him there for a short time until arrangements were completed for his transfer to the Nassau County jail. Detzler had removed all of Stan's personal effects, itemizing them for the record. An old gold Elgin wristwatch. Tattered leather billfold containing two one-dollar bills, an outdated New York State driver's license, three state lottery tickets, all losers, and a boat rental stub from the Glen Cove Marina across the bay. Also in the pathetic little pile of possessions was Stan's class ring from Yale.

Detzler let out a snort of amazement. "I guess you missed the boat and anchor course when you were up there at Yale, huh? I'll give it to you now. To keep the boat on shore, you got to take the anchor out and drive it into the sand or hook it on a rock or something."

One of the cops laughed. "You couldn'ta gotten away anyway. Even if the boat hadn'ta drifted off. We'da just radioed over to Glen Cove, and they'da nabbed you there."

"Leave him alone," said Carol. "This isn't doing any good."

"I just wanted my daughter back," Stan said, almost sobbing. "I just wanted—"

"You gonna read him his rights, Chief?"

"How does that go? Oh, yeah. Anything you say can be held against you, Walsh."

Stan nodded.

"Your old dad would be turning over in his grave to see you here like this, you know that?" Detzler prodded. "God, what a guy he was. Used to go with him down to the horse races, at Roosevelt Field. At Belmont. What a guy. The 'Inner Tube King,' we called him. You sure are a stain on the family name. Jesus!"

Carol was about to interrupt again. She saw no good purpose in tormenting Stan with his inadequacy. Then she understood what Detzler was trying to do. *Goad* Stan into talking, perhaps into an admission, confession.

"Where've you been hiding out all this time, Walsh? Fellow like you, seems to me he could hardly figure out a way to get his pants on frontwards."

Stan took the bait. The old strain of arrogance that Carol had noticed when she'd first met him, that the-world-owes-me-a-living attitude surfaced now, and Stan smirked.

"Almost two months, Walsh," Detzler continued, "and us dumb cops couldn't get a tag on you. What's your secret? How does a loser like you finally get so smart? No, not smart. Just lucky."

Stan frowned. The quick anger of the smug.

"You know those big old abandoned estates in Brookville? Up along the shore? I hid out in a carriage house there," he said.

"Oh, did you now? Why'd you feel you had to *hide out?*"

Stan saw the mouth of the trap into which he'd fallen, saw the steel jaws of logic close around him.

"Well, I wasn't actually hiding from anything . . ."

"And coming around here, to the school. Sneaking around like some—why'd you kill your wife, Walsh, you loser? You had a wonderful father. You have a lovely little girl, whose life you may well have ruined. And your dear sweet wife, the beauty queen, she was a darling if there ever was—"

Stan snapped. He could not bear others being praised, and himself ridiculed. "Valerie was nothing but a cheap shrew!" he bellowed. "Miss Lobster Festival! What the hell is that? Nothing! Always criticizing, bitching. *'We don't have any money in the account, Stan! Why can't you remember to transfer the funds?'* Why? *Why?* Because I didn't have any goddam money anymore. Because the

· 247 ·

great 'Inner Tube King' spent his time at the races with third-raters like you, instead of studying which way the tire market was going—"

"Why'd you kill your wife, though, Walsh? Huh? Money? Was that it?"

Stan pulled himself together, looking canny.

"I didn't touch a hair on her bleached head," he said.

"Stan," Carol told him softly, "you did. Lisa remembers. She remembers everything."

Stan sat there for another moment, trying to look cool and haughty. But he had expended so much effort trying to look cool and haughty over the years that now, when he needed them most, his reserves of energy were depleted. His face twisted, and his shoulders began to tremble, then to shake.

"She'll never forget it, Walsh," Detzler put in, "your own little girl. Think what you've done. And now you're not even man enough to own up to what you did! Why, Walsh, your daughter has more strength than you, and she's only in the first grade . . ."

"All right," Stan admitted, sobbing now, "all right. Yes. I killed Valerie. I threw her over the balcony, into the pool." He paused, sobbing, but then gave them his great justification. "Yes, I killed her. *But she had it coming!*"

Stan was broken now. Carol asked him one more question. She had asked him over the phone the night he'd called the house. But she had to make sure.

"Stan, did you put lilacs in Johnny's schoolbag? That day in Mrs. Pilaf's classroom?"

He registered the question. But it made no sense to him. "Johnny? Mrs. Pilaf?" he asked, through bitter tears.

"All right," Carol said. "I believe you."

"*'She had it coming,'*" Detzler repeated, after Stan had been driven away in the Nassau County Police van. "My God! What a reason! The wonders of the human brain. Do you even want to guess how many people there must be, planning revenge and thinking, it'll be all right because my victims *have it coming to them?*"

"No," replied Carol, shuddering. "I don't want to guess."

She knew for certain that Stan had never been a real threat to her or her family. He had had nothing to do with the lilacs. He had not evoked even a note of *The Waltz of the Dead.*

Cleophus Watts was long dead. Vic Brand more recently so.

Anton Semlac did not have to bedevil her with lilacs. All *he* had to do was call a strike.

Stu Inkspell was still a possibility, but then it wouldn't be Stu, really, it would be Gertie Kiefer. And, upon scant reflection, it seemed most unlikely that blunt, forthright Gertie Kiefer would invent any form of harassment more subtle than a punch in the stomach.

So who else was there to suspect?

Who else was Out There, waiting?

5

In the hours after midnight, sleepless and trembling, the stalker had always been supremely convinced. Convinced that he had every right to take revenge. During daylight, though, with the world moving normally and normal people going about their business, the stalker was, in the beginning anyway, given to doubt. Questions arose within his mind. *Is there something wrong with me? Must I carry through and settle with Kenton? Why can't there be some other way to ease my grief? Is there something wrong with me that I want revenge?* And the answers kept coming back at him, from the black void of his hatred and despair. *The lilacs meant nothing to Kenton. He uses people and discards them. He is utterly callous and cold. Of course you have the right to revenge. Who could blame you? Kenton has it coming.*

A DEATH FOR A DEATH! *Two* deaths!

So there came a time when the stalker was bent upon utter revenge, both in the daytime and at night.

During the daytime, he went about his business, thinking coldly, happily, *Nobody knows; nobody will ever guess, nobody.* Just going about his job, the greatest cover of all, and nobody knowing what was going on within his body, heart and mind, haha. During the daytime he was cool and professional and *had no face* except that which he chose to show. But at night, when there was no need to show the world a face, when all of the darkness was his heart, the stalker read. He read stories and histories and biographies, books of vengeance and of great avengers. The stalker was sure he was one *of* them; he was absolutely certain that he was one *with* them.

The stalker's favorite was Joseph Stalin, who waited and waited and waited until the time was right. You had to learn to wait. You had to pick the right time, and the best time of all was night. Had the victims known what was coming? How could they not have? How could they not have seen the signs, and fled? Scores of extant photographs show Stalin with his victims. They are looking straight into the camera, often smiling. But Stalin is not looking at the camera. He is looking at *them*, with a slow half-smile on his face, partially obscured by a heavy moustache. That smile was The Sign of Death. How could they not have seen? All they had to do was look at the picture.

How could Jack Kenton have ignored The Sign? Did he not know what the lilacs meant? He who was supposed to be so smart. And who was obviously so lucky.

IT WASN'T FAIR!

But what if Kenton were to die? Or be killed?

Then the bastard would probably go to heaven, if there was a heaven.

And if there wasn't, they would probably build one so he could live in it.

But what if . . . ?

What if Kenton went on living?

And his *loved ones* died? Or were killed?

That's right, thought the stalker. *Do to him what has been done to you. He'll be a living dead man. Let him suffer.*

Survivors are for suffering, the stalker knew. The dead are only dead.

Choose a time, the stalker thought, reading the *New York Times*.

According to reports, Governor Higgins was going to have something important to say, at the Waldorf-Astoria, on the night of the Fourth of July. If the stalker was right, that announcement would have to do with Jack Kenton. So Jack Kenton would be there.

But would his family be there? His family might not. His family might be at home. And, even if his wife were not at home, the children would almost certainly be.

Choose the time, thought stalker. *Night.*

Choose the date. That was easy. The *Times* had given him the date. A fine historic date, a lovely night.

Lilac Night, the stalker thought.

Wait until they believe themselves to be safe and secure. Wait until all is prepared, the web spun, until Kenton thinks victory is in his hand. Stalin was right: wait. Let a man believe himself to be safe, give him his full belly and his bottle and his woman and his bed. Give him his healthy children asleep in a safe place, warm and without tears. Wait until he has those things, until he has forgotten that you ever lived. Then strike! Put the knife in, and twist it. And go home to a good night's sleep.

And after that night, there would be one more luminary in the pantheon of avengers sworn and proven.

The man who evened his score with Jack Kenton.

The Stalker, of Long Island, New York.

6

The desk in Jack's study was strewn with charts, notepads, sheets of yellow legal paper, pens, pencils, a tape recorder, and phone directories.

He was building a model of the past, his past and Carol's too.

"A model isn't the real world," he told her. "Life is too detailed and chaotic for us to see or remember everything that happens. But if enough facts are collected, and organized in the proper way, the result is a reasonably accurate model of reality."

"And that model will tell us who in the world might plan to harm our family?" Carol asked.

"Maybe." Jack sighed. "Maybe. If we have the right facts and put them together correctly."

In preparation for building the model, Jack and Carol had reviewed their past lives, careers, and travels. Events long forgotten were recalled; people known years ago or yesterday were disinterred from memory and brought up to the light.

"There is a crucial question," Jack decided. "Are we being harassed by a man or a woman?"

"A woman," Carol declared.

"Why do you think that?"

"Who but a woman would use lilacs as a—as a sign? Or whatever they're supposed to represent."

"Haven't been any lilacs lately, though, have there?"

"That's because the season ended. They aren't in bloom any-more. But that doesn't mean the person who—who *gave* them—it doesn't mean that *woman* isn't still around."

"All right. But a model must be completely logical. No intuition. No hunches. If, as you think, a woman is behind this, who? Karyn? She just returned to the United States. I can't even get in touch with her—"

"It might be someone else."

"*Who?*"

"I don't know . . ."

"Wait," Jack exclaimed, "Gisela Twister!"

This time it was Carol's turn to ask, "*Who?*"

"General Twister's widow. She swore vengeance against me once, and later she tried to take me to court. Let's get down to serious work here."

Jack and Carol worked together all through the day and into the evening, turning stones and following threads, extrapolating, deducing, and pursuing.

Gisela Twister, now *Frau* Thuringer, was the mother of three little Thuringers. She had never visited the United States. Frank Brewster, who acquired this information, told Jack that the general's widow did not recall former Lieutenant Kenton fondly, but she had found happiness in her family and no longer bore him ill will.

Sergeant Big Ben Potts, one of Twister's accomplices, had been knifed to death in a fight over a package of cigarettes six months after being sentenced to the military prison at Leavenworth.

Major Adolph Olk was still incarcerated there.

"Shouldn't he have been paroled long ago?" Carol asked, when Jack ended his phone conversation with a Pentagon officer.

"He killed a man while serving his term. A captain named Kuffel. It was one of those shower-room incidents. You know, the kind that can occur in a men's prison? Well, Olk was sentenced to life for homicide. Lilacs are the last thing on his mind."

"And General Twister is dead?"

"Lo, these many years."

"What if a friend of his . . . ?"

"If that's the case, we've no way of knowing."

"Then what good is the model, if it can't reflect reality?"

"Smart girl. When a tree falls, with no one to hear it, is there a sound? What we have to do is create a forest, fell a tree, and listen."

Carol brewed coffee, and brought it into the study. Jack was reading a volume of the encyclopedia.

"How much do you know about lilacs?" he asked, looking up.

Carol poured coffee, black for him, milk for her.

"What's to know? They're pretty. They're common. They have a lovely bouquet."

"Also, they're found all over the world, in two colors, pink and white. That's about it. Do they have any emotional significance for you?"

Carol thought about it. She'd had a few lilacs in her bridal bouquet, but that was because lilacs had grown on her family's property at Wescott Cove. There were lilacs here in Royall Beach, too, and there had been at Miss Blaisdell's. But other than that? "No," she said.

"Nor for me," Jack shrugged. "But they do mean something to whoever is making a signal with them. And if I had to come up with a major hypothesis right now, I'd say whatever threat might be on its way to us comes out of your past, not mine."

"Jack, why?"

"Vic Brand," Jack said.

"He's dead."

"I know that. But even the dead have survivors. Did lilacs mean anything to him? To the two of you?"

"No. Not at all. He sent me flowers once. After I'd—met him at Cornell. But it was just a bouquet. I can't even remember what kind of flowers were in it."

"Okay. Let's go over it once more. Lilacs on the beach. In Johnny's schoolbag. No intruder reported at school that day, was there?"

"Are you saying it's someone in my school?"

"And another time in the mailbox, along with the big branch at the door. I don't know what I'm saying."

"What about your business? A lot of people have gone to prison, or been fined, or gotten fired, because Kenton Diversified uncovered corporate theft or embezzlement."

"I've been through my files with a fine-tooth comb. No solid leads there at all. Not one."

"What do we do now?"

He handed her a yellow legal pad. "Categorize your life," he said. "Break it down. Childhood. School years. Family. Romantic involvements. Career. Anything else you can think of. List every person you can remember in each category. Then we'll see."

They worked quietly, remembering their pasts. Jack worked in the study, Carol upstairs in the bedroom. *"Dead end,"* she wrote on her yellow pad, *"dead end dead end dead end."*

The black silhouette of the man on the beach stood before her, arrogant and mocking.

But he had existed! He had been there on the beach, close enough to *touch* her!

Suddenly, she had an idea and ran downstairs. Jack was lying on the couch in his study, surrounded by discarded sheets of scribbling.

"Any headway?" he asked.

"No, but I thought of something. Maybe the police out near Montauk ran into somebody strange that day."

"Somebody strange enough to hand out lilacs?"

"Don't police record just about everything? Every encounter?"

"If they're alert."

"Isn't there some way we can check?"

"CiJi, that's been over a month ago."

"But it's all I can think of. What if? What if there *is* some information they have."

He sighed. "It's worth a try. Anything is, right now. I know Chief O'Melia, out in Riverhead. I'll give him a call."

"Did you think of anyone?" She wanted to know.

His expression was dark, a combination of bewilderment, tenderness, and regret. Carol leaned down to look at his notations. The name stood alone, beneath a category Jack had labeled "Loose Ends":

Pauline Yates???

"I have no idea what ever happened to her, and she's the last person on earth who would think to harm anyone, but I'm going to try and find her, so we'll know for sure."

Carol was aware that Jack had known Pauline in Germany for a short time. Pauline Yates was a ghost, and it would be very nice if she were to remain one. A spouse's old lovers are much more charitably regarded if they remain incorporeal.

"If you think you have to," Carol said.

The phone rang, and Carol answered. That rich and perfect voice sounded friendly and all too familiar.

"Mrs. Kenton, this is Karyn Bari. May I speak to Jack?"

Not *your husband*, not *Mr. Kenton*. But *Jack*.

"Yes, he's right here."

Jack's head tilted slightly to the side, his eyebrows raised in query, as he took the receiver.

"Jack, I must see you, and I know this is a sensitive time for you. I'm at the Pierre, but you oughtn't to come here. One of my men will arrange a time and place, and contact you."

"Karyn, yes, of course, I—"

"I'm so much looking forward to seeing you, darling. We have a million things to discuss."

"That's what I've heard," he managed to say. Before Karyn said good-bye.

7

Thirty years and three thousand bottles of booze earlier, there might have been, on the face of Mrs. Felix J. Yates, widow, a sign of the beauty she had passed on to her daughter Pauline. But now her face was bloated folds of fat, shrouding rheumy eyes and blue, puckered, petulant lips.

"What the hell do you want?" she demanded, her odoriferous breath coming out into the tenement hallway. She had unbolted and unlocked the door, but remained well protected by three chain-locks, behind which she regarded Jack suspiciously. In the narrow open space between door edge and doorjamb, Jack could see the shambles of a tiny apartment. Mrs. Yates was making her last woozy stand in life on the fringes of the South Bronx, to which Jack had tracked her down. She had no phone, and no one in her old Pelham Parkway neighborhood knew her whereabouts, but through Social Security, Jack learned her address.

"Go away," she whined at him. "I didn't see anything. I didn't do it. I don't want any."

"I'm Jack Kenton," he told her.

"Yeah? What do I care?"

"I used to know your daughter, Pauline."

The woman's eyes showed faint interest. Very faint.

"So?" she asked.

"I'd like to get in touch with her. It's important. I hope you can help me."

"I can't." Mrs. Yates started to close the door.

"Please," bargained Jack. "I have to know. I'm willing to pay for the information."

"Yeah?" A canny glimmer of avarice appeared in the woman's watery eyes. "How much?"

"First of all, do you know where your daughter is?"

"First of all, how much you gonna pay me for that information? Second, why do you want to know?"

"How about twenty dollars? I used to be a friend of hers. When she worked with the Red Cross, in Germany."

Mrs. Yates laughed at him. "I can't recall that Ina ever was in Germany—oh, no, wait. She was somewhere overseas. But that was a long time ago."

"But I'd like to see her now. It's quite important. How about forty dollars? You're sure you know what's happened to her?"

The old woman's cackle was almost sad. "Oh, yeah. I know. Only one of my kids I do know about. Rest of 'em ran off and left me to die. Give them a fine home and the chance for a good life, and what do they do? They run away and leave you to die. Sixty dollars," she said.

Jack reached for his billfold, slid three twenties from it. Mrs. Yates stuck her fat hand out into the hallway and grabbed them. "You got a lot more of them. How about two more and I'll tell you."

Jack took out one more twenty, and held it up. Mrs. Yates grabbed for it, but missed.

"This is it," he said. "I want to know, and I want to know now. Where is Pauline?"

"Get smart with me, buster, and I'll call the cops," the woman shot back. "Think I won't, huh?"

Jack thought no such thing. She probably would. He could just imagine one of the poetic, inventive *Post* headlines: *Tax Champ Decked in Bronx Bribe Bid*.

"You tell me, and you get this," he told her, tough in his turn. "And who knows? I might be in a position to cause you some discomfort. From what I see of your apartment, there, it might interest a fire inspector . . ."

His negotiating strategy—carrot and stick—worked. Mrs. Yates wanted the extra twenty dollars, and emphatically did not want dealings with authorities of any kind, even had Jack any intention of summoning them.

"Okay," she shrugged, "you want to know, and I'll tell you. Pauline is dead. She got hit by a cement truck."

It was the truth. Jack could tell by the finality in the wasted woman's tone, a small spasm of mother-love and loss in her voice.

He stood there, stunned, assailed by old memories of Munich and tenderness and regret.

He was thinking of the night Pauline had fled *Die Vier Jahreszeiten*, the night he'd met Karyn. Mrs. Yates snatched the bill from his hand and slammed the door shut.

"Go away," she muttered behind the door, as locks turned and bolts shot to. "Go away and leave a poor old woman in peace."

8

Ace (in his personal opinion) Suffolk County Patrolman Bruce Toole was sweating more than a little. He had been ordered to report to Chief O'Melia at headquarters in Riverhead, and he knew what for. He was going to get his ass chewed royally. He didn't care for the prospect at all, because he didn't have the slightest idea what other line of work he might get into, not having accumulated a particularly sterling academic record at Hauppauge High School. Bruce knew, though, way deep down, that he deserved a good ass-chewing. While attempting to break up a teenage brawl outside a Montauk disco, Bruce's .45-caliber weapon had been taken from him by some hairy punk wild with the courage of beer. Everybody knows a cop who loses his weapon is a goddam clown, and Bruce would hardly have been in more trouble had he actually *shot* the punk. He halfway wished he had. In fact, maybe he still *would*.

"Awright, Toole, chief'll see you now," grunted the desk sergeant.

Still sweating, Toole went into the chief's office, gave his name, saluted, and stood at attention before the officer's desk. O'Melia let him stand there for quite a while, and then looked up with feigned, distasteful surprise, as if to say, "Hey, how'd this piece of shit get into my office?"

"Patrolman, where is your sidearm?"

"Sir, they—ah—they took it away from me over at the precinct."

"They *took it away from you?*" This in a tone of slow, sarcastic astonishment.

"Yessir." Toole was still at attention.

"My, my, everybody is taking your weapon away. Isn't that so?"

"Yessir."

"Well, let me enlighten you a bit, Patrolman. They took it away from you at precinct because I told them to. Do you know why? I said DO YOU KNOW WHY?"

"Nosir."

"FOR YOUR OWN PROTECTION, THAT'S WHY!"

Toole said nothing, and tried to keep from staring cross-eyed at the drop of sweat on the tip of his nose.

The chief let him stand there for a while, then: "You plan to remain on the force, do you, Toole?"

"Yessir. That is, I hope so, sir . . ."

"Well, well. I am pleased to hear that. I am really pleased to know that such fine talent is working its way up the ranks. Did you like it out on patrol?"

"Oh, yessir," said Bruce, enthusiastically. He had liked it, very much. Driving around with a new car, flashing lights on her, and something new every minute. He had busted his *ass* to get through police academy, but it had been worth it just for the fun of driving around on patrol.

"Well," said the chief, "*someday* we may get you back out there on the street. But for the time being, I think it would be educational for you to learn, shall we say, clerical procedures."

Clerical procedures? Oh no, that meant sitting at a desk. Oh, Jesus, he wouldn't be able to stand it.

"Ever hear of Jack Kenton?" Chief O'Melia was asking.

"Nosir."

"Ever read the daily papers?"

"Yessir," said Bruce, offended. Every day, religiously, he read the sports, the comics, and Ann Landers.

O'Melia shook his head. "For your information, Jack Kenton decided what your next assignment will be."

"He did?"

"Yes. He wants you to check out everything that happened in the Montauk sector on Mother's Day."

"Mother's Day, sir?"

"I can repeat it for you if you like."

"Oh, that's not necessary, sir."

"Well, I'm glad to hear that. I really am. Now, you report down to East Hampton. I want a list of everyone in the whole area who encountered or was encountered by a Suffolk police officer on the afternoon of Mother's Day. Every name, every incident, every license plate. You got that?"

"Yessir."

"Check every summons, every traffic ticket, every NAME. You understand?"

"Every NAME, sir!"

"I know you're going to be a real whiz in clerical work, Toole. I just want you to know if I thought this was important, and not an off-the-wall idea by a wet-behind-the-ears politician who's going to try to lower taxes and keep our salaries down, I would assign somebody with at least half a brain to do the job. You got that?"

"Right, sir. Half a brain sir."

"Any questions?"

"This is—ah—isn't this going to take pretty long, sir? I mean, there are a lot of records, and—"

"Toole, Toole," replied the chief, with exaggerated sympathy and patience, "I do so want you to learn *all there is to know* about clerical procedures. And, anyway, it will take *you* longer than it would most people."

Bruce was offended. "Why is that, sir?"

"Because, even while you take care of this assignment, I have arranged for you to keep your hand in day-to-day police work. Or, I might say, to keep your feet in. You will also walk a beat in East Hampton town. Wouldn't want to sit at a desk all day now, would you, Toole?"

The chief was grinning, but somehow he didn't seem very friendly. "Get back to me when you get it done. Which better be damn soon. Now, DISMISSED!"

9

Buster knew it was Bernice pounding on the goddam door, because Bernice had a special way of pounding. She pounded like she talked.

It was Saturday morning, and Buster had his usual Saturday morning hangover. He'd stopped at Mel and Irma's Tavern for a quick one after leaving the Royall Beach stakeout, but the quick one had multiplied, and Buster'd finally flowed out of there at about two-fifteen.

Buster listened to the pounding and tried to judge how bad his hangover was. He could make a fist, so it wasn't the worst kind, and there seemed to be enough oxygen in the air, so it wasn't the second worst. But he couldn't quite focus his eyes, and he felt like he'd just run the New York Marathon with a backpack full of lead, so he knew it was going to be a long fucking day.

"Waddya want?" he yelled from the bed.

The pounding ceased. "Buster, you open this door. I want to talk to you."

I want to talk to you. Jesus, how many times had he heard *that?* What could she want? Wasn't the end of the month yet, so she couldn't be over here to bitch about not getting her check. Wasn't anything he could think of. Curious in spite of himself, he rolled over, shot his legs out over the edge of the bed, and let his feet touch the floor. He groaned, squinted around, and came wide awake. On the floor next to the bed was his microwave decoder, electrical cords, and sprawls of printout sheets, full of conversations at the Kenton house. Sheee-it, she couldn't see that. Who knew what she'd think, and who she might babble to? He shoved the decoder under the bed, along with its electrical attachments, folded the printouts and put them on a chair next to the bed.

"Buster, you open up, or I'll bang this door down."

Bang it or blow it, he thought miserably, covering the printouts with yesterday's (and the day before's) dirty shirt. Through the iridescent haze of a dozen beer-and-balls (daiquiri culture having faded fast in the harsh reality of Queens), Buster lurched over, flicked the lock, and opened the door. There she was, all right, the ex-queen of Grover Cleveland High. Her hair was red again, after tours of duty masquerading as blonde, silver, black, blue (once, for a week), and orange. Her ass was a lot bigger and her breasts a lot lower, but her mouth was just the same. This was the woman who, long ago, while blowing him, had said, "Buster, let's get married. Let's get married, Buster. Just get me that little bitty carat-and-a-half diamond, and I'll do this to you all the time. All the time, Buster, 'cause you taste so good!"

And Buster had fallen for it. How stupid could one guy be? He'd never learned not to give a sucker an even break.

"Well," observed Bernice, stepping into the room, "you look like something the cat dragged in. Mel and Irma's, I bet?"

He didn't deny it, but he didn't admit it either.

"What do you want?" he asked, while she started ass-swaying around the room, poking her nose everywhere. He wouldn't put it past her to check his sheets for come stains.

"I got good news for you," she informed him. "I wanted you to be the first to know."

Buster shut the door. "Oh, yeah? What's that? You getting married again, so I can stop paying you?"

She was over by the bed now, and sure enough the nosy bitch leaned over and looked underneath.

"Buster, what the hell is this?"

"None of your business. Get away from there."

Never one to listen, especially not to him, she was already on her hands and knees, dragging the decoder out from under the bed.

"I said get your hands *off* it," he snarled, swatting her ass real hard.

Bernice howled, released her grip on the decoder, and cracked her head on the bed frame as she jumped up. Then she really howled.

"Oh, shut up, for Christ sake," said Buster. "You'll wake the fucking neighbors."

"You hit me! I'll scream."

"You scream, and you'll find out what hitting is. You stay away from my stuff."

Bernice glanced down at the decoder, her little mind working hard. "You're up to no good again, aren't you?" she accused. "That ain't no typewriter. Buster, I bet you are going to get in real big trouble this time. You just can't keep away from it."

"Another precinct heard from. You came over here; I let you in. You got something to tell me? Go ahead. I got work to do."

"Work! The day you work will be—"

"Bernice, this is it. Speak your piece, or I'll chuck your fat ass out of here for all the neighbors to see."

Bernice considered whether to get offended or not, then decided against it. She smiled sweetly. "I came over to tell you," she said, "that I fell in love. I'm getting married again."

Old Buster stood there in his pajamas and his bare feet, and could not believe his ears. This was just about the sweetest news he'd heard since his bookie'd called with the word that Spinks had beaten Ali.

"It was, like, love at first sight," Bernice was saying.

"Who's the lucky guy? If that's the right phrase?"

Bernice grinned real wide. Her big surprise. She thought it would knock him dead.

"Bernie Lipschitz," she said. "You remember him?"

Buster just stood there for a moment and let it roll over him, like a wave of sweet water on the shores of paradise. There was justice in life after all, and maybe even a God. Buster could never have dreamed a revenge this sweet.

"I ran into him at that Chinese place in Rego Park. He was having a Zombie at the bar, and I had just finished some shrimp and lobster sauce. It was love at first sight, like I said." She looked doubtful now. Her big announcement wasn't having the intended effect. "Buster, did you hear me? I said it was—"

"Love at first sight. I heard. Bernice, nobody could be happier than me. I'm glad you came. You got any more good news?"

Bernice, aware of her miscalculation, cast about wildly for something to wound him with. "You just weren't much of a provider, you know. And Bernie runs the brewery now, that his father left him."

"That's great," said Buster, easing her toward the door.

"And you weren't very good in bed either, you know that?"

"Sorry, Bernice. But look what I had to work with."

He got the door open and positioned her in front of it.

"This doesn't mean you can stop paying my alimony right away. You have to pay right up until the wedding. That'll be in October, I think."

"Sure. Send me an invitation," chortled Buster, and swatted her on the rump again as he sent her through the door.

God, life was looking up! He felt so good that he almost forgot his hangover and that he had work to do.

The good mood didn't last, though. He got to work with the decoder, determining what Jack Kenton and his old lady were talking about in their house. He felt like some cheap hired shyster. Which was what he was.

It had all started up again, that old guilt thing about Jack Kenton, the fight with Lipschitz in the park, and Buster running his ass off to get away while Kenton took the heat.

And Charlie Kiefer was being adamant. "I got that young bastard right where I want him," Charlie kept saying, over and over. "Buster, you go out there to Royall Beach. You go every day. Keep tabs on that young bastard. I want to know every word he says."

That's what Buster had done. He'd bought himself a new three-hundred-dollar suit, rented a Mercedes. Once inside the Royall Beach enclave, Buster got real canny. None of this crawling around in the hedges, not this time. This time he parked on quiet side streets close to the Kenton house, turned on the machine, and cranked up the power. Not enough to interfere with any of the electrical appliances in their house but enough to pick up any conversation inside the place. There were quite a few, and their subjects bothered old Buster.

But he felt cheaper and cheaper, spying on Kenton. The guy might be rich and everything, but he had his problems, just like everybody else. He and his old lady were having trouble with that little girl, Lisa, they'd adopted. And Kenton's old lady was having trouble at work. And Kenton had this Karyn Bari to worry about, and her son, who was Kenton's too. And now—he learned while decoding the conversations—the Kentons were worried that somebody unknown might be out to get them, somebody who left lilacs as a message, but they didn't know what the message meant.

Buster felt like a jerk eavesdropper, listening in on them. He'd tried to maneuver Charlie out of the plan. "Every time I go out to Royall Beach, I get the same old stuff," he'd said. "Whyn't we lay off Kenton for a while?" He'd even invented a few lies about close run-ins with the cops, telling Charlie he was sure to get caught one of these times.

But not only had Charlie been unimpressed, he had been nasty. "I'm calling the shots," he'd said. "And I think you know your position well enough."

Buster did. He was strictly a bought man, a tool, a *thing*. When Charlie paid you, Buster was learning, he had already *bought* you. Buster felt, while monitoring the Kentons, like a used rubber left in the grass in Lovers' Lane.

That goddam Charlie Kiefer, so jaunty now that he thought he'd get the nomination! Buster took to calling Charlie every day and saying things like, "Nothing new" or "Sorry, nobody home today."

Because how would Buster feel if somebody in a Mercedes was humping around outside of *his* apartment, trying to find out what was happening inside?

Not too fucking happy.

But Buster still made the daily trek to Royall Beach. After all, it was a job. And maybe he could help find out who was hassling the Kentons with the flowers.

10

The open forum of the Royall Beach School District is now in session," called Mrs. Crispus, board president, banging her gavel decorously.

A crowd of citizens jammed the library. Money was an important subject in Royall Beach, and money was the subject of this meeting.

Carol glanced at her watch. Sometimes board meetings lasted an hour, sometimes four or five hours, until, weary and battered, the participants slunk homeward to hiss bitterly or crow gloatingly, depending upon how their pedagogical wisdom had been received. Carol made a quick check inside her purse, touching the few note cards on which she'd jotted some thoughts.

Jack was at home with Lisa and Johnny. He and Carol had agreed that one of them would always be with the children, at least until the lilac business was satisfactorily explained or until Mrs. Wenthistle, the housekeeper, returned from England.

"We have a most serious situation in the district," Mrs. Crispus orated from a long table positioned in front of the book checkout desk. "Next week, as you all know, the district is scheduled to administer state exams to our children. This is the . . ." she was about to say "climax" but amended herself in midflight ". . . *pinnacle* of the year, toward which we shoot from September onward. Yet, we are faced with a cessation of teacher activity."

Blanche Dunphy, local union leader, jaw square and mouth taut, looked determined and self-righteous from her chair in the front row. Next to her, tough and laconic, Anton Semlac seemed bored.

Carol, seated next to Mrs. Crispus, kept her face carefully blank. She had made her final decision.

"By drawing straws," Mrs. Crispus explained, "it has been determined that Miss Dunphy will speak first. Blanche, you have the floor."

Blanche spoke a little too fast, but she had rehearsed her speech so often and was so convinced of its overwhelming logic, did it even matter if people could follow it or not?

". . . and so as representative of the teachers' union," she concluded, "I am here to tell you that we have taken the position that those who work *for* the community, namely the teachers, have a greater claim to support than do outsiders, even if children, even if *poor* children, even if meritorious. The days of pilot programs, and bootstraps, and bleeding-heart liberalism are over. Now is a time of first things first!"

Returning to her seat, she gave Carol a *So there!* glare, while, throughout the audience, murmurs of assent arose.

"Mr. Semlac?" Mrs. Crispus said, gesturing for him to stand. "Anton Semlac," she told the assemblage, "is a state union coordinator. As such, I felt it would be helpful to have him offer his position, even though he is not a Royall Beach resident."

"Nor do I want to be a Royall Beach resident." Semlac glowered, opening his remarks.

The audience was startled. Semlac certainly knew how to get attention.

"I don't get sick much anymore," he told them. "But you people *do* make me laugh. I see the wall around your community, and your big lawns, and your quarter- or half-million-dollar homes with the three cars parked carelessly out front like expensive dogs. I see all those things, but do you know what I really *see?*"

A couple of businessmen in the audience were red in the face, and Mrs. Crispus was staring with her mouth open.

"I see a moral and sociological cesspool," he told them. "I doubt there are more than a dozen or so people in this whole . . . community who are even smart enough to figure out the basic equations of life."

He turned to Carol, nodded, and said, "Dr. Kenton, much as I disagree with her on the specific needs of the moment, is one woman who has thought about the important things. She knows *what* she thinks, and she knows *why*. Most of you people couldn't think your way out of a paper bag. That's why we're here tonight, discussing whether the pittance you are willing to pay for education will go to the people who teach your children, or to poor kids who were not clever enough to be born in Royall Beach. And if you want another piece of news, I'll tell you this. Let just one of you businessmen stop yowling about what pillars of the community you are, let just one of you clubwomen stop fighting about who's going to head the Snowball at the Royall Beach Yacht Club, and teach for a week. Really *teach*. Do *all* of it. Study the curriculum and read the books. Figure out how best to get a point across to some of your kids, who are convinced by the time they're in the second grade— because you're all so loudmouthed and proud—that they are already superior to their teacher. Get to school early. Decorate your room. Teach the lessons. Don't forget to stop the fights, take Johnny to the nurse, quiet Susie who is worried that her parents are getting a divorce, or soothe Tommy whose dog died. And don't forget, you've got playground duty this week, and lunchroom duty next, and the parent-teacher meeting Thursday night. And *then* you might begin to understand what work is—and what's *really* important in life."

He paused, looking at the people. He smiled his grim, unsettling smile.

"I see that I have your attention," he went on. "Good. Now I'll talk to you in a way you understand, because it's the way you've presumed to talk to those you've considered your inferiors: If we don't get the pay raise, we're striking. If it takes a strike to make you realize what good people need, to make you *think*, well, it will probably do you some good.

"Thank you, Mrs. Crispus," he said, returning to his seat.

There was a long moment of offended silence followed by indignant babble. Mrs. Crispus banged her gavel like mad.

Carol stood up. She might as well speak her piece now. It took several minutes, but the people finally noticed her standing there and began to quiet down.

"I have only a few things to tell you," she began. "It has been a long and difficult year for me. I have been trying to sort out what we call 'priorities,' trying, as Mr. Semlac put it, to think my way out of my personal paper bag."

Mrs. Crispus looked surprised, and so did a lot of the people. They had expected Carol to make a spirited defense of her position.

"In a way," Carol continued, "the burden of this imminent strike is on me. I have taken positions. I have done things, acted. I cast a shadow. People who stand up to face the world usually do.

"I want you to know, Mrs. Crispus, members of the board, parents, that I realize a great deal of our current problem is tied to me. I have been thinking my life over and sorting it out. It's good to see where you've been, and it might even help you to decide where you want to go. I entered education to serve, to teach, to do some good. Now, however, there seems to be nothing I can do or say that won't in some way antagonize or disappoint someone, and nothing I can do, as principal, that will very much please anyone, least of all myself.

"So I have decided to return to teaching. I don't want an office anymore. I want to decorate my classroom, and see a child's face light up when I have touched his or her mind.

"So I am resigning as principal, effective immediately. The board will wish to consider the matter of my successor."

"Carol, no . . ." Mrs. Crispus murmured.

"All right, go," hollered someone, from the anonymity of the audience, only to be shouted down by a score of his fellows.

"I think it would be best if I left now," Carol told them.

"Are you serious?" asked a worried Mrs. Crispus. She had relied on Carol for so long to handle the details of the school that, now, to be on her own was a little frightening. "What's going to happen?"

Carol sensed the mood of the community, Royall Beach, face to face with its potential.

"They can afford teacher salaries *and* the pilot program," she told Mrs. Crispus, "and I think they know it, thanks to Mr. Semlac. But no one knows what's going to happen until it does."

*　　*　　*

Anton Semlac gave her an abrupt nod as Carol left the library, his manner of conveying professional respect. Before the meeting, Carol had been wondering just how she would feel if she offered her resignation. There was a measure of regret, because a certain stage of her life had ended, but she was ready for something new. She felt good. *Very dramatic of you*, she laughed to herself, indulging in a bit of self-congratulation, recalling Blanche Dunphy's surprise and Mrs. Crispus's jittery realization that she would have to take some responsibility for a change.

The school corridors were clean and bright, and Carol admired the astonishingly good artwork that children had hung on the walls. She walked toward the exit. The classrooms were closed and dark. Her high heels *clicked on the corridor floor* . . .

How quiet the school was, how vast and empty and antiseptic! Exactly as the ballroom in her dream had been, vacant and waiting . . .

The exit was closer than the library, so Carol ran toward it, her heels clattering like brittle castanets. The entryway was brightly lit; there was not a soul around; yet, as Carol ran, she heard above the racket her heels were making, the thin, ghostly echo of *The Waltz of the Dead*, and she felt a cold chill all around, as if Death were running beside her, pacing her in an eerie marathon of time and night.

Then, breathless, she was in the entryway. Outside, arced fluorescent lights bathed the parking lot in glow. Her car was there, in its parking slot. Carol ran down the steps and across the asphalt toward it. She fumbled in her bag as she ran, found the keys, had them ready when she reached the car. She yanked the door open, slid quickly behind the wheel, slammed and locked the door.

She was just about to turn the ignition switch when she noticed the fresh sprig of lilacs stuck beneath the windshield wiper. How could that be? The lilac season was over, yet these blossoms were crisp and thriving. They might just have been cut; they looked wet with dew.

A small, hand-lettered note had also been inserted beneath the wiper blade, the message turned toward the glass, so Carol could read it:

NEXT TIME LILAC NIGHT.

11

$\mathbf{J}$ack stood at the curb in front of
the Museum of Natural History, looking around for Karyn. She
had promised to meet him here an hour earlier, and he had almost
decided to give up the wait. Cabs flashed by, Metro buses, cars.
The sidewalks were filled with people, moving slowly in the heat.
Across the street, in Central Park, others enjoyed the shade of trees.
Cars pulled to the curb; people got out. Cabs stopped. People got
into them. But no Karyn. Jack gave up, and turned down the street
to find a phone. He would call the Pierre and see if something had
gone wrong.

"I believe we met in Budapest, did we not?"

A black limousine inched slowly along curbside. And in the car
was Karyn.

"Get in." She laughed. He did. The tinted window glided up,
closed. In the car was cool and dark and Karyn.

Her presence, as always, struck Jack with the force of a blow. She
seemed not to have changed at all. Her smile was dazzling, and it
drew him back within the spell of her radiance and wild will. She
wore her hair long and straight, like an Egyptian queen. A simple
black dress accentuated the animalistic lines of her body. She was
Karyn Bari, and there was no other.

The driver pulled smoothly away from the curb and swung west
on a crosstown street.

"Darling," said Karyn, and kissed him.

Unbidden, all memory roared back out of the past. Jack felt her
body pressed against him, every curve and promise. Time did not
matter; nothing mattered, and he was lost and spinning in her kiss.

They drew apart. The car was moving northward on the West
Side Highway.

"Where are we going?" he asked.

"To meet your son, Tyler Bennington."

Jack remembered the feeling he'd had, looking at the photo in the

Post on that lost day, long ago. *Rudolf Bennington and Karyn Bari board jet for Venezuela.*

"Why are you sad, darling?"

"Why did you leave me?"

Until he heard himself ask the question, Jack had been sure he had mastered the hurt she had dealt him. But now he heard a ragged edge in his voice, and he knew he had been kidding himself.

"Why. . . ?"

". . . did I not tell you I was pregnant? I know you, darling. If you had realized I was having your child, you would have kept me from doing what I wanted." She gave him a quick kiss. "And that I could not have abided." She smiled. "You see, I wanted to experience what it was like to be as rich as Bennington, to be within his white walls. I wanted to learn from him what I would have to learn, if I am to do what I have set out—but let us not discuss that yet. You have a family now, and I read about you in the newspapers!"

"What was it you thought you could learn from Rudolf Bennington?" Jack demanded.

"Not now, darling. How will your wife respond when you return to me?"

"*What?* Karyn—"

"Oh, you will," she smiled, "but not just yet. First there are things I must do."

"Naturally, I'd like to work out an arrangement regarding Tyler. Perhaps he'll be able to live with me at least some of the time—"

"Don't be ridiculous. We'll all be together. You and I and the boy."

Karyn was completely sure of herself, as always. Didn't she grasp the fact that a decade had passed? That everything had changed?

Apparently not. She was smiling as she had in Munich long ago, saying, "Marry me and take me to America, darling. I want to be a Broadway star." She had absolute conviction that life would work out as she wanted it to.

Why should she not be certain? Jack reflected. So far, life had gone exactly Karyn's way.

"Have you ever created an aura with anyone but me?" she asked him.

"No," Jack admitted, remembering the unearthly delight they had shared. And, remembering, he wanted that pleasure again.

She knew it. "That is a part of our bond, darling. We will always have it, and it is something no one else can share. When I return from India—"

"India?"

"When Tyler and I return, and you come to live with us—"

"Karyn, it *can't be that way.*"

"Oh, darling, don't be silly. Take this exit, Juanito," Karyn told the driver, who switched lanes and took the ramp leading to The Cloisters, an abbeylike museum at Manhattan's northernmost point. Juanito eased the car slowly up park drives and circled The Cloisters itself, a dark palace behind green leaves.

"Over there, Juanito. Park near those benches."

The driver nodded, took a microphone from a dashboard hook, and said something in rapid Spanish. Juanito braked to a halt. Jack got out of the car. Karyn followed.

"Let us sit down," Karyn said, leading him to a bench.

"Where is the boy?"

"He will be here. Do not worry."

From the park bench, they looked down a tree-laden cliff. Sunlight sparkled on the Hudson, far below, moving in its wide valley like a ribbon of light. Beyond it lay the vast empire called "Upstate."

"So you want to be governor, darling?" Karyn said.

It occurred to Jack that she might bargain with him now. Bargain or blackmail, using the boy as a pawn. *You do what I want, or your chances for political life will be ruined.*

But Karyn placed no value on high office. "How boring *that* would be," she told him now. "I do hope you'll change your mind."

"You mentioned India. . . ?"

"In a moment. Here comes the car now."

Another limousine circled The Cloisters, and approached Karyn and Jack. It halted, and a uniformed driver got out, went around, and opened the rear door.

Then Tyler emerged, straight and handsome. He walked across the grass toward Jack and Karyn. He wore a blue blazer, light gray slacks, and a white shirt open at the collar. He seemed very calm. Karyn's amused self-possession; Jack's looks. The best of both parents, or vice-versa? But this was his son, and Jack knew it. His throat tightened. His eyes felt hot.

"Tyler," Karyn said, "this is your father."

"Hello, Father," said the boy, offering his hand. "I am proud to meet you. Mother has told me that we will be seeing much of you when we return from India."

Jack didn't know what to say. He held the boy's hand for a long time, put his other hand on Tyler's shoulder, trying to communicate the love he felt. "Your mother and I have things to discuss," he said finally, "but I know we'll see a lot of each other. I want you to come visit at my house—"

"That will be all, darling," Karyn said to the boy.

Unruffled, plainly curious about Jack, Tyler looked him over thoroughly before walking back to the car. "Good-bye," he called, waving. "It was a pleasure to meet you, sir."

Then the car pulled away, and was gone down the drive.

"He has your looks, of course." Karyn smiled.

"Karyn—"

"Yes, darling?"

"What are your plans, anyway? You can't just bring that child into my life and take him out again."

"But I'm not going to do that. We are going to India, and when we return . . ."

"No. It can't work. I'm not going to leave my wife, my family—"

Karyn laughed. "Darling, I know your weakness," she said. "Such knowledge makes anything possible. I learned that from Bennington. I was his weakness. I doubt he even knew it."

"What's my weakness then?"

"Love," she said. "I saw it in your eyes when you looked at Ty."

"And you would use that . . . ?"

"You have another defect, too," she went on, not at all harshly.

She was being playful with him. "You want the best there is. And that is me."

"Naturally, you have no weaknesses, do you?"

"Oh, yes," she said. "I also want the best. Or maybe it's the most. With Bennington, I had the most money. I still have it. On Broadway, I was the greatest star. You loved me best, and I will want that back, after India . . ."

"What's in India?"

Karyn's coal-black eyes darkened, gleamed. A desire long smoldering now burst into flame. "Revenge," she told him, her eyes hard and her lovely mouth taut. "I can do it now. I have the money, the power. And from Bennington I learned how to proceed. I am going back to India and get even with the people who dispossessed my family and took our great house away."

"But that's been years ago. Many of them must be dead, or very old—"

"Then I shall even it with their children!"

Jack recalled something he had once told Pauline Yates.

"Nobody really gets even, Karyn," he said. "All they do is create a whole new mess."

"I don't care," she said.

"Think about it. Why dwell in the past? People bent on revenge don't know the trouble they're going to cause."

"It doesn't stop them, though, does it, darling?"

"No, it doesn't," Jack admitted.

"And it's not stopping me, either," Karyn said.

"Leave the boy here, anyway."

"No."

"Please. He's my son too."

"His name is Tyler Bennington. I am Mrs. Rudolf Bennington." She was in control again, presenting him with the facts. Her position. Her prerogatives. Her plans. Jack saw that she could not be dissuaded, and he realized he did not have the power to stop her.

"You have always gotten what you've wanted," he said, "but before you make a great mistake, please think once more. Is revenge really what you want? Deep in your soul?"

"Yes!" she cried, with absolute conviction, and with hunger too.

"Revenge is not at all bitter. Revenge is very sweet. I shall have it, and then I will come back to you."

"Karyn, it can't work—"

"But, darling, I always get what I want. And in Ty I have what I need to get you back." She came toward him, and opened her arms for an embrace. He took her wrists, holding her off. He used no force. He did not have to. She looked at him, surprised. "You mean it, don't you?" she asked, in wonder.

He nodded.

"We shall see." She rallied. "We shall see. Get in the car now, and let's go back to the city."

"That's all right. You go. I want to stay here awhile and do some thinking. I'll call for my car when I'm ready."

"As you wish."

Jack saw her to the limousine and helped her inside. She did not look up for a good-bye kiss, and he did not bend down to give it.

"*Auf Wiedersehn*, darling," she said.

The car pulled away.

Angry, and still in love with her, Jack turned back to the bench. He stayed at The Cloisters for a long time, thinking, looking out beyond the Hudson, where the green fields of America rolled on under the sun.

12

Ed Peters watched and fretted, watched and prayed, but finally computer programmer Bambi Bush left on her afternoon coffee break. Ed had been afraid she wouldn't take one at all, and he wanted to use the computer on his own. He was certain he'd mastered all he needed to know, and if he didn't do the proper programming today, the funds would not be ready for pickup tomorrow. Fourth of July loomed, banks would be closed. If he didn't get the money transferred, all his plans would be ruined. Ed had watched so many people, executives included, botch chances to do jobs right simply because they had planned poorly. No excuse for that sort of thing. Ed Peters had not made one mistake yet, and he was not about to start now.

Repeatedly consulting the account numbers he'd written on a three-by-five-inch card, Ed punched codes into the Stuyvesant Mutual computer, which was tied to existing accounts at Citibank, Chase Manhattan, and Marine Midland. Then, glancing around to make certain Bambi had not yet returned, Ed punched one more number code, connecting the Stuyvesant Mutual treasury to The Bowery Savings and Loan, where Ed had opened a personal account the previous week. Former baseball star Joe DiMaggio did television and other media ads for The Bowery, and Ed, a Yankee fan, Bronx-born, Bronx-bred, was loyal to an old hero.

Ed, as Stuyvesant treasurer, had been issued a personal code number, which, when he pressed the proper buttons on the computer console, informed the computer that anything he might command it to do was totally authorized. The computers at the various banks, connected to their Stuyvesant sibling, received and considered Ed's orders, checked their propriety, and opened their circuits—and, in turn, the vaults of their respective banks—to Ed's deposits. By punching buttons for two minutes, Ed transferred $98,600 to Citibank, $231,590 to Chase Manhattan, $190,350 to Marine Midland, and a healthy $790,000 to The Bowery.

"Why, hi, Mr. Peters!" Bambi Bush exclaimed. "Something I can do for you?"

She gave him her very widest, brightest Loni Anderson smile. Mr. Peters *had* been visiting the computer section quite a lot. Maybe he was really interested in her, but just a little shy. She had heard that was the way it was sometimes with these older guys who had to start dating all over again.

"No, no," he said, polite but formal as ever. "I was just running a few computer checks. Everything is in order."

"Oh, I'm glad, Mr. Peters," Bambi chirped.

He gave her a little smile, and it was kind of sweet. Sad, but still sweet. At least he had smiled. Bambi felt she was making some progress. From computer programmer to wife of a vice-president and treasurer? Could that happen? Stranger things had.

Bambi went back to work, humming an old Buddy Holly tune. "It's so easy to fall in love," she began to sing, wondering whether Mrs. Edward L. Peters or Ms. Bambi Peters sounded better.

When Ed got back to his desk, the completed insurance forms for Lisa Walsh were finally ready. Terrific. That was a burden off his mind. He'd take them over to the Kenton house as soon as he got the chance. You can't get the job done right if you leave loose ends all over.

Chief O'Melia of the Suffolk County Police called that evening just after dinner.

"Mr. Kenton, I'm calling late in the day, I know, but I wanted to try and catch you at home . . ."

"Perfectly all right, Chief. What's up?"

"Well, sir, I had an officer, Patrolman Toole, working on that request you made? To check anything that might have happened in or around Montauk on Mother's Day? We have a few items you might want to consider. Naturally, we don't know what you have in mind . . ."

"Chief, we're not sure, either. Wait a moment, please, and I'll put my wife on the other line."

When Carol was on the extension, Jack told the chief to go ahead.

O'Melia related many items, essentially similar in nature, distinct only insofar as the individuals involved were different. A man arrested prowling about the beachfront homes at Amagansett. Two teenagers overturning a stolen car a mile west of Montauk village. Numerous summonses issued for speeding or careless driving. A lone man stopped for illegal hitchhiking in East Hampton.

"What was his name?" Carol asked. "What did he look like?"

"Let's see," drawled O'Melia. "Bellis, Harvey. Itinerant from Utah. A poet, he said. Looking for a commune. Dark hair. About five-four."

"No," said Carol. "The man with the lilacs on the beach was taller."

After a while longer, the police officer had run through the names on all summonses and arrests given or made that Mother's Day.

"Nothing else?" Jack prodded.

"Okay," sighed the chief. And he proceeded to what he called "tape record items." Sometimes a patrolman would leave his cruiser to check out something suspicious, or merely to assist a motorist. When so doing, the patrolman routinely explained what he was about to do, calling it in on his car radio. His message went onto the permanent recordings made at the headquarters desk. The chief read a number of these incidents or encounters, then said: "Officer stopped and investigated Chevrolet sedan, New York license number four-one-three QFH parked on Montauk Highway, vicinity Gurney's Inn, fifteen hundred hours. No summons issued."

He went through several more items, and then said, "That's all, Mr. Kenton, Mrs. Kenton."

Carol had been struck by the mention of Gurney's. "That Chevrolet? Who was driving it?"

"No record. As I said, there was no summons."

"Would there be—would there be any way to find out, for example, what the man looked like? The driver?"

"Only if the officer remembered. Let me check." Jack and Carol heard the riffling of papers. "Jesus Christ, it was Toole," Chief O'Melia said, as if to himself. "You're interested in this one?" he asked Jack and Carol.

Carol was.

"All right," O'Melia agreed. "I'll have Patrolman Toole get in touch with you. Perhaps he'll remember the incident. If not, you can have him do a trace on the license number anyway. We always like to help out if we can, Mr. Kenton."

Jack thanked him, and the call ended. Next morning, Officer Toole called bright and early. "Sure, I remember, ma'am," he told Carol. "The guy wished me a happy Mother's Day. It struck me as unusual, so I wouldn't forget it."

"What did he look like?"

"Nice-looking guy. Very polite, as I recall. Oh, well dressed. He was well dressed."

"How tall?"

"I didn't ask him to get out of his car. I wouldn't know his height."

"Biggish? Fat? Skinny?"

Toole thought it over. "Neat," he said then. "Neat and trim."

At the phone in the Kenton home, Carol nodded. "Officer," Jack asked, "would you check out that license number and get back to us as soon as possible? I'd like the name of the driver and his address."

"Sure thing, sir."

Bruce Toole really planned to run the tracer on the license number, but it was a pretty nice day. And he *hated* clerical work. Besides, when he called Motor Vehicle Registration, somebody always gave him a hard time. "Cruising with a desk, hey, hotshot?" "Hey, rookie, arrest your chair, it's holding you up!" Everybody thought it was hilarious that he was humping a desk.

So when it came time for lunch, Toole signed out and wandered over to the Deli. There he ran into Callie Fox, from his old high school, who would go down for anybody anytime. She was out here on the East End to "beach it" for the day, she said.

"Jeez, Bruce, you sure look . . ."

"It's the uniform," he admitted modestly. "And you look . . ."

"I took off a coupla pounds."

"In the right places."

So Bruce took a little detour from his lunch hour, came right to attention at a secluded spot out on the dunes, and did his duty thrice in very creditable time. Callie Fox paced him all the way, cleared the same hurdles, and, in fact, just barely beat him to the final wire. Then, naked and drowsy, enjoying the sun, they both fell asleep.

"Got a little sun on your nose, eh?" The desk sergeant grinned, gleefully marking Bruce "late in reporting for duty" when the sun-scorched patrolman came back to the precinct.

That's not all that's burnt, moaned Bruce to himself, as he tried to sit down. *Let's see, got to do a license check . . .*

13

The stalker was ready.

It was late afternoon on the Fourth of July; tonight was Lilac Night.

He had read the papers, and now he was watching the six o'clock news. All the waiting was ended; all the days were gone. Now, at last, the score would be settled. The newscaster was on camera, reporting the Democratic gala planned at the Waldorf-Astoria for that night. "Governor John Higgins, it has been learned, is scheduled to speak first, after which he will introduce John Tyler Kenton, of Long Island, fueling speculation that the chief executive will pass on his mantle . . ."

The stalker snickered and grimaced. He was sure Kenton would declare candidacy. And probably win the election.

So what?

". . . Kenton plans to leave his Royall Beach home by helicopter this evening, and speak to party faithful in the Waldorf ball-room . . ." the newscaster went on.

But when he returns home, shrugged the stalker, *he will have lost everything. Because I will have been there.*

He fought back a burst of sudden tears. *I will kill those he loves and leave him alive to grieve.*

So he will know what it is like to be me.

In his basement workshop, its walls padded with blankets and mattresses, the stalker readied his machine, hoping that nobody in the neighborhood would hear him screaming. His cries had to sound absolutely authentic, and he would set the playback for top volume. He took a deep breath and pressed the "Record" button.

"HELP, HELP!" he screamed. "Help, oh, help me, *pleasssse! FIIIIRRRRREEE!*" he yelled into the tape recorder, at the top of his lungs. "Oh, my God, help me. I can't get out!"

When he played back his screams at low volume, he was pleased. The howls sounded very convincing. They would do the job just fine.

Next, the stalker went to work on the tape and the recorder itself, splicing and rethreading so the tape would play continuously, or at least until the flames destroyed equipment or tape. Cool and detached, pleased as always to adjust and invent and improvise, the stalker wondered how the last screams would sound as the tape melted. *Another tragedy for that poor man*, the neighbors would think. *First his wife and now him.*

By the time the ashes cooled enough to sift the debris for some leftover shard of his bones, the stalker would be in another country. Costa Rica. Costa Rica did not have an extradition treaty with the United States.

The stalker would be rich and safe in Costa Rica, forever. He would be at peace, too, hurt extirpated, violation avenged, all debts settled.

The stalker was too excited to be hungry, but he hadn't eaten anything since breakfast. It would be after 11:00 tonight before his plane was airborne, and the flight attendants started offering food. So he made himself a hamburger with fried onions. He ate his "last supper" at the table in the little breakfast nook where he'd shared so many happy hours with his wife.

"I'm doing it for you," he said, talking to the empty chair, *her* chair. "I'm not only doing it for me. I know how much he hurt you."

No, nothing would ever be the same again, and the stalker really did not know what Costa Rica would be like. But at least he would be avenged. And *she* would be avenged. And the baby that would have been a son, had it been born, would be avenged too.

Thinking about it made him morose. Stop thinking. Act. It was after seven o'clock now, with much remaining to prepare. He washed the plate, cup, and silverware he'd used, and the frying pan. Things ought to work out fine, timewise. He took a quick shower and from his closet selected a dark blue Hart, Schaffner and Marx. Dark blue was "sincere," as everyone in business knew, and the stalker did not want any problems, since he would be boarding the plane with $520,000; withdrawn just before closing time this afternoon from his account at The Bowery bank.

He knew now that he could go through with all of it; he knew now that he would kill tonight.

Long ago, he had selected the means by which ultimate revenge would be achieved. He had planned both a primary strategy and a secondary strategy, should the first fail. Ed went to his closet, pulled each of his dozens of neckties off the rack, judging them for strength and appearance. The necktie would be his primary weapon. It had to "do the job," and it still had to look good when he wore it onto the plane at JFK. He finally chose a heavy polyester tie, maroon with a conservative dark blue stripe. It was wider than the current style but it was tensile. It shouldn't tear and it wouldn't wrinkle. Moreover, Ed recalled that his wife had always liked it. There was the justice of bitter poetry in his selection of this tie.

Then, from beneath the bedroom mattress, Ed withdrew his secondary weapon, a blunt object of black metal, with only one small movable spring-steel piece. It consisted of a short, narrow hollow tube, a squat black handle, and a flick switch to drive a small spring piston. A "zip" gun. It fired, one at a time, .22-caliber bullets. Ed was sure he would not have to use the secondary weapon, but if he had learned one thing in business it was never to take chances. He was sure he would not have to use the zip gun, because his tie—and his hands—could do the job.

Ed had good hands.

Tonight he would kill with them.

Ed packed his bag, checked the money Stuyvesant Mutual would not find missing until after the Fourth of July holiday, made certain he had his plane ticket and passport. Leaving the house for a moment, he put his bag into the Oldsmobile and checked his watch. It was 8:07 P.M. He would leave here at nine. Twilight came at about nine-thirty, and in half an hour, he could be at Royall Beach. It had always taken Ed's wife twenty or twenty-five minutes to get from their home to her job as nurse at Community Hospital in Glen Cove. Except for the fact that he would swing westward to the Royall Beach peninsula, Ed was taking the same route his wife had taken on the day of her death.

He didn't want to think of that right now. He went back inside the house, down into the basement again, and gingerly began to splash gasoline onto the mattress with which he had soundproofed his workroom for the recorded screaming. He took care not to get any of the fuel on himself. An earlier, rejected version of his master plan called for sprinkling the gasoline before he showered and dressed, but the chance that the house would catch fire with him still in it forced him to a revision.

Ed did not want the fire to become obvious too soon. Bill Crooker, his neighbor, was at home, barbecuing hamburgers in his backyard for a bunch of relatives and their kids, and Crooker was sure to spot smoke or flames right away. Ed wanted to be in Royall Beach, or almost at Royall Beach, before Crooker noticed anything amiss. So he splattered gas lightly on the mattress, a little on the floorboards, some on the wooden basement beams. Then, to make sure the fire spread upstairs, he trailed a last thin line of gasoline up the stairs, and sprinkled it onto the wooden basement door. Last, he tossed the empty jerrican back down into the basement itself.

Now it was 8:37 P.M. Twenty-three minutes until departure.

But those twenty-three minutes were a rebirth of agony for Ed, minutes that served to commit him even more strongly to the deadly course on which he had embarked.

He positioned the tape recorder in the little den he had built for his wife, plugged a timing device into a socket, and then plugged the recorder into the timing device. He calculated how long the fire might smolder in the basement before it flashed into the upper part of the house, made his decision, and set the recorder to activate at 9:35 P.M.

By 9:35 P.M. he ought to be loosening his polyester tie, ready to do the job.

Ed sat down, waiting, but this time he entertained, rather than tried to hold at bay, the ceaseless recapitulation by which he was tormented. Thinking about the day of his wife's death would steel him for action. He wanted to be all steel tonight, and not to falter.

She had left for Community Hospital that morning, just like any other morning, heading north on Glen Cove Road. She enjoyed her hospital job and wanted to keep working through her fifth month of pregnancy. It had been an easy pregnancy; she was feeling fine and looking forward to the birth of the child almost as much as Ed was. She was merely overjoyed; Ed was getting to be—she'd told him laughingly—"a fanatic about it." Why not? "It" was going to be his son.

Ed had always marveled at his wife's innocent loveliness and at his luck in winning a girl with such beauty and style. She was sometimes sad for no apparent reason, and she lacked what he had expected would be a natural self-confidence in so gorgeous a woman. But he explained this insecurity as a result of her dismal childhood in the Bronx.

She'd loved flowers, and so Ed built a greenhouse for her, right in the backyard, regulated for moisture and temperature, at any time of the year. She might have grown orchids in there. But she hadn't. She'd grown lilacs. Lilacs planted at different times, grafts of lilac bushes, and flowering lilacs replanted, so that every month of the year, the sweet, fragrant pink and violet flowers were in bloom. Ed would be raking leaves in the autumn, and he would see his gentle, gorgeous wife behind the moisture-fogged panes of the greenhouse, on her knees among her creations, her face buried in the pink and shimmering blossoms. It made her happy, and so he was happy, in the autumn when her lilacs bloomed, and in the winter, in the spring, and summer too.

He had had no idea. He was a workaday man, a literal man.

She'd kissed him good-bye that morning, and left the house in their five-year-old Olds. Ed was commuting by train to the city, and he had plenty of time for another cup of coffee, a glance at the paper, and then the walk to the station in Garden City Park. But the phone rang.

"Mr. Edward L. Peters?"

"That's right." But he didn't like the voice. The voice had something in it . . .

"Are you married, Mr. Peters, to a woman named Pauline Y. Peters, and who drives a four-door Oldsmobile sedan?"

"Yes, I am. She does. Who is this?" And in the voice was . . .

"Sorry, Mr. Peters. Lieutenant Bentpudlian, Nassau County Police. I'm afraid there's been an accident . . ."

And in the voice was death.

No, Edward L. Peters had never been a poet, nor would he ever be, but he had loved totally and completely once in his life, and that love had gone to the woman who had been his wife. She was a shy and beautiful thing, never seemed sure of anything, not even of his love, which was entire and free and full.

Ed had rushed next door, and asked to borrow his neighbor's car. But Bill Crooker was more than good neighbor, he was an observant man, and he saw that Ed was too upset to drive anywhere. So it was Crooker who drove Ed to the intersection of Glen Cove Road and Northern Boulevard. There, hard by gasoline stations, a bank, Burger King, and Roy Rogers, Ed's wife lay bloody and dead on the roadway. Her chest was crushed. Splinters of rib and spine and pelvis had pierced her lungs, heart, womb. Killing her and killing, in her womb, what an autopsy disclosed to be the fetus of a male child. Ed would not be a father. Never would he know, with Pauline, the joyful times a child can give to life, an enhancement of ordinary celebration, a happiness added to jack-o'-lanterns on Halloween, wreaths and gifts at Christmas, flowers on Mother's Day . . .

> Mrs. Pauline Peters, of Garden City Park, was killed today when her car was struck broadside at the corner of Glen Cove Road and Northern Boulevard by a truck bélonging to the Mid-Island Concrete Construction Corporation. Mrs. Peters, a registered nurse working at Community Hospital in Glen Cove, was a member of the American Nursing Association, the First Methodist Church of Garden City Park, and the Independent Citizens Committee of Nassau County. Prior to her nursing career, she served with the American Red Cross, stationed in Munich, Germany. She is survived by her husband, Edward L. Peters, of Garden City Park, and her mother, Mrs. Felix J. Yates, of the Bronx . . .

But Pauline Peters, née Yates, was survived by her husband only in the sense that he possessed biological life after the car crash. In spirit he was dead, altered, changed. It was not merely Pauline's death that did this to him. After her death, Ed went through her clothing and belongings, to sort them out, keep what he could, discard what he must. First, he tackled her wardrobe in the closet, and then he turned to her dresser drawers. There, beneath a pile of lingerie, he found a picture that killed in him whatever spirit had survived the crash. Pauline, in the picture, had her arms and long lovely legs around a man, making love to him amid the lilacs, her eyes closed tight, and her mouth open. The picture was so clear he could see her tongue and that her teeth were wet.

On the back of the picture, in Pauline's hand, Ed read:

> *John Tyler Kenton*
> *and Pauline Yates*
> *were once in love.*
> *Germany, 1966.*

Now, on Lilac Night, Ed went to his desk, took the photo from a drawer, and placed it next to the recorder, checked the timer again, and turned on the switch. The photo would perish to the screams of Ed Peters, who was already dead. From his desk, Ed picked up the insurance forms covering Lisa Walsh and slipped them into his coat pocket. At the basement door, he struck a match, edged the door open slightly, and tossed the match downstairs, slamming the door against a ripple of flame. Locking and double-locking the front door behind him, he took one extra moment to stop by the little greenhouse and clip a sprig of lilac for his lapel. A calling card.

Will you know the meaning then, Kenton? Think. Think real hard.

Then he climbed into his new gold Oldsmobile—be a shame to leave it in the parking lot at JFK—and started toward Royall Beach.

The night was cool and mild and clear.

There was a moon.

On Lilac Night.

14

Jack's chartered chopper came right on time, fast and low across Manhasset Bay. The moon was up, but pale, pale as the white beach below the house.

"Here it comes," called Johnny, watching the helicopter through the thick glass of the living room window. "Where's it going to land?"

"Right down by the beach," Jack said. He hung up the phone, on which he'd been keeping in touch with proceedings at the Waldorf. Governor Higgins had just arrived, Charlie Kiefer had been there for over an hour, but party stalwarts had not yet begun to take their seats for dinner. There was plenty of time. Higgins wouldn't speak until dessert, and Jack would be after him. The governor had called Jack earlier in the afternoon to say, "Jack, I'm giving a pretty standard speech. Got some little surprises, but nothing you won't be able to handle with a few ad libs. Then you'll introduce Charlie, and he'll wrap up the evening."

Jack was silent for a moment, and Higgins sensed unease. "Jack, don't worry. By the time we're through, the only thing left for Charlie to do will be to give the party his patented pep talk."

The helicopter hovered now just above the beach, then it dropped slowly and easily to the sand.

"Can we go see it?" asked Lisa, with a note of eagerness in her voice, as she joined Johnny at the window.

Carol and Jack exchanged glances. Lisa was improving. The worst, at least, seemed over.

"Okay. But just for a minute," said Jack.

The children went out the front door and across the wide, sloping lawn, bathed in the big floodlights. The pilot was climbing out of the craft.

"You have your speech, honey?" asked Carol.

"Sure do."

"And you're really going to suggest that the party nominate Charlie for lieutenant governor? Is that what you want?"

"No. But it's a good move, and Charlie's too proud to take the second slot anyway. Also, it'll make his ma happy, and she's sure to be there on a big night like this."

"I wish I could be there too."

"I know. But it's better if one of us is with the kids."

"You're right."

They embraced and kissed.

Jack went to the door and called the children. They started slowly up toward the house. The pilot waited next to the helicopter.

"Did that cop call?" Carol remembered. "The one who was running the license check in Suffolk County?"

"If he tried, he wouldn't have been able to get through. I've had the phones tied up most of the day."

Johnny and Lisa came in, and Jack gave them a good-bye hug. "You guys get to bed before midnight, all right?"

"Okay, Dad," said Johnny.

"Okay . . . Dad," decided Lisa.

He gave Carol a quick kiss good-bye. "Looks like this is it. Just stay locked up here, and don't hesitate to give Chief Deztler a call if anything suspicious happens."

"I hope I don't have to call him *again*."

Jack made sure the front door was locked, waved, and trotted across the lawn, down to the helicopter. The guttural blat-blat-blat of the idling engine turned into a roar, and the machine shot up into the air, spun easily for a moment, then veered off to the west and New York City.

Carol touched a button, and the draperies moved soundlessly along their tracks, covering the windows and shutting the house off from bay and beach and lawn. She felt the pressure of Jack's last kiss still on her lips. And she felt—or thought she felt, or merely imagined she felt—another kind of pressure, at once tender and eerie, like being caressed by a feather, by thistledown, by the memory of the touch of a long-dead lover . . .

No, she told herself. "Tell you what," she said to the kids, "let's play a game for a while before bed. You can choose. It'll take our minds off . . ."

They were both looking at her. "Off what, Mom?" Johnny asked.

In the helicopter, Jack Kenton looked down upon the North Shore, which fell away beneath him as the aircraft rose higher. To the west was New York City. To the east lay the heavily forested peninsulas of Long Island. The moon was up now, bathing the Island in soft, eerie light. And in the pale glow of that moon, Jack Kenton saw a car creep up the driveway toward his house. The car's headlights were off.

"Sorry," he said to the pilot, a young mesomorph with a "Bomb the Cong" tattoo on his forearm, "I forgot something. I'll have to go back for a minute."

"You're the boss," returned the flyer, above the engine's roar. He moved the stick and swung the chopper in a beautiful flowing arc, back down toward the luminous beacon of the Kenton house.

The car had stopped in the yard.

"Patrolman Toole, ma'am, Suffolk Police. I tried to get through to you before. I really did . . ."

"That's all right, Officer. The phone's been in use. Did you find anything on that license number. . . ?"

"Yes, ma'am. The car that was stopped near Gurney's Inn on Mother's Day afternoon is registered to a Mr. William S. for 'Story' Crooker of Garden City Park, Long Island."

"William Crooker," Carol repeated, writing the name down. She could not recall anyone named William Crooker. "Thank you, Officer."

Toole, sounding relieved, said if there was anything else, be sure to call, don't hesitate. When he had hung up, Carol took the Nassau County phone directory out of the drawer, and riffled forward to the C's. Cassin, Chambers, Craddock, Crooker . . .

She dialed. The phone rang five times, and she was just about to hang up when a man answered. He sounded breathless.

"Do you have a Chevrolet, license number four-one-three QFH?"

"What? Look lady, I ain't got time . . ."

In the background, over the phone, Carol heard the sound of a siren in Garden City Park. In her own house, she heard the front doorbell. A quick glance out of the kitchen window, next to the phone, showed a gold-colored Oldsmobile in the yard. Mr. Peters's car. That was funny. She hadn't heard him drive up.

But now, with the phone still in her hand, she heard that first tremulous murmur of air, prelude to *The Waltz of the Dead.*

Oh, God! No! Jack!

". . . so, yeah," William Crooker was telling her. "That's my license number and that's my car. So what about them?"

He had a deep, rasping baritone, peremptory and tough.

"What were you doing out near Montauk on Mother's Day?" she demanded, suspecting that this tough-talking stranger was the mysterious lilac messenger.

Yes, she thought. *I must be right.* Because now, even as the doorbell sounded again, she heard within her mind, within her being, another blood-chilling note of Death's organ. Across the living room, the doorbell rang again.

"Look, are you there or not?" William Crooker was asking, on the phone. "Montauk and Mother's Day? What the hell are you talking about, lady? There's a fire . . ."

Unsteadily, Carol reasoned that she must be hearing the *Waltz* because she was talking to Crooker, who was somehow its composer-conductor. She heard, as if in confirmation of her logic, yet another chord of the secret song. The doorbell rang again, too. She pressed a button on the console, and the drapery covering the front door slid back a little. There was Mr. Peters with his nice smile, holding up some papers. The insurance forms! Yes, he'd said he'd drop them by. Thank God he was here now!

"Look, lady," Crooker was saying, "it's my car you're talking about, God knows why, but . . ."

"Johnny," called Carol, "would you go to the front door and let Mr. Peters in, please?"

". . . but on Mother's Day I loaned it to my neighbor. His wife had wrecked his, and—look, I've got to go—the poor bastard . . ."

Johnny came out of the den, where he and Lisa were setting up for a game of "Battleship," and started across the living room. Outside the glass door, Mr. Peters was smiling and loosening his tie.

"I know this sounds very odd," Carol told William Crooker, "but I have to know. It's quite important. Who is your neighbor? What's his name? The man you loaned the car to?"

Johnny released the door latch. Edward L. Peters pushed the door open and stepped into the house. He reached for Johnny. It seemed unusual when he took Johnny's shoulder in his hand and gripped it, hard.

". . . you mean who *was* my neighbor," William Crooker told Carol. "His house is on fire! The poor guy is screaming his head off, and the fire department's trying to get him out. Ed Peters, Jesus Christ, the poor bastard . . ."

"I think you'd better hang up, Mrs. Kenton," commanded Ed Peters. Still holding Johnny, whose face was twisted with fear and alarm, Ed used his free hand to pull off his tie. With a quick gesture, he flicked it full length, slipped it around the boy's neck, crossed the ends, and pulled it taut.

"A neck snaps as easily as a matchstick," Peters said to Carol. "Now, hang up. Where's the girl?"

"She's . . . not here."

"You're lying. Son, where's the girl? Point." He tightened the necktie around Johnny's throat, and the boy choked and struggled for air.

"She's in the den," cried Carol.

Peters yanked the draperies back over the glass door. What was that noise? An engine? The *helicopter* engine? How could that *be?*

Pushing Johnny ahead of him, he motioned Carol toward the den. He would do it in there. He would be quick. He would not think about it. First the boy, that would be easy, one quick yank and his neck would crack. Then the woman. Then the girl. Don't think about it . . .

But the sound of the engine. The helicopter *was* returning. What was happening? Ed Peters yanked Johnny back to the door, glanced outside. Yes, goddammit it all to hell, the aircraft was slowly settling to earth.

"Don't hurt him!" Carol cried. "Please don't pull him like that."

Why Ed Peters? she was thinking. *What possible reason. . . ?* But it *was* Ed Peters, and he had death on his mind, because chords of abyss pounded within the walls of Carol's soul.

"What's the matter?" asked Lisa, coming out of the den. "Oh!" she exclaimed, fear leaping to her eyes as she remembered another night, another assault. But she did not panic. Her glance shot to the burglar alarm button on the kitchen console.

Ed Peters followed her eyes. The alarm. He knew. He had inspected the house prior to the original insurance policy. No one must reach that button. Outside, the sound of the helicopter grew louder and louder. Kenton was coming back. Every cell in Ed's body screamed with tension. What to do? The necktie would do for Carol and the children. But he would have to use the zip gun on Kenton. And what about the pilot?

Then Lisa made her move. She was not going to stand by, powerless again, while another person was killed. She dodged a chair, raced for the alarm button. Peters, releasing Johnny, dived for her. He grabbed the cuff of her slacks, and she crashed down, face-first, on the kitchen tile, screaming in pain. Blood burst from her nose and mouth and spilled across the floor.

. . . *Miss Blaisdell, dead upon the marble, red blood running like cream* . . .

Johnny was choking for breath. Peters leaped to his feet, as Carol grabbed a kitchen knife from the counter. The waltz of death was swirling into maniacal rills and flourishes. Carol struck with the knife, but Peters was faster. With a backhanded blow, he slapped Carol, slamming her against the wall. The crack set off pink-and-violet pinwheels behind her eyes. Johnny, with the necktie still around his neck, but with some of his breath back, rushed Peters, trying with his inadequate child's body to protect his mother and Lisa. But Peters grabbed the ends of the tie again, and yanked taut.

"Into the den, all of you," he ordered, pushing Lisa and dragging Johnny cruelly.

Carol, still dazed by the blow to her head, found herself half jerked, half carried. Peters flung her onto a chair in the den and pushed the children down onto the couch.

The doorbell rang. Jack.

Ed Peters switched off the lights. He twisted the necktie, looped it, forming a sliding knot over Johnny's Adam's apple.

"Carol?" called Jack, in the living room now, having opened the door by the voice-code device. "Carol, what's wrong?"

In his chopper, the pilot was momentarily startled when the house went dark. What the hell. Kenton had probably hit the wrong switch when he went inside. The pilot shrugged, lit a cigarette, and relaxed. Nice night. Real nice moon tonight, too. He puffed his Camel and listened to the engine go blat-blat-blat.

In the house, Jack glanced around. All the lights were extinguished. He stood just inside the front door, in the living room.

"Carol?" he called. "CiJi?"

No answer.

"John? Lisa?"

Dead silence.

He knew already that something was very wrong, but he did not quite know what it was. He had caught a glimpse of the car in the yard, but it meant nothing to him. He had never seen Ed Peters's car. The car indicated that a stranger was here, but whether inside or outside the house Jack did not know.

In the den, Carol wondered why Jack could not hear *The Waltz of the Dead*, frenzied and triumphant now, or why he could not hear her heart, which banged like a signal drum of warning against her fragile rib cage. Peters yanked Johnny up from the couch. "Make a sound, Mrs. Kenton, and the kid's dead," he hissed. He reached into his coat pocket, gripping the zip gun.

Only trouble was, he did not trust the weapon's accuracy. He would have to get very close to Kenton before firing. And Kenton was all the way across the living room.

Jack's impulse was to go to the control console and turn on all the lights. But he calculated. The house was dark. If Jack turned on the lights, he would be an instant target to anyone hiding. Darkness made things closer to even.

Ed Peters stood just inside the door of the den, with the boy trembling beside him. Ed's hands were wet with sweat. Terror assaulted him. What if the tie slipped through his fingers when he tried to pull it taut? What if the weapon wavered in his jittery grasp? It could fire only one cartridge at a time, after which he would have to reload. He had three more cartridges, true, but time—time he did not have.

Just remember Kenton with Pauline, he told himself. *Just remember that.*

Down on the beach, the pilot got out of his chopper, dropped the butt, and ground it into the sand with the heel of his boot. He glanced at his watch and then up toward the house. Dark. Silent. He began to feel a little uneasy. But, what the hell, it was none of his business. Give it a minute, he told himself. Give it a—hey, wasn't that someone moving in the hedges right by the house? Naaaa.

Ed Peters stood inside the den doorway, holding the boy, covering Carol and the girl with the zip gun. Gloomy darkness, electric with tension, dazzled his overwrought senses, assaulted his resolve. *Act, Act!* he told himself. Johnny shivered in his grasp.

Inside the front door, Jack waited. His fear was rising now, like a red current inside a tube, toward a tension he had never felt. His body, his heritage, impulses long buried in the aeons of human experience, flooded back. Dark senses, capacities he had never used, flickered into life. He sensed that death was in his house. In the beat of his blood, he began to feel something that possessed the cadence of a song . . .

"*Dad!*" croaked Johnny, trying to warn his father.

Ed Peters moaned. *Do it now. You have to.*

"Jack!" screamed Carol. "He's got a gun."

Ed released Johnny, swung toward Carol, raising the zip gun. The boy squirmed away, out of the den. He was going to . . . he was heading for the console! And the alarm!

Jack unlatched the door, slid it open, ready to fight or flee. Johnny and Carol were alive; he knew that much. Lisa?

Ed Peters saw Jack in the doorway, silhouetted against moonlight. *Now. Now! Get close!* He raised the zip gun as he ran across the living room, taking aim . . .

Johnny reached the console and hit all the switches. The house exploded in light.

Ed Peters was no more than ten feet from Jack, and closing. His weapon was up and ready. He flicked the switch that released the spring-action firing device.

Jack saw the man coming toward him, saw someone he *knew!* Of all the people in the world! Ed *Peters?*

Reflexively, his head tilted slightly to the side.

Ed's weapon cracked.

Jack felt a lance of fire slice his skull apart, felt himself flung backward out the door. He struck the earth with an impact that left him breathless. This was what dying was like. No air to breathe and your mind on fire. Ed Peters was standing in the doorway, fumbling with a squat, ugly weapon. He was . . . he was reloading. Jack tried to move, could not. Ed Peters was raising the weapon again.

"*Why* . . . ?" Jack heard himself asking.

If he heard the question, Peters did not choose to answer. Perhaps he would not have been able to answer, even if he had had the time. A ruddy crater of blood and tissue appeared in the middle of his forehead. He danced convulsively there in the doorway, as if an eerie power had suddenly come to earth to seize and shake his soul. He fell to the ground beside Jack, his eyes open in a final, baleful glare.

Ed Peters was dead. Jack knew it. Knowing it, Jack figured he himself was still alive.

Everything was silent for a moment, bathed in light.

Then a burly man crawled out of the hedges. He slipped a large black pistol into a shoulder holster.

Jack saw Peters's weapon in the dirt. His throbbing brain commanded an arm to move. To his surprise, it moved. His hand closed around the zip gun.

Carol appeared in the doorway, the children behind her. "Don't look," said Johnny, looking. Lisa covered her eyes.

"Jack!" Carol screamed.

Jack aimed the weapon at the man coming out of the hedges. But he couldn't focus. The pain in his head was shattering.

"Don't shoot," the man yelled, lifting his hands. "It's okay."

He came closer, bent down. "Jesus fucking Christ, Kenton," he said, "you almost bought the farm that time. Lucky you opened that door so I could get in a shot."

The Foulest Mouth in Grover Cleveland.

"Pauley," Jack wondered, in a voice that sounded to him like an echo of an echo of an echo. "I heard you were working for Charlie Kiefer. What in the hell are you doing out here?"

"I had to settle a kind of a score," Buster Pauley said, almost shyly. "Let's just say I owed you one, okay?"

Then he examined Ed Peters. "Know this guy?"

"He's our . . . he was our insurance man," said Carol, kneeling beside Jack, patting the thin bloody ridge that ran along the side of his head.

"Jesus," muttered Buster Pauley. "You never know. Classy guy, though."

They all looked at Buster.

"What?" Carol managed.

"Classy guy, I said. Look, the dude's even got a little sprig of flowers in his lapel."

15

Nothing is ever over, reflected Jack, *not as long as one person is alive to remember.*

He opened his eyes and lay there for a while, listening to the hum of the air-conditioning system and watching dawn turn the bedroom air from dark blue to light blue to pink to gold. He had a headache, but it was fading, and his wound burned beneath a dressing applied late last night at the North Shore Hospital in Manhasset.

"You're on borrowed time now," the doctor had said.

Jack decided he would pay whatever the rate of interest was; small change to Chance, which had gifted him with one splendid unconscious reflex, a quick tilt of his head whenever he was surprised.

Ed Peters. *Why?*

Outside the house, Jack heard the putt-putt whine of the paper boy's moped, coming up the drive. He lay there in bed and waited as the sound grew louder. Then there was a *thock* as the rolled-up *New York Times* struck the side of the house, followed by the moped's receding whine.

It seemed a waste not to get up and enjoy the tender dawn. Quietly, Jack eased out of bed, leaving Carol undisturbed, sleeping there with her golden hair loose on the lavender pillowcase. He looked in on Johnny and Lisa before going downstairs. His son slept facedown, sprawled out, a young cub growing rangy and long. The marks left by Ed Peters's tie were still on Johnny's neck, but they would disappear, and then nothing would remain but memory. *Nothing but memory!* Jack smiled, shaking his head. *Memory is everything, and nothing is ever over.* Lisa, in her room, slept on her side, one arm extended over the edge of the bed, her palm easy and open, waiting for someone to place within it the golden apple of beauty and love.

"Good for you," Jack said quietly. "If you don't dream it, it won't happen."

Ed Peters. *Why?*

He went downstairs, plugged in the percolator, and walked outside to get the *Times*. He had been on the phone to the Waldorf last night, to say he wouldn't be speaking at the gala, so he already knew what the news would be. Higgins had sprung his surprise after all.

GOVERNOR DECLARES THIRD-TERM CANDIDACY
Praises Kiefer, Kenton

Jack grinned ruefully. Carol had been right about Higgins all along. Still, reading the Seymour Hochzeit story, he learned that Higgins thought well of him.

> ". . . I would be proud to have, as my Lieutenant Governor, either John Tyler Kenton or Charles Kiefer. Both are admirably qualified to seek the office, and here at the Waldorf-Astoria, on this splendid celebration of our nation's birth, I invite them to contest vigorously and openly for the prize . . ."

Jack went back inside the house. The percolator's red light was on, so he poured himself a cup and sat down at the table. Nothing is ever over. One person suffers an injustice and is forever embittered. Another suffers in the same way and becomes abject, a walking doormat for anyone who might be disposed to stroll on over and wipe soiled boots. Still another transforms his hurt into devotion to All Humanity, becoming a crusader.

There is also the person who coddles and nurtures hurt, finds it an abomination, and turns toward revenge.

And so there is another hurt, more grief, and the process begins again.

Because nothing is ever over.

Ed Peters. *Why?*

And why *lilacs?*

Nothing made sense, but yet everything must have been perfectly logical to Peters . . .

Carol came downstairs then, tying her robe. "Oh, honey," she said, kissing him, "how could you get up so early?"

"I decided I like life."

She poured herself some coffee, sat down at the table, and glanced at the headlines.

"Lieutenant Governor Kenton," she said. "It doesn't sound so bad."

"It doesn't sound so good, either."

"What'll you do?"

"Think about it tomorrow. Maybe next week."

"Good idea."

Jack read the business section, and Carol tackled the political news. But it didn't hold her interest. *Yes,* she was thinking, *I have a perverse gift, a prevision. But so what? Even when I am aware of disaster, I must still decide what to do about it.*

Like a mere mortal.

And, like a mere mortal, she would take whatever love and joy life brought her way. She was the sum of her past, of every day that she had lived, and there was no mind alive upon the earth brilliant enough to unravel the lost incidents buried within those days. Death, as Miss Blaisdell had promised long ago, came out of the past. Yet the living possess the power to flee toward the future.

Knowing they will lose one day.

But with courage, and full heart, and hope.

Safe with her husband and family, Carol understood. She moved and had her life in corridors of time. There was no turning back. Her day would come. One day, one unimaginable moment, and she would hear again, to its last throbbing note, *The Waltz of the Dead.* She was no longer afraid of the song.

The phone rang. Jack answered. "Chief Detzler," he said. "What have you found out?"

He listened. Carol saw him grow tense at the phone, then sad. Finally, he thanked Detzler and hung up.

"Bad news?"

He sat down again, sipped cold coffee. "It came out of my past," he said. "Pauline Yates. The girl I knew in Munich. She was

Peters's wife. She was killed in an accident just before Mother's Day."

"But why would Peters turn on you? On us?"

"I don't know. At least we have a connection, though, even if we can't decipher it."

"And what about the lilacs?"

Jack thought for a long time. "I just don't know," he said. "I can't recall that lilacs meant anything, either to Pauline or to me."

The phone rang again. "I'll get it this time," Carol said.

"Mrs. Kenton?" A truculent rasp.

"Yes."

"Mrs. Jack Kenton?"

"Yes."

"This here's Gertie Kiefer. You read the paper? About what Higgins said?"

"Yes, I have. I—"

"Well, you tell your husband he better not try to get that loo-ten-ant governor job away from my boy, you hear?"

"I hear you, Mrs. Kiefer."

"You tell him he better not ruin it for Charlie. Let me tell you. And let me tell you something else. If you people over there think you can ruin it for Charlie, you got another think coming. I'll fix you. You won't know when. You won't know how. But just you wait. You try to ruin it for my boy, and I'm gonna figure out a way to fix you good. You got that?"

Carol had been listening intently, and Jack, watching her face, looked a little worried. What now? But then she smiled at him, and he relaxed.

"Mrs. Kiefer," Carol asked, "what's your favorite flower?"